Dear Reader:

Welcome to SILHOUETTE SUMMER
SIZZLERS! Summer isn't just a season, it's a
state of mind. Summer means a willingness to
step away from the familiar into the new—and
that's just what we're inviting you to do.

Come join us! You are invited to open these
pages and step into an adventure in reading.
Three wonderful authors will sweep you into
three different worlds. Explore the possibilities
with Diana Palmer, Patricia Coughlin and
Sherryl Woods, and you'll discover it's not just
the summer sun that can sizzle!

So take a moment to yourself. Put your feet
up. Relax. Cool off. Then heat up with a
summer romance with the man of your dreams,
courtesy of Silhouette Books!

Happy reading,

Isabel Swift
Editorial Manager

SILHOUETTE SUMMER

Sizzlers

Diana Palmer
Sherryl Woods
Patricia Coughlin

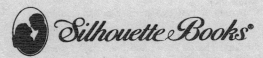

Published by Silhouette Books New York

America's Publisher of Contemporary Romance

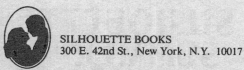

SILHOUETTE BOOKS
300 E. 42nd St., New York, N.Y. 10017

Silhouette Summer Sizzlers 1990
Copyright © 1990 by Silhouette Books

ISBN: 0-373-48229-9

First Silhouette Books printing June 1990

The publisher acknowledges the copyright holders of
the individual works as follows:

Miss Greenhorn
Copyright © 1990 by Diana Palmer
A Bridge to Dreams
Copyright © 1990 by Sherryl Woods
Easy Come . . .
Copyright © 1990 by Patricia Madden Coughlin

®: Trademark used under license and registered in
the United States Patent and Trademark Office and
in other countries.

Printed in the U.S.A.

Contents

MISS GREENHORN
by Diana Palmer   11

A BRIDGE TO DREAMS
by Sherryl Woods   133

EASY COME . . .
by Patricia Coughlin   235

MISS GREENHORN

Diana Palmer

A Note from Diana Palmer

I spent one of the most delightful weeks of my life in Arizona, and I hope I've managed to convey some of the magic in "Miss Greenhorn."

Though I didn't get to look for lost artifacts, I did get to see a lot of beautiful country and many historical places that I never dreamed I'd get to visit. For instance, I stood in the O.K. Corral in Tombstone where a fellow Georgian stood in October of 1881. His name was John Henry "Doc" Holliday. He was actually born around Griffin, Georgia, although his family moved to Valdosta soon thereafter. He left Georgia after attending dental school in Maryland and being diagnosed with tuberculosis. He has been called a cold-blooded killer, but even his enemies credited him with at least two virtues—he was loyal to a fault, and he had nerves of cold steel.

I have spent years collecting information about Doc Holliday, and the more I learn, the more fascinating I find him. I can't describe the thrill of standing on the streets of Tombstone, Arizona—or the shock of finding that it sits on a mesa, surrounded by mountains.

Tucson was just as interesting, and so was a dude ranch we visited. I will never forget Arizona, and I hope you enjoy reading about some of what I learned.

Vacations are so much fun, and I always learn a lot. I've just come back from a trip to Montana and Wyoming with my friend, Ann. She says that going on a research trip with me is like seeing Europe in three days. We go from dawn until late at night, and we come home exhausted. My son, Blayne Edward, who is turning ten this year, wanted to go with us. I said sure. But I reminded him that it would mean two hours in the car to the Atlanta airport and seven hours on the plane to Billings, Montana. Blayne is looking forward to teleportation being invented, because he feels that five minutes in a car is long enough to get to any point short of Mars. So he thought about that for a minute, grinned and said, "Mom, I'd really like to go with you, but I have to stay here and feed the chickens."

My husband, James, agreed. I went to Montana. Ann and I got lost in Wyoming after an eight-hour drive through Yellowstone and the Rockies, and wound up on a dirt road at an oil refinery twenty miles from anywhere with a quarter of a tank of gas at ten-thirty at night. I was driving. Next time *I'm* going to stay home and feed the chickens!

Chapter One

It was the second day of the dig, and Christiana Haley was having the time of her life. She'd signed up with Dr. Adamson's Pastfinders team earlier in the year, planning the three-week trip to coincide with her summer vacation from teaching. It was a long way from Jacksonville, Florida, to Tucson, Arizona, but as Christiana had pointed out to her worried older sister, sand was sand.

However, she was learning the hard way that ocean sand and desert sand were amazingly different. She'd forgotten to wear a hat yesterday morning, and he had given her hell. In fact, *he* gave her hell at every possible turn, and had ever since she and the team had registered at his dude ranch. If only Professor Adamson had picked *anywhere* other than the Lang Ranch for the dig. It was pure bad luck that the *Hohokam* ruin the professor was interested in was on property owned by Nathanial Lang, who seemed to hate science, modern people, and Christiana with a passion.

Christy had actually daydreamed about meeting a handsome, charming, eligible cowboy out West when she'd paid the group rate for joining the private archaeological expedition. And what did she get? She got Nathanial Lang, who was neither handsome nor charming even though he was eligible. He'd barely looked at Christy at the Tucson airport and his slate-gray eyes had grown quickly colder. Men had really started noticing her just recently. Her new image gave her a confidence she hadn't had, and it had helped her to overcome her former demeanor—which was shy and awkward and old-fashioned. She had a nice figure anyway, and the new wardrobe really did emphasize it. She was slender and had pale green eyes and long silvery blond hair, a soft mouth and a delicate oval face. She looked very nearly pretty. But Nathanial Lang had stared at her as if she had germs, and he'd made sure to keep his distance from her, even while he was being charming and courteous to the rest of the twelve-member group.

It wasn't her fault that she had two left feet, Christy kept reassuring herself. Just because she'd tripped over her suitcase at the airport and sent its contents flying—and her bra had landed on top of Nathanial Lang's dark head and given him a vague resemblance to a World War I flying ace—well, why should he have been so insulted? Lots of people spilled things. Everyone else had found it simply hilarious. Including, unfortunately, Christy herself.

He hadn't spoken directly to her after that. At supper, a delicious affair served on the ranch's sprawling patio facing a range of mountains that became a shade of pale burgundy in the setting sun, she'd managed to spill a bowl of tomato soup on the lap of her white skirt and while frantically trying to wipe it up with the tablecloth, she'd pulled that off her table—along with most of her supper. It was good luck that she'd been sitting alone. Mr. Lang's mother had been caring and sympathetic. Mr. Lang had fried her with his slate-gray eyes.

The first morning they went out to the dig, she'd tried to get on a horse and had to be helped into the saddle. The horse, sensing her fear of it, helped her right back off again and reached down to bite her.

She'd screamed and accused it of cannibalism, at which point the increasingly irritable Mr. Lang had put her into his Jeep and promptly driven her to the dig site, where he'd deposited her with bridled fury. After a day in the sun, her skin was fried and she'd been no trouble to anybody, preferring a bath and bed to supper.

Somehow, she'd managed to avoid Mr. Lang this morning. Two other members of the party hated horses, so the three of them had begged a ride with the equipment truck driver. It was almost noon, and so far no Mr. Lang. Christy mentally patted herself on the back. She'd avoided him for several hours now; maybe her luck would hold.

Just as the thought occurred, a Jeep climbed over the distant mountain and threw up a cloud of dust as it barreled toward the dig site. A lean man in a creamy Stetson was driving it, and Christy knew just by the set of his head who it was. With a sigh, she laid down the screen box she'd been manipulating for fragments of pottery. It had been too good to last.

He got out of the Jeep and after a few terse words with Professor Adamson, he headed straight for Christy.

"At least you had enough sense to bring the sun hat," he muttered with a pointed stare at the floppy straw brimmed hat that shaded her pale skin. "Sunstroke is unpleasant."

"I'm not stupid," she informed him. "I teach school—"

"Yes, I know. Grammar school, isn't it?" he added, insinuating with that thin smile that she wasn't intelligent enough to teach older students.

She bristled. "Second grade, in fact. I have thirty students most years."

"Amazing," he murmured, studying her. "They carry medical insurance, presumably?"

She got to her feet. Too quickly. She tripped over the screen box and cannoned into a startled Nathanial Lang, tipping him headfirst into another amateur archaeologist. They collided in an almost balletic sequence, toppling down the small rise and into the small trickle of water in the creek.

"I'm sorry, Mr. Lang!" Christy wailed.

He and the other man got to their feet as she made her way carefully down the small incline, her hand against her mouth.

Nathanial Lang's once-immaculate pale blue pinstriped shirt was muddy now, along with the deep blue sports coat he'd worn with it. There was a long trail of mud down one sharply creased trouser leg, and a smear on his creamy Stetson. He stared down at Christy with eyes that she couldn't meet.

"Things were so quiet around here before you came, Miss Haley," he said through his teeth. "And this is only your second day, isn't it?"

Christy swallowed down her fear. He was tall and very intimidating, not at all the hero type she'd been hoping to meet. "I'm doing my best, Mr. Lang."

"Obviously," he said without inflection.

She reached out to brush off a few spots of dust on his jacket, but he caught her wrist. His touch, even firm and irritable, was exciting.

"Gosh, Mr. Lang, I'm sorry about that," George, the young student archaeologist, apologized. George had gone down the hill with the older man.

"Not your fault," Nathanial said curtly.

"Not Christy's, either," George defended her bravely. He was tall, thin, blond and wore glasses. He was studious and shy and had a habit of going scarlet when he was embarrassed—like now. He managed a smile for Christy and plodded back to his table, where he was sorting and matching pottery shards.

"A fan of yours, I gather," Nathanial remarked as he brushed angrily at his Stetson while his slate-gray eyes pinned Christy.

"A friend," she corrected. She shifted. He made her nervous.

"What are you doing out here?" he asked unexpectedly.

Glad for an opportunity to really talk about her work, she said, "I'm searching for pieces of *Hohokam* pottery. We've mapped this area and we're doing a pottery search."

"I know that," he said with forced patience. "What are you doing in Arizona?"

"I had a vacation and I like ruins."

"There's Rome," he pointed out. "They have lots of ruins over there."

"They've all been dug up," she replied. "I wanted to go someplace where everything hasn't already been discovered."

"You might try the North Pole." He frowned. "On second thought, don't do it. There's a theory about the calamity that would strike if it melted. With your background, who knows? You might trip over some forgotten thermonuclear device and blow it up."

She glared at him. Anger gave her delicate features added beauty and color, and her green eyes blazed up. "I can't help having the occasional accident!" she said angrily, wishing she could see him better. He was very tall and his face seemed far away.

He put his spotted Stetson back on his head and cocked it at an angle across his brow. "I'll bet your insurance company has prayer every morning."

"I don't have an insurance company," she managed under her breath.

"Why doesn't that surprise me?" He tipped his hat and started to walk away.

"I'm really sorry about your hat and all," she called after him.

"Lucky for me that it was a little creek instead of an old mine." He stopped and turned, his expression very serious. "That reminds me, there are a few old mines around here, so for God's sake stick to well-traveled areas. If you go down a shaft, you could disappear forever."

She sighed. "Okay. I'll stay where I'm told."

"You'd better," he said firmly and kept walking.

The thought of a mine shaft opening under her kept Christy nervous for the rest of the day. So far all they'd found had been little bits and pieces of pottery, mostly gray. But the fact that it was over a thousand years old made her giddy. Imagine holding something in her hand that a *Hohokam* potter had held in his or hers that many centuries ago! She held one shard up to her nose and drank in its earthy, dark scent with her eyes closed.

They were a very special race, the *Hohokam*. They'd had irrigation and a unique form of peaceful government here in southeastern Arizona about the same time people were hitting each other over the head with battle-axes in Europe. They had a religion which united and uplifted them, a society which was equal for rich and poor alike. They were a poetic people, with a reverent attitude toward the land and each other. From this ancient people, it was said, the *Pima* and the *Papago (Tohono O'odham)* tribes evolved.

"Exciting, isn't it?" George asked, squatting down beside her as she laid the shard back down. "I've read everything I could find about the *Hohokam*. What a pity that their way of life had to vanish."

"At least there are offshoots of it—the *Pima* and the *Papago*," she reminded him. "The *Anasazi* left no trace of themselves as far as we know."

He sighed. "I've dreamed all my life of coming here," he remarked, his eyes lifting to the surrounding sharp, lifeless mountains and the blue sky. "Isn't it clean? Like it might have been a thousand years ago."

"They have pollution alerts in Phoenix these days," she said, "and water and soil pollution are just as big a threat. Toxic waste and radioactive debris and chemical spills..."

George glowered at her. "You're a real thrill to have around."

"Sorry. I have a soapbox. I got hooked on conservation when I was just a little girl. I've never lost the fire. I think the Indians had the right idea—to live in harmony with nature. All we've managed to do is pollute it out of existence. We've destroyed the delicate balance of predator and prey that once sustained the whole planet. Now we're trying to recreate it by synthetic means. I wish we'd left it alone."

"If that had happened, you would be pounding maize to make cornmeal and chewing deerskin to make it soft enough for clothing. I would be hunting buffalo and dodging bullets trying to provide meat for somebody's lodge." He grinned. "In between there would be prairie fires, attack by enemy tribes, rattlesnakes, dust storms, floods and droughts and rabid animals—"

"Stop." She held up her hand. "I agree wholeheartedly that there are two sides to every story." She grinned back. "How about helping me organize these pottery shards?"

"There's something we can agree on," he said.

That night, Christy managed not to do anything remotely clumsy at dinner. She sat out on the patio watching the stars, munching a cookie while Hereford cattle grazed and lowed in a fenced pasture just a few yards from where she sat. The gauzy white Mexican dress she was wearing was cool and comfortable, and her long hair was blowing in the soft wind.

Footfalls behind her made her start. She knew almost without looking who was going to be there when she turned around.

"There's a pool game going on and several people are playing bridge," he said. "I saw a chess match and a checkers tournament. There are books in the library and a television and several new movies to watch."

"Thank you, Mr. Lang, but I find this much more entertaining."

"Waiting for George to show up?" he queried, pausing beside her chair.

"George is playing chess," she informed him.

"And you aren't going to cheer him on?" he asked with cheerful mockery. He lit a cigarette and straddled a chair across from her. He was wearing jeans and boots and a silky blue shirt that clung to the hard muscles of his arms.

She lowered her eyes shyly. "George is just a colleague."

"Not quite what you expected when you signed on?" he probed. He lifted the cigarette to his lips. "Didn't you come out here looking for adventure and romance? And what did you find? George."

"George is intelligent and kind and very nice to talk to," she faltered. "I like him."

"He's not likely to throw you over his saddle and carry you off into the hills," he pointed out.

"Thank God," she replied. Her fingers clenched the arms of her chair. Her heart was going crazy. Why wouldn't he stop baiting her?

He turned his head and watched her, his eyes missing nothing as they ran down her body to her long, elegant legs peeking out from the skirt of the white dress and to her strappy white sandals. "No taste for excitement, Miss Haley?"

"Being carried off like a sack of flour is hardly my idea of excitement, Mr. Lang."

"Ah. A career woman." He made it sound like a mutated strain of leprosy.

"I'm not a career woman. I have a job that I like and I'm very satisfied with my life and myself."

"How old are you?" he persisted.

"Twenty-five," she said after a minute.

"Not a bad age," he remarked. He blew out a cloud of smoke. "I'm thirty-seven." She didn't say anything and he smiled mockingly. "No comment? No curiosity about my life?"

"What do you do, Mr. Lang, besides run this ranch?" she asked politely and folded her restless hands in her lap.

"I'm a mining engineer. I work for a company near Bisbee. You've heard of the Lavendar Pit, I imagine? It was the biggest mine around in the heyday of mining here in southeastern Arizona. Of course, now it's little more than a tourist attraction. But we have plenty of other mining interests, and I work for one of them."

"I've heard about the Lavendar Pit, but I haven't seen it yet. I don't know much about Arizona. Do you like your work?"

"Sometimes. I like geology. Rocks fascinate me. I was a rock hound as a kid and as I got older, I found that I liked it enough for a career. I studied it in college for four years, got my degree, worked briefly for an oil company and finally wound up here." He took another draw from his cigarette. "I might have gone to Alaska to work, but my father died and mother couldn't manage the dude ranch alone."

"You . . . never married?"

He shrugged. "No reason to," he said honestly. "It's a great time to be a man, in a world where women would rather be lovers than wives. All the benefits of marriage, no responsibilities."

"No security, no shared life, no children," she added.

He shifted in his chair. "That's true. Especially, no children. How about you, Miss Haley? Why are you still single yourself?"

"I haven't ever been in love," she said simply, smiling as she glanced his way. "I've had proposals and propositions but I've never cared enough to give my heart." *Or my body*, she could have added.

"I can understand that."

She glanced at him, but she couldn't see him well enough to gauge his expression.

He leaned toward her, his eyes narrowed. "Why did you come out here?"

"I wanted to do something wild just once in my life, if you must know," she replied. "My sister—she's five years older than I am—leads me around like I'm a lost soul. She's so afraid that I'll have a terrible accident and die. Our parents are gone, and that would leave her alone in the world. I can't seem to breathe without Joyce Ann asking if I've got asthma. I haven't been out of Jacksonville in my whole life, so I thought it was time. I escaped on a plane and didn't tell Joyce Ann where I was going. I left her a note and told her I'd call her in a week and tell her where I was."

"I imagine she's worried," he said quietly.

"Probably." She stared at her hands. "I guess it was a cowardly thing to do."

"Why don't you go inside and call her? You don't have to tell her where you are. Just tell her you're all right."

She hesitated, but only for a minute. "I should, shouldn't I?" she asked softly.

"Yes, you should." He got up and reached a lean, very strong hand down to pull her up. For a few seconds, they were almost touching and she had her first really good look at his face.

He had a lean face with a jutting chin and thin lips and high cheekbones. His eyebrows were dark over deep-set eyes and there were little wrinkly lines at the edges of his eyes. His hair was thick and very dark and he combed it all straight back away from his face. He was a hard-looking man, but appearances could be deceptive. He was much more approachable than she'd imagined.

If she was looking, then so was he. His gaze was slow and very thorough, taking in her delicate features like a mop soaking up water. The hand still holding hers contracted with a caressing kind of pressure that made her stomach tighten as if something electric had jumped inside it. She almost gasped at the surge of delicious feeling.

"Don't stay up too late," he said. "You're two hours behind your time in Jacksonville. It will take a couple more days for you to get used to the difference."

"All right. Thank you, Mr. Lang."

"Most people call me Nate," he said quietly.

"Nate." She liked the way it sounded. He must have liked it, too, because he actually smiled. He dropped her hand and stood back, letting her move around the chair and back to the small guest cabin she occupied. She paused at the corner of the patio and looked back. She made a little farewell gesture with her hand, smiled back self-consciously, and went on her way.

Chapter Two

Joyce Ann was outraged when she found out where Christy was.

"You might at least have asked my advice," the older woman said. "Honestly, Christy, I don't know what's gotten into you lately. The new clothes, the new hairstyle, and going without your..."

"Now, Joyce Ann," Christy soothed, "you said yourself that I was getting into a rut. I'm fine. There are some very handsome men out here," she added, dangling the sentence like bait.

Joyce Ann swallowed it whole. "Men?"

"That's right. Especially one. He's very dashing and romantic, and he's always talking to me." Well, that was true, except that the way he was talking to her wouldn't sound very romantic to her sister.

"Well, he couldn't be much worse than Harry, I guess," came the reply.

Christy didn't like thinking about Harry. He was more of a last resort than a suitor, the kind of man her more staid image attracted. Harry probably wouldn't have cared for the new her. "Harry's been nice to me," she said. "It's just that he wants a mother for his sons more than he wants a wife."

"You aren't desperate enough to marry Harry," Joyce Ann said firmly. "Now tell me about this Arizona man."

"He's sexy and very nice."

"That's different," Joyce Ann said, and laughed. "In that case, I'll forgive you for worrying me to death. How long are you going to stay?"

"Another week or so."

"Good, good. Darling, do let me know how things go. And do, please, wear your—"

"Goodnight, Joyce Ann. I'll keep in touch, I promise!"

She hung up with a long sigh. That was out of the way. Now she could enjoy herself, without having Joyce Ann hang over her shoulder trying to shove men in her path.

The image change was her own idea, though, not her sister's. She was tired of the routine her life had become. She wanted to do something wild, something different. And people had to take chances and do outrageous things once in a while if they didn't want to stagnate. So she'd signed on for this expedition, something she'd always longed to do, she'd bought new clothes unlike anything she'd ever worn before, and she'd changed her appearance. There were a few little minor drawbacks, like walking into people, but in the meantime she was having a ball. Until tonight, she'd actually forgotten Harry and his plans for her.

As she got ready for bed, she thought about Nathanial Lang's attitude toward her. For a man who found her an impossible trial, he'd certainly changed his tune. He'd been almost companionable tonight. She remembered how nervous she'd felt around him at their first meeting, and compared it with the ease of talking to him earlier. It was as if he'd wanted her to be curious about his life, to want to know him as a person. And, she discovered, she honestly did. He wasn't quite the stick-in-the-mud she'd thought he was. He was much more. She went to sleep on that tantalizing thought.

The next morning, she was the first one at the breakfast buffet, to her embarrassment. She'd slept fitfully and her dreams had been confusing and vivid, mostly about the elusive Mr. Lang.

But if she hoped to find a new beginning with him, it was a dream gone awry. He stared right through her as he walked past the buffet and kept going. She stood gaping after his tall figure in the tan suit and cream-colored Stetson, wondering what she'd done to antagonize him now. Probably, she sighed as she put a tiny amount of food on her plate, she'd breathed the wrong way.

"Here, now, Miss Haley, that's not enough to keep a bird alive," Mrs. Lang tut-tutted. The small, dark-eyed woman shook her head. "You'll make me self-conscious about my cooking."

"Your cooking is delicious," Christy protested, embarrassed. "It's just that the, uh, the heat is difficult for me."

"Oh." The white lie produced good results, because Mrs. Lang smiled and lost her worried look. "I forget that you're not used to the desert. But don't you worry, you'll adjust soon enough. Just take it easy, drink plenty of fluids and don't go into the sun without a hat!"

"You can count on me," Christy said with a jaunty smile.

She sat down alone at a table, picking at her food, while the much older Professor Adamson and his wife Nell smiled politely as they passed and went to their own table. The others drifted in one at a time, yawning and looking dragged out. George noticed Christy sitting alone and made a beeline for her.

"What a beautiful morning." He grinned as he sat down with a disgustingly full plate and proceeded to eat every bite. "I never get this hungry back in Wichita. Great food, isn't it? You're not eating," he added with a frown.

"I'm so hot," she said and smiled at him. "I'll get used to the climate in a day or so."

"Lots to do today," he murmured between bites. "Mason's going to use the laptop to match the pottery fragments we've found so far. He spent the night writing a program for it."

"Computers make me nervous," Christy confessed. "We have one at school that we're teaching our second-graders to use, and I'm terrified of it."

"You should see Mr. Lang's," he confided. "He's got one of those mainframe jobs—you know, the kind that cost twenty grand or so. He uses it to keep his cattle records on, and he's got some great graphic software that he uses in his mining work. What a setup!"

"He must be pretty smart," she said.

"Smart doesn't cover it. The man's a wizard, they say. A couple of the gang tried to beat him at chess last night. Talk about ego problems...he could checkmate the best of them in three moves or less."

"I'm glad I don't play chess."

"Well, I wish I didn't," he said with a grin. "Eat up. Time's awasting."

They went out to the dig in the equipment truck again, and Christy settled down to another day of sifting through sand to find pottery fragments.

She was sitting in the shade of the truck with a soft drink from the cooler at lunchtime when the Jeep roared up. Nathanial Lang climbed out of it, still wearing his suit, and looked around the relaxed camp until he located Christy. He studied her from a distance for one long minute and then went and said something to Professor Adamson before he came to join her.

"You're alone," he remarked, going down on one knee beside her. "Did George die?"

She gaped at him. "I beg your pardon?"

"I'm going into Tucson for some supplies I ordered. Come with me."

Her heart jumped into her throat. "Are you sure you aren't mistaking me for someone else?" she asked, staring into his eyes at point-blank range. "You walked past me as if you hated the very sight of me not five hours ago."

"I did, but that was five hours ago," he said pleasantly. "I've checked you out with the professor. He says you can go."

"I'm not a library book that you can check out . . . Mr. Lang!"

He'd pulled her up by one hand with apparent ease and she was protesting on the run. He lifted her by the waist, soft drink and all, and put her inside the Jeep, smiling a little as he noticed her attire. Long khaki walking shorts and high beige socks in saddle oxfords, with a lemon cotton shirt that buttoned up and a yellow tank top under that. She'd tied a jaunty yellow-and-white scarf around the band of her hat and she looked very trendy with her long silvery blond hair falling down around her shoulders.

"You look like a teenager," he said, grinning.

She smiled back, shocked by his attention when she'd given up on ever getting it. "Thank you," she said, feeling and sounding shy.

He let go of her, shut the door, and got in beside her. "Hold on," he instructed as he started the Jeep and put it in gear.

It shot off like a gray bullet, bouncing her from one side to the other so that she had to hold her hat to keep it on her head.

"Doesn't this thing have shocks?" she cried above the roar of the engine.

"Why do we need shocks?" he asked with lifted eyebrows.

She laughed and shook her head. Even a simple thing like going to town took on all the dimensions of an adventure with this man. She held on to the dash with one hand and her hat with the other, drinking in the peace of the desert as they sped along the wide dirt road that led to the paved road to Tucson. Fields of saguaro and creosote, prickly pear cactus and ocotillo, cholla and mesquite stretched to the jagged mountain chains that surrounded Tucson. It was a sight to pull at the heart. So much land, so much history, so much space. She could hardly believe she was really here, sitting beside a man who was as elemental as the country he lived in. Her head turned and she stared at him with pure pleasure in his masculinity, little thrills of delight winding through her body. She'd never felt such a reaction to a man before. But then, she'd never met a man like Nathanial Lang.

He caught that shy scrutiny. It made him feel taller than he was to have such a pretty woman look at him that way. He was glad he'd let his mother talk him into changing his staid bachelor image, and he was especially glad about the improvement when he was with Christy.

"How are you enjoying your stint in the sun?" he asked.

"It's harder work than I expected," she admitted. "I'm stiff and sore from sitting in one place and using muscles I didn't know I had. It's rather boring in a way. But to sit and hold something a thousand years old in my hand," she said with faint awe, "that's worth all the discomfort."

He smiled. "I find the *Hohokam* equally fascinating," he said then. "Did you know that the *Tohono O'odham* are probably descended from the *Hohokam*? And that their basket weaving is so exacting and precise that their baskets can actually hold water?"

"No, I didn't! I'll bet they cost the earth."

"Some of them do, and they're worth every penny. I know an old woman who still practices the craft, out on the *Papago* Reservation. I'll take you out to see her while you're here."

"Oh, would you?!" she exclaimed, all eyes.

"She'll be glad to find someone more interested in her craft than in the price of it." He pulled out onto the paved highway and shot the Jeep smoothly into high gear.

She gave up trying to hold her hat on her head and took it off, clutching it in her lap.

"Not nervous are you?" he taunted gently. "I'd have thought a grammar school teacher would have nerves of steel."

"I need them from time to time," she agreed. She twisted her hat in her hands, enjoying the wind in her hair and the sweet smell of clean air. It was different from the smell of the Atlantic, and not as moist, but it was equally pleasant.

"I suppose you miss the sea," he said, and she started.

"Well . . . a little," she admitted. "But the desert is fascinating."

"I'm glad you think so." He turned the Jeep on the road that led directly into Tucson. "How do you like Tucson?"

"My first sight of it was staggering," she told him. "I never realized how big and sprawling it was."

"We like a lot of space," he said with a quick smile. "I can't stand to go back East for long. I feel cramped."

"Too many trees, I expect," she replied with a wicked glance.

"That's about it." He sped past fast-food restaurants, modern shopping malls, motels and empty lots. "Did anyone tell you about the coyotes?"

"In the mountains, you mean?" she asked as she looked toward them.

"No. Here in the city. You can hear them howling early in the morning. The tourists get a big kick out of it."

"I wouldn't," she said, shivering.

"Sure you would. You can hear them out at the ranch, can't you?"

"I thought the howling was wolves."

"Coyotes," he corrected. "The Indians used to call them 'song dogs.' There are all sorts of legends about them. One says that they would sometimes stay with a wounded man and guard him until he healed."

"You know a lot about this country, don't you?" she asked.

He smiled. "I was born here. I love it." He turned down a side street and into a parking lot.

Before she could ask where they were, he'd cut off the engine and extricated her from the Jeep.

She almost had to run to keep up with his long strides. In the process of getting into the store, she managed to run into the door and overturn a barrel of hoes and shovels.

With her eyes closed, she didn't have to see the expression she knew would be on Nathanial Lang's face. If she'd had the courage, she'd have stuck her fingers in her ears to keep from hearing him. But no sound came, except a clang and a thud here and there, and hesitantly, she opened one eye.

"No problem," Nathanial murmured dryly. He'd replaced the barrel and its contents and he had her by the arm, an expression on his face that she couldn't decipher.

"I'm so sorry..." she said, flustered.

"Stand over here and look pretty," he told her, leaving her against the fishing tackle counter. "I'll pick up my tags and be back before you miss me."

He did and he was, giving Christy time to gather her shredded nerves and manage some semblance of dignity. Of all the times to do something clumsy, she moaned inwardly, and she'd been doing so good.

"Don't look so worried," Nathanial chided as he came back with a large box over one shoulder. He took her by the arm. "Let's go. How about lunch?"

"I had a soft drink," she began as he hustled her out the door and back into the Jeep.

"No substitute for a good meal," he returned. "How about some *chimichangas* and a taco salad?"

"A chimi-what?"

"*Chimichanga*. It's a...Oh, hell, I'll buy you one and you can see for yourself. They're good."

They were. He took her to a nice restaurant near one of the biggest new malls in town, and she had food she'd never heard of back in northern Florida.

The *chimichanga* was spicy and delicious, beef and beans and cheese and peppers in a soft shell that melted in her mouth. She'd had great fun studying the menu before they ordered.

"What's this?" she asked, pointing to the breakfast entrées.

"*Huevos rancheros*," he translated, "or ranch eggs. It's a little misleading," he said with a smile. "Scrambled eggs and refried beans with salsa. If you eat it, you don't want to sit upwind of any potential victims. It's harsh on the digestive system if you aren't used to it."

She burst out laughing. He was so different than she'd imagined. He was good company and a lot of fun, and best of all, he didn't seem to mind that she couldn't walk five feet without falling over something.

"Like it?" he asked when she'd finished most of the taco salad and was sipping her huge glass of ice water as if it was the last drop on earth.

"Love it!" she enthused. "I could get addicted to this food."

"That's nice to hear." He finished his soft drink and leaned back in his chair, one lean hand toying with his napkin while he studied her at his leisure. "I'm still trying to figure out how a woman who looks like you do manages to stay single."

"I haven't really wanted to get married," she confessed. She smiled at him shyly. She wanted to add that until recently, she'd looked more like a violet than a rose. She'd bought some new clothes and had her hair styled and she'd even taken a brief modeling course to learn how to move and walk. But she couldn't tell Nate that. She didn't want him to think she was a phony. It was just that he wouldn't have looked twice at the woman she'd been. Nobody ever had— except Harry.

His eyes narrowed as he listened to her. So she didn't have marriage in mind. Good. Neither did he. And looking the way she did, there'd been men. He was almost sure of it, despite her old-maid shyness. That could be an act, of course. He'd seen some performances in recent years, despite his lack of looks. He had money. It made him a target for all sorts of women, but especially for the pretty, fortune-hunting variety. God knew, there had been plenty of those around. The dude ranch drew them in droves. He'd always enjoyed the game while it lasted, but he was looking especially forward to playing it with Christy. She was a dish and he wanted her feverishly. Going slow was the hardest thing he'd ever done, but she seemed to want a slow pace, and he didn't want to spoil things.

"Have you always taught school?" he asked.

She nodded. "Ever since I graduated from college. I don't know if you ever really graduate, though," she added on a laugh. "You have to constantly take refresher courses and upgrade your education. I don't mind it. I like learning new things, new techniques. It's quite a challenge to get young minds to enjoy being taught.''

"I can imagine."

"You must have studied geology," she said when a short silence fell between them.

He nodded. "I always loved rocks. The feel of them, the history of them, the colors, the forms." He smiled at her over his glass. "I was a rock hound even when I was a kid. As I grew older, mining sort of stood out as a possible profession. It's hard to ignore mines in this part of the country. Tombstone was started as a mining town, and Bisbee with its Lavendar Pit mine was known all over the country for copper mining in its heyday. Even today, seventy percent of all the copper mined in the U.S. comes out of Tucson and Pima County, Arizona. This is the greatest place around for finding profitable minerals, and I don't mean just gold and silver.''

"I guess everyone in the world has heard about the Lost Dutchman's Mine in the Superstition Mountains," she agreed.

"Yes. And that's far east of here. But there are rumors that another kind of gold can be found in Colossal Cave, and that's just outside Tucson. It's the biggest dry cave in the country, you know. Outlaws once used it as a hideout, you see," he said, leaning forward to whisper conspiratorially. "And they say the gold's still hidden in there!"

"Wow!" She smiled with excited delight. "Could we go there and look?"

"And here I thought you weren't a mercenary girl," he chided, and the cynicism in his eyes almost gave him away.

"It's the adventure of it, not the prize," she replied, blissfully unaware of the undercurrents. "I'd rather find an old six-shooter or some Apache arrowheads than the gold, if you want the truth.''

"I've got a whole collection of Apache arrowheads," he told her. "And if you like, I'll run you over to Cochise Stronghold one day while you're here. Cochise and his band used to camp there. He and his people fought the U.S. Cavalry to a standstill and legend and the historical people say he's buried in an unmarked grave on the site. The Indian agent, Tom Jeffords, who was his friend, was the only white man who was privileged to know the old chief's burial place.''

"What is it like there? Desert?" she asked.

"No!" he denied, shaking his head. "It's way back in a canyon with plenty of trees and good water and mountains behind. It's a beautiful spot.''

"Imagine that." She sighed, staring at him. "You know, before I came out here, I thought the desert was just a lot of sand stretching to the horizon. But it's not like that at all. It's full of creosote and cholla, ocotillo and prickly pear cactus, and cottonwood and mesquite. And the birds! The red-winged blackbird is so beautiful.''

"Not to mention the cactus wren, the roadrunner, and the owls," he agreed, smiling back at her. "Yes, there's life out there. Other kinds, too. Lizards and snakes, coyotes, wolves, deer, game birds—"

"How long have your people lived in Arizona?" she interrupted.

He shrugged. "I don't really know. An ancestor of mine was living in Tombstone around the time of the O.K. Corral, but I don't know when he actually came here. All I know is that he was a Southerner. He came here after the Civil War.''

"Someone told me that the city of Tucson once flew the Confederate flag just briefly.''

"And it's true. A lot of Southerners settled here in the old days. There's plenty of history here in this part of the state."

"I grew up reading Zane Grey," she recalled wistfully. "I never dreamed I'd actually get to see any of the places he wrote about. But the most exciting part of this trip has been looking at the *Hohokam* ruins."

He nodded. "They fascinate me, too. In 300 B.C., the *Hohokam* farmed here using a 150-mile system of canals. They were an inspiring people."

"Yes, I'm learning that."

He glanced at his watch. "I've got to get back to work. Are you through?"

"Yes, thank you. How can you take off whenever you like?" she asked hesitantly as they got up.

He grinned. "I'm vice president of the mining company. My uncle owns it."

"Oh."

"I'm rich," he said, and a mocking smile touched his lean, dark face. "Haven't you noticed? Most women do."

She flushed and turned away, flustered by the point-blank bluntness. In her haste to move, she backed into the chair he'd pulled out for her, tripped, and went face down across it, plowing into a table full of tourists and their children.

Milk shakes and hamburgers went everywhere. So did the contents of Christy's purse. She sprawled on the floor, feeling unbearably foolish and embarrassed.

"That was my fault," Nate said quietly as he helped her up and proceeded to patch up the incident with a charm and diplomacy that Christy was just beginning to realize was an innate part of his personality. Flinty he might be, but he was a gentleman, and he had a knack for putting people at ease. The tourists were more concerned about Christy than the mess she'd made, and even the restaurant people were understanding and kind.

All that sweetness only made Christy feel worse. She was in tears by the time Nate helped her into the Jeep.

"Now, now," he said gently, mopping up her tears. "I shouldn't have cut at you like that. It was my fault, not yours."

"It was mine," she wailed. "I'm so clumsy...!"

He finished clearing away the tears and tilted her face up to his searching gaze while he surveyed the damage. "Red nose, red eyes, red cheeks," he murmured dryly. His eyes fell to her mouth and lingered there until she felt her toes curling in her shoes. "Red mouth, too," he said, his voice deepening. The hand holding her chin contracted a little. "Red and soft and very, very tempting, little Christy," he said, half under his breath. He lifted his eyes to catch the look in hers, and his gaze held hers until she was breathless from the tense excitement he created.

The interior of the Jeep was quiet with the canvas top on, and they could barely hear the traffic noise outside. The heat was stifling, but neither noticed. His dark eyes lanced into her pale ones and even as he looked at her, he moved closer, looming over her, the spicy scent of his cologne filling her nostrils as his mouth began to move down toward hers.

She felt her nails clench on the expensive fabric of his jacket while her heart tried to climb into her throat. His mouth was very masculine, and it looked hard and ruthless for all its sensuality. She imagined that he knew a lot more about kissing than she did, and the thought of being kissed by Nathanial Lang was far more exciting than she'd ever dreamed. She felt her lips parting for him, waiting, her body in a tense expectation that was suddenly, painfully, shattered by the car that pulled up alongside Nate's Jeep with a noisy roar.

Nate sat up, glaring toward the new arrivals. "Just as well, honey," he said when he noticed Christy's expression.

"What we were leading up to wouldn't have been appropriate in a public place. I don't want an audience when I kiss you for the first time."

She choked on her own reply, but he only smiled and started the Jeep.

"Fasten your seat belt," he said easily, and pulled out into the road with apparent ease, his expression as relaxed as if he'd been on a leisurely outing with no excitement at all.

He let Christy out at the dig, and try as she might, she couldn't quite manage to be as blasé and sophisticated about what had happened as he was being.

Fortunately for her, George saw them drive up in the Jeep and came loping toward them, all smiles, with a laptop computer under one arm.

"There you are!" he called to Christy and waved. "I missed you!"

Nate glared toward him. "George, again," he murmured darkly. "Does he have radar, do you suppose?"

"He's lonely," she stammered, surprised by his antagonism for the younger man.

"Is he?" He glanced at her curiously and then shrugged. "Well, to each his own. See you later."

He let her out and pulled away with a shower of dust, without even looking back. In another man, she might have suspected jealousy. But a man like Nathanial Lang wouldn't be jealous of her in a million years, and certainly not of sweet egghead George. She turned with a smile painted on her face to listen to what George was rambling on about. But her mind was still on what had happened in the parking lot of the restaurant, her lips hungry for a kiss she'd wanted so desperately and didn't get.

Nate's behavior was puzzling to her. He seemed genuinely interested in her one minute, and he looked at her with such cynicism the next. She didn't quite know how to take him. She hoped she wasn't letting herself in for a big heartache. Nate Lang appealed to her. She liked to think that the reverse was also true, but she was going to have to watch her step. He was a worldly man with a real sophistication. She couldn't afford to fall too deeply under his spell unless she was certain that he felt the same way she was beginning to. Holiday romances might be the norm here, and she might not be the first Eastern tourist to catch Mr. Lang's sharp eye.

That thought was so depressing that she gave George a beaming smile, and he returned it with interest, thinking it was the lure of his charm finally getting to her.

Chapter Three

Christy had expected Nathanial to ignore her again that night, because he seemed to go from friendly companionship to cold animosity with relative ease where she was concerned. But that evening after supper, he pulled her to one side before George could appropriate her for a chess game in the recreation room.

"Do you dance?" he asked, his level stare disconcerting.

"Why . . . yes, a little," she stammered.

"There's a bar and grill in town. They have a country-western band and dancing every night. We could sit and drink beer and dance."

"I don't drink," she said, sounding apologetic. Then she held her breath, because he might not want to take her along at all.

"That's all right. You can have ginger ale." He smiled then, and her heart did a dance all its own.

"Then, in that case, I'd like very much to go with you," she said.

"Put on a skirt," he instructed. "Better for dancing."

Was it, she wondered, or did he just like feminine women? But she had to agree when she changed that her full white Spanish dress did a lot more for her than jeans and a loose, short-sleeved sweater had. She brushed her hair out long and wore sandals instead of high heels. When she was ready, she went looking for him. He was wearing dress slacks with a long-sleeved, Western-cut blue-print shirt and a turquoise and silver bola tie, and his feet were decked out in cream-colored boots that matched the Stetson slashed over one dark eyebrow. He looked cocky and arrogant and every inch a sophisticated, mature man. She caught her breath at the thought of spending an evening alone with him and dancing to boot.

"There you are!" George broke in just as she started to speak to Nate. "Why are you dressed up? I thought we were going to play chess."

"I'm going into town with Mr. Lang," she said firmly. "Sorry, George."

The younger man looked unsettled for a moment. He glanced from Christy to Nate Lang, as if it hadn't occurred to him that the other man could possibly be interested in Christy. "Oh, a date," he said hesitantly.

"That's right," Nate said easily. "A date."

"Well, then I, uh, I'll see you later, Christy. Or tomorrow." George smiled nervously before he loped off in the direction of the recreation room.

"He's smitten," Nate told her as he took her arm and propelled her toward his Mercedes.

"He's very nice," she said, defending her colleague. "He's sort of shy and he doesn't mix well. I'm his security blanket."

"You're too much woman to be wasted on a kid who's wet behind the ears," he said.

She waited until he'd put her in the passenger seat and had climbed in beside her to start the car before she answered him. She wasn't quite secure herself, and this man was older than anyone she'd ever dated and very obviously experienced. She didn't quite know how to take his interest in her.

"I'm a little wet behind the ears, myself," she began.

He glanced toward her. "Are you?" he asked, and there was a cynical note in his tone that was lost on her. He grinned. "Fasten your seat belt. Your virtue is safe with me, Miss Greenhorn. For the time being, anyway," he added.

She wondered how to take that, and decided that he was kidding. She laughed softly. "Oh." She fastened the seat belt and tried to look satisfied.

"You're a new experience," he remarked as he pulled the car onto the main highway and sped toward Tucson. "The women I usually attract don't set limits."

"You sound very cynical," she told him.

He shrugged. "I'm a target. I wish I was a little better-looking. Then I might think it was me instead of my bankbook that appealed to the fair sex."

"You must be looking in the wrong kind of mirrors," she said before she thought. She smiled self-consciously at the look he gave her. "Well, you're not exactly repulsive, you know." Her eyes fell to her lap. "You have this way of making people feel safe and at ease with you, and stirring them up all at the same time."

"There's an interesting remark. You can explain it to me a little later on. How do you like the desert at night, little tourist?"

She glanced out the window and sighed as the reddish glow on the horizon threw the jagged mountains into stark relief past the shadowy silhouettes of vegetation across the flat fields. "It's beautiful. Chilly," she added, smiling toward him. "I didn't expect that. The desert is so hot during the day that I thought it would stay that way."

"It doesn't, though. Why do you think cowboys pack blankets in their saddle rolls?" he asked, chuckling. He sped down the highway with absolutely no regard for the posted speed limit, noting her nervous glance at the speedometer.

"Sorry," she muttered. "Back home in Florida, the state patrol will get you for that."

"So will our law enforcement people," he agreed. "But we're pretty far from town here and it's a straight, uncongested highway. I don't take chances, and I can handle the car. In fact, I used to race them when I was in my early twenties."

"Really?" she asked, fascinated.

"Just stock cars," he added. "I did some rodeo, and once or twice I tried my hand at steeplechase. In those days, living dangerously had a special appeal. These days, there's enough excitement in just trying to keep up with taxes and tax shelters, in between prospecting for new finds."

"I don't suppose I've ever done anything really dangerous," she remarked, her pale eyes sparkling with faint humor. "Except maybe riding in that Jeep with you," she added, glancing deliberately at him.

He laughed with pure delight. "You were holding on hard enough, that's for sure. Well, we won't do anything that exciting tonight."

She wanted to tell him that just being with him was exciting, but she didn't quite have the nerve.

The bar and grill was in a nice part of town, and it wasn't a dive at all. It was one of those big, airy places with a distinctly Western atmosphere that catered to city cowboys. It featured a mechanical bull, a dance floor and band, and a light show that was a delight in itself. Nate found them a table facing the band and dance floor and seated her before he went to get them something to drink.

"What do you fancy? Just ginger ale?" he asked politely.

"Just that," she agreed.

He pursed his thin lips and stared down at her speculatively. "Do you like the taste of beer?" he asked with a deep, dark kind of velvet in his voice.

Her breath jerked a little. "Well...not really," she admitted.

"In that case, I think I'll stick to ginger ale, myself," he said and smiled slowly. He left her and went toward the bar.

She sat trying to get her breath back while she watched the people on the dance floor and listened to the music. Shortly after Nate left, a young, good-looking cowboy stopped by her table and smiled at her.

"Hi, pretty girl," he said. "Care to dance?"

"No, thank you," she said, smiling back. "I'm with someone."

"Hell, so am I, but that's okay. We're friendly here." He moved a little closer, and looked as if he didn't mean to take "no" for an answer. "Just one dance, and I'll bring you right back."

She didn't want to dance with him, but it didn't look as if she could find a way out without causing a scene.

Just then, Nate came back with two glasses of ginger ale and moved deliberately between Christy, who was still seated, and the cowboy, who wasn't.

He put the glasses down and straightened to face the cowboy, who looked a little less confident. Talk about body language, Christy thought dazedly, watching. Nate's was emphatic and frankly threatening, especially the way he stood, legs slightly apart, both hands by his sides. He was smiling, but it was not a polite smile. This was a side of Nate that Christy hadn't seen before, and she began to understand that ranching wouldn't be a job for a city cowboy. Neither would mining. Nate had mostly been pleasant and easygoing with her, but there was a toughness in him that she was seeing for the first time.

The young cowboy looked a little nervous now. He could see, as Christy could, that Nate was half a head taller than he was and a good bit more muscular, and had an arrogance and authority that the younger man lacked.

"We came here to dance and have a good time," Nate told the cowboy. "But her idea of a good time and mine are a little different. Now, me, I like a good fight, and I really enjoy making holes in glass. In fact, you're just the right size to make a nice big hole in that plate glass window out front..."

"I see my girl over there," the cowboy said suddenly, making as if to look over Nate's shoulder. "Hi, hon!" he called. "Sorry, but I'd better go now," he told Christy. He tilted the brim of his hat respectfully, looked at Nate and cleared his throat, and made a quick exit.

Christy blew out the breath she'd been holding. "I didn't know what to do," she said as he sat down. Her face was red and she was almost babbling with nerves. "He asked me to dance. He wasn't insulting or anything, but he just wouldn't go away."

"Can't say I blame him," Nate said, smiling gently. "You're a dish."

Her face grew radiant. "I am?" she asked shyly.

That attitude amused him. She was good, he'd give her that. The way she'd refused the cowboy and pretended to be frightened was a nice touch. Not that it worked. He'd seen other women use the same tactic. In fact, he was a veteran. One too many sophisticated Eastern women had come out here pretending to be innocent for his benefit. He was too worldly wise to be taken in, unfortunately for Christy.

"Come here." He stood up and pulled her into his arms, moving her out onto the dance floor to the rhythm of a slow love song. "Relax, honey," he said gently when he felt her slender body tense, going along with the deception to put her at ease.

She bit her lip. "I haven't danced much..."

Sure, he thought cynically. "You'll get the hang of it. Here, put both arms around me. Just like this." He pushed her arms under his and around him and slid his own arms around her shoulders, riveting her body to his so that the only space between them was at the hips. He chuckled at the shiver that went through her, his breath warm and amused at her ear. "Don't you like dancing close? I do." He wondered why she insisted on pretending to be shy and innocent, but perhaps it was part of her act. He didn't care. She was like all the other women who came on to him, this was just a different ploy. It wouldn't matter in the long run. She'd be gone soon, so he was going to enjoy her while he could. She appealed to his senses in a shockingly fierce way. He wanted her as he'd never wanted anyone else.

Christy felt his arms contract and her knees threatened to give way beneath her. Nate smelled spicy and manly and she loved the warmth of his lean body and the hard, heavy beat of his heart at her ear. He was so much taller than she was that her cheek lay against his breastbone. He felt like hard muscle all over and she loved the safety and excitement of his arms. Her eyes closed and she relaxed all at once, letting him take her weight.

He let out a breath himself when he felt her breasts soften against him as she let go. He tugged her a little closer, lifting her into a warmer embrace as he moved her to the music. It had been a long time since he'd felt so exhilarated from a simple dance.

He was no fancy Dan on the floor, but he wasn't bad, and Christy laughed as he whirled her around to the music. She'd been lonely for so long. It was incredible to be here with this man, to feel like a woman, to be free of all the old restraints. This holiday was worth every penny it had cost, and it still would be when she went back home to Florida, back to her old life. She pushed away the thought of leaving Nate, because it stung. She closed her eyes and pressed closer into his hard arms, oblivious to everything except the music and the man.

He felt that tiny movement and his arms tightened protectively. She appealed to everything masculine in him. It was like an avalanche; he was in half over his head already. He couldn't stop what was happening, and he didn't want to, anyway. What harm could there be in another holiday romance?

"Having fun?" he murmured.

"Oh, yes!" She sighed and nuzzled her cheek against his chest, faintly curious about the way he stiffened when she did it.

He stopped in the middle of the dance floor and lifted his head, looking down at her regardless of the amused glances from passing dancers.

"What is it?" she asked.

He wasn't smiling. He looked somber and very adult as he held her eyes. "Nothing," he said after a minute.

He swung her back into the dance, but his behavior had unsettled her. She stumbled and he caught her, the action bringing one of his long legs briefly between both of hers. She clutched at his arms and gasped out loud at the intimate contact.

He stopped dancing again and stared into her soft eyes, holding her shocked gaze while the throng of dancers around them passed by in a blaze of colorful movement.

"Christy," he said huskily.

With fascinated disbelief she watched his dark head bend. He couldn't; he wouldn't! Not here!

But he could, and he did. His thin, hard lips touched hers in a soft, searching kiss while his eyes held hers and the world seemed to spin away.

"You taste sweet," he murmured deeply. His mouth found hers again and this time his arm came up behind her head to force her lips into his. The kiss became swiftly intimate and intense and she moaned with the warm crush of it. "It's all right," he bit off against her lips. "I feel it just that strongly...." The pressure of his mouth increased and she gasped under it.

He lifted his head, leaving the taste of ginger ale and mint on her lips as he looked down at her. His eyes had darkened and his face was totally without expression.

"I want more than a kiss on a dance floor. I'd rather park the car on a ridge and make a little love to you than shuffle around here all night. How about you?" he asked tersely.

She couldn't believe what he was saying, and her face registered that. "I...I..." was all she could get out, when she wanted to tell him that she'd go anywhere, do anything he asked of her. That slow kiss had knocked the resistance right out of her, and he had to know it. His eyes told her that he did, that he knew and understood everything she was feeling, including her faint apprehension.

"I won't rush you," he said. His voice sounded deeper and a little husky. His hands tightened on her upper arms. "Come on, Christy."

He took the decision out of her hands, which was just as well, because she was in no condition to make one. She followed him like a lamb out to the Mercedes, not protesting when he drove quickly and silently out of town and up a winding mountain road to stop eventually by a rock wall overlooking the city.

He cut off the engine and turned to her, his face quiet and somber in the faint light that drifted up from the city streets far below.

"Come here, honey," he said gently. And he reached for her.

She felt the cool mountain breeze drift over her face while he kissed her, savoring the mingled scents of clean air and Nate's spicy cologne as his lips brushed leisurely all over her face. She lay in his arms, across his lap, with his breath sighing out heavily through his nose while his mouth began to possess hers with relentless intent. She tangled her fingers in the thick, cool hair at his nape with more instinct than experience, her nails faintly abrasive.

"I like that," he said under his breath. He lifted his head and studied her rapt face. His lean fingers traced the soft lines of her chin and throat, making her tingle with new sensations. "I'm glad you came to Arizona, Christy."

"So am I." Her pale eyes searched his dark ones in the faint light. "Kiss me, Nate," she whispered unsteadily.

His blood surged in his veins like a tidal wave. His lean hand lifted her head and he bent, crushing her mouth under his in little, biting kisses that made her gasp, arching her body against his as she gave in to the experienced caresses.

He guided her arms around his neck and his warm hands stroked up and down her back while he deepened the kiss in a way that brought a shocked gasp from her. He could almost feel the surprise in her, as if a kiss had never affected her so strongly. But after a minute, she relaxed and her lips began to respond, shyly, to his.

The response went to his head. He had a pretty good idea that she was feeling a desire for him that she'd never felt for anyone else. Perhaps even sophisticated women were vulnerable once in a while, but he didn't want love from her. He didn't want forever. He only wanted a night. He looked down at her with a deep scowl. She was still and shaken, her eyes enormous in her pale face, looking back at him with a curious kind of expression. He wondered if it would be too soon to make a move on her, and decided that it would. She didn't seem like the kind of woman who made quick decisions about a man. Just as well, he assured himself. He didn't want to start something until she was almost ready to leave for home. It would be easier for both of them if it was a brief affair, quickly over.

She didn't know what he was planning. She saw a dark, intent look in his eyes that thrilled her, because she mistook it for the beginnings of love. She knew that she was falling in love with him. It could have been because no other man had ever paid her any real attention. Well, except for Harry, she thought ruefully. She wondered what he'd say if she told him that there was a widower named Harry with three kids who wanted to marry her? He needed a mother for his sons more than he needed a wife, and he was about as exciting as a worn pair of sneakers. But he was a teacher with a stable income, he had a nice house, and the kids weren't bad. She'd have a comfortable life. Except that she didn't love Harry, and she was beginning to love Nate. Despite the differences between them, his wealth and her lack of it, his Western heritage and her Eastern one, she thought there might be a chance for them. And heaven knew, he did seem to want her desperately, if that expression on his face was any indication of what he was feeling.

Even as she thought it, he was easing her back into her own seat, fastening her seat belt.

"We'd better get back," he said quietly. He started the car and they turned toward the ranch.

He didn't speak as he drove. She was getting to him. Now that he'd had a taste of her, he knew he was going to want more. She delighted his senses, but he had to be careful not to let himself be taken in. She was just a tourist, he reminded himself, and not a permanent resident. She could be a big headache if he didn't handle this right. Sometimes that act of hers almost fooled him, but no woman her age could be that innocent and ignorant of men. He had to keep that in mind.

Christy felt as if she'd done something unforgiveable. She wondered what had disturbed him, because she could feel him drawing away from her. She wrapped her arms across her breasts and stared quietly out the window all the way back.

He walked her to her cottage with a minimum of conversation, as silent as the palo verde trees that lined the walk.

She unlocked her door and turned on the light inside, turning to Nate with a question in her eyes.

"I'll see you in the morning," he remarked. He touched her cheek with his fingers and abruptly turned and walked away.

Christy went inside and closed the door. She felt as if he'd already closed one in her face, and she didn't even understand why.

George hovered at breakfast the next morning until she had to invite him to sit with her. At least he was consistent, she thought bitterly. Nate had gone out earlier on his way to work, apparently, and he'd spared her no more than a glance and a curt nod. His behavior was the most puzzling she'd ever seen.

"Did you have a good time with Mr. Lang last night?" George asked, a little too casually.

"It was all right," she said, downplaying it. She smiled at George over a forkful of scrambled eggs. "How was the chess game?"

"I won." He laughed. "First time, too. Mrs. Lang played several games with me. She's very nice."

"Yes, I like her, too. What are we going to do today?"

"More of the same thing we did yesterday," George said. "Archaeology is a very exacting science. I used to think it would be glamorous and adventurous to go searching for ancient ruins. Now that I've discovered you do most of the work with a sifting box and a toothbrush, it's lost a lot of its appeal. I think I'll stick to anthropology.''

"Isn't that the same kind of thing?''

"Basically, but an anthropologist can go and live in Third World cultures that have their roots in the past. He can experience first-hand the kind of lives they live. Remember reading about Margaret Mead and all the exciting places she went? That's what I'd like to do.''

"You could wind up in somebody's stewing pot in the jungle,'' she felt obliged to point out.

He shrugged. "Death is nothing more than transition from one plane of existence to another, Christy. Why be afraid of it?''

"That's a different way of thinking about it,'' she said, taken aback by his easy acceptance of something that was, to her, formidable.

"My parents were missionaries,'' he grinned. "I grew up in places where you could wind up in a stew pot. That's why I'm not afraid of it.''

"Oh, I see.'' She smiled at him. "I guess your childhood was a lot more exciting than mine.''

"You're from Jacksonville, aren't you?'' he asked.

She nodded. "It's a great place to live. But I like Arizona,'' she added, and her eyes went dreamy.

George grimaced. It wasn't hard to see why she liked it. He sipped his orange juice and wondered why he couldn't be more dashing.

Later, Christy sat with him while they worked at the dig, poring over pottery pieces. He didn't know that her mind was on the way Nate Lang had kissed her the night before and his strange behavior afterward and today.

Nate didn't come around all day, and he wasn't at supper. Christy called Joyce Ann because she was bored and sad and nervous and needed to talk.

"Are you getting homesick?" her older sister asked hopefully.

"Not really," Christy began.

"Well, Harry must miss you. He's called three times already. Look, Christy, I know he leaves a lot to be desired, but he'd take good care of you..."

"I know that, Joyce Ann," she told the older woman gently. She couldn't blame her sister for wanting to see her settled and secure. But Harry was not at all her idea of the husband she wanted to spend her life with.

"Tell me you aren't getting involved with that man you told me about," Joyce Ann said suddenly. "A holiday romance is one thing, but you won't do something silly like getting in over your head with a stranger, will you?"

Christy's heart jumped. Amazing, how easily her sister read her. "Of course not," she protested. "I mean, there are a lot of men out here. George works with me at the dig. He's a college senior and a very nice boy."

"But he isn't the one you've got your eye on. Who is?"

She gave in to the need to tell someone. "His name is Nathanial," she said. "He's a miner."

"Oh, my God! A caveman!"

Christy burst out laughing. "No! He works in an office, not down a mine shaft. He's tall and rugged-looking, and very smart. He has a huge computer."

"And money?" Joyce Ann asked shrewdly.

"He and his mother own this ranch," she said.

"A mama's boy!"

"No!" She shook her hair back. "Joyce Ann, he's a very mature—"

"How old?"

"I don't really know. I guess he's in his middle thirties."

"So is Harry."

"Harry is forty and paunchy and about as romantic as Jell-O!"

"Speaking for myself, I find Jell-O with whipped cream on top very romantic indeed."

Christy sat back in her chair, curling the telephone cord around her fingers. "Harry doesn't love me, and I sure don't love him."

"Well, don't tell me you love the Arizona caveman," Joyce Ann scoffed, "because you don't fall in love in just a few days."

"Don't you?" Christy asked sadly. "I don't suppose it matters anyway, because he doesn't seem to feel that way about me. He takes me places and then goes off and ignores me."

"Does he?" There was new interest in her sister's voice. "Gets mad, does he?"

"He seems to stay that way. And he looks at me in the oddest way." She crossed her long legs. "Anyway, I don't suppose he'd be interested seriously in a schoolteacher from the East. He's rich and good-looking and has his pick of women. I don't imagine he has any trouble finding them, either. This ranch always has women guests, and most of them are rich."

"Rich doesn't buy love."

"So they say, but it makes it easier to digest, I'll bet. Joyce Ann, how would you like to hear about the *Hohokam*?"

"Not long-distance, darling, you'll go bankrupt. You can tell me about them when you come home. When are you coming home, Christy?"

"In another week," Christy replied, feeling already the pain of parting from Nate. She'd only known him for a few days, but it felt like years and she couldn't bear the thought of leaving him.

"Don't sound so morose. Harry says he's going to meet you at the airport with a dozen roses."

The thought of Harry with a dozen roses in his arms made her burst out laughing. She got Joyce Ann started, and then they began to reminisce about the old days, when their parents were still alive. Joyce Ann could be a pain, but it was so nice not to be alone in the world.

As she said good night and hung up, she wondered how she was going to manage if she had to go home and fight off Harry's practical proposal all over again.

Chapter Four

The next day was Saturday, and the team was given the weekend off. A trail ride was planned for guests at the ranch, along with a shopping trip to town, a small rodeo, and a camping trip that night in the mountains behind the ranch. It would be a full day, but all Christy saw were the regular wranglers. She hadn't even caught a glimpse of Nate, and some of the joy and excitement went out of the activities because he wasn't around.

George, of course, stuck to her like glue. He was delighted to have a partner for the trail ride. The only thing was, he apparently couldn't ride at all. He was allergic to horses and obviously terrified of them. What happened was probably inevitable, Christy thought as she watched the horse he was on begin to buck. George came off the horse, landing flat on his back in the dust, with the breath knocked out of him.

She and Mrs. Lang fussed over him while one of the men was delegated to take him to town to be X-rayed. He was limping a little, but Christy was almost sure no real damage had been done. George was just enjoying the attention he was getting. He asked her to ride into town with them, but before she could answer, Nate came striding up and appropriated her with only a brief sympathetic word to George and a nod to his mother.

"George is hurt," she protested.

"George is a blithering idiot," he said shortly. He glared down at her as he propelled her back toward the barn. "And

I'll be damned if he's going to monopolize you with that fake fall."

"But it wasn't fake...!"

He turned her to him within sight of the other guests mounting their horses. "Listen. Your friend George hit hard, but he knew how to fall, surely you noticed that?"

She had noticed, although she hadn't suspected that George had done it on purpose. She stared up at Nate curiously.

He hated that look. He couldn't decide if she was sophisticated and trying to pretend she wasn't, or if that innocence was real. She was full of contradictions and he didn't know whether he was coming or going lately.

Frowning, he stared down at her, his eyes suddenly kindling as the look took on new dimensions, made her knees weak, her breath come in faint gasps. The magic was there again, as potent as ever.

"Where are we going?" she asked, trying to break the spell before she gave in to it again.

"Riding," he said.

"But, I can't...!"

"I'll teach you." He took her hand and led her into the stable where two of the cowboys were busily saddling horses for the guests. "Bud!" he called to one of them. "Saddle Blue for Christy."

"Yes, sir!"

The young cowboy moved toward an older horse, a palomino, and Christy watched with delight as it was saddled and led to her.

"This is Blue," Nate told her, thanking the cowboy as he took the reins. "Blue was my birthday present when I was fifteen. He's twenty-two now, and he doesn't get ridden much, but he likes a leisurely trail ride now and again. He's very gentle. He won't throw you."

She moved toward the horse and lifted a hesitant hand to his soft muzzle. He let her stroke him, his big brown eyes kind and watchful.

"Oh, he's beautiful!" Christy exclaimed. "What a nice boy," she cooed as she stroked his forehead. "Nice old fellow."

"Here, give him this and he'll be your friend for life. Mind your fingers, though." He handed her a sugar cube, which she fed to the horse. "We don't let him have much sugar these days. It isn't good for him to get overweight, but he's got a sweet tooth."

"I guess you could ride from the time you could sit up," she mused.

"Almost," he agreed. "My dad put me in the saddle when I was four and kept me there until I learned to ride the way he thought I should. He was a former rodeo star. His son had to be the best, at everything, on horseback."

The deep, angry note in his voice caught her attention. She looked up at him.

He laughed when he saw the way she was looking at him. "I'll bet your dad spoiled you rotten," he murmured.

"My parents died when I was twelve," she said. "Joyce Ann raised me. She's been more mother than big sister all my life."

He brushed the hair back from her face, gently. "My kids aren't going to be pushed into doing things they don't want to do," he said.

"Neither are mine," she replied.

He searched her eyes. "We're different in coloring," he murmured, lifting her hand in his to study it. "My skin is much darker than yours, like my hair and my eyes."

"I take after my mother," she said. "Her grandmother was Norwegian."

He smiled. "I take after my mother, too. Her mother was Spanish."

"I thought she might be. She's still very lovely."

"Yes." He let go of her hand, disturbed at the images that had been dancing around in his brain. He couldn<u>'t</u> help but wonder if he and Christy had kids, which one of their parents the children would favor. Those weren't thoughts he should be considering. This was just a holiday romance, he told himself firmly.

He helped Christy into the saddle, trying not to laugh as she tugged and panted her way onto the horse with his help.

"My goodness, it's much harder than it looks on television!" she exclaimed.

"Oh, you should be overweight and try it," he murmured dryly. "Riding a horse is pretty easy compared to getting on and off one. It just takes practice."

She was still panting, pushing her hair out of her eyes. "I guess so."

"You shouldn't ride longer than an hour, either," he added as he went to get his own mount.

"Why?"

He swung into the saddle with the ease of years of practice and moved his horse up to hers. "Because you're going to discover that you use muscles you didn't know you had. By tonight you'll be walking bowlegged, and tomorrow you'll be stiff as a board."

She fingered the reins. "I don't suppose there's a van going to church?"

He chuckled. That was a nice touch, he thought to himself. She was really putting on the act for him. "No. Most of the guests like to sleep late on Sunday. But mother and I go, if you'd like to come."

She beamed. "Thanks."

His slate-gray eyes ranged over her face with pure mockery, but she was too far away to see the expression. All she saw was the smile. "Don't pull too hard on those reins."

He rode off ahead of her, more disturbed than he wanted to let on. If she'd been a hometown girl, if that pose of hers was real, she'd have been everything he'd ever wanted in a wife. As it was . . .

They headed around the valley and through a small canyon, and while they rode, he told her about the vegetation that grew in the desert and how it held water.

"Notice the leaves," he said, reining in, indicating one of the prickly pear cacti beside the trail. "If the leaves are fat, it means we've had rain. If they're skinny, we haven't. The leaves on desert plants usually stay thin during periods of drought so that the plant won't require as much moisture. Now, the saguaro is pleated, like an accordion, to allow it to expand with water when it rains." He crossed his forearms over each other on the pommel and stared at her. "Did you know that a saguaro can weigh up to ten tons? There's a skeleton inside it to support that weight, and most of it is just water. The saguaro doesn't grow an arm until it's from seventy to seventy-five years old. They can live to be two hundred years old."

She caught her breath. Just looking at the huge cacti in the Saguaro National Monument outside Tucson had fascinated her as they drove through the monument to get to the ranch. But Dr. Adamson hadn't known a lot about the giant cacti, so conversation had centered on the dig, not the vegetation.

"That's not a fraction of fact on the plants here," he mused, staring out over the desert. "My God, a botanist could spend his life learning about desert plants. The *Papago* use them for medicine, for food, for liquor. They make flour from the dried pods of palo verde and mesquite. They fry or boil the leaves on prickly pear cacti for food. They make a kind of beer from the fruit of the prickly pear and the saguaro. I could go on for hours.''

''I could listen for hours,'' she replied. ''I'd like to take pictures of those plants for my class back home. The children would enjoy learning about a different kind of vegetation than they're used to.''

He frowned as he looked at her. If she really was an elementary school teacher—and everything pointed to it—that one fact didn't jibe with what he thought she was. If she led a wild life, wouldn't the education department protest? And how could she settle for such a tame career, if she was the pretty little flirt she'd convinced him she was? It didn't make sense.

''Why do you teach school?'' he asked bluntly.

''I don't know. It just sort of fell into my lap. My father was a teacher. He loved the life, and I loved him.'' She smiled. ''My mother was an artist. They were terribly mismatched, but it was just as well they died together.'' The smile faded. ''They were so devoted to each other that one wouldn't have thrived without the other. I suppose I've spent my whole life looking for that kind of love, but maybe it's so rare that it only happens for one couple out of ten thousand.''

''Maybe,'' he agreed. ''My parents never got along. My father married my mother because he wanted this ranch. He managed to drive it into bankruptcy with his extravagant ideas of how to make an empire of it. He died when I was twenty-five,'' he added curtly, and his dark eyes glittered. ''He never forgave me for preferring geology to ranching. When he couldn't browbeat me into doing what he wanted, he tried freezing me out. I don't think he said ten words to me after I started college.''

She wondered if he'd ever told anyone else that, and decided that he was such a private person that he probably hadn't. It flattered her that he felt so at ease with her. "Your mother is very proud of you."

His dark gray eyes searched hers. "Yes. She was the one person who ever cared enough to let me be myself." He pushed back the creamy Stetson he was wearing. "Most women go into a relationship with the idea that they'll change a man to suit them. It's not that easy to restructure a person's personality, and not much of a man who'll allow a woman to do it."

"If you change people, sometimes you change the things you love most about them, without realizing it," she replied.

He stared at her blatantly. She was beautiful with the sun making a golden fire of her wavy hair as the wind moved it around. Her pale green eyes were soft and warm as she looked back at him, and there was an attractive color in her cheeks. She was wearing a gaily striped blouse with puffy sleeves that buttoned up the front with her tight jeans and tan boots, and she looked like the Eastern tourist she was. But she had a lovely figure and Nate remembered so well how she felt in his arms. Fires began to burn deep inside him as he looked at her. She knew the score, for God's sake, and she wanted him, too. He knew by the electricity that sparkled between them when they were alone. So why was he holding back?

His jaw clenched. He glanced past her to the shade of some palo verde trees by the wash that was, infrequently, a running stream during the rainy season. "Let's rest a bit," he said.

She followed him into the shady area and watched him tether his mount to a palo verde tree. He reached up to help her down from her own horse, deliberately letting her slide against him, so that she could feel the corded muscles in his body, feel the warm strength of it, feel his breath sighing heavily against her face as he helped her down.

The nearness was unnerving, especially when his dark eyes looked down into hers and time spun out between them.

"I'll tie Blue for you," he said huskily. "Then you and I are going to make love."

She wasn't quite sure she'd heard that last bit, because he turned away as he said it and probably she'd misunderstood. He tethered Blue and came back to her, and then she knew that she hadn't mistaken what he'd said. His eyes were blazing with raw desire.

He bent and lifted her easily in his muscular arms and carried her, holding her fascinated gaze, to the shelter of the tree. He laid her down in the soft sand and stretched out beside her, pausing just long enough to let his hat sail to one side before he bent to her mouth.

She knew then how much he'd been playing with her. The teasing kisses of the past were totally eclipsed by the blatant, demanding hunger of the kiss he now gave her. His mouth was hard and rough, pushing her lips apart with fierce command, making her submit with the threatened pressure of his body while he deepened the kiss into something far beyond her slight experience.

"Relax," he said against her soft mouth. "There's nothing to be afraid of. I may be a little rougher than the men you're used to, but I won't hurt you."

That didn't make sense at first. Then she felt his tongue go into her mouth, felt his hands sliding under her top, against her bare skin. Her eyes flew open and she tried to speak, but his mouth grew rougher.

He moved, one long leg insinuating itself between both of hers, and she felt the power and strength of him in an embrace she'd never shared with a man before.

"Please...you're going...too fast!" she whispered, frightened.

He lifted his head, searching her eyes. He frowned, because she actually looked frightened. Odd, when she was such a pretty, outgoing woman. Men must have been camped on her doorstep for years now, and she surely didn't reach her present age without some experience. Not the way she looked. It must be part of the act, but that fear seemed real.

"How old are you, Christy?" he asked, his voice deep and faintly husky with desire. He knew, but he asked anyway.

"I'm twenty-five," she said uneasily.

His fingers were against her ribcage, gently caressing her so that unknown sensations began to work in her body. He made her feel odd, uneasy, excited, especially when he worked his way up to the band of her bra just under her breasts and lingered there. She shouldn't let him touch her this way, but something was happening to her that she didn't understand.

"I'm thirty-seven," he murmured, holding her eyes while that hand moved again and his fingers touched her breast, making her jump. "We're both plenty old enough to know what we're doing, aren't we?" he added.

"I...guess so," she managed. Her heart leaped. He was touching her, his fingers warm through the thin fabric of her bra, and she lay there docilely, letting him caress her. She couldn't imagine why she was permitting the intimacy, except that it was making her head spin and her body blaze up with pleasure. She made an odd sound and raised her back, shocking herself with the sensuous little movement.

He smiled, bending to her mouth again. "That's more like it," he whispered. "I wondered how long you could keep up the act . . ."

Her thoughts dissolved as his mouth covered hers again. His thumb rubbed over her nipple and she felt it tighten until it was almost painful, but every time he touched it, her body flinched with helpless pleasure. She moaned, tangling her hands in the hair at the nape of his neck, pulling his hard mouth even closer against her own. She opened her lips for him, inviting the thrust of his tongue into the soft, warm darkness of her mouth.

Fever, she thought while she could. It burned like a vicious fever. She wanted to be closer to him. She wanted to be without her clothing so that he could cool her hot skin by touching it with his lean, strong hands. She wanted his touch as she'd never wanted anything.

He seemed to know it, too, because he lifted her and snapped the fastening of her bra. Then he looked into her eyes and slid his hand over her naked breast, watching the expression that washed over her face.

"Yes, it's good, isn't it?" he asked gruffly. "Feeling my hands on your body, my mouth on your mouth. And this is just the beginning. Hasn't it been like this before?"

"No," she whispered brokenly. She shivered as he began to raise the hem of her blouse.

"There isn't another soul within twenty miles of us," he breathed, letting his eyes slide down to the bareness of her white skin as he pushed the offending fabric away and left her bare to the collarbone. His breath caught at the sight of her pretty breasts, pink-tipped, firm and peach-colored. He couldn't get enough of the sight of her. But it wasn't enough. Not nearly enough. He bent his head and opened his mouth, taking her inside.

Christy wept. It was the sweetest agony she'd ever known. His eyes on her body, the expression on his face that told her she was beautiful to him, the feel of his mouth against her tender skin. She clung to him, arching herself up to his lips, begging for the feel of them on her body. She thought she wouldn't survive the pleasure, and then he turned her into him and brought her hips against his with one fierce jerk of his lean hand.

She'd never experienced the feel of a man's aroused body. It terrified her. She cared for him and she didn't want to ask him to stop, but it was going to be too late if she waited much longer. Judging by the feel of him, and the faint shudder of his powerful body, he wasn't going to be too eager to stop anyway. He was sophisticated and he seemed to feel that she was, too. She didn't understand why he was letting things go this far. She'd told him she was a greenhorn, but perhaps he'd misunderstood.

She had to force her lips not to cling when he lifted his head. She could imagine how she looked, with her mouth swollen and her body half bare to his eyes. It was agony to stop.

"Please," she whispered, putting a trembling hand against his broad chest.

"Unbutton it," he said, his voice rough, his eyes glittering with desire.

"What?"

He snapped open the buttons, disclosing a chest thick with curly black hair. "Here." He dragged one of her hands to the hard, warm muscles and buried her fingers in the thick hair. "This is what I like," he breathed, moving her hand against him, groaning at the delicious touch.

She felt her other hand joining the first one, too entranced by the forbidden delight to deny it to her starving senses. She touched him, fascinated with the way he felt under her hands, the wiry abrasion of hair tickling her fingers. He arched under her touch, just as she had under his, and she caught her breath to know that she could give back the pleasure he was showing her.

"Christy," he groaned. He bent to her mouth, dragging her body against his so that they melted together, skin against hair-roughened skin.

She cried out at the surge of feverish pleasure the contact gave her, at the hunger it rekindled to feel his aroused body so close to hers. But when he rolled her onto her back and moved over her, trapping her beneath his powerful legs, she panicked.

Her eyes flew open. "No!" she whispered shakily, meeting his hot gaze. "No, Nate, please! I can't!"

"Can't, the devil," he said, his voice biting as he stared down at her, on fire with the need to bury himself in her. "You can stop playing. You don't have to ply me with virginal wiles. I want you like hell."

"It isn't . . . playing," she said. "I'm a virgin."

He laughed coldly. "At your age? The way you look? Like hell you are!" He bent to kiss her again.

But she turned her face away. "I didn't always look like this! Nate, I've never . . . done this!" she said frantically. "You don't understand!"

"Do you expect me to believe that?" he demanded, jerking her face back to his furious eyes. "My God, you've teased and flirted and had one 'accident' after another to get my attention. You've thrown yourself at me ever since you got here, so why act shocked when I make a move on you? You want me. I've known that from the first."

She bit her lower lip, so horribly embarrassed that she could hardly get the words out. He still had her pinned and now his arousal was becoming a terrible punishment.

"Yes, I wanted you," she confessed miserably. "But I thought . . . I thought you felt something for me."

He glared down at her, furious with her and with himself for what she was doing to him. "Felt something?" He laughed coldly. "Can't you feel what I want?" he asked with cruel mockery and moved his hips deliberately against her, watching the flaming color come into her face. "Yes, you know what that is, don't you? Why pretend it's such a shocking experience?"

"Because it is." She swallowed and closed her eyes, wishing she could just disappear. Her hands clenched on his shoulders. "Until a week ago, I looked like somebody's old maid aunt. I got my hair done and bought new clothes and . . . and revamped my personality. I thought for once in my life, I'd try to be like those women I admired on television. You know, the independent, sophisticated, outgoing women that men . . . that men want." Tears welled in her eyes. "I didn't know, didn't realize, that I'd be mistaken for a . . . for a tramp!"

Her voice broke and it finally got through to him that he was treating her like one.

His lean hand jerked her face back up to his while his body throbbed in anguish over hers. "Are you serious?" he asked curtly. "Are you really trying to convince me that you're a virgin? That you've never been intimate with a man?"

"Nobody ever wanted to be intimate with somebody who looked like I did," she whispered, her voice shaking as she met his accusing dark eyes. His weight was formidable and she just wanted to get away from him. He looked as if he hated her. "I was just a dull little dishwater blonde. I had my hair lightened and my face done, I bought new makeup and new clothes and forced myself to try and be outgoing. I thought . . ." She closed her eyes. "I thought maybe if I were pretty, men might notice me. I've been alone all my life. I just wanted somebody to love me," she whispered in a fever of embarrassment.

His jaw clenched. It sounded too genuine to be a lie, but he hated her for what he was hearing. "Love is a rare commodity," he said tersely, easing his body away from hers. "I don't have any to give. All I wanted was one night with you, Christy, not happy ever after. I'm thirty-seven. If I wanted to be married, believe me, I could be."

"Yes, I know that," she said. She heard him move away and she managed to sit up without looking at him, embarrassed at her disheveled clothing, at the way she'd responded to him. Her trembling fingers gathered the fabric to her taut, swollen breasts. She could still feel his mouth on them, like a brand.

"I can't believe a woman could be that green," he said, his voice cutting as he glared down at her, trying to get his breath. "Surely you knew what I was leading up to? The way you kept stumbling around me, the way you smiled and teased, added to the way you looked was enough to make any man want you."

"Yes. Well, I didn't know that," she managed. She sighed miserably. "I'm sorry. I just wanted someone to love me."

He looked at her with pure fury, his fists clenched at his sides while he breathed unsteadily. "And all I wanted was a little sex," he said coldly, forcing himself to say the words, to make her understand. It was cruel, he knew it, but it would be the kindest thing in the long run. He didn't want commitment. All he'd wanted was a night in her arms, but he hadn't bargained for this! "If you want love and marriage, honey, you won't find either one with me. I thought you were in the market for a holiday romance, and I was willing to oblige. My mistake."

What she saw in his face made her feel ashamed. She averted her eyes from the condemnation of his, embarrassed and wounded. Her hands trembled as she got her bra and blouse back on and scrambled to her feet. She brushed the sand from her jeans without looking at him. She couldn't say anything, because her mind had stopped working.

He hated her. He hated himself. He glared at her trembling body and wanted to throw things. Why hadn't he realized that it was no act? No experienced woman would have behaved as she had, and no actress was good enough to keep up the masquerade so consistently. It was no act. She really was a virgin. Imagine that, he thought furiously. A real live innocent who looked like she did. She'd said something about changing her image, but he couldn't imagine that she'd been less than beautiful before.

Then a terrible thought occurred to him. He tried to push it away, but it wouldn't go.

"How are you set financially?" he asked bluntly.

"I teach school. How do you think I'm set?" she asked miserably. She pushed back her disheveled hair. Her eyes lifted to his. "What difference does it make?"

"None, now that I've found you out," he replied coolly. "I'm rich. I guess the money really appealed to you, didn't it?"

She gaped at him. Could he honestly believe that? Probably he could. He seemed to enjoy thinking the worst of her today. Maybe it made him feel better. She was aware that getting stirred up was painful to men, and he'd been pretty stirred.

She turned away, toward her horse. "I'd like to go back now," she said in a defeated tone.

"We might as well," he agreed curtly. "You've had your shot at the brass ring, but you fell a little short, didn't you, honey?"

She cringed at the mockery in his tone. She loved him, and he could treat her like this, with such coldness. It was just as well that she'd found out now, before she let herself hope for anything more. He wanted sex, not love, and she wasn't capable of a purely physical liaison. What irony. She'd come to Arizona looking for love, and she'd found a man with a heart as barren as the desert he lived in.

She let him help her into the saddle, noticing absently that he'd fastened his shirt back up. She didn't want to remember how his chest had felt under her caressing hands, or how his mouth had felt on her body. She had to put it into perspective. It had been physical attraction, nothing more. He didn't want her for keeps, he just wanted to make love to her. She sighed wearily. If that was all he wanted, then why hadn't he just left her alone? It would have been kinder for both of them if he'd never touched her.

He swung into the saddle, disturbed by his own feelings of guilt. He'd been the pursuer, not she, despite the accusations he'd made. He should have known how green she was and left her to George. Damn it, he'd backed her into a corner and then attacked her for refusing to let him use her. He was vaguely ashamed of his own behavior. But he didn't want to get married, he told himself firmly. He'd escaped the noose too many times already to voluntarily put his head into it now. No, he'd get over Christy and she'd get over him. It was just one of those unfortunate interludes that was best forgotten.

"Don't look so dismal," he said, riding along beside her as they headed back. "We'll forget it happened."

She didn't answer him. She didn't want to look at him or talk to him ever again. It might not be a mature attitude to take, but she didn't feel very mature. She felt cheap and ashamed. Perhaps he was right, and she had led him on with her false image. Perhaps men looked at things differently than women did, and her pretty appearance gave the impression, along with her unfortunate clumsiness and teasing, that she was "available."

Joyce Ann was right, she decided. She should go home and marry Harry and settle down. This disguise she'd adopted was nothing like the woman she really was, and she should be ashamed for giving a false impression. Starting tomorrow, the old Christy was going to be very much back in her proper place. She wasn't going to hurt anyone else with her stupid ideas of changing. Besides, she thought sadly, she couldn't change, not really. She wasn't vivacious and outgoing and beautiful. She was serious and introverted and plain. She'd do well to remember it from now on. Nathanial Lang didn't want her as she appeared to be, then he certainly wouldn't want her as she was. It had been a lucky escape for both of them.

He glanced at her, disturbed because she wouldn't answer him. She looked . . . devastated. He dragged his eyes back to the trail in front of them. He shouldn't have been so cruel to her. She was more sensitive than he'd realized.

"Christy . . ." he began.

"It's all right, Mr. Lang," she said gently. She didn't look at him, but at the reins in her hands. "I'm sorry for everything. I won't bother you anymore, I promise."

"Oh, for God's sake . . . !" he raged.

She would have burst into tears at his tone, but a party of riders approaching cut into the tense silence between them and she gave a huge sigh of relief when she saw George. Sanctuary, she thought, heading old Blue in his direction. George had recovered enough to come on the trail ride, and Christy was going to stick to him like glue, she promised herself. At least George only wanted companionship, not to get her into bed!

Nate watched her ride away with mixed feelings. It looked as if George was going to get her after all. Just as well, he assured himself. He had nothing to offer her. George was steady and dependable.

Nate lifted his chin and glared as the younger man beamed when Christy joined him. Damn it all, he thought furiously, life had been so simple before this archaeology outfit pushed itself into his privacy. Now he was confused and hurt and he didn't know what he wanted anymore. He wheeled his own mount with a silent curse and rode away, leaving his foreman to conduct the group on its trail ride without him. He couldn't stand the pain in Christy's soft eyes one more minute!

Chapter Five

Christy was never as glad to see anyone as she was to see George. She rode up beside him and stuck like glue, trying not to notice the abrupt way Nate Lang made his departure. She was still shaking inside from what had happened.

"Are you all right?" George asked when they stopped to water the horses on the mountain trail.

"Of course," she said brightly, brushing back her disheveled hair.

"You look funny," he said, frowning. "Upset."

"I almost fell off my horse," she lied. "It unnerved me. But I'm all right now. Are you?" she added, remembering his fall.

He smiled sheepishly and adjusted his glasses, an action that Christy found all too familiar, as they slipped down his nose. "Well, actually, that was a planned fall. I'm good with horses, but I thought you might notice if I got hurt."

"Of course I noticed," she chided gently.

He cleared his throat, toying with his horse's reins and looking at them instead of her. "Christy, I like you...a lot."

"I like you, too, George," she said gently. She put a hand on his forearm. Nathanial Lang was right, she thought as she studied the flustered young man. It was better to be honest with people. "George, I have to tell you that I'm going to be married when I go back to Jacksonville. I hadn't made up my mind when I came out here, but I sort of had it made up for me."

He looked wounded for a moment, then he got himself back together and straightened. "I'm sorry, for myself. He'll be a lucky man. Have you known him long?" he added, and forced a smile.

"Since I started teaching," she said. "He teaches sixth grade at the elementary school where I work. He's...he's a good bit older than I am. He's divorced and he has three sons. They're all in high school, but they like me and I like them."

He tried not to show how dismayed he felt. Surely Christy deserved better than that! "You'll have one big family, what with his kids and the ones you'll have together," he said cheerfully.

She seemed to wither before his eyes. She even looked momentarily older. "Oh, Harry doesn't want any more children," she said. "He's made sure he won't have any, so there's no question of..." She turned away, hating the thought of never holding a child of her own in her arms. It was too painful to think about. "We'd better go."

George helped her to mount and then got on his own horse. What she told him was enough to keep him depressed all the way back to the ranch.

Christy refused to go on the overnight camp out. Nate went, and she was glad to have the recreation room pretty much to herself. She was so engrossed in a book that she hardly heard Mrs. Lang come in and sit down across from her.

"You'd have enjoyed the camp, Christy," the small woman said, smiling at her gently. "It's quite something, the campfire on the desert and the taste of freshly brewed camp coffee. Our foreman, Terrance, plays guitar and he has a marvelous voice."

"I didn't really feel up to it," she said, and it was the truth in several ways. "I got pretty sore from the ride earlier today."

Mrs. Lang's dark eyes were persistent as they searched the younger woman's face. "Nate hasn't said two words all day. He snapped at me when I asked if he was going camping, and he stayed in his study until it was time to leave. When he found out you weren't going along, he used language I won't even repeat. It got worse when George volunteered to stay behind with you. I think Nate might have roped and dragged him with them if he hadn't changed his mind."

Christy flushed, fumbling with the book. "George is a nice boy. But I explained things to him this afternoon. I had to make him understand that...well, that there was no chance of our being more than friends."

Mrs. Lang smiled. "I had an idea that you'd have to speak to him eventually. I assume your affections are engaged elsewhere?" she fished delicately.

Christy nodded. "I'm getting married when I go back to Florida."

Mrs. Lang dropped her dishcloth and bent to pick it up, her expression astonished. "I had no idea that you were engaged," she said haltingly.

"I'm not," Christy told her. "I came out here to think things over. I changed the way I look, but not the way I think and feel," she added sadly, lifting a ravaged expression to the older woman. "I'm still old-fashioned and full of hang-ups and unsuited to the modern world."

"In other words, you don't sleep around."

In spite of herself, Christy laughed at the twinkle in the other woman's eyes. "No, I don't sleep around," she agreed. She leaned back against the sofa. "Men don't really want marriage anymore. They don't need it unless they want children or belong to some conservative organization that likes settled executives. It's not that easy for even a pretty woman to find a husband, but it's doubly hard for an unattractive one. I can't live a breezy, rootless existence with only a career for comfort. I want a home of my own and children, even if they aren't my own," she said firmly, for her own benefit. "I'm twenty-five. If I don't marry while I have the chance, it might never come again." She looked up. "I don't want to live alone until I die."

"Tell me about this man you've decided to marry."

Christy did, her eyes dull and lackluster. "He's almost forty," she added. "But he's a kind man, and he'll give me security and a good life."

"Do you love him?"

"I'm very fond of him," Christy said hesitantly.

"Do you want him?"

She thought of Nate's mouth on hers, his hands holding her against him with passionate need, and she closed her eyes. "I can endure that part of the marriage."

"Oh, my dear," Mrs. Lang sighed heavily. "My dear, it's more than just endurance. Men know when you feel nothing. It will hurt your husband. Eventually, it will kill your marriage. It isn't fair to either of you to marry without desire."

"The way my life is going, I can have either but not both," she said with a humorless laugh. She looked up. "Mrs. Lang, I've done a bad thing. I've pretended to be something I'm not, and now I'm having to pay for it. I wish I'd stayed at home and been satisfied with what I had."

"If everyone took that attitude, America would never have been discovered," Mrs. Lang returned. She leaned forward and patted Christy's hand. "Don't worry so, child. Let each day take care of itself. You still have a week to go, you know."

"I thought I might go home Monday..."

"No!" Mrs. Lang stood up. "Don't you dare. Running away from a problem never solved it. Besides, you've already paid for your holiday. The least you can do is stay and enjoy it."

Christy wasn't sure that it was the right thing to do, but in her heart, she didn't want to leave Nate yet. She wondered if his mother had guessed how she felt about him. She was a wise little woman with keen eyes, and she didn't miss much. It was flattering that his mother didn't want her off the Lang ranch. Since she didn't, it blew up Joyce Ann's theory that Nate was a mother's boy. No, he wasn't. Not by a long shot. But he would never be Christy's, either. He'd as much as said so. Every day she remained here would be painful and too long. But running wasn't really her style, either.

"I suppose I should stay," Christy said finally. "It would leave the others in a bind if I go early." She forced a smile. "And you're right. Running doesn't really solve things, I guess."

"That sounds more like it," the older woman replied. "Now I have to get back to my dishes. Why don't you have an early night? Nate mentioned that you wanted to go to church with us in the morning?"

"If you don't mind, Mrs. Lang, I think I'll pass. This time," she added, trying not to give too much away.

But Mrs. Lang was shrewd. She had a fairly good idea of what had happened. "I understand. Another time, perhaps. Goodnight, Christy."

Christy smiled gently. "Goodnight."

She knew it was cowardly to back out of church because she couldn't face Nate after what had happened the day before, but it was too much to ask. She was too ashamed of herself. He said that she'd led him on, and maybe she had. She hadn't realized that she was doing it, that was what made it so terrible. She was a greenhorn, all right, in just about every respect.

She got up the next morning after a sleepless night fraught with erotic, violent dreams that kept her tossing all over the bed until dawn. She dragged herself up and took a shower. Then she glared at herself in the mirror, wondering if she shouldn't go whole hog with her repentance and turn herself back into the pitiful wallflower she'd been before she came out here. But that would be silly, she decided, and it wouldn't bother Nate. It would just make people feel sorry for her, and that was the last thing she wanted. But she didn't go to a lot of trouble with the careful makeup she'd used before, and she didn't spend half an hour curling her hair with the styling rod.

She decided to give breakfast a miss, because she might run into Nate. Then she decided to give lunch a miss for the same reason. She had some cookies in her purse. She ate those and drank some water, hating her own cowardice. This wasn't like her, really it wasn't, but her pride and her heart had never been crushed so terribly.

When she didn't come out for lunch, Nate was disturbed because he knew she hadn't had breakfast. She couldn't starve herself, for God's sake! He felt more guilty by the minute for the way he'd hurt her the day before. He should have been a little less cruel, but then, hindsight was a great asset. He wondered how he was going to bear being around her for the rest of her stay, seeing that hurt look in her eyes and knowing he'd put it there. But then, she shouldn't have flirted with him so much, he told himself. And there was still the matter of those clumsy antics to get his attention. She'd asked for it. He had to keep believing that, or he was going to go crazy.

He went into the dining room where guests were going through the buffet line and started to fill a plate for her when he encountered George holding two.

"I thought I'd take Christy something," he told Nate. "She's feeling kind of low. I guess the man back home called and upset her or something, because she was really depressed yesterday. I don't think she's even come out of her room. I haven't seen her at all."

Nate felt as if he'd been frozen in his boots. "The man back home?" he prompted.

"The one she's going to marry," George said miserably. "He's forty and settled, and she says he'll look after her—Here, Mr. Lang, you're about to spill that chicken..."

Nate set the plate on the table and walked out of the room without speaking. He found himself, eventually, out on the desert behind the ranch, standing bareheaded in a stand of spreading creosote bushes in the dirt. The wind whipped through his hair and he felt it, but it hardly registered. Christy was going home to marry someone. She'd been engaged all along and she hadn't told him. She'd let him take her out and make love to her, and then she'd fought free and started spouting excuses.

Was she a virgin? Or was it just guilty conscience because she was betraying the man she'd promised herself to? He wanted to jerk up a creosote bush and beat the desert with it. It might help alleviate some of his bad temper. The woman was driving him crazy! Well, let her go home and marry her settled man, he didn't care! He'd be glad when she was out of his hair and in someone else's, he told himself. Of course he would!

He was so angry and irritable that he locked himself in his study for the rest of the day and didn't even go in to the office. In fact, he didn't even stop working to eat. Let her marry her settled fool. He didn't give a damn.

Christy avoided the house all day, having an early night. Bless George for bringing her food, because she'd rather have starved than have to face Nate until she'd gotten her nerves settled. George had admitted that he'd told Nate about Harry, and she imagined what Nate was thinking now. He probably had a good picture of her as a two-timing Jezebel. She couldn't win for losing, she thought miserably.

Sure enough, Nate looked at her the next morning as if he hated the sight of her. She was wearing her jeans and a white embroidered smock top for coolness and comfort. She'd put her hair up and she hadn't used any makeup at all. But if she'd hoped to look plain again she didn't succeed. Her face looked young and innocent with her clear complexion, and her hair in its soft bun, leaving her nape bare, gave her a vulnerable air. Nate found her every bit as attractive now as he had when she worked at her makeup and her hairdo and dressed to the hilt. That made him feel even worse. He strode toward his car and went to his office without one single word to her, or to anyone else.

George stuck with her when they went out to the dig, encouraging and kind. Why, oh, why couldn't she have given her heart to him? He wouldn't throw it in the sand and stomp on it the way Nate had!

It was a long day, as Mondays always seemed to be, and the heat was oppressive. She was glad when they were able to go back to the ranch to have lunch under the palo verde trees. But when they got there, everything was in a frenzy. Mrs. Lang was nowhere in sight and one of the maids was trying to set the buffet table, muttering to herself in rapid-fire Spanish.

"What's wrong?" Christy asked gently.

But the answer came in Spanish and Christy had only a little French to her credit. She smiled apologetically, going out to sit with George.

Mrs. Lang, looking harassed and haunted, came out of the house just as everyone lined up for the buffet.

"What's wrong?" Christy asked gently.

"Nate," came the reply. "There was a cave-in at one of the mines this morning. He was in it when it happened, part of an executive tour."

Christy went stark white. "Is he alive?" she asked, her voice shaking.

Mrs. Lang studied the young face for a long moment and then she smiled gently and touched the thin shoulder. "Yes, he's alive. Very much alive. Just a little bruised and scratched, but the doctor wanted him to spend the rest of the day in bed, to make sure there are no complications."

"Oh, thank God." Christy bit back tears, embarrassed at the way she'd blown her cover. She shook her head to clear the tears, glad that she and Mrs. Lang were standing apart from the archaeological group, so that no one could see her face.

"I've got to go to town and get some prescriptions filled for him," the older woman said with a calculating stare. "Could you sit with him for me?"

"He wouldn't like that, Mrs. Lang," Christy said quietly. "It would be better if you asked someone else."

"No, I don't think so." She took Christy by the hand and led her firmly down the hall and into Nate's room, where he lay smoldering in his bed with his chest bare and the sheet lying precariously across his lean hips.

"I've asked Miss Haley to sit with you while I go to town for your prescriptions, Nate," Mrs. Lang said, pretending innocence. "I'll have Nita bring a tray so you can have lunch while I'm gone. I won't be long."

She was out the door before Christy could argue any more, before Nate could voice the words hanging on the tip of his tongue. He glared at Christy from cold slate eyes, a slash across his forehead and another across his cheek making him look even more dangerous than before. The gashes had been treated with antiseptic, and the one on his forehead was stitched. It would probably leave a scar. There was a bandage on one shoulder, white against the dark tan of his skin. He looked bruised and a little groggy, but formidable just the same.

"I'm sure one of the men wouldn't mind sitting with you..." she began hesitantly, so shy with him that it was painful just to talk to him.

"Sit down," he said. "I won't bite."

She colored as she slid into the chair near the bed, sitting stiffly on the very edge of it with her hands folded in her lap.

He studied her with more interest than he wanted to show, from the color in her cheeks to the rapid movement of her blouse. He made her nervous. He could see her eyes darting reluctantly over his bare, hair-roughened chest and away, as if the sight of him fascinated her. Once it would have amused him, even flattered him. But now he knew the truth about her, and he hated her attention.

"What's his name?" he asked, drawing up one knee under the white sheet to rest his wrist on.

"His... name?" she faltered.

"The man who's waiting for you back home. The one you're going to marry," he returned, his voice cutting.

"Oh. Him." She looked down at her hands. "His name is Harvey White, but most people call him Harry. He's forty, he teaches sixth grade, and he's... settled and mature."

He was also fifteen years older than she was, he thought angrily. Too old. Of course, he himself was twelve years her senior. He pushed that thought to the back of his mind and glared at her.

"A bachelor?"

"No," she replied. "He was married. His wife left him to marry another man. He has three teenaged sons. They're very nice," she added helplessly.

His jaw tautened as he stared at her. "A ready-made family. What about your own kids, how will they fit in?"

"We won't have any," she said, refusing to look at him. "Harry had an operation. He...doesn't want any more children, he said three was enough for us to look after financially."

"Oh, my God," he ground out. "You little fool, is that what you want?"

She lifted her face, aware that most of the color had drained out of it. She had a little pride left. "I'll have a secure life. I might not have made a good mother. Some women aren't cut out for it."

He was certain that she was. There was a nurturing quality about her, a tenderness, that a child would sense and respond to. He hated the thought that she wouldn't have children. It wounded him.

"There are other men in the world," he said shortly.

"No, I don't think so," she said sadly. She smiled. "I'll be fine, Mr. Lang, you don't need to be concerned about me."

"Don't call me that," he said, his voice harsh as he stared at her. "My name is Nate."

She didn't know how to answer that, but she didn't have to. Nita brought in the tray and set it on the table by Nate's bed. There was coffee and tea and cups with cream and sugar, a platter of cold cuts, salad and dressing and fruit, with two plates and utensils so that Christy could make whatever combination they wanted.

Nate spoke to the little Mexican woman in her own tongue, very fluently. She laughed and left them.

"I want coffee, black, and salad with ham and cheese and Thousand Island dressing," he said, leaning back on his pillows.

She almost smiled at his assertive tone. He was, at least, consistent. He never pulled his punches, even when he ordered lunch. She fixed his plate and handed it to him, putting his coffee cup and saucer within easy reach.

She fixed herself a fruit salad and coffee, also black, and went to sit in her chair.

They ate in a companionable silence. When they finished, she collected the plates and stacked them on the tray, then poured second cups of coffee.

"How did the cave-in happen?" she asked.

"Damned if I know. One minute the ceiling was overhead, the next I was wearing half of it," he said simply. His dark eyes narrowed as he searched her face. "I don't spend a lot of time in the mines, but the occasional inspection is a necessary part of my work."

"Yes, I suppose it would be," she said. She sipped her coffee.

"I don't like your hair like that, Christy," he said unexpectedly.

She steadied the cup that was trembling in her hands. "I'm sorry, but I don't wear it to suit you."

"Christy." He said her name, savoring it. "What's it short for?"

"Christiana," she said. "I was named for my grandmother."

"It's pretty." He stared at her until she felt like a butterfly on a pin. "Get up and close the door, Christiana," he said, his voice husky. Despite what he knew about her—perhaps even because of it—she stirred him to his bones. He wanted nothing more than the feel, the taste of her. It was suddenly exciting to know that no other man had touched her. He knew instinctively that even this man she was going to marry had never been allowed the intimacies he had. It made him feel a foot taller.

"I won't," she said quietly. She closed her eyes, so that the sight of him that way, his skin dark against the white sheets, his face sensually inviting, wouldn't tempt her. He had nothing to offer except an affair, and she wasn't built for affairs, even with a man she'd grown to love.

"Afraid of me?" he asked, his voice deep and soft and slow as he watched her.

She lifted her haunted eyes to his. "Please stop it," she asked softly. "I can't play the game. I'm not brave enough."

He wasn't taking no for an answer. His lean fingers went to the sheet and he smiled at her in a way that made her nerves leap. "Close the door, or you're going to get an eyeful," he said, and moved the sheet so that it inched down his ribcage.

She couldn't believe he'd do it, but she knew he didn't make threats. "That's not fair," she accused.

"Live dangerously. I might only want to talk."

"Really?" she asked in disbelief.

"Are you that conceited?" he murmured, letting his eyes run over her as if she hardly interested him at all. "You really aren't that desirable, honey," he lied.

She flinched and got to her feet. "All right," she replied. He'd cut her pride to the bone, but she wasn't going to let the hurt show. She went to the door and started to go through it.

"Do it," he threatened, "and I'll follow you, just as I am."

That would be interesting, she thought, having a naked man follow her out to the tables. But they were all men out there and she was the only person who was likely to get embarrassed.

She closed the door firmly and turned, leaning back against it. "You're no gentleman," she said shortly.

"That's a fact. Come here."

She hesitated. But he stared at her and the sheet inched down again.

"It's blackmail!" she accused. But she went, her face scarlet. She could see enough to embarrass her already, despite the fact that he was a little blurry at a distance.

"And I thought you were sophisticated," he said, shaking his head as she approached him warily. "My God, I was blind as a bat, wasn't I? It sticks out all over you."

"What does?" she queried.

He caught her hand and jerked her down beside him on the bed. "Your chastity," he said. He drew her hand to his hair-covered chest and pressed it there. "Take your hair down."

"Please..."

"Come on, honey," he said gently. "There's nothing to be afraid of. Mother won't be gone that long, and I'm not going to do anything you'll be ashamed of later. Okay?"

She still didn't quite trust him, but his nearness was working on her will power. Again. She lifted her hands to her hair and let it loose, so that it curved gracefully around her shoulders.

He reached up. His strong hands lifted and turned her across him, so that she was lying beside him on the cool, crisp sheets.

"Nate, don't," she whispered, her eyes pleading with him.

"Life is too short to settle for crumbs, Christiana," he said quietly. His eyes fell to her soft mouth. "I want the whole cake." His mouth settled gently on hers, probing, coaxing her lips to open for him, so that he could taste their warm fullness. He arched over her, one hand sliding under her back to lift her even closer while the kiss grew slower and harder and then, deeper.

She stiffened. His head lifted and he looked down into her eyes.

"Why are you afraid of that?" he asked softly. "Deep kisses won't make you pregnant."

"I don't... want to be that intimate with you," she said miserably. "You're just playing!"

His fingers curled into her thick hair and tugged. "Like hell I'm just playing," he murmured. "Has Harry held you like this?" he asked suddenly. His slate eyes blazed up dangerously and his hand tightened in her hair. "Answer me. Has he?"

"No, but..."

"Have you let him touch you the way I did the other afternoon?" he persisted.

"Please, you're hurting my hair."

"I want to know if you've been intimate with him," he breathed roughly.

"I don't... feel like that with Harry," she blurted out.

He could feel himself tautening, but with pure pleasure, not with anger. He searched her face with eyes that glittered. "And you're going to marry him?" he asked coldly.

"I'll learn," she said mutinously.

He touched her soft mouth with his free hand, bending over her with silent intent. "You don't learn desire," he said softly. "Either it's there or it isn't. You feel it for me, don't you?"

She reddened. "I won't stay here and let you... Nate!" she gasped.

"You won't what?" he asked, as his hand smoothed deliberately down her body, trespassing under the waistband of her jeans to stroke her smooth, flat belly. "Go ahead. Tell me."

But she couldn't. Her mind was in limbo. She stared up at him helplessly, too entranced to even struggle.

He liked that helplessness. His hand smoothed back up, under her embroidered smock top to the lacy covering of her bra. He traced the whirl of lace, watching her face color, feeling her breath quicken.

"This is what you like most, isn't it?" he murmured, and his hand slid gently under the lace, to touch her bare skin, to trace the hard nipple that was screaming her response. "You like me to touch you here. But you like my mouth more than my hands, don't you, Christiana?" he whispered, bending. "Even through the fabric, it drives you mad . . ."

It did. She whimpered at the feel of his mouth on her. Her fingers clung to his thick hair and she shivered with the fire-hot brand of his mouth even through two layers of cloth.

"To hell with this," he ground out. He found the fastening underneath her and pushed the offending barrier out of his way, jerking up her smock so that he could find her with his mouth.

It had never been like this, so intense, so heated. She felt the hungry mouth fasten on her breast and she began to weep with reaction. The pleasure was almost pain in its intensity. She clung to him, pressing closer, begging for his touch.

He lifted his head, pausing to look down at his handiwork with blazing eyes before he lifted his gaze to lock with hers. She looked loved, he thought dazedly. Her misty pale green eyes were half-closed, her face a study in absolute surrender. He thought he'd never seen anything half as lovely in his life.

"Can Harry give you that?" he asked huskily.

"Don't," she pleaded in a broken whisper. "Don't...play with me. I can't help it."

He let out a rough sigh. "You might not believe it, but neither can I." He rolled away from her, his face hard and drawn.

She turned her head and only then noticed that the sheet had come away. He was as beautiful as a sculpture, all long elegant lines and powerful muscle. Even where he was most a man, he was beautiful. She couldn't see him with a great deal of clarity, but her eyes found him fascinating, dark skin with a tangle of black hair all over him, the very epitome of masculinity.

He felt her eyes and turned his head, watching her gaze wash over him. It aroused him to see her pleasure in his nudity, and the arousal took a physical form that she saw with dawning realization and then flaming embarrassment.

"You don't have to be afraid of it," he said gently when she averted her gaze jerkily. "It's a reaction I can't help, but I won't hurt you."

"I've never seen a man like...that," she whispered.

"Yes." Her reactions were too drastic to be faked. She was virginal all right, and her innocence excited him so much that he could hardly control the need to drag her under him and slake his thirst. But that would be wrong. "Christy."

She darted a glance at him, feeling threatened.

"It's all right to look," he said, his voice slow and tender.

She hesitated, but curiosity was too strong. Her eyes slid over him and back up again, her face scarlet. "You're so beautiful," she whispered, her voice hopelessly adoring.

The look on his face fascinated her. He frowned slightly, his eyes searching and curious. It wasn't a comment he'd expected from her.

Because she didn't understand the look, she was afraid she'd put her foot in her mouth again. She sat up, rearranging her disheveled clothing with hands that trembled.

He sat up, too, turning her to him. He didn't speak, but his eyes did. They were eloquent. He turned her across his legs, so that she could feel him intimately against her. When his mouth settled over hers again, she opened her own willingly, adoringly, and gave him complete access. His tongue thrust inside and she went limp in his arms.

"I can't take any more," he whispered, his voice deep and shaken as he lifted his head. "Cover me."

He held her up so that she could tug the sheet over his hips, concealing what he couldn't help.

He held her then until the faint tremor went out of his powerful body, until he could breathe normally again. "I want you," he said at her ear. "You'd better cut your trip short and go back to Florida."

She bit her lower lip. "Why?"

"You know why," he said with a bitter laugh. He tilted her face up to his mocking eyes. "My mother raised me to be a gentleman, but what I feel isn't so easily controlled. This time I mastered it. Another time, I might not. If you want to go to your marriage bed a virgin, you'd better get as far away from me as you can."

Chapter Six

Her mouth was swollen. She could barely get words through it at all. "I love you," she whispered miserably.

His jaw tautened. "No."

Her eyes lowered to his bare chest. "Are you . . . so certain?"

"Certain enough." He moved her over him and off the bed. "If you've never been intimate with anyone, it's easy to delude yourself into thinking physical attraction is love. I know. I did that once. But it doesn't last," he added quietly, his dark eyes cutting into hers. "This is nothing more than an interlude, and my fault. I shouldn't have touched you."

She looked down at him with anguish. He wanted sex and she wanted love. It was an impossible situation, and he was right. She should go home. She turned away toward the door.

"I'll get my things packed," she said.

"I didn't mean you have to leave today," he said tersely. Good God, what was wrong with him, he thought furiously. He knew it was the best thing all around, for her to go quickly. But the thought of her leaving was like a knife in his chest.

"I should—"

"Not today!" he said curtly.

She turned around, her back against the door. She couldn't really see him clearly, but she could feel his rage. "You said it would be better," she reminded him.

He leaned back against his pillows, still taut with unsatisfied desire, and raked a hand through his thick black hair. "Probably it would, but you've got a responsibility to the group. I don't want to cost them a worker they need," he said, not looking at her. "I'll make sure this doesn't happen again. Despite what I said about your chastity, I'll send you home in your present condition. There won't be any more...interludes."

Could he know how much it hurt to think of never being held by him again, kissed by him? She sighed shakily.

"All right," she said. "Can I bring you anything?"

"No, thank you, honey," he said gently. "Go on. I'll be all right."

"I'll get back to work, then." She hesitated as she opened the door, not looking at him. "I'm glad you're not hurt," she said huskily. She closed the door behind her.

She didn't see Nate again until the next day. She'd been too embarrassed to go near him. It seemed to be that she went from shame to shame with him. First giving in so easily, then confessing that she loved him. She couldn't imagine what had possessed her to admit it, knowing that he felt nothing like that for her. But it had seemed so natural at the time.

George had been helping her sort pottery shards, in between doing his own search of the area. She loved what she was learning about the *Hohokam*, despite the sting in her heart over Nate.

"One school of archaeologists believes that the *Hohokam* society thrived for over nine thousand years," George murmured as they studied the design on a large shard. "Imagine a society that stable, that unchanged."

"I can't," she said, brushing aside a stray wisp of hair. She was still going without makeup, without fixing her hair except into a soft bun, and without...

Well, what harm was there, she asked herself bitterly. She only had a few days left and she wasn't hurting anybody with this last little deceit. Besides, it was her own business.

She and George were still buried in their discoveries when it was time to go back to the ranch for supper. She piled into the equipment van beside George and thought about all that had happened since she'd come to Arizona, and wondered how she was going to live the rest of her life without Nate. She'd marry Harry and help get his kids through college, and then . . . and then what? The thought of being touched by Harry's pudgy hands made her sick.

She still looked nauseous when she got to the buffet line. Nate was standing in the doorway watching her, curious about the reason for that expression. He waited until she'd placed a meager portion on her plate and then he walked over and drew her by the arm to the table where his own coffee and food were waiting and seated her.

"What prompted that God-awful expression?" he asked, letting his dark eyes slip to the deep neckline of her sleeveless magenta blouse before they held hers.

"I was thinking about Harry's hands," she said without considering her words, and then blushed as Nate's eyebrows went up to the neatly stitched cut on his forehead.

"Comparing them to mine?" he asked quietly.

She grimaced. "I wish you wouldn't," she murmured, glancing nervously around to see if anyone had heard. But the others were at the opposite end of the patio, talking shop as they sat together at three grouped tables.

He lifted a forkful of steak to his mouth, his smile faintly smug. "You'll pay a high price for that wedding ring if you don't enjoy having him touch you."

She stared down at her plate, hardly seeing anything on it. "I don't want to spend the rest of my life alone. I've had enough of that already. There will be compensations."

"Name one."

"I'll have someone to watch television with," she murmured dryly.

"Buy a dog. He'll have the added attraction of being someone to take on walks and buy presents for."

"I can take Harry on walks and buy presents for him," she said stubbornly.

His eyebrows arched. "Sure you can, honey, but the dog won't expect you to put his kids through college. Or can you tell me that Harry won't expect your help financially?"

"Harry and I agreed . . ." she began.

"Damn Harry," he said, his eyes kindling. His gaze fell to her soft mouth and lingered there. "I don't want supper. I want you."

"Don't," she moaned. She had to drag her eyes away from his. She forced herself to taste the steak. It was probably delicious, but she couldn't really savor it with him looking at her like that.

"I don't think I slept five minutes the whole night," he continued quietly. "What we did together haunted me."

"I don't want to have a love affair with you," she said, glaring at him.

"If you love me, why not?" he asked.

"Because sex is sordid without mutual feeling," she returned icily. "Don't you ever listen to the sermons when you go to church?"

He shrugged. "Not usually. You could go with us next Sunday and I'll try."

"I won't be here next Sunday," she said, and went white when she said it, because it was only then that she fully accepted that the group was leaving Saturday. Tears stung her eyes and made them suddenly bright, and her throat felt as if it had a pincushion in it.

His jaw tautened at the look on her face. "Don't look like that," he warned gruffly. "I'll come right over that table after you if you do, and to hell with gossip. I can't bear to watch you cry!"

She lowered her face and struggled for composure. "Why do you do this to me?" she wailed.

"Why do you do it to me?" he countered. "My God, do you realize I've been stuck out here in the sand for over three years without a woman? I've been celibate so long, I'm surprised that my body even remembered how to react when it had a half-naked woman against it!"

She looked up, shocked. "What?"

"I've been celibate for three years," he said, slowly as if she was too thick to understand words of more than one syllable. "You aren't the only one who had to do some renovating on yourself. I've never been much to look at, but I had money, so there was the occasional woman who gave her all for a few luxuries in the past. But I hated being bedded for my wallet, so I gave up on the fair sex. Then it dawned on me that a man can work on his appearance if he wants to, so I lost some weight and had my hair styled, got some new clothes and...other things...and my life changed overnight. But suddenly sex for its own sake wasn't enough. I seemed to lose my taste for it. Until you came along," he added darkly, "and complicated things."

"What did you look like before?" she asked, fascinated.

"Never mind. I'll show you a photo one day." His eyes narrowed. "Saturday is too soon. You can stay."

"I can't, you know," she replied sadly. "Joyce Ann made me promise to help her with her husband's banquet. She's a hopeless cook, you see, and it's going to be a major occasion for him. He's a junior partner in his business and two of the big bosses are expected."

He smiled at her lazily. "Can you cook?"

"Yes. I'm not *cordon bleu*," she murmured, smiling back, "but I used to win prizes at the fair for my pies and cakes." She lowered her eyes. "I'm doing some French haute cuisine for the banquet."

"You could come back, when it's over," he suggested.

She couldn't tell him that she wouldn't be able to afford the plane fare again. Her pride wouldn't let her. She just shook her head. "I have commitments."

"To Harry," he said icily.

She lifted her eyes. "Yes. To Harry. He may not be the world's greatest lover, but he's kind and I'll have security."

"You'll have nothing," he said. "Nothing, except the memory of what it was like to lie in my arms."

She bit her lip. "That's not fair."

"I can make it more than a harmless memory," he said, his voice deepening. "I could give you one long, endless night to carry back with you. We could go all the way."

Her eyes closed. She loved him, and he knew it, but it wasn't fair to taunt her like this. "I can't," she moaned.

"Look at me!"

The commanding tone brought her pained eyes up to meet his.

"I won't let you get pregnant," he said roughly. "And there's no danger of anything else with me, because I've never been promiscuous. I've been careful, in every way. I can give you something you'll never have with your stodgy prospective husband."

"I know that," she replied quietly, averting her eyes. "But I'd be cheating him out of something that's his due if he marries me. And you can sit there and harp on the new morality and my old-fashioned hang-ups until hell freezes over," she added when he started to speak, "but it's a matter of honor with me. If a man is willing to give me his name and be faithful to me, I owe him something in return. He has every right to expect fidelity in me.''

He caught his breath. She was right. But he'd never thought of it like that. Fidelity. Honor. She was quoting words he'd said without understanding them. Now, suddenly, he did. She felt that she had to be faithful, even when there was no ring, when no vows had been spoken. A woman like that would never settle for any convenient bed partner after she was married, or indulge in casual affairs without seeing the harm in them. She'd marry one man, love one man, die faithful to one man. She'd have his children. . . .

He stopped there. No, she wouldn't have Harry's children. He didn't want any more. She'd die without having known the beauty of an infant in her arms, and it was so pointless. She was made to be a mother. He watched her ardently, trying to imagine how she'd look big with his own child inside her body, blooming in the fulfillment of motherhood. A scalding need surfaced in him, one he'd never realized he possessed. He wanted a family of his own. A wife. Sons. Daughters. He was thirty-seven years old and, except for his mother, totally alone. He had no one, really. But he wanted to have someone. He wanted Christy. His eyes narrowed. He hadn't really expected her to take him up on his offer of one wild night of love, although at the time, it had seemed perfectly sensible to offer it. Now he wasn't sure that he should have. She was a woman completely out of his experience. A woman with principles. He felt suddenly proud that a woman like that could love him.

''Fidelity,'' he repeated, watching her. ''One man, one love. But if you don't love him, aren't you going to be cheating him, just the same?''

''I'll learn to love him,'' she said stubbornly.

"You said you loved me," he returned, and the words warmed him as he saw them hit the target.

She shifted restlessly in her chair. "You yourself said that that was just a cheap physical interlude," she returned, her voice wounded.

"I never said it was cheap," he returned. His eyes kindled. "That was the one thing it could never be, between you and me. My God, just the idea of letting a woman see me without my clothes was unthinkable only a week ago!"

She gasped. "You're not serious!"

"Why not?" he asked, his expression dark and formidable. "Do you think you're the only one with hang-ups? It was the most natural thing in the world to let you look at me, but I'd never have pulled that sheet away with any other woman."

Her eyes looked everywhere except at him, because the memory of what she'd seen was potent.

"And you needn't look so shocked," he replied. "You can't pretend that you've ever let your heartthrob back home look at you the way you let me."

She couldn't, she thought. She gazed at him across the table and her eyes adored the blurry line of his face. He was almost ugly, despite the self-improvement he'd mentioned, but it wasn't for his looks that he attracted women. There was a very definite masculinity in his personality, a take-charge attitude that was reassuring and comforting. Added to that was a tenderness she could feel in him, and a compassion that was deep and certain. He had qualities that appealed to everything womanly in her.

She picked at her meal halfheartedly. She had little appetite, and she was all too aware of time passing. She'd have to go home Saturday, back to her familiar world, but it was no longer an eagerly anticipated trip. She didn't know how she was going to survive leaving Nate.

"I've enjoyed being here," she said absently.

"It must have been a change for you," he replied.

"Sand is sand, they say," she murmured and smiled at him. "But there's such a difference between mine and yours."

"I suppose so."

She glanced up, her eyes lingering on the stitched red gash on his forehead, half obscured by his shock of dark hair. "How's your head?" she asked.

"Hard," he returned dryly. "I guess that's what saved me."

"I've never even been in a mine," she said.

"You haven't missed much." He leaned back with his coffee cup in his lean hand, watching her. "What does your Harry look like?" he asked.

He seemed to be pretty curious about Harry. Odd, when he didn't want a permanent relationship with her anyway. "He's a little taller than me," she replied. "Graying. He has a beer belly and he's sort of red-faced. He isn't handsome, but he's nice."

"I'm not handsome, and I'm not nice to boot."

She lifted her eyes to his face. "I wouldn't mind being trapped in a cave-in with you," she said simply. "Because I know you'd get us out one way or the other. Harry would sit down and give up. He isn't a fighter."

"You can do better than Harry," he said.

"Can I? I put on my best clothes and came out here with my changed image, and you thought I was a hooker," she reminded him.

"I did not," he returned, his eyes blazing. "I thought you were a gold digger."

"Thanks a lot."

"I didn't know you," he reminded her. He smiled slowly. "The real you came as quite a shock. I didn't plan on stopping that afternoon, out on the desert, you know," he added bluntly. "At that time, I had every intention of seducing you. Then I found out why you were so embarrassed when I looked at you."

"I'm sorry I gave you the wrong impression," she told him. "I wasn't trying to tease, even if it did seem that way."

"Yes, I've figured that out," he murmured, and there was a curious, knowing look on his face. "Are you going to be free tomorrow afternoon?"

The question thrilled her. She should have said "no" and played it safe, but she couldn't resist him. "Yes," she replied.

"I thought we might take in a movie in Tucson." He toyed with his cup. "There's a murder mystery that I've wanted to see."

He named it and she beamed. It was one she'd been looking forward to herself.

"I'd like that," she said.

He put down his cup, studying her long and hard. His slate eyes narrowed. "I'm too much a bachelor to offer you marriage," he said honestly. "And too much a gentleman to seduce you. I suppose we'll have to be friends, since that's all we have left."

"I wouldn't mind that," she lied.

"Neither would I. It gets lonely here." He turned the cup carefully on the table. "An occasional one-night stand doesn't do a thing for me anymore. I suppose I'm getting old." He looked up. "What we did together in my bed yesterday was a memory I'll treasure for the rest of my life."

"But we hardly did anything, really," she stammered.

"Didn't we?" He stood up, towering over her, his gaze long and steady on her uplifted face. She couldn't know how adoring her eyes were, how warm and caring and soft. They made him feel humble and guilty, all at the same time. He wished he was more of a gambler. If he had been, he'd have taken her away from Harry and married her out of hand and trusted to luck to keep them together. But it would be more of a risk than she realized. She was too unworldly, and her emotions were in a state of flux. He was afraid to take the chance that what she felt might only be infatuation.

"Sleep tight, honey," he said gently. He touched her hair as he passed her. "I'll see you tomorrow."

"Goodnight," she called after him.

She finished her meal and went into the recreation room to watch the chess game with the group. She didn't want to be alone just yet with her thoughts, because they were too painful already.

The next afternoon, George left her alone while he helped Dr. Adamson with some measurements. She closed her eyes and felt the wind in her face, smelled the clean air with its faint scent of ancient pottery and desert vegetation. It was marvelous, the freedom she felt here, in this vast expanse of land. It seemed endless and wide open. Except for the total lack of trees in most places, it was very enticing. Of course, there were places in Florida where trees were scarce, too. But there was ocean and salt air all around, there.

It didn't get dark until late, so she wasn't aware of the passage of time. She sat down on a big boulder to brush sand off the design on a piece of pottery when two sounds impinged on her consciousness. One was the sound of an approaching Jeep, and she smiled to herself, because it had to be Nate coming after her. It touched her that he cared enough to do that, when she could have ridden in with the van.

But the other sound, the one that followed, was enough to chill her blood. She knew so well the noise that a rattle-snake makes. The Eastern diamondback is fairly common in south Georgia and northern Florida. The sound its rattle makes is unforgettable, like sizzling hot grease. This was the same sound, and she was aware that there was a Western diamondback, a counterpart to the snakes she knew.

She knew better than to move. She sat very still, like a statue, and waited for Nate while she prayed that the snake wouldn't decided to sink its sharp fangs into her leg. Even if they got her to the antivenom in time, she would still be very sick until she recovered from the bite.

Nate would know what to do, thank God. She felt safer just knowing he was nearby. It would be all right.

"Christy?" She heard his deep voice calling her.

Did she dare answer, or would that venomous reptile be irritated by the vibrations of her voice and strike? If she didn't say something and Nate made much noise when he approached, it might happen anyway. She had nothing to lose, really.

She closed her eyes and bit her lip nervously. "Nate, there's a rattlesnake!" she called.

There was a rough curse and the sound of running foot-steps. Barely a minute later, a lifetime later as she sat stiffly and prayed, the footsteps returned.

"Where is it?" he asked curtly.

"Somewhere near my left," she said, trying not to move a muscle. "I'm afraid to look."

"Sit still," he murmured, moving into her line of view. "Just sit still. You're doing fine. Managed to find a rattler, did you? I suppose you were camped on the only available shade. That rock you're sitting on juts out to keep the sun away. Good girl, you're doing fine, Christy."

She saw him move, his stride sure and deliberate. He was holding a rifle in the firing position, his eyes open and watchful as he moved slowly around in front of her. He looked like an old-time cowboy, she thought through her terror, with his Stetson pulled low over his eyes, wearing a Western-cut gray jacket and dark slacks. The snake was going to be sorry he'd tackled her now, she told herself. Nate was going to make a hatband out of the sneaky creature.

"Don't move, now. I see him."

She clamped her teeth together, steeling herself for the report when he fired. She knew without being told that he was a dead shot. It was in his confident aim, in the steely glitter of his eyes as he sighted, in the way he stood and shouldered the rifle.

He fired once and the rattling stopped. Christy jumped up and ran to him, throwing herself into his arms, shivering all over.

The lean arm that wasn't holding the rifle hauled her closer, bruising in its ferocity. "God Almighty, that was close!" he said harshly. "Didn't you look before you sat down? Not that it would have mattered, anyway, because what could you see?" he added, his voice cutting. "That's the last damned straw. You come with me."

He led her back to the Jeep, ignoring her questions, and put away the rifle. "She's all right," he told the others, who were gathered around, concerned. "Just a rattler, but he didn't strike her. I'll run her back to the ranch."

"I'm glad you're all right, Christy," George said with relief.

"So am I," she said, but she didn't get time to talk. Nate put her in the Jeep, got in beside her, and set new speed records for covering distance.

But he didn't stop at the ranch house. With his face hard and set, he screeched to a halt in front of her cabin and dragged her out of the Jeep to the door.

"Key," he said.

She fumbled it out of her pocket and gave it to him, puzzled by his attitude. He hadn't said one word to her all the way back, and he looked odd.

He unlocked the door, threw it open, and drew her inside. He pushed her gently down into a chair and began to go through drawers, oblivious to her shocked protestations. Minutes later, he found what he was looking for. He turned, with her huge-rimmed glasses in his hand and stuck them none too gently over her eyes.

"Now wear the damned things," he said shortly, glaring down at her with pure fury. "You little fool, you can't see five inches in front of you without those, can you? Did you think you could keep it up indefinitely? If you hadn't had good ears, you'd be in the hospital by now! Those rattlers are deadly."

"I know that..." she began, aghast at having been found out. Now that she could see him properly, she was a little afraid of him. He looked far more formidable with the lines stark and hard in his lean face. His eyes were much darker than she'd first thought, and there was a hardness, a ruthlessness about his face that intimidated her. If she'd been able to see him properly, like this, that first day, she'd never have had the nerve to even smile at him. He looked what he was—a hard-bitten desert man with no time for idiot tenderfeet.

"No wonder you fell over everything in your path," he muttered as he looked down at her. "If you don't want people to see you in specs, why don't you get contact lenses?"

"I tried," she confessed wearily, pushing her glasses up on her nose when they began to slip—as usual. "I had one eye infection after another, because I was too haphazard to keep them antiseptically clean, so they said I couldn't wear them. It's this or go blind." She looked at him mutinously.

"I changed my whole image to come out here. The glasses spoiled it."

"What's wrong with glasses?" he asked carelessly. "I think you look better with them on. They make your eyes look bigger. Much sexier," he added with a grin.

Her green eyes widened. "Really?" she asked, forgetting her protests. He didn't think she looked awful!

"Really. Glasses aren't a cosmetic nuisance in your case, they're a necessity. Now keep them on. I don't want to lose you to a rattlesnake. I'm responsible for you."

That took a little of the pleasure out of his interest. She hesitated, her eyes sweeping over his hard features with quiet pain.

"You don't believe that bull about glasses making you less desirable?" he persisted.

She shrugged. "Men never noticed me before."

"I can understand that," he replied easily. "You're shy and introverted and you probably dressed to hide your body. Now you've put it on display and had your hair done and learned to use makeup. Glasses don't have anything to do with the qualities that make you desirable, Christy." He pulled her up against him and stood holding her, with his lean hands smoothing her bare arms in the white sleeveless top with the bulky yellow overblouse that kept her from burning in the sun. "Glasses or no, you're the sexiest woman I've ever known."

"You're only saying that to make me feel better...!"

He caught the words in his mouth and breathed them back into her own. She gave in immediately, too hungry for his touch to fight it now. Her arms reached under his and around him beneath his jacket and she pressed close, delighting in his instant arousal, in the sudden crush of his mouth against hers.

"That's it," he bit off. "Kiss me. Open your mouth. Yes. A little more. Don't hold back," he murmured roughly as he bent and lifted her. "Harder, baby. Do it harder!"

She felt him put her on the bed, felt his weight as he joined her on its narrow surface. His mouth was doing impossibly arousing things to hers, and his body was hard and urgent as it pushed her into the mattress. She felt the force of his heartbeat against her breasts, inhaled the faint scent of his cologne until she was drunk on it, drunk on him. His mouth was minty and hard and warm, and she never wanted to be free of it. She lifted closer into his embrace, feeling him shudder in response.

But even as she yielded, he lifted his head and muttered a curse.

"My God, it's impossible," he said huskily, sitting up as he struggled to catch his breath. His dark eyes swept over her prone body with possession and hunger, lingering on the thrust of her breasts under the low-cut white sleeveless top beneath her yellow overblouse. "We can't make love here. The damned bed's too flimsy for two people. It would fall through with us the first time we started moving back and forth on it."

She blushed scarlet. He smiled down at her with a knowing look in his dark eyes that got worse when her reaction was so transparent.

"Does it bother you to hear such blunt descriptions of lovemaking, Christy?" he asked, leaning over her to nip her lower lip gently with his teeth.

"Do you enjoy embarrassing me?" she demanded.

"Indeed I do. It's a rare treat to watch a woman blush in this day and time." He smoothed his hand blatantly over her breast, possessive demand in his touch while he gauged her helpless reaction. "You can't imagine how it feels, to watch you and know that what you're feeling is totally new."

"I guess it makes you feel conceited," she said defensively, embarrassed by his arrogance.

"No. It makes me feel proud." He let his eyes fall to where his hand was caressing her. "It means everything to me, being your first lover."

"But you aren't . . ."

His eyes went back up to hers. "I will be." He held her gaze for one long, endless moment before he slowly got to his feet and helped her up. He held her against him gently, his breath in her hair. "Did you hear me, Christy?" he whispered. "I'm going to be your first man. When it happens, it's going to be me."

"I'm marrying Harry," she whispered miserably.

"I don't think so." He drew her closer, sliding his hands to her hips and pulling them gently to his, letting her feel how aroused he was. "No, don't pull away from me," he said against her ear. "This reaction is yours alone. You don't have to be afraid of it. I told you I wouldn't seduce you and I meant it."

She relaxed finally and let him hold her. "I'm sorry about the snake," she murmured. "I know I should have worn my glasses. I could hardly see the boulders, although close up, my vision is very good."

He smoothed her hair gently in its disheveled bun. "You'll wear them from now on, do you hear me? I won't risk you twice. My God, when I saw that snake, I thought your number was up!"

"We both seem to be accident prone," she said on a forced laugh. "First you get caved in and then I get rattled at."

"We both need our heads examined." He drew back, glancing down at her. "Want to take a shower and change before we leave for Tucson?"

"Yes, if you don't mind."

"I don't mind." His thin lips tugged into a wicked smile. "I could wash your back."

She colored delicately. "No, you couldn't. I don't take showers with strange men."

"I let you look at me," he pointed out.

She glared at him. "Shame on you!"

He shrugged. "All right, be a prude. I'll have you out of your clothes one of these dark nights and under a sheet with me."

"I won't let you," she replied.

He tilted her chin up and brushed his mouth tenderly over hers. "Yes, you will. Have your bath. I'll be back in thirty minutes to get you." He searched her wide, soft eyes. "Harry can't make you pregnant. I can. If you loved him, that wouldn't matter. But if you don't love him, you might give that point some thought before you make up your mind."

She stiffened. "There's nothing to decide. He wants to marry me."

"No, I don't think that's a good idea," he said somberly. "He wouldn't enjoy raising my son as much as I would. Get your clothes changed, honey, I want to get an early start. We'll eat in town."

"Nate!" she said, exasperated.

But he left her there, trying to make sense of what he'd said. She finally gave up and got into the shower, still completely in the dark. He didn't want to marry her and here he was talking about his son. Sexist, she thought, how did he know it wouldn't be a daughter?

Which was beside the point, because she wasn't making any children with him when she was going to marry Harry!

Chapter Seven

Christy didn't have a large selection of dresses with her, and she'd already worn two of them. The third, and last, was a soft pink synthetic with a full skirt and button-up bodice, a large collar and cap sleeves. It suited her coloring beautifully, and emphasized her delicate complexion. She wore a scarf with complimenting colors and left her hair long. She glared at the glasses, but she put them back on. If Nate thought she looked all right, she supposed that was all that mattered.

She started to wear sandals, but mindful of the sand, she put on some white pumps instead.

Nate was waiting outside the cabin, still wearing his gray suit. He smiled at the picture she made in her dress. He couldn't imagine how she'd remained single so long, even if she hadn't prettied herself up. She had a sweet, caring nature and so many good traits that her looks were just a fringe benefit—not the reason he liked her.

"Nice," he pronounced, helping her into the car. "I hope you feel like Chinese food. I've got a yen for it tonight."

"I love it," she said. "Sweet and sour pork and egg rolls and hot mustard sauce! Yum!"

He chuckled. "My favorite, although I'm partial to pepper steak."

"Did I even thank you for rescuing me from the snake?" she asked as they drove along. "I was so shaken up, I don't remember."

"You aren't the only one. I was pretty shaken myself," he admitted. He glanced toward her. "Rattlers can kill, even in this day and time. And even if they don't, it's a painful experience. I took a bite in the leg when I was in my teens. They barely got me to the doctor in time, and I spent three days in the hospital. Damned thing still swells at the same time I was bitten every year," he chuckled. "They can't explain that, but it happens all the same."

"No wonder it bothered you that I almost got bitten," she murmured, thinking the memory would have resurfaced for him.

"It bothered me because I don't want anything to happen to you, Christy," he said.

"Because I'm a guest on your property," she nodded, understanding.

He scowled. "My God, do you believe that?" he asked angrily. "Hasn't it dawned on you yet that I was worried about *you*? It didn't have anything to do with your being a guest, or my old memories."

"No, it didn't occur to me," she said honestly. She smiled. "I'm not much to look at, even with my glad rags on..."

He muttered something violent under his breath and pulled off the road, into the privacy of the shade of a palo verde tree and stopped the car.

"I care about you." He said it slowly, looking straight into her eyes. He watched her blush. "That's right. I care. I don't want to, and it's interfering with my life and all my notions of freedom, but there it is. I just haven't quite decided what to do about it yet."

Her lips parted. She couldn't believe what she was hearing. Her heart was beating like a tom-tom deep in her chest, and the look in his eyes made her want to climb on top of the car and dance a jig.

"I'm glad. That you...like me, I mean," she added shyly. She looked down at his chest, noticing its heavy rise and fall. "I'm still sorry that I gave you the wrong impression at first."

"You didn't. I read what I wanted to read into the way you looked and acted. That was a defensive action." He sighed and traced her cheek with a lean, strong hand. "Oh, Christy, you're under my skin, girl. But there are so many reasons why I should let you go back to Jacksonville that I don't have a single argument for keeping you here," he said, and there was finality in his voice. That, and an expression that she couldn't quite understand in his eyes—a bleak look that puzzled her.

"I know that you don't want anything permanent," she said gently. "It's all right, Nate. I'm not asking for a single thing."

"That makes it harder to let go," he replied. He sighed softly. "Come here and kiss me, Christy."

He unfastened her seat belt and pulled her into his arms, kissing her slowly, and with a new tenderness. He wrapped her up in his lean arms, and his mouth asked things of her that it hadn't before. It asked for comfort, for reassurance. It asked for love.

She slid her arms around his neck and gave him back the soft, slow kiss without a thought of withdrawal. Even when his hands found her breasts and cradled them with quiet possession, she didn't protest. She belonged to him. He had every right to touch her.

His head lifted. His arm tightened around her while his free hand loosened the buttons of her bodice and slid inside. He watched her face while he touched her. "Anything I want?" he whispered softly.

"Yes," she confessed.

He bent and brushed his mouth lazily over hers. She felt the cool air wash over her, because the bodice had been pulled away and so had her bra. Her breasts, hard-tipped and swollen, lay open to his warm gaze in the dim light of the setting sun.

He looked down at her body with reverence, his hand going slowly to trace the exquisite curve of one firm breast. "It's never been like this with a woman," he said huskily. "There was never time...like this." He tried to put it into words. His dark gray eyes slid up to hers. "There was always urgency and haste, even when I thought my emotions were involved. There wasn't this tenderness, this need to cherish, to give."

Her lips parted. He didn't seem to understand what he was describing, but she did. It was what she felt for him. It was love. Perhaps he hadn't realized it just yet. She smiled gently, her eyes so soft and caring that she heard his breath jerk when he looked into them.

"Christy, you're exquisite," he breathed. His eyes moved back down to the beauty his hand was exploring. His fingers trembled on her body. "Exquisite, and I want you so badly, honey...!"

She touched her lips to his throat, feeling him quiver at the contact. He caught his breath and bent to take her mouth under his. He groaned, his hand suddenly warm and insistent as he cupped her.

"Nate," she whispered ardently.

She arched her back, pulling his mouth down to her breasts. She cried out at the pleasure his hungry touch gave her, moaning as the pressure increased and his hands contracted on her waist.

He said something violent under his breath and buried his face in her warm throat. His arms enveloped her roughly and he rocked her in the heady silence of the car, his arms faintly tremulous with the force of his passionate need. God, she was sweet to love! But she was grass green and in the throes of her first physical intimacy, and he didn't trust her feelings enough to take a chance on them, despite the fact that he couldn't bear the thought of letting her leave him.

Christy smoothed his dark hair, guilty that she'd let things go this far again when she hadn't meant to. It was hurting him to hold back.

"I'm sorry," she whispered at his ear. "I seem to keep saying that. I don't want to hurt you."

He actually laughed, deep in his throat. "You can't imagine what a sweet hurt this is, for a man," he whispered. "A kind of slow, throbbing ache laced with vicious pleasure."

"I feel that way, too," she confessed shakily. Her arms contracted and she was tempted beyond imagination. "Nate, you said that you could...keep me from getting pregnant," she blurted.

He stiffened. She wanted him. God, he wanted her, but not like this. Not in a parked car, in desperation. No. He wanted her honorably, or not at all, and his own scruples stopped him.

His mouth brushed her ear. "No." He kissed her closed eyes, feeling her puzzlement. "I can't."

"But..."

"Don't tempt me," he breathed. "Don't ask me to tarnish something this beautiful by reducing it to raw sex."

Her breath stopped in her throat. So he did feel something! He had to, or why would he have refused when she could feel his need?

His head lifted, and her eyes were full of awed adoration.

"And that's the first time I've backed away from satisfaction," he said flatly. His eyes searched hers. "There isn't another woman on earth I wouldn't take right here, sitting up if I had to. But it's different with you, Christy. So different."

She smiled, and her face radiated love. "Yes."

He smoothed back her hair and his eyes involuntarily dropped to the open bodice of her dress. "No white lines," he whispered, smiling at her shyness.

"It's too hot to sunbathe," she murmured. "And I haven't been to the beach this year."

"Do you sunbathe topless?" he asked.

She laughed self-consciously. "No. I'm too inhibited."

"I'm glad. I don't like to think of other men seeing you this way," he said slowly. He bent and put his lips reverently to her breasts before he rearranged her clothing to cover her.

When she'd brushed her hair with the small brush in her purse, and restored her lipstick, she had a radiance that made her beautiful enough to stop Nate's breath in his throat.

"I'm going to have to let you go home, Christy," he said through his teeth. "You know that."

She looked at him. "Yes. I know." He could have loved her, she was sure of that, but it was commitment that stopped him dead. She could understand it, too. He was thirty-seven. He'd been a bachelor too long, and now the thought of giving up his freedom was impossible. She didn't know how she was going to manage to go on living without him, but there was no question of her staying here and they both knew it. Like an amputation, it would be better to get it over with as quickly as possible.

He looked at her long and hard, with a dark, unfathomable expression in his eyes. "We'd better get going," he said, turning away finally to start the car again.

Christy fastened her seat belt with steady fingers. She could take it, she told herself. And at least she'd have beautiful memories of this trip, and dreams of how it might have ended. Perhaps they'd sustain her through the years ahead.

The one thing she was certain of now was that she couldn't possibly marry Harry. Nate had been right about that. It would be cheating him as well as herself, feeling the way she did about Nate. But she needn't go into that, she thought, glancing at Nate. Let him think she'd be married and settled and not dying of love for him. She didn't want him to be concerned for her happiness, or guilty because she wanted more than he could give. It was better if he thought her marriage plans were final.

They ate, but without any real enthusiasm, and Nate kept the conversation on a strictly impersonal level. Inside, he was on fire. He wanted to tell her she couldn't go home and to hell with Harry, that he'd take care of her, that he'd love her. But she had to have time to make sure that what she felt was going to last, that it wasn't just the adventure and different environment blinding her to reality. He owed her that. He owed himself that, he added. Marriage was forever to him. He wasn't going to risk it on a brief infatuation. She had to be sure.

Nate took Christy back to her cabin and kissed her good night, but gently and without lingering. And for the rest of the week, he was pleasant and polite and mostly too busy to spend any time with her. Christy understood that he was making the parting easier for her, so she didn't complain. She stuck with George and did her best to blot out the memory of Nate's lips and arms while the last few hours of her holiday ticked away with relentless speed.

Saturday came before she was ready. She was packed and dressed for travel in her jeans and a loose white sweatshirt and sneakers, because the plane was air-conditioned and frankly cold with her arms uncovered. She joined the others at the front of the house, where the van was waiting to take them to the airport.

Nate came out to say goodbye, saving Christy for last. She looked at him with pain and longing, wishing that she could hide her despair well enough to make him think she didn't mind going. She didn't want him to feel sorry for her now, even though she'd hoped right up until the last minute that he'd change his mind, that he'd confess undying love and propose marriage. But that didn't happen, and she knew she shouldn't have expected it. He wanted her, but he'd get over that. Desire and a little tenderness weren't enough to build a future on, although she'd have tried it if he'd been willing. She loved him so much that she had no pride at all.

He drew her to one side, his eyes lancing over her face like a paintbrush, memorizing every soft line of it. He was hurting, but he didn't dare show it. She had to be free.

"Take care of yourself," he said quietly.

"You, too." She bit back tears and laughed self-consciously. "I'm sorry. I promised myself I wouldn't do this."

He cupped her faced in his lean hands and his thumbs brushed away the tears. His dark eyes were soft with concern and something deeper that she was too blurry to see. She hadn't put on her glasses this morning, because she didn't want to see too clearly.

"Don't fall down the steps. You should have your glasses on," he said gently.

That concern in his deep voice almost brought the tears back. "I won't fall." She reached up and brushed his lean cheek with her lips. "Goodbye, Nate. Thanks for a lovely holiday. I'll never forget it. Or you."

He didn't return the caress or the sentiment. He looked down at her with his heart like lead in his chest, feeling empty and alone already.

His hands fell away from her face. "You'd better get on board," he nodded toward the van.

Her lips trembled into a smile. "Yes, I had." She'd hoped that he might at least kiss her goodbye, but with all these other people around, he probably felt it would be too public a demonstration. He was letting her go, wasn't he? "Well, goodbye," she faltered. She smiled again and, dragging her eyes away from him, she shouldered her pocketbook and climbed into the van.

Nate didn't wait to see it leave. He climbed into his car and headed for work without looking back. He couldn't have borne seeing the van drive away, taking Christy out of his life.

Christy put on the one pair of prescription dark glasses she had, wondering why she hadn't thought to wear them sooner. That way her fellow travelers couldn't see the tears.

George, bless him, knew what was wrong. He sat beside her, holding her hand unobtrusively.

"I'd like to keep in touch with you," he said. "We could write each other at Christmas, at least."

"That would be nice," she said, and meant it.

He smiled. "Fine. I'll write down my address for you."

She settled back into her seat. Only a few hours more and she'd be home in her own apartment. Then she could have a good cry and try to put the past three weeks out of her mind. She had a few souvenirs that she was going to put in a drawer until she could stand to look at them and remember. Meanwhile, it was going to be trouble enough just to walk around normally.

In the weeks that followed, she wondered how she survived the black depression that settled over her. Joyce Ann was openly concerned, and more so since Christy had said a definite and final "no" to Harry.

"It's the Arizona caveman, isn't it?" the older woman demanded, pushing back her gray-streaked blond hair with an angry hand as they sat in Joyce Ann's immaculate living room drinking coffee. "You haven't been the same since you came back. Honestly, Christy, it's been two months, and you walk around like a zombie! You won't go anywhere, you just sit at home and moon!"

Christy had lost weight. She knew she looked bad, but she had no interest in life anymore. Odd, that, when she'd loved the simplest things before. Things like sitting on the beach, listening to the gulls while the salt breeze whipped through her hair and the whitecaps foamed onto the damp sand. Things like going to art galleries to browse and sitting in small cafes drinking coffee and watching people. But she'd changed since her trip to Arizona. She wasn't the same woman who'd gone on an archaeological expedition looking for lost civilizations.

"Pre-planning starts the end of the month," she told Joyce Ann, barely listening to what her sister was saying. "School will be good for me."

"I hope so. Darling, you're positively skeletal, and you don't even bother to dress up and fix up anymore. There are the most terrible dark shadows under your eyes." She shook her head. "Christy, I'm worried about you."

"I'll get over him," Christy assured her. "Really, I will."

Joyce Ann sighed, frowning. "I've never had the courage to ask, but is there any chance, well, that you might be pregnant?"

Christy smiled. "No. That would make the Guinness Book of World Records for sure. He was a perfect gentleman, even when he didn't want to be."

That made it all worse somehow, Joyce Ann thought. Why would a man with sex on his mind bother to hold back? On the other hand, why would a man in love be willing to let her go?

"Oh, Christy. What can I say?" she asked helplessly.

"Just that you love me," Christy replied, and hugged the older woman tight.

Joyce Ann sighed as she returned the embrace. Somehow it seemed unfair that Christy should finally find a man to love and lose him in so short a time. But that happened sometimes. She could only hope that Christy would recover in time.

It was almost dark and Joyce Ann's husband was due home when Christy left for her own apartment. She got in her compact car and drove home without paying any attention at all to her surroundings. If she had been, she might have noticed the vehicle sitting across the road from where she lived, and the man watching her from the driver's seat.

But, oblivious, she parked the car, got out, and went to unlock the door. As she turned on the light inside, she heard footsteps behind her and turned.

Her heart stopped beating; at least, that was how it felt. Her heart had fed on memories for weeks. She hadn't taken a camera to Arizona, due to an oversight in packing, so she hadn't even a photograph of him to keep. But here he was, in the flesh, looking every bit as terrible as she did.

He came closer, and she felt her jaw drop. This wasn't the Nate she remembered. He was wearing glasses with silver rims, sporting tan slacks with a white shirt and a conservative gray and tan sports coat. He wasn't wearing a hat or boots, and his hair was unruly and a little long.

"Nate?" she asked hesitantly.

He was doing some staring of his own. She had her hair in a bun, no makeup on. She was wearing a green dress that did nothing for her, and with her glasses on, she could see him very clearly. He looked thinner, too, and there were dark circles under his eyes that matched those under her own.

"It's me," he said, pausing to tower over her in the doorway, with night falling rapidly over his shoulder. "The real me," he added with a faint smile. "This is the way I looked before you saw me."

Her eyes adored him. "I like you this way," she said softly. "This way, the other way, any way!" Her voice wobbled and tears burst from her eyes.

"Come here!" he groaned, reaching for her.

His arms enfolded her even as his hard, hungry mouth found her own. He held her and kissed her with all the anguish of two months of loneliness, glorying in her headlong response, in the softness of her body in his arms, the sweetness of her open mouth accepting the hard thrust of his tongue. She trembled, and he felt that, and smiled against her lips.

"What a welcome," he breathed against her smiling mouth. "You'll make me conceited."

"You know how I feel. I made no secret of it," she said huskily, her eyes telling him everything.

"And I had to," he said, his eyes dark and possessive. "I had to keep my feelings to myself until I was sure of yours. My God, you look terrible! Almost as bad as I do. Has it been hard?"

"Impossible," she confessed. Her eyes adored him. "I thought I was going to wither and die."

"Same here." He held her close, rocking her, his lips in her hair. "I suppose your neighbors will think you're harboring a lover,'' he mused, glancing around at the other buildings.

"I am,'' she whispered. "Because that's what you're going to be.''

"Eventually,'' he agreed, lifting his head to smile down at her. "I want you like hell, but we're going to do this the right way around. First we get married.''

"Oh, Nate!'' she said, feeling heaven in her grasp.

"I hope that idea appeals to you as much as it appeals to me,'' he said, his voice deeper, softer as he looked down into her eyes. "I don't want to live if I can't have you.''

"Neither do I.'' She reached up, touching his lean cheek, adoring him. "Why did you let me go?'' she asked in anguish.

"I had to, honey,'' he said gently. "I was your first real beau. You were so vulnerable, especially in a physical sense. I didn't want to take advantage of you. You had to have time to be sure that you loved me.''

"What do you think?'' she murmured. "Do I?''

He chuckled at her saucy scrutiny. "Yes, I think so,'' he said, his eyes kindling. "I think so, Miss Haley.''

"Have you had anything to eat?''

His eyebrows arched. "No. Can you find us some bread and mayonnaise and sandwich meat, or do you want to go out and eat?''

"I've got quiche in the refrigerator and the makings of a delicious fruit salad. If you'd like that,'' she added hesitantly.

"Oh, I don't believe that bit about real men not eating quiche,'' he said easily, and grinned. "It's one of my favorite dishes.''

"Mine, too.'' She sighed. "My sister will be surprised.''

"Joyce Ann?" He laughed out loud, ushering her into her apartment and closing the door behind them. "No, I'm afraid the surprise is yours."

She put down her purse and turned to him. "What do you mean?"

"Who do you think called me long distance to ask why the hell I was killing her baby sister?"

"Joyce Ann didn't!" she burst out. "She couldn't!"

"She did," he interrupted. "Thank God she did, I was at the end of my rope. Another week and I'd have been sitting on your doorstep anyway. But it was nice to have some advance notice of how you were taking my absence." The humor went out of his lean, dark face. "I want you to love me," he said huskily. "I've never wanted anything so much. So will you please tell me you don't believe in long engagements, even if you do?"

She slid into his arms and lifted her mouth to his. "I think three days *is* a long engagement. Can I go home with you?"

"Is that what you want?" he asked, frowning. "Arizona is pretty different from what you're used to..."

"I love Arizona," she said softly. "I love the land and the people and the history of it. Most of all, I love it because you do. I can teach anywhere, Nate. I have a feeling teachers are pretty important in your neck of the woods. I'll be doing work that will have meaning, important work."

"In that case, yes, you can come home with me. Do you want to be married here?"

"Joyce Ann would never get over it if we didn't," she murmured. "But what about your mother?"

"She adores you. She'll look forward to having you around. But I thought we might build a house of our own," he began.

"Who's going to help your mother and Nita if we desert them?" she asked reasonably. "Do be sensible. I don't have a mother. Yours is super. I don't want a house of my own."

He shook his head, adoring her with his eyes. "Whatever you want, honey," he said quietly. His face hardened with passion. "I love you," he whispered, bending toward her.

Her lips met his and she closed her eyes, reaching up to him. He lifted her and carried her to the nearest armchair, sitting down with her in his lap. The kiss deepened and lengthened, and Christy thought she'd never been so happy in all her life.

By the time he finally lifted his demanding mouth, she was trembling and more than a little bare flesh was on view. He smiled at her with dark appreciation and laughed at her shyness.

"Three days," he said. "I'll get a motel room and we'll spend every available hour together. Then, on the third night, I expect to get as little sleep as possible."

She laughed and pressed her face against his bare chest, enjoying the abrasive sensuality of the rough hair that covered it. "So do I," she said. "I hope I won't disappoint you too much."

"Well, let me put it this way," he said, tilting her eyes up to his amused ones. "Having a greenhorn along on a cattle drive would be hard on the nerves. But having a pretty greenhorn in bed . . ." He brushed his mouth lovingly over hers. "Now that, Miss Haley, is a prospect that I look forward to with pure delight. Enough said?"

She sighed and traced his hard mouth with a slow forefinger. "Enough said," she whispered.

They were married exactly three days later, with Joyce Ann and her husband for witnesses. Christy wore a white satin dress with a short lace veil, and as Nate lifted the veil to kiss her for the first time as her husband, the look in his eyes brought tears to her eyes. Love was there, and tenderness, and desire, all three as radiant as the sun outside the small church. Christy lifted her lips to his, and gave him her heart.

* * * * *

Diana Palmer

I was born in Randolph County, Georgia, and grew up on a small farm near the small town of Edison. Most of my people were Scotch-Irish, and all of them on my mother's side were farmers. I grew up with a love for animals and the land that I've never quite lost. I still like to have a small garden every year and plant flowers. I have taken this hobby to such extremes that it is now very difficult to find enough room in my acre yard to plant anything new!

I have been writing for Silhouette Books for ten wonderful years, and in that time I've made some very special friends among my readers. And not only in America. I have friends in Australia, South Africa, England, Jamaica, India and Canada. My parents are no longer living, although I have a married sister and she has a super husband and little girl. I, too, have a loving husband and a young son. I always think of my readers as the rest of my family. They are as dear to me as if they were my own blood.

Mail is the best fringe benefit of being a writer (besides having a marvelous agent, great editors, production people and artists and supportive booksellers). I learn a lot about people and places and cultures. It's very educational, and I hope I give as good an opinion of my country as my pen pals overseas give of theirs. Suzanne in Alice Springs, Australia, has taught me about the outback. Rose-Anne Marie of Capetown has taught me about Africa and how to play the thumb piano. Swathi in Bangalore is a student of Sanskrit and a computer whiz. Betty in Queensland has given me the grand tour of the beautiful Australian Gold Coast and introduced me to one of Australia's great humorists, Jolliffe. Jo in England is teaching me about the fascinating Gypsy culture. Alice and Flo in Canada have taught me about that vast, beautiful country. And there are more.

In this country I have Mama Alice in Chicago, Dorothy in California, Ophelia in Georgia, Stephanie in Arizona, Diane in New York, Sandra in Louisiana, Rozanna in Oregon, Doris and Kay and June and Kathleen and Helen and Aurora and Mary in Texas, Helen in Colorado, and so many more in these states and others that I could spend a week naming them. These are not just acquaintances; these are readers who have stuck with me for almost ten years, since my first books were published.

Loyalty and friendship such as this make me feel humble. I can only say that I love each and every one of my readers. Thank you for your devotion and your friendship. I will work hard to deserve both. God bless.

Your biggest fan,

Diana Palmer

A BRIDGE TO DREAMS

Sherryl Woods

A Note from Sherryl Woods

When I was growing up outside of Washington, D.C., my family spent every summer and most long holiday weekends at our vacation cottage on the shores of the Potomac. It made for consistency and wonderful friendships but did very little to feed my sense of adventure. That may explain why I never really felt I'd been on vacation unless I'd traveled a great distance and done something I'd never in a million years do back home. It has made for a few memorable moments.

There was, for instance, the cruise to Mexico, during which I managed to wind up on an island far from the ship with a gentleman who had the insane notion that we would leap off the edge of a cliff into a waiting boat—a very small waiting boat—to get back. After scouting the island for a lifetime supply of berries and finding none, I leaped. To my amazement, the boat didn't sink, but the relationship was doomed.

In Jamaica a friend made the mistake of assuming that a woman who spent hours at a racetrack would know how to ride a horse. This particular woman is unable to even get on a horse. After a little humiliating assistance, we rode to the top of a mountain at a pace just slightly faster than a dead stop. The view of the distant Caribbean was spectacular. I had survived. I was content.

Then they told us to get off the horses, an idea that might have been less horrifying had I known getting back on was going to be easier the second time around. For others in a similar quandary, please note that it is infinitely easier to get on a horse when it is parked by a knee-high stone wall.

Then there was the adventure that got away. Practically on the eve of my departure for Mexico, this time to the southernmost rain forest on the Guatemalan border, I had a call from my traveling companion, a correspondent based in Mexico City.

"We have this wonderful opportunity!" he said, immediately setting my suspicious brain on alert. "We've been invited on an archaeological dig in the jungle."

Then began the litany of things we'd need: a snake-bite kit, malaria pills, sleeping bags, mosquito netting, canned food, bottled water—all this for a woman who believes in traveling with carry-on luggage. Double it, since I had to bring all of his supplies from Miami, along with my own.

Then came the day of reckoning. *We* had to make the arrangements to reach this inaccessible jungle dig. My Spanish vocabulary has some rather significant gaps in it, but even I could tell that the arrangements were not going well. It seems that we would have to charter a plane. No problem, my friend said. His company would pay for it. The hitch seemed to be that there was no guarantee exactly when the pilot would come back for us. Nor did we know exactly where in the jungle this dig was located. We could, however, rent a mule to take us there. If you recall the incident with the horse, you can imagine how thrilled I was with that news.

With my reputation as a good sport at stake, I was smiling through it all...and praying like crazy. At 6:00 a.m., packed and ready to go, I wandered into the courtyard of our charming little hotel in San Cristobal de las Casas.

"We're not going," he announced.

"Oh, really," I said, while staring heavenward, silently and fervently giving thanks. "Why not?"

It seems there was one little detail he'd neglected to mention. To get out of the jungle we were expected to stand in the middle of the runway and signal the pilot with a mirror. If he saw the bright flash of light, he'd stop for us. The glitch in this modern-day version of hitchhiking? It was the height of the rainy season.

Of course, there was also the icy February night that I'm fairly certain I became engaged to a Russian painter on the dance floor of a Moscow nightclub, but I'm sure you don't want to hear how that happened. It's just as well. Since I don't speak Russian, I'm a little vague about the details myself.

Despite all of this, I'm still looking for faraway places to travel, for romantic adventures to pursue. I've discovered, however, that sometimes the very best romantic adventures take place right in your own backyard.

Sherryl Woods

Chapter One

The fog rolled in, gray and thick, but not nearly dreary enough to dampen Karyn's enthusiasm. She could barely see the Golden Gate Bridge in the gloomy twilight, but beside her she had shimmering, golden sunshine in the form of at least a dozen travel brochures for Hawaii, from the exciting, sun-drenched beaches of Honolulu to the more private, but equally tropical sands of Maui. She'd spent the past hour in the travel agency sorting through the colorful, tempting photographs of places she'd only seen on television. Finally the impatient travel agent had grown weary of her dreamy expression and her indecision and had handed over the entire assortment, suggesting that she take her time before making her reservations.

Karyn intended to do just that. She was going to spend the entire weekend savoring every minute of planning the first real, away-from-home vacation she'd taken in her entire twenty-six years. She was choosing far more than a destination. She was searching for romance and adventure and a dash of excitement all rolled into one seven-day vacation.

As her car began the steep climb up the narrow, winding road to her apartment, the engine coughed and sputtered.

"Come on, Ruby, you can do it. You climb this hill every night," she reminded the aging engine. The response was a wheeze that would have put a human in the hospital. Karyn felt the first pang of panic. "Don't you dare give up on me now," she ordered. "It is cold and wet outside."

Ruby responded with an apologetic murmur, then choked and died. Karyn yanked on the emergency brake as the car started to roll backward. Then with a familiar sense of resignation, she put the car into neutral and tried to restart it. Tonight, however, the red Volkswagen did not respond. After several futile attempts to encourage the ancient car back to life, Karyn sighed and rested her head against the steering wheel.

"Why now, Ruby?" she said, admitting that the signs of a permanent collapse were all too ominous. "Couldn't you have waited another month? Another year? What did I ever do to you except feed you oil and wax you? Is this any way to repay me for taking you off the junk heap and giving you a new coat of paint?"

On the off chance that the car would react favorably to her pleas, she turned the key one last time. Nothing. Not even a muted grinding noise to indicate that there might be a hint of life stirring under the hood. Resigned, Karyn let the car roll to the curb, reset the emergency brake, then got out and went to hunt for a pay phone so she could call a tow truck. Thanks to Ruby's growing number of quirks, she knew the number at the garage by heart.

"When are you going to give up on this old heap?" her gray-haired mechanic grumbled when he had the car hooked up and Karyn was bouncing along in her all too familiar spot beside him.

"One more year," she said wearily.

Joe, who'd bandaged every part in the car half a dozen times over the past eight years, shook his head. "It'll never make it. It's getting too dangerous for you to be out in this thing, especially at night. One of these days you're going to get stranded after the shop's closed. Then what'll you do?"

"Abandon it. Call one of my brothers. Take the bus. Whatever," she said. It was exactly the same thing she'd said last week and the week before. "Joe, you know I can't afford a new car now."

"But you can afford some expensive trip?" Joe knew all about Hawaii. He didn't approve. "What's more important? Your safety or a few days away from home in some foreign place where you don't know a soul?"

"Hawaii is hardly foreign."

"Might as well be. You have to cross a mighty big ocean to get there, don't you?"

Karyn sighed. Joe had considered his own move from Oakland to San Francisco risky business. He was even more protective of her than her family was, something she hadn't thought possible. "I am going on this vacation," she said with a stubborn glare in his direction. "I have waited a lifetime to save enough money to get away on my own and see another part of the world. I will not give up this trip. Please, Joe, just fix the car this one more time."

Still grumbling under his breath, he chomped down on his unlit cigar. "Okay. Okay. I'll do the best I can."

But on Saturday when Karyn returned to the garage to pick up Ruby, the car was sitting forlornly at the back of the lot in a spot obviously chosen because it wouldn't block traffic. Joe wore a funereal expression. Even his cigar drooped at a downcast angle. Karyn's heart plummeted.

"The engine's blown," he said. One thing about Joe—he didn't waste words or sympathy.

"Can't you fix it? You're the best. There must be something you can do."

"Not worth it," he said, poking his head back under the hood of a car that apparently had more of a future.

"It is to me. Please, Joe."

"It'll cost you more than the car's worth."

"How much?"

"Five, maybe six hundred. More if I can't find the parts in some junkyard."

The figure represented half of her savings, half of the money she'd set aside over the past year and a half for the long-dreamed-about trip to Hawaii.

"I know you was counting on taking that vacation, but it ain't worth it." He even managed to sound vaguely sympathetic, which told her far more than she liked about the state of the car. Joe was a genius with engines. He never willingly sent one to the junk heap. If he couldn't fix Ruby, then Ruby was beyond repair.

"Use the money to put a down payment on a new car or at least a good used one from this decade," he urged. "Pick one out and I'll go over it for you. You can take the trip next year."

Karyn knew the advice was well-meant and probably sound, but it sent her spirits sinking straight down to her toes. More dejected than she'd ever been, she walked over to the scarred red VW. She wanted badly to kick the tires, but couldn't bring herself to do it. Unlike Ruby, she still had a certain amount of loyalty.

"How could you do this to me?" she said plaintively, taking one last resentful look before gathering the Bay area maps, sweaters and umbrellas that had accumulated in the back seat. She started across the parking lot. As she reached the gas pumps in the center, she opened her purse, took out the travel brochures for Hawaii, ceremoniously tore them into shreds, then dumped them into the oil drum that served as a trash can. They were only pieces of paper, but as they fluttered away she felt as though she were destroying her dream.

It took Karyn until the following Friday after work to accept the inevitable. With a sort of grim determination she went to a car dealership she'd passed every day. She walked past the sporty new convertibles, past the serviceable sedans, beyond the new car showroom to the used car lot. She tried very hard to tell herself that buying a replacement for Ruby was going to be exciting, that it would be terrific to drive something that didn't quit at stoplights and balk at hills. All she could see, though, was the dimming vision of Diamond Head.

"May I help you, miss?"

Karyn sighed heavily and returned to reality, which in this case happened to be an eager salesman who was practically rubbing his hands together in glee at the prospect of making a sale before the day ended.

"I'm looking for a car," she said without enthusiasm.

He chuckled as though she'd made a terrific joke. "Well, you've certainly come to the right place," he said with so much forced enthusiasm that Karyn reconsidered the possibility of taking the bus for the rest of her natural life. Only the fact that she often needed her car for work kept her standing right where she was.

"Now we have a real beauty over here," he said. "Take a look at this convertible. Only a couple of years old, real low mileage. Just right for a pretty little thing like you. It's flashy. Sexy. It projects a certain image, if you know what I mean."

Karyn glanced at the bright red car that reminded her all too vividly of Ruby in color, if not in style. Used or not, the car looked expensive. She didn't want to get her hopes up so she shrugged indifferently. "How much?"

"Well, now, I guess that's something we'd have to discuss. Why not take it for a test drive and see how you like it?"

"How much?"

"Just look at this interior. All leather and it's like new. Not a mark on it. Only twenty-five thousand miles on her, too."

"How much?"

"You have a trade-in?"

She shook her head.

"Hmm."

"How much?" she persisted.

"What sort of budget do you have?"

"Limited."

His enthusiasm staggered after her terse response. "I see. Perhaps we ought to take a look at something a little more basic. We have a classic right here, a good solid car. Dependable. That's important." He led her to a dull blue two-door the size of a large can of tomato sauce. There was rust around the edges of the door. A dent marred the left front fender. "Nothing fancy, mind you, but reliable transportation. I'm sure we can bring this in on your budget."

Karyn studied the car without interest, then glanced back at the convertible. If she was going to blow her vacation on a car, why not get something with a little style? Why not go for something that suggested the owner was a daring adventurer, instead of a recently graduated paralegal, who dutifully watered her geraniums every Thursday and took her vitamins every morning?

"Tell me again about the convertible."

The salesman's eyes lit up. "Absolutely. Let me get those keys and you can take her for a little spin. Get the feel of her. Once you've driven that beauty, nothing else on the lot will do."

Of course that was exactly what Karyn feared. Her nervousness increased when the salesman put the top down and settled her in the bucket seat behind the wheel. The engine turned over on the first try. The damn thing purred. As the rare, late afternoon sun caressed her shoulders and the gentle breeze whispered through her hair, a spark of excitement was born. She recognized that spark. She'd felt it gazing at pictures of Waikiki and dreaming of tall, dark, handsome strangers. That spark was very likely to be her downfall.

Back in the salesman's office, she braced herself to negotiate. He ran through the car's virtues as lovingly as a proud father trying to pitch his daughter to a blind date.

"You don't have to sell me," she said. "Just give me a price."

He looked crestfallen. Apparently it was not going to be that simple.

"Why don't you give me a figure," he suggested. "We can start from that."

Start from? The phrase had an ominous ring to it. Why not start with the bottom line? "A thousand dollars," she said finally.

The salesman appeared to be suitably aghast. He shook his head and swallowed hard. "I'm afraid that's a little out of line. I don't dare take it back to my manager. He'll laugh me off the lot."

"Then it's your turn. I've given you my starting figure."

"Come on," he pleaded, beginning to sweat. "Give me something to work with here."

"I just did."

"I can't take that to the boss. A thousand dollars is nothing for a car like that."

Karyn stared at him and her apathy began to return. She wasn't going to get the convertible. She would not go into debt for a car, not when she was finally getting on her feet financially. Growing up as she had on the cutting edge of financial disaster had taught her the dangers of living on credit. "Maybe we should just forget it." She stood. The dealer was surprisingly alert and swift for a man at least thirty pounds overweight. He moved to block her way.

"Wait a minute. Don't be too hasty." He flashed another of his thoroughly insincere smiles at her. "I'm sure we can reach an agreement on this, if we go about it right."

"I don't think so," she said, slipping past him.

"But, miss," he began frantically, running along behind her.

She cast one last, regretful look at the convertible, then turned—straight into a rock solid wall.

"What's the problem, Nate?" To her amazement, the wall talked. She glanced up and discovered it also had shoulders. Very broad shoulders, in fact. A deep dimple slashed one tanned cheek at a rakish angle. A scar knit a tiny white thread through one dark eyebrow. The result was uneven, unique and totally devastating. Even though she had no experience with car salesmen, Karyn recognized at once that this had to be the dealership's top gun. This man could have sold Fords to stockholders at General Motors. Those dark green eyes could have seduced her eighty-year-old spinster aunt. His hand rested at the small of her back, presumably to steady her after their encounter. It felt as though she had been touched by lightning. She simply stared, while Nate tried to explain the difficulty.

To Karyn's dismay tears welled up in her eyes. All she'd wanted was a car. The process should have been no more complicated, if slightly more costly, than buying a toaster. Instead, she'd discovered that it required the skills of a nuclear summit negotiator and the patience of a saint. She had neither, nor was her purse exactly brimming over with the third necessary ingredient—cash.

"Look, I really think this was a bad idea. I'll come back another time."

"You like the convertible," the wall said, studying her expression.

She nodded.

"What did you offer?"

"A thousand dollars," she said with a trace of defiance.

Brad noted the stubborn tilt of her chin, but, more important, he caught the shimmer of tears in her huge blue eyes. He was a sucker for a woman's tears. It had gotten him into trouble more than once. He had a hunch this was going to be another one of those times.

"I see," he said very seriously. "Can you make it twelve hundred?"

"But . . ." Nate protested, only to be silenced by Brad's fierce look. He watched a spark of excitement return to those wide, innocent eyes and felt his heart do an unexpected flip. She glanced longingly at the convertible.

"If I live on peanut butter sandwiches for a while," she said slowly.

"Fine," Brad said before she could change her mind or Nate could start whining about the loss of commission. "Nate, take care of the paperwork. Miss . . ."

"Chambers."

"Miss Chambers and I will be in my office having coffee. Come and get us when the car is ready. Make sure it's washed and waxed and that the inside is vacuumed."

"Certainly, Mr. Willis."

He watched as recognition dawned on her face. "As in Willis Motors?" she said.

"Heir apparent," he confirmed, taking her arm and steering her back into the main showroom, down a corridor and into an office that was decorated with plush carpet, mahogany furniture and a wall that featured too many photographs of him standing beside various race cars.

Brad glanced at those photos, which were a taunting reminder of a past he'd only recently had to give up. The sacrifice still hurt. Left to his own devices, he'd have stripped the walls of every last picture, but they were his father's pride and joy. Ripping them down would have shown his father just how much sacrificing his racing career had meant. Since that would only cause his father pain, there was no point in it.

Brad focused his attention on the petite, dark-haired imp before him. Before she could vanish like a woodland sprite, he settled her into a chair and gave her a cup of coffee. She was probably in her midtwenties, but she seemed so young compared to the sophisticated women he usually met. He wondered fleetingly if he ought to be offering her milk instead. He perched on the side of his desk and studied her with blatant interest. The fact that she was obviously flustered by the intense scrutiny fascinated him.

"You won't get rich making deals like that," she told him sternly. "Not that I'm not grateful, you understand, but it's bad business."

"I'm already rich," he confided. If his father hadn't seen to that, his own success on the racing circuit would have ensured it. He'd discovered long ago that money was useful, but it didn't solve all the world's ills by a long shot.

"Plan to stay that way?" she said, obviously still worried about his rash decision to make a deep slash in the price of the car.

"Absolutely. Another few hundred dollars from you won't make that much difference in our bottom line for the year, so don't worry about it," he said, minimizing the cut. He had a hunch if she knew exactly how much he'd subtracted, she'd have demanded to know what he expected in return and bolted from his office in a huff.

"But why'd you do it? For all you know I could make a habit of going around, conning men into giving up their cars at rock bottom prices."

He laughed at the idea of anyone with a face that innocent being a con artist. "I doubt it."

"Why?"

"I saw you get off the bus. I watched you walk through the lot. You obviously needed cheering up. You looked as though you were on some sort of grim mission." In fact that was what had brought him out of his office in the first place. He'd been drawn by that aura of dejection. He probably should have lived a few centuries earlier, so he could put on his armor and ride off to save damsels in distress. The knight in shining armor syndrome was definitely out of step in this day and age. Most women had no interest in being saved from much of anything—except maybe dragons, but they were in short supply.

"Very perceptive," she was saying with a hint of surprise.

"You didn't really want to buy a car?"

"I wanted a trip to Hawaii."

He nodded sagely. "There aren't many of them on the lot today. Did you think of trying a travel agent?"

"I did," she said with a heartfelt sigh. She held up her hand, her finger and thumb a scant inch apart. "I was this close to going. This close," she repeated mournfully.

"What happened?"

"Ruby died."

She sounded so sad again that he felt instantly sympathetic. No wonder she'd looked so forlorn. No wonder he'd wanted to rush to her rescue. "I'm sorry. Ruby was your...?"

"My car."

"Oh." His sympathy waned, but not his fascination. "So you're buying a car, instead of taking a trip you'd badly wanted to take."

"Exactly."

"You can always take the trip next year. Hawaii will still be there."

"That's what Joe said."

The mention of this Joe unsettled Brad in a surprising way. For some reason it bothered him that she ran around quoting some other man as though his opinions really mattered to her. "Joe?" he said cautiously.

"My mechanic. We've been on very friendly terms the past couple of years."

He scowled. It was worse than he thought. "I see," he muttered.

"I doubt it, unless you've had a '68 VW recently."

"Good heavens." With understanding, there came an astonishing sense of relief.

"Exactly. I'd hoped to keep it alive one more year, just until I had a chance to take this one little vacation." She gazed at him wistfully. "Was that so much to ask?"

"It was a lot to ask of a '68 VW. Why was the vacation so important to you?"

"I'd never taken one."

He regarded her disbelievingly. "You mean to Hawaii?"

"I mean ever, to anywhere. I am twenty-six years old and I have never been south of San Francisco. North, east or west either, for that matter. With seven kids in the family, we're doing good to get everyone together on Sundays for church. We went on a picnic once. It rained."

"But you just said you're twenty-six. Surely you've been on your own for a few years now."

"I have never been on my own, not the way you mean. I am the baby in the family. I have six older brothers who regard the idea of my being out after dark as worrisome at best. When I finally got through school and started earning enough to get my own apartment, they took turns standing guard at night until I threatened to call the cops on them. Now they just keep calling until I get in. Heaven knows what they'd do if I ever. . ." Her voice trailed off in obvious embarrassment. "Well, you know."

He chuckled. "I certainly do. I think I understand why you wanted to get away."

"Don't be mistaken. They're really great brothers. I just wish they all had a couple of dozen kids of their own so they'd leave me alone."

"You're very loyal."

"Yeah, that's what I told Ruby." Suddenly she blushed. He loved it. "You must think I'm an idiot talking about my car as though it were a person."

Actually, Brad liked that about her, too. Things obviously mattered deeply to her—cars, as well as people. It beat the shallowness he usually encountered all to hell. He leaned toward her. "Mine's Ralph," he whispered confidentially. "Of course, I don't dare call him that in public. I'd be laughed off the racing circuit."

"Then those aren't just publicity photos on the wall. You actually do race that car?"

"I did up until a few months ago."

"You quit?"

"More or less. My father had a heart attack. The doctors told him to lighten up his work load or die within the year. We have ten of these dealerships around the state. So, here I am, making my monthly pilgrimage. Between paperwork, problem solving and trying to keep my father from sneaking into his office, there's not a lot of time left for entering Grand Prix events."

"You're very loyal, too. It must have been hard to give up something you obviously loved."

"I did it grudgingly, sort of the way you bought that car."

"But you did it, just the same. I think what you did is very noble. I never gave up anything."

"Except Hawaii."

"That wasn't noble," she said ruefully. "That was a necessity and I did it kicking and screaming all the way. If I could have managed without a car, I would have."

Brad had a sudden inspiration. "When's your vacation?" he asked.

"There is no vacation."

"I mean the dates. Have you told your boss you're not taking off?"

"Not yet. I think it's called denial."

"Then don't tell him. You're going to have your vacation."

"But I can't afford to go anywhere."

"You can take a vacation right here."

"This isn't a vacation. This is home. I don't want to waste another perfectly good vacation sitting around in my apartment cleaning the closets."

"Who said anything about cleaning closets? Thousands of people come to San Francisco every year. Songs have been written about this place. It's one of the most romantic, exciting cities in the world. If you want a taste of the Orient, it's here. A suggestion of the French wine country, it's here. A quaint, cliffside city by the sea like Italy's Portofino, it's across the Bay. Why should you go anywhere else?"

"To get away from my brothers."

"Turn off your phone. Tell them you're leaving town, if that's what it takes. Take a fresh look at this place. Have you ever looked at the Golden Gate Bridge at twilight?" His own enthusiasm was definitely mounting as the impulsive notion took hold. He hadn't felt this carefree and excited in all the months since his father's heart attack. He was talking with the fervor of a tour guide. The chamber of commerce would love him. "Well," he persisted. "Have you?"

"Every night when I'm stuck in traffic."

"But have you ever really seen it?"

"Not really," she murmured.

"Then for one entire, fun-filled week you and I are going on vacation in San Francisco."

She looked thunderstruck. To be perfectly honest, he was feeling a little that way himself.

"You?" she whispered.

Brad shrugged. "Why not? I've been noble for the past year myself. Even you said so. I deserve a vacation," he said emphatically.

"But you could go anywhere."

"I could," he admitted readily. "But I can't imagine a better way to spend a vacation than with a woman who just bought her very first, very flashy convertible."

The words rolled off his tongue with all of his practiced charm, but to his amazement he realized that somewhere deep inside he'd never meant anything more in his life. Seeing the world through her fresh, unjaded eyes just might turn out to be the best investment of time he'd ever made. Maybe they'd even turn up a few dragons for him to slay.

Chapter Two

Karyn had never made an impetuous, throw caution to the winds decision in her life. She'd certainly never had to make one involving a man who was heart-stoppingly handsome, witty, rich and apparently famous enough to know at least half a dozen very sexy actors, if the framed photos and clippings on the wall were any indication. But during twenty-six years of nonstop struggling just to survive, the longing for adventure and storybook romance had flourished. She'd never quite gotten over "Cinderella." From what she'd observed, the man sitting across from her had all the qualifications of a handsome prince.

She studied him closely as she considered his unexpectedly tempting suggestion. She ticked off his attributes with the nervous anticipation of a certified public accountant hoping a column of figures would add up correctly. He had spoken of his father with genuine affection, despite the sacrifices he'd made on his behalf. He was boldly confident without being arrogant. He was impeccably dressed without being flashy. And there was an energy and vitality about him that counterpointed her own quiet personality.

Most important, he seemed to be trustworthy, even if points were deducted for that unnerving glint in his eyes. She had a feeling that glint was exactly the sort of thing her brothers had been worrying about since she reached adolescence. She rather liked the champagne-sparkly feelings those eyes set off inside her.

He'd been very kind, very compassionate to her. She had felt an almost instantaneous rapport with him, which was all the more incredible considering the man apparently traveled in celebrity-studded circles. The closest she'd ever come before to anyone famous was when she'd subbed for the executive secretary to the senior partner in her law firm on the day his picture had been in the *Chronicle*.

There was, of course, a negative side to all that fame and obvious sophistication: Brad was probably very experienced at portraying whatever image circumstances called for. Maybe in his circles it was even acceptable for him to pick up and discard women as casually as other people tossed aside old clothes. Since Karyn had never followed auto racing, she had no way of knowing for sure what sort of reputation the Brad Willis of those bold sports page headlines had in the more scandalous tabloids. Just thinking about the possibilities made her doubt her own judgment. She hadn't exactly dated extensively. She hadn't had time. Would she even recognize a rogue before it was too late?

Still, she reminded herself, there were only cars and men in all those pictures on his office wall, no women. She glanced instinctively at his ring finger. It was tanned, well-manicured and unadorned. That was promising, but hardly conclusive.

"Are you married, Mr. Willis?" she asked with the sort of bluntness she'd heard her boss use successfully in taking depositions and cross-examining witnesses in court.

It didn't seem to rattle him in the slightest. He grinned, in fact. "It's Brad," he corrected pointedly, "and obviously some of your brothers' caution has worn off on you."

The evasive response made her nervous. Though Karyn kept her tone light, she persisted with a deliberateness that would have done her brothers and her bosses proud. "Isn't it considered proper to know a little about the person one plans to spend an entire vacation with? Even if we aren't going to be sharing hotel rooms, surely it's important to know if we have anything in common.''

"So you want to know if we have my marital status in common?"

The return of that devilish glint of amusement in his eyes was plain. Karyn hoped that was a good sign. "Something like that," she admitted. "Doesn't it matter to you whether or not I'm married."

"We wouldn't be having this conversation, if you were."

"How do you know, though? You didn't ask."

"No ring."

"Not conclusive."

"No hovering husband on the car lot to poke his head under the hood."

"Maybe I'm mechanical. After all, I did keep a '68 VW alive."

"Joe did that," he said, his knock-your-socks-off smile emerging again.

"Which still doesn't answer my question."

"Which one? How I knew you weren't married or whether I am."

"Both, but if I have to make a choice, the latter."

Brad folded his hands on his desk, leaned forward, met her gaze intently and said solemnly, "No, Karyn Chambers, I am not married. There are not even any serious entanglements to speak of, now or ever. I'm afraid I've lived in the fast lane in more ways than one."

There was an intriguing note of regret in the honest admission. "Do you still?" she asked with a mixture of curiosity and trepidation.

"Live in the fast lane? I told you I'd given up racing."

"And women?"

"I'm not a monk, but the times are changing, in case you haven't heard. And I'm older and wiser."

She felt like purring with satisfaction. She doubted her brothers would view the comment the same way. "How much older?"

"I'm thirty-two. Want to see my birth certificate?"

"No. Your driver's license will do."

Never taking his eyes from hers, Brad reached for his wallet. He moved very slowly, obviously expecting her to back down from the impertinent request. Karyn determinedly held out her hand. "I'm not about to let a total stranger drive my new car, until I'm sure he has a valid driver's license."

Laughing, Brad handed over his wallet. It had enough credit cards in it to charge the entire stock of clothing at I. Magnin without putting a dent in his credit limit. The license told her far more than his driving status in the state of California, badly minimizing some of his best points and elaborating on a few of her own impressions.

His eyes, which she could see for herself, were a rich fascinating shade of emerald and were listed simply as green. Obviously the clerk who'd put it down had no imagination. He was six feet two inches tall, one hundred eighty pounds and, by her assessment, all muscle. He lived in Malibu at an address that inspired images of redwood sun decks, which were draped in vibrant pink and purple bougainvillea and opened onto wide expanses of sandy beaches. His birthdate, May 15, told her he was a stubborn Taurus, which suggested that she might as well give in now about this vacation.

She'd known for the past fifteen minutes she was going to do it anyway.

Her brothers were going to kill her. Or maybe they'd kill Brad, she conceded, if they ever found out about him.

"What's the itinerary?" she asked before she could start worrying about how Brad would fend off the six angry Chambers men, who made up in sheer numbers and street-fighting savvy what they lacked in health club fitness.

"You haven't said when your vacation begins."

"Technically, a week from Monday."

"Perfect. That gives me time to get back down to LA, take care of a few details and free up my own time. You just leave the itinerary to me. I promise you the vacation of a lifetime."

"I'm not sure I can afford anything that dramatic."

"I promise this will be first-class all the way and it won't cost you a dime."

"If you can accomplish that, maybe you should go into the travel business."

"I have more business than I'd like now. I certainly don't want to get into another one."

That statement raised a nagging concern. "Are you really sure you want to do this?" Karyn asked. "Maybe you ought to think about it. I mean it's a lovely gesture, but you don't even know me."

He stretched a hand across the desk, palm up, and waited for her to put her hand in his. When she did, he folded his long fingers around it in a grip that was warm and strong and reassuring. "I've never wanted to do anything so much in my entire life."

His voice practically throbbed with apparent sincerity. Karyn's unsophisticated pulse skipped several beats and a pleasant warmth stole through her. This was definitely a man with a knack for selling. She was about to take the charm with a grain of salt, until she looked into his eyes.

His green eyes glinted with golden sparks and his gaze never wavered. This was not the cold sheen of a precious metal, but the romantic allure of the moon and the brightness of a thousand stars.

This was the magic she'd been waiting for all her life.

Trying to explain her vacation plans to her brothers, who were sprawled around her tiny studio apartment like so many muscular, intense security guards, went about as well as Karyn had anticipated. They probed. She evaded. If it had been a chess game, they would have played to a draw. If only circumstances hadn't kept her living at home so many years longer than most of her friends, Karyn thought with a sigh. Her brothers had gotten into the habit of watching over her. She'd been so busy trying to manage school and work, she'd had little time for dating anyway. Their protectiveness had never mattered all that much. Breaking them of it now was going to take either extraordinary tact or dynamite. Judging from their scowling, wary expressions, she should probably start hunting for someplace to buy the dynamite.

"I thought you had to cancel Hawaii to get the car," said Frank, the eldest and the one who'd led all family discussions since her father's death when she was still in elementary school. He had obviously sounded the alarm for the others the instant he'd realized that she was going ahead with her vacation. They had arrived on her doorstep within fifteen minutes of each other. Not one of them had been surprised to find the others there. Unity was a Chambers motto, especially where their baby sister was concerned. Maybe it would have been better if she'd been a gloriously tall, assertive redhead, instead of a barely over five-feet shrimp. Maybe then, they'd understand that she was way past due to take charge of her own social life.

"I did cancel the trip," she admitted.

"Then what are you going to do?" asked Peter.

"Stay right here," she said.

The cheerful tone was obviously a mistake. Jared regarded her suspiciously. "I don't get it. I thought you'd be upset about this."

"She was upset," Daniel confirmed. "When I was here last Saturday, she was moping around."

"Yeah," Kevin agreed. "When I called on Sunday, she sounded real depressed."

Karyn rolled her eyes as they continued to discuss her recent moods as if she'd left the room and they all had degrees in psychology. Eventually, they'd get back to her. They always did. It was Frank who finally turned to her again and said, "Okay, sis, what happened to perk you up?"

She shrugged with exaggerated innocence. "Nothing happened. I'm just resigned to my fate, if you must know. What's wrong with that?" Resignation was so far removed from the tingles that swept through her every time she thought of Brad Willis, it was all Karyn could do to keep a sappy, lovesick grin off her face.

"Nothing," Timothy interceded quickly. If Timothy had had half a chance to go to an Ivy League college, he'd have been a perfect diplomat. He was wasting his skills as a transit worker, handing out transfers and reminding tourists which stop was closest to Ghirardelli Square. By the time he worked his way through college at night, he'd probably be too old to go traipsing around the globe for the State Department.

"I'm sure Karyn can find lots of things to do right here in San Francisco," he said.

"Well, of course, she can," Jared grumbled. "For one thing this apartment needs to be painted. Why don't we all come over tomorrow night and help? I can get the paint on sale."

"No way," Karyn said adamantly. Six startled faces stared at her, stunned by her sharp tone. She backed off at once. She did not want to arouse their suspicions. "I mean, I can paint this place myself. Besides, I do not intend to spend my vacation working around the apartment. That's not a vacation—that's drudgery." At that moment, an untimely recollection of Cinderella flitted through Karyn's head, along with an even clearer image of the prince. He looked so much like Brad, she almost smiled.

"Then what are you going to do?" Frank said, clearly bewildered. His last vacation had been spent taking apart their mother's shuddering, fifteen-year-old washing machine and putting it back together. He'd actually enjoyed it. Their mother had been thrilled. The incident had convinced Karyn it was past time for Frank and his girlfriend of five years to get married. Now was not the time, though, to plague him about it.

"I don't know. Maybe sleep in a little." She came dangerously close to blushing at that one. She raced on, "Go to a couple of museums. I'll just play it by ear. That's what a vacation is all about."

She hoped she sounded noble, self-sacrificing and just sufficiently contented that they'd leave her alone for the next week instead of setting out to keep her company. It would not be the first time that they'd considered it their duty to protect her from boredom.

"I'm off Tuesday," Peter began.

"No, really," Karyn said, patting his knee and trying not to show her alarm. "You should be spending your day off on your own social life, not worrying about mine. Besides, I already have plans for Tuesday." She hadn't talked to Brad since the previous Friday, but she knew in her heart that he would show up on Monday.

"What plans?" asked Frank, his gaze narrowing.

"With a friend."

"What friend?" he persisted.

"Frank, she obviously doesn't want to tell us any more about it," Timothy said.

"Well, I don't care what she wants," her eldest brother blustered with something akin to parental indignation. "If she can't introduce us to her friends, then I have to wonder why not. What's wrong with them?"

"Nothing is wrong with any of my friends," Karyn said, thoroughly exasperated. She was worn out from the whole exchange. Although she had been prepared for her brothers' objections, the prospect of using dynamite to break them of their habit became more and more appealing. "Will you all please go away. I want to get some sleep."

"It's only eight o'clock," Jared pointed out.

"I think that just means she's tired of arguing with us," Timothy said. "Come on, guys. Let's go and leave her in peace."

She looked over at him gratefully. "Thanks, Timmy."

He winked. He was the youngest of the brothers and had had more than his share of protective custody, as well. He'd been so grateful to have her come along when he was six that he'd come to her rescue more than once through the years.

Still grumbling, the pack finally vacated the premises.

"If you change your mind about the painting," Frank said at the door.

"I won't change my mind."

"But you might. By Wednesday you could be bored to tears."

Another image of Brad popped provocatively to mind. She would not be bored by Wednesday. In fact, if she had her way, by Wednesday her life would be just beginning to reach fairy-tale status.

* * *

When the pounding on the door began, Karyn moaned and pulled a pillow over her head. It did not shut out the sound. She lifted the pillow and peeked at the clock. It was exactly five minutes before six.

In the morning.

On the first day of her vacation.

She was going to kill whomever was on the far side of that door, assuming that it wasn't someone who planned to kill her first. Killers, she reassured herself as she dragged on her bedraggled terry-cloth robe, probably did not knock. Her brothers, to her everlasting regret, all had their own keys.

As she stumbled the few feet from the sofa bed to the door, she called out, "Who's there?"

"It's Brad."

The announcement sent her adrenaline surging faster than three cups of straight caffeine. She'd counted on him showing up sometime today, but not before she'd even taken a shower.

"Brad? What are you doing here? It's the middle of the night."

"Wrong attitude. It's the first day of your vacation. You don't want to waste a minute of it."

She sagged against the door. Had it been only ten days ago that she'd actually admired his energy? Why hadn't she suspected that it was not nearly as attractive at 6:00 a.m. as it was twelve hours later in the day? Maybe because she'd never before had a man outside her door at 6:00 a.m.

"Are you going to let me in?"

She glanced down at her faded, baggy T-shirt, her shapeless, beltless robe, her unshaven legs and the chipped polish on her toenails. "Not on your life. Come back in an hour."

"In an hour the sun will be up."

"That's the general idea."

"If the sun's up, it'll ruin my plan."

"We don't know each other well enough for any plan that requires the dark," she said, sliding to the floor in embarrassment as the implication sank into her muddled brain. She drew her knees to her chest and tugged the shapeless shirt over them. Thank heavens the man couldn't see her. What had gotten into her? Sweet, innocent Karyn Chambers did not say daring, dangerous things like that. Brad's low, silky laughter, however, confirmed that she apparently did and that he was enjoying the banter. No wonder her brothers worried about her. At heart, she was obviously capable of becoming a brazen flirt. The idea made her smile.

"I'll be ready in ten minutes," she compromised finally. "Wait for me."

"Out here?"

"Out there."

"I suppose it's what I deserve for not calling ahead."

"Exactly."

"Is this indicative of your overall attitude toward surprises?"

"Pretty much. I haven't had a lot of experience with them."

"We'll have to work on that. Hurry up, now, or your coffee will get cold."

"You have coffee out there?"

"Of course."

Karyn opened the door as far as the chain would allow and poked her hand out. "Please."

"I've always loved women who beg." The bold taunt sent a shiver down her spine.

"In your dreams," she retorted, pleased that her voice didn't waver. She wondered if it was possible to develop a jaunty, sophisticated attitude in a week simply by praying for it.

"Now hand over the coffee," she added forcefully.

He put the take-out cup in her hand. "Want the croissants that go with it?"

She was tempted, but the prospect of eating her breakfast alone on one side of the door, while Brad remained locked in the hallway did not appeal to her, any more than the idea of letting him see her before she'd pulled herself together. "Hold the croissants. I'll be ready in five minutes."

It actually took her closer to fifteen. She refused to skip shaving her legs. As it was she had four nicks on one knee and a gash on the opposite ankle from hurrying. When she finally opened the door, she almost swooned. It could have been from the loss of blood, but more likely it had to do with the dark-haired rogue who was sitting placidly on the steps waiting for her. In a business suit, he'd been gorgeous. In jeans and a navy-blue-and-lime-green rugby shirt, he was devastatingly sexy.

To his credit, he didn't say a thing about the fact that she was most likely standing there with her mouth hanging open. He merely stood, popped a piece of buttery croissant into her mouth, then brushed a friendly kiss across her cheek. The croissant was melt-on-your-tongue good. The kiss, innocent as it was, was delicious.

"Where are we going?" she asked, when she could finally collect a sufficient vocabulary to form a coherent sentence.

"For a walk."

A walk? "You woke me out of a sound sleep at six o'clock in the morning to go for a walk?"

"A very special walk," he confirmed, steering her unresisting form down the steps and through the door before she could rally a strenuous objection.

Karyn stopped dead still in the middle of the sidewalk. She looked up into emerald eyes in search of the remembered warmth, the remembered promise of romance. There was a spark of something in the returning gaze, a responding flutter of awareness in the pit of her stomach.

She nodded in satisfaction, linked her arm through his and muttered in her sweetest tone, "It better be one hell of a walk."

Chapter Three

The walk was spectacular! Awesome!

It was the drive that almost killed her.

Brad Willis roared through the predawn streets of San Francisco as if he had a particularly challenging Grand Prix course spread out in front of him. Her VW's aged engine had never permitted speeds this fast, even had Karyn been tempted to try attaining them. Karyn clutched at the edge of the seat with fingers that were rigid with fear. The wind whipped through her short black hair and lashed color into her pale cheeks. Her heart beat wildly. She'd hoped for a few thrills, not this death-defying race around impossible curves.

She wasn't certain of the precise moment when exhilaration replaced panic. Perhaps it was when Brad clasped her hand in his and gave it a reassuring squeeze. Perhaps it was the instant when she caught the glimmer of excitement in his eyes, heard the low rumble of his laughter as they crested an incredibly steep hill.

Most likely, though, the evolution took place when she learned to trust, when she realized that he knew exactly what he was doing and precisely how far he could push the car. By the time they reached the waterfront, her eyes were sparkling with delight and her pulse raced with the wind. Never had she witnessed such an incredible blending of man and machine. Her car had become an extension of Brad, subject to his whims, mastered by his skill and daring.

"You've just tripled the difficulty of impressing me with this walk," she warned as they got out of the car. Her pulse was finally settling into a more comfortable, sedate rhythm.

Brad smiled with serene confidence as he led her along the street. When she realized where they were headed, she regarded him in amazement.

"The Golden Gate?"

"Can you think of a more appropriate place to begin a San Francisco vacation?"

"Most people simply drive across it or look at it from one of those little tour boats in the Bay."

"You and I are not most people. We are adventurers," he reminded her.

"Right," she said. There was more hope than conviction in her voice as she studied the magnificent span that linked San Francisco and Marin County.

"Did you know that on the day this bridge opened in 1937, two hundred thousand people walked across it and that they paid a nickel for the privilege?"

"It must have been crowded," she observed as she stared up at the art deco towers disappearing into the fog. The steep cliffs of Sausalito weren't yet visible in the dawning daylight.

Brad ignored her unimaginative observation. He took her hand and tugged her along. He rattled off a steady stream of historical tidbits about the bridge. Her favorite was about the Englishman who'd proclaimed himself monarch during the Gold Rush era and declared that such a bridge should be built.

"I thought you were down in LA cleaning off your desk. Obviously you spent the past week studying some encyclopedia," she said.

"Travel brochures and guide books," he corrected. "You keep forgetting we're on vacation. Lesson one—a vacation is always enhanced if you do your homework."

"I'll try to remember that," she said solemnly.

"It'll come with practice."

Karyn wondered if she'd ever have enough travel experience to make any trip and its planning seem routine.

As if he'd sensed her discouragement, Brad said, "You'll see. I promise. Now, let's hurry. We don't want to miss this."

As they reached the middle of the bridge, he drew her close to his side and gestured around them. Karyn was so absorbed by the newness of having Brad's arm around her waist, she was hardly aware of their surroundings. As his hand settled lightly on her hip, she found she was holding her breath as her body accustomed itself to the excitement of his touch. Not one of those rare dates she'd permitted herself during the demanding schedules she'd had in high school and college had prepared her for the sensual possibilities of the right man's touch.

"Now wasn't this worth getting up for?" he prodded.

She had to force herself to focus her attention on something other than the man beside her. Because he expected it, she glanced dutifully around.

Fire-engine-red cables rose thousands of feet above them, splashed like colorful ribbons across the thick, impenetrable layers of fog. Karyn could hear the pounding of the surf below, but she couldn't see it. Even though she could feel the throb of rush hour traffic just beginning, it didn't dispel the notion that they were isolated in a world of shadows and imagination. The early morning air made her shiver, which was apparently incentive enough for Brad to wrap his arms around her. An unexpected burst of fire deep inside warmed her. A feeling of contentment that was at odds with the wild, howling wind and bone-chilling dampness stole through her. It was definitely awesome.

"What do you think?" he murmured against her hair.

Her senses sang with exhilaration. "I think I've died and gone to heaven."

"It is a little like being above the clouds, isn't it? Is it any wonder people have left their hearts here?"

"You realize, of course, that I will probably be late for work every day for the rest of my life," she said, relaxing in the warmth of his embrace.

"Why's that?"

"I'll want to stop and take this walk."

"Then do it."

She sighed with regret. "No. If I did, I suppose it would become old hat after a while. It would lose the sense of enchantment."

"Not if you keep your mind open to the subtleties, a change in the direction of the wind, the shimmer of color when the sun begins to reflect off the metal. The slow lifting of the fog. The threads of sunlight lying in silver pools on the water."

The poetic words spun a web of magic around her heart. "You should stop peddling cars for a living and write guide books."

"You inspire me."

His embrace tightened ever so slightly with the quietly spoken and seemingly heartfelt compliment. Karyn lifted her gaze to his and caught a faint suggestion of wistfulness that tugged at her heart. She turned slightly and, with fingers that trembled, touched his cheek. His skin was warm and smooth from a morning shave, his jawline angular. He was flesh and blood male, not a daydream, but she didn't understand him any more than she could capture an illusion. Her experience had been with honest, down-to-earth, hardworking men whose level of gallantry extended no further than opening a car door. Men like that talked about football point spreads and baseball batting averages. They did not wax eloquent about threads of sunlight.

"What makes you tick, Brad Willis?" she wondered aloud.

He refused to take her question seriously, shrugging it off with a laugh and a grin. "I'm driven by demons," he said flippantly, but Karyn heard the odd note in his voice that warned her the description fit in ways she couldn't begin to fathom. Before she could pursue the truth, Brad released her and opened the bag he'd been carrying. He plucked a bottle of champagne from its depths.

"To toast the sunrise," he said, popping the cork.

"Sunrise?" Karyn repeated with a lift of an eyebrow as she surveyed the endless vista of gray. The sky was lighter now, but no less muted.

"It's out there," he promised. "It's just one of those things in life you have to take on faith."

"That's a dangerous practice. I learned long ago not to count on anything I couldn't see or touch."

The edge of cynicism sobered him. He caressed her jaw with his thumb, while gazing deep into her eyes. "You haven't had an easy time of it, have you?"

Now it was her turn to shrug off the serious moment, the unwanted sympathy. "Not easy, no, but far better than some. I've had to work hard for it, but I have an education. I have an interesting job with plenty of opportunity for advancement. Most important, I've always had a family who loved me."

"Those are all the basics, but that's not always enough to take away the hunger."

Karyn tried again to lighten the tone. "Hey, it wasn't that bad. We had food on the table, just not much else in the way of extras."

"People can hunger for more than food, my literal one," Brad said, sounding like a man who knew such hunger firsthand. "Hawaii, for example."

"And Grand Prix victory?" she guessed.

"I had my share." The statement suggested Brad took pride in his accomplishments, but his tone was flat, drained of all emotion.

"That doesn't mean it was enough. People with a craving for pickles, for instance, never seem to get enough."

"Pickles?" he repeated, grinning at the comparison.

She laughed. "It was one of the extras. Like picnics and vacations. To this day I can't pass up a juicy, fat dill pickle. Thank heavens, I didn't develop a craving for diamonds."

Despite her laughter, his grin died. "I'll add pickles to the agenda this week," he promised. "As long as you don't want them for breakfast. I'm not sure I could bear that."

"No, for breakfast, champagne in the middle of the Golden Gate will do very nicely." She watched him closely. "What else do you hunger for, Brad? Besides another race?"

The burning glint in his eyes intensified and Karyn's heart thundered in anticipation. "Until right this minute, I haven't known for sure, but this, I think," he said softly and bent his head, capturing her lips with a hunger that took her breath away.

Karyn had never known such need, never experienced such powerful masculine possession. She gave herself over to it with a passion that very nearly overwhelmed her. Joy burst inside her. It was as though she were discovering springtime after a hard winter. It was the heat of fire after the chill of snow. It was . . . awesome.

Shaken and vulnerable in the aftermath of that kiss, Karyn couldn't bring herself to meet Brad's eyes. He tilted her chin up, until she had no choice. "Don't hide from me, Karyn. Please," he said softly.

Dazed, she shook her head. "I won't."

"I was right, you know."

"About what?"

"You are what I've been hungering for. There is a freshness about you, an innocence, that I haven't known for a very long time."

It wasn't his words or the tone of his voice that dazzled Karyn. It was the blaze of fire in his eyes. She reached out to touch the icy, bright red metal of the bridge, to ground herself in reality. Even that couldn't rob her of the sensation that the bridge was falling away beneath her; that Brad Willis, a man she'd known for such a short time, held her fate in the palm of his hand.

"You're trembling," he observed, his expression troubled. "Am I going too fast for you?"

"A little," she admitted shakily. Boldly, though, she looked into the depths of eyes the same deep green shade as the churning water below and said, "But don't stop."

With a heavy sigh, he drew her close. "I don't think I could if I wanted to."

Brad tangled his fingers in her hair and rested his chin atop her head. She could hear the steady, thumping rhythm of his heart. The tangy scent of his soap filled her senses. His warmth surrounded her. When he spoke again at last, the words rumbled up from deep in his chest.

"Where would you like to go next on your vacation?" he asked. "Italy? China? France? Take your pick."

Smiling, Karyn lifted her gaze to his and gave herself over to the fantasy. "Italy, I think. Will it take long to get there?"

"Not long at all. In fact, if you look closely enough, you can see it from here."

"Oh, really?"

"Yes, you can," he said, chiding her for her skepticism. He pointed toward the cliffs of Sausalito. "Look there at the flowers tumbling down the hillsides, the little twisty roads. Doesn't that remind you of an Italian seaside village?"

"My imagination must not be as vivid as yours. It looks like Sausalito to me."

"Then I think our first stop should be to buy you some rose-colored glasses. Any true romantic could see what I see."

"I haven't had a lot of time for romance in my life," she said, unable to prevent a wistful note from creeping into her voice.

Brad's fingertips were warm against her cheek as he vowed, "Then that's about to change."

Hand in hand, they returned to the car. With Brad's dangerous promise still ringing in her ears, Karyn sat silently looking out the window as they crossed the bridge. Her world was suddenly spinning like a top, reeling away from reality as she had known it—dull, consistent, unchanging. What was emerging was a way of life colored with vibrant, passionate shades and throbbing with excitement. After a few days of this, would she ever be content with her humdrum existence again?

It didn't matter, she told herself staunchly. The taste of enchantment was worth whatever heartache might follow. Determined to savor it all, Karyn put her hand trustingly into Brad's as they left the car near the ferry dock and began the walk through the winding streets of the quaint village.

With the total enthusiasm of a dedicated shopper, Brad dragged her in and out of one boutique after another, watching her closely as she tentatively touched the unique jewelry, studied the paintings, or ran her fingers over the fabric of handcrafted woolens or delicately screened silks. She fell in love with a scarf in shades of gold and red, but Brad shook his head and reached instead for one in bright blues and boldest turquoise. When he held it close to her cheek, she could see at once that he was right. It brought out the warm peach tones in her skin and emphasized the unfamiliar sparkle in her eyes.

Astonished by the difference, she teased, "You have quite a knack at that, Mr. Willis. Have you spent a lot of time picking out women's clothes?"

"Some," he murmured and Karyn's heart fell. "But never as successfully as this." He turned to the salesclerk. "We'll take it."

"Brad, no," she protested, glancing at the exorbitant price tag. "It's far too expensive and impractical."

He shook his head. "What am I going to do with you? Vacations are meant for frivolous purchases. Now pay attention and repeat after me—for the next week, if I see something I really, really want, I'll buy it. That's lesson two."

Karyn laughed at his serious expression. "And who will pay the bill for all these extravagances?"

He waved aside the practicalities. "That's something you worry about over the long months between vacations. Besides, this is a gift from me to you."

"I can't accept it. It's one thing for you to be entertaining me all week long. This is too much."

"Don't you want me to enjoy this vacation as much as you do?"

"Of course."

"Then you'll have to accept the gift. It makes me happy to give it to you, to see your eyes light up when you look at it and at me."

The rich colors and cool silk of the scarf tempted, but not nearly as much as the hopeful gleam in Brad's eyes. For a fraction of a second, Karyn could almost believe it really mattered to him whether she accepted the present. "Thank you," she said finally.

"You're welcome," Brad replied, his eyes locked with hers as he wound the scarf loosely around her neck. His fingers brushed her nape, then trailed along the neckline of her sweater. Against her bare flesh, his touch blazed a path of fire and new, unfamiliar emotions burst forth deep inside her.

Karyn had never experienced such tenderness before, such attentiveness to her needs. It wasn't so much Brad's gift that mattered, as the fact that he'd caught the longing in her eyes, that he'd cared enough to recognize how rare such treasures were for her. She reached up and touched the delicate fabric. The emotions born this morning were just as fragile, just as unique.

Was there any way, she wondered, to tell how long either would last?

Chapter Four

The sun burned away the last wisps of fog and like more magic, San Francisco emerged across the Bay as Karyn and Brad lingered over coffee in one of the cafés that dotted the Sausalito waterfront. Though Brad kept her entertained with innocuous stories of past travels with his family and on the racing circuit, she was not unaware of the speculative looks constantly cast in their direction. The reminder of Brad's celebrity status was disconcerting at best to someone used to remaining quietly in the background.

It was one thing when a boy of about twelve asked hesitantly for an autograph. It was quite another to have a flashy redhead in a skintight miniskirt wiggle over, drape herself around Brad's neck with obvious familiarity and kiss his suddenly flaming cheek. Karyn couldn't quite tell whether Brad's blush was caused by embarrassment or outrage. Her own reaction was even more confusing. Not only did she feel uncomfortable in the presence of such intimacy, she discovered that she was also capable of gut-wrenching jealousy.

"Brad, honey," the woman whispered in a throaty, all-too-sexy purr. "It's been too long."

Brad shot an apologetic look at Karyn as he tried to disengage the woman's fingers, which were threaded through his hair. Quickly, he stood, threw some cash on the table for the bill and reached for Karyn's hand. "Nice to see you," he mumbled to the woman, then headed for the door at a determined pace that could have earned him first place in a marathon.

"Sorry about that," he said, when they were finally alone and a full block from the restaurant.

"The run or the interruption?" Karyn asked, drawing in a ragged breath.

"The interruption."

"Who was she?"

"Beats me."

"You didn't know her?"

"Let's just say I don't remember her."

Karyn stiffened at his cold, dismissive tone. "It's not particularly gallant of you to say so. She certainly seemed to know you."

He stopped and turned her around to face him, his hands on her shoulders. "There are a lot of women who follow professional sports, including racing. They show up at parties. They claim an intimacy that may or may not be real. I probably have seen that woman before. I may even have had a conversation with her, but I guarantee you that it's never gone any further than that. I may have had some wild moments during my years on the circuit, but I remember all of them."

At Karyn's doubtful look, he repeated, "All of them, sweetheart."

Karyn felt the knot that had formed in her stomach finally begin to dissipate. She supposed what Brad said was entirely possible, but the woman had spoken in such a familiar way. Such brazen public behavior was beyond her experience. It emphasized once more the wide chasm between her level of sophistication and Brad's. He might not like what had just happened, but he was apparently used to it.

"Does that sort of thing happen to you a lot?" she asked as they started to walk again, his arm settled comfortably across her shoulders. She liked the way it felt there, liked the hint of possessiveness.

"Not as much as it used to. I've been away for a while now. People start to forget. New faces have taken my place."

"Did you enjoy all the attention?"

"I enjoyed winning. The rest was unavoidable. To be perfectly truthful, there were times I took advantage of it. It can be very lonely, if you don't. Women like you don't want to get involved with a man who's always on the run. The glamour wears thin very quickly. They want someone they can count on when the kids get sick or when the washer breaks down."

"Someone like Frank," Karyn said, unable to restrain a grin.

"Frank?"

"My oldest brother. He's very handy. He turns positively rapturous at the sight of something broken."

"Just the kind of man I meant," Brad concurred, laughing at the description.

"I want more," Karyn countered, warming to the subject. "I mean I know there's a lot to be said for stability and responsibility, but I'm perfectly willing to rely on myself for those. They weren't traits that did my mother any good. My father was as responsible as they come, but he died when he was barely fifty and she was left on her own with little education and no marketable skills. It's not smart for a woman to count on anyone other than herself."

"That's a pretty cynical attitude."

"Not cynical," she contradicted. "Realistic. I'm not dismissing the value of love, mind you. I'm all for romance and storybook endings, but not solely for the purpose of providing a safe, secure future.''

"Ah," he said. "I think I'm beginning to catch the distinction. I think it puts you somewhere between feminism and fairy tales.''

"You're laughing at me," she said indignantly.

"No, sweetheart. I'm envying you. You're so certain about what you want out of life.''

"Is that how I seem to you?"

"Absolutely. I've never known anyone more confident in herself and her goals. All that self-reliance is a little intimidating to a man who's going through a mid-life crisis that's not of his own choosing.''

"Only if you think the only way to maintain a relationship is for the man to control the purse strings. Are you that insecure, Brad? Can't you conceive of a relationship with a woman that's a full partnership in every sense of the word?''

"I've never thought about it before," he said. "I guess we'll just have to wait and see how deep my macho chauvinism runs, won't we?''

"When do you anticipate knowing?"

"Oh, I'd say I should have a better idea by the end of the week. Now why don't we talk about your insecurities for a minute.''

"Mine? I thought you just said I was intimidatingly confident.''

"With one exception that I've discovered so far. You turned practically green with jealousy when that woman came up to our table. Why?''

"She seemed like exactly the kind of woman who knows how to go after everything she wants and get it." *Including you,* she thought to herself.

He shook his head. "I guess I'll just have to spend the rest of this week proving to you that you have absolutely nothing to worry about from a woman like that." His fingers combed back through the short curls of her hair until his palm rested against the curve of her cheek. "You are a beautiful, vital, exciting woman. No man who's out with you would ever turn his attention to someone else unless he's a damn fool."

The attempt to still her self-doubt was sweet, but Karyn wasn't crazy enough to believe she could compete with the full-figured, flamboyant redheads of the world. "It's very nice of you—"

He pressed his finger against her lips. "No doubts."

"Brad, how can I not have doubts?" she said, trying desperately to cling to reality, when he was leading her toward fantasy at a dizzying pace. "I'm not glamorous."

"So what?"

"I'm not sophisticated."

"Thank God."

"There are so many things I've never experienced."

"Which will make it all the more fun for us to do them together. Now are you quite through denigrating yourself?"

"I am not putting myself down," she argued. "I don't believe in self-pity. I'm just trying to make you see my limitations. I am what I am. I'm proud of what I've accomplished. It just may not be enough for someone like you."

"Sweetheart, those things you mentioned are only limitations to you, definitely not to me. Do you want to know what I see when I look at you? I see spirit and determination. I see the innocent delight that makes your eyes sparkle. I see someone who's not afraid to laugh, who still takes pleasure in little things like pickles or a scarf. I see excitement at the prospect of discovering new things."

All the things he mentioned were traits that Karyn thought of as merely an irritating lack of experience. "You really mean that, don't you?'' she said, searching his expression and seeing nothing but heartfelt sincerity.

He nodded. ''I really do. Now let's go. We have an entire city to explore and only a week to see it. Think you can keep up with me?''

After the tiniest hesitation, she smiled and a weight lifted from her heart. If Brad Willis was content with her company, who was she to suggest that he would soon grow bored? ''Absolutely,'' Karyn said with renewed confidence. ''What's next?''

''Fisherman's Wharf. We began the day as tourists. I think we should end it the same way.''

The honky-tonk atmosphere of the famed waterfront area, along with the Cannery and Ghirardelli Square was exactly what Karyn needed. The sidewalk entertainment, the diverse shops and outdoor cafés set against the backdrop of the Bay gave them a chance for more leisurely, hand-in-hand strolling in an environment that defied depressing thoughts.

She discovered that while Brad was knowledgeable about the offerings of the exclusive boutiques in Sausalito, he was just as enthusiastic about inexpensive tourist trinkets. He insisted that she have a San Francisco T-shirt and was endlessly patient while she chose one. When the purchase was made, he promptly tugged the shirt over her head, his hands lingering for just a moment beneath her breasts. The light, casual brush of his fingertips set off waves of shivering delight. It was a sensation Karyn knew she'd remember weeks from now when Brad was gone and she was alone in her bed, wearing the oversize shirt.

''You're trembling,'' he noted, his gaze locked with hers.

Her throat too dry to respond, Karyn nodded, terrified he could tell how his touch aroused her.

''I think that calls for some Irish coffee,'' he decided, apparently misreading the cause of the shudders sweeping through her. She was relieved at first, until she caught the knowing glint in his eyes and realized that he had deliberately taken her response lightly to set her at ease. Karyn realized then what she should have known all along: Brad knew all about seductive pacing, just as he did about negotiating the curves and hills of a Grand Prix course. It should have made her cautious. Instead, it filled her with anticipation.

They walked to the Buena Vista Café on Hyde Street, where they were finally able to find a table for two squeezed into a corner of the crowded restaurant famous for its Irish coffee. When the steaming coffee was in front of them, Karyn clung to the cup and searched for something witty to say. Her range of repartee seemed all too limited. She doubted he would want to hear about her class in interrogatories or her struggle with taking depositions. For the first time in her life, she regretted not taking more time away from her classes and work to develop the social skills that were second nature to most women her age.

"You're retreating again," Brad accused gently.

"You're right," she admitted. "I don't have a lot of practice making small talk."

"Small talk is between strangers. Surely we're more than that by now."

"Not really."

He settled back, crossed his legs at the ankles and grinned. "Okay, fire away. What would you like to know?"

She seized the opening with enthusiasm. Leaning forward, Karyn propped her chin in her hand and said, "Tell me about your family."

"You already know about my father. My mother is a bit of a socialite in her own right. Her parents had money. They thought she married beneath her, when she married my dad. I think that's probably why he became such a workaholic. I think he's always been trying to prove himself. Ironically, he never needed to prove anything to my mother. She adores him and she stopped caring what her parents thought the day she walked down the aisle."

"Any brothers or sisters?"

"A younger brother."

"Does he show any inclination to take over the family business? Couldn't he relieve you of some of the responsibility, so you could race again?"

"Unfortunately, Brian is only interested in making sure that he gets his share of our father's estate. If he had his way, I'm sure it would be sooner, rather than later."

"That's awful," she said, genuinely appalled. "Don't they get along?"

"It's not that. Brian is a gambler, a real high roller. It's an addiction, but he doesn't see it that way. Dad gave up on him a long time ago. He put money in a trust fund for him so that he'd never have grounds to challenge his will, but he won't allow him access to the business. He's afraid he'd lose it in a high-stakes poker game or use it for collateral to bankroll a bet on the races at Santa Anita. Brian gets a healthy amount from the interest on the trust, but it's never enough. He's always borrowing from Mom or me or our grandparents. He only dares to turn to dad when he's desperate."

Karyn listened carefully for some evidence of anger. She heard none. "You don't sound bitter. Why? He's keeping you from your dream."

"I feel sorry for him. Gambling is a sickness for him, but until he realizes it, he'll never change. As for me, Brian's not keeping me from anything. I made a choice about how I wanted to handle my life and my relationship with Dad. I owe him a lot. Without him, I'd never have been on the race circuit in the first place. I'm going through a rough period of adjustment now, but I know what I'm doing is right.''

''I saw that picture of the two of you that's hanging in your office. He looked very proud.''

''He was. I think he feels tremendous guilt about what's happened. I've tried not to let him see the frustration I feel, but sometimes I'm sure he does. Fortunately, for all of us, it's getting better.''

Brad took her hand in his and rubbed his thumb across the knuckles, before raising it slowly to his lips. That sense of shivery anticipation raced through Karyn again as he lingered over the tender caress. ''I'm finding more and more to like about this more stable life-style,'' he said in a low voice that skimmed across her senses with the fire of whiskey.

''Brad.'' With the roaring of her blood in her ears, she was barely able to choke out his name.

''Umm?''

''Maybe . . . I'd better go home. It's been a long day and it's getting late.''

He smiled ruefully. ''Why am I so certain that you mean to go alone?''

''I'm sorry.''

''You needn't be. It's part of what makes you special. Come on, then. I'll walk you to your car.''

''I'll give you a lift,'' she offered, suddenly reluctant to put an end to the day, fearful the joyous feelings she'd been discovering would vanish like a wisp of fog in sunlight.

''No. If I get into that car with you, I may not want to get out. It's better if I walk back to my hotel.''

She felt oddly hesitant. What if sending him home alone proved to him just how silly and unsophisticated she was? ''I will see you in the morning, won't I?'' Though her tone was light, she knew there was no mistaking her doubts. She regretted it, but she couldn't stop it.

"Maybe not at dawn again, but I will be there," Brad promised. "Count on it."

His arms slid around her then and his lips found the sensitive spot on her neck before claiming her lips one last time. "It's been a special day, Karyn. One I'll never forget."

"Do you really mean that?" she asked, anxiously searching his eyes.

"Every word, sweetheart."

With his words warming her heart, Karyn got in the car, turned on the ignition and started to back up. A bus pulled part of the way past and stopped, blocking her way. She hit the brakes and waited. The bus didn't move. Finally growing increasingly irritated, she turned and glared toward the driver.

It was Timmy—and the expression on his face as he scowled down at her and Brad, who was still waiting nearby, was not filled with brotherly love. She had no doubts at all that the only thing keeping him from climbing out of the bus and pummeling Brad right then and there was the fact that the bus was filled with passengers. Even so, he appeared torn between expressing his indignation and his professional responsibility.

"Brad, I think you'd better go on," she whispered urgently.

Brad heard the odd nervousness in her voice, but more than that he saw a quick flicker of panic in her eyes. It shook him. He reached out to touch her cheek reassuringly, but she backed away a step. Puzzled, he asked, "Karyn, what's wrong?"

She again glanced anxiously toward the bus that was blocking her car. "The man driving that bus," she whispered, "the one with murder in his eyes..."

"Yes?"

"He's my brother, Timmy."

Brad turned around slowly and looked toward the bus. He studied the driver and caught the hint of brotherly outrage on his face. For the first time he fully understood just how protective her family was. A part of him appreciated such deep loyalty and concern and liked the fact that someone had been looking after Karyn as he himself would have done. What worried him was the effect it seemed to have on her. One minute she had been all woman in his arms. The next she had been as skittish as a kitten.

In an attempt to disarm Timmy and relieve Karyn's nervousness, Brad waved. As Brad had intended, the friendly gesture obviously disconcerted her brother. Timmy gave him a halfhearted wave then, with obvious reluctance, responded to the noisy, irritated rebukes from his passengers. He pulled into traffic and drove on.

With his departure, Brad could see Karyn's tension visibly abate, though she continued to shiver. He realized then that he couldn't possibly let her go home alone, when it was obvious she was going to spend the night worrying herself sick over the prospect of a confrontation with her brother. Before she could put the convertible back into gear, he leaped over the door and settled into the passenger seat.

Clearly startled, she stared over at him. "Brad, what do you think you're doing?"

"Going home with you."

"You can't," she protested.

"Why not?"

"Because—"

"Because your brother is going to show up with a thousand and one questions, right?"

"If I'm lucky," she said with a sigh of resignation.

"And if you're not?"

"He'll also have the *rest* of the family in tow."

"That's exactly why I'm coming along. We've done nothing wrong. The fact that he saw me kiss you good night is hardly grounds for hysteria."

"You've obviously never encountered anyone like my brothers. They plopped me on a pedestal at birth and I can't seem to get down. They definitely don't want anyone up there with me."

"Very Victorian," he said, and laughed at her grimace. "I'm looking forward to meeting them."

She turned and stared at him in apparent astonishment.

"I am," he repeated emphatically.

She looked glum. "You don't have to do this, you know."

"I know."

"Then why are you?"

"Because you and I are going to continue seeing each other and your brothers and I might as well get that straight right now."

A bright spark of hope lit her eyes. It was almost as bright as the desire he'd seen there earlier. The combination was too much for a mere mortal like him. Brad felt himself falling wildly, crazily in love. Karyn had presented him with one more dragon to slay and judging from the expression on her face, he'd done just fine.

Chapter Five

Karyn awoke with a crick in her neck and a pain in her back. It was just after 7:00 a.m. and once more someone was pounding on her door. Obviously any opportunity to sleep late during her vacation was doomed. Still groggy, she stumbled halfway across the room before she remembered that Brad was sprawled on her sofa, where he'd fallen asleep sometime shortly before dawn. Since the pounding didn't seem to be fazing him at all, she doubted that there was anything she could do to get him up and out a window before the person on the other side of that door barged in.

She swung open the door. "Keep it down, please. My head hurts," she grumbled.

"More than your head is going to hurt by the time we finish talking," Tim growled right back as he stalked into the living room.

He was halfway to the kitchen when he caught sight of Brad, who was just beginning to stir. Tim's expression went from shocked to outraged to thoughtful in a matter of seconds as he watched Brad kick the quilt to the floor. Fortunately, he was fully clothed beneath it.

Tim locked his hand around her elbow and propelled her into the kitchen. "Okay, sis, who the hell is he and what is he doing here at this hour?"

"We were waiting for you," Karyn said, plugging in the automatic coffeepot and dumping in an extra scoop of coffee. She had a feeling they were going to need the strongest brew she could make. "When I saw you last night, I figured you were upset about seeing Brad and me, well, you know.'' She gazed at him beseechingly.

"Kissing? Right in the middle of the street? Were you out of your mind?"

She figured the question was rhetorical. "Anyway,'' she went on, "Brad came back here with me so I wouldn't have to face the music alone. Not that there should have been any music to face, mind you." She gazed at him pointedly. He scowled. "By the time it dawned on me that you were working the night shift, we were both too exhausted to move. Before you ask, he slept on the sofa. When he offered to sleep there, I didn't have the heart to tell him that was actually my bed. I guess he figured there had to be a bedroom somewhere. Most people do have them, you know." She couldn't seem to stop rattling on.

Tim nodded. "Okay, so far. What I'm more concerned about is where *you* slept."

Something inside Karyn snapped at the inquisition. In the past she'd simply shrugged them off. She'd certainly had nothing to hide. Now, however, it was definitely time to put a firm stop to these ridiculous intrusions into her personal life once and for all.

"Not that it's any of your business," she began well enough. Her resolution wavered under Tim's penetrating gaze. "Okay, I slept on the floor, which is why every bone and muscle in my body is protesting this morning. If you're going to act brotherly, do it in a hurry and get out, so I can stand in a hot shower for an hour or two."

"Alone?" Timmy inquired.

"Yes, dammit, alone. I hardly know Brad Willis, but I might add, if I were not going into that shower alone, that, too, would be none of your business." She faced him with hands on hips. "What is wrong with you? I thought you were the one brother I could count on not to behave like an overly protective jerk.''

"Call me anything you like, sis. I can take it. Just tell me this, why haven't we met this guy?'' Tim was still scowling in the direction of the living room, where Brad was finally sitting upright and looking as though he might be able to get his cramped body on its feet any minute now.

"Because I just met him a week ago,'' she admitted reluctantly.

"A week ago? Are you out of your mind letting a total stranger into your apartment in the middle of the night?'' Tim scrutinized Brad from head to toe. No suspect in a criminal investigation had ever been studied more closely. Karyn didn't have a doubt in the world that Tim now felt competent to identify him should he walk off with the family silver or, to be more precise in her case, the stainless steel.

"He looks familiar,'' he said finally.

"He used to be a race car driver.''

"A race car driver!'' His tone made the profession seem comparable to ax murdering. "Where the hell would you meet a race car driver?''

"Thanks for the vote of confidence in my appeal.''

"That wasn't what I meant and you know it. Stop evading and answer me.''

"We met when I bought my car.''

"You bought a convertible, not some souped up hot rod.''

"I don't think Brad drove souped up hot rods in Grand Prix events.''

"Brad Willis?'' Tim said with dawning understanding. "Of course. I've seen his picture in the paper. Sis, he's not your type.''

"What is her type?'' Brad inquired curiously, pulling a stool up to the bar that separated the kitchen and living room and reaching for a cup of coffee. He looked perfectly at home.

Tim wasn't the least bit taken aback by being overheard. "Someone less . . . I don't know, less . . ."

"Experienced?"

"Yeah. That's exactly it."

"Your sister is twenty-six years old. Most of the men she's likely to meet are going to be experienced."

"I wasn't referring just to sex," Timmy said bluntly.

Karyn put her head down on her arms and groaned.

"Neither was I," Brad countered.

A very tense silence ensued. When Karyn could stand it no longer she got up, put bread into the toaster, then coated it with butter and slammed it down in front of the two men. They continued to study each other as if they were prospective sparring partners.

Brad dumped sugar and cream into his coffee, then stirred it slowly. He ignored the toast and looked directly into Tim's suspicious eyes.

"I'm glad you've always taken such good care of your sister," he told him, then added gently, "But it's time to let her go."

This time Tim *did* look thrown by the blunt pronouncement. His gaze narrowed. "Exactly what are your intentions toward her?"

"Timmy!" Karyn protested, moaning inwardly. Embarrassing moments were piling up so rapidly this morning, she'd never live them down.

"Keep quiet, sis. I want to know how this man feels about you."

"This man doesn't even know me!"

"He knows you well enough to sleep on your sofa."

"On my sofa," she reiterated. "Not in my bed."

"Your sofa is your bed," Timmy reminded her.

"It is?" Brad said, staring at her. "Where did you sleep?"

"On the floor and that's not the point. There is a difference, Timothy Michael Chambers, between having a man fall asleep on the sofa and inviting him into my bed!"

After another moment of tense silence, her brother nodded sheepishly. "You're right. I apologize."

"Maybe you should go home and get some sleep," Karyn suggested. She wanted him out of there before he began cross-examining Brad about his career prospects and bank balance.

"Are you sure?"

"I'm sure."

Tim directed another measuring glance at Brad. He seemed to visibly relax finally, though that didn't keep him from warning, "If you hurt her, Willis, the world won't be big enough for you to hide in."

Brad gave him a faint smile. "I wouldn't have it any other way."

Karyn's heart tumbled at the tenderness in his voice. It was almost impossible for her to draw her gaze away, but finally she was forced to walk Tim to the door, since he didn't seem inclined to get there on his own.

"You're not going to say anything to the others, are you?" she pleaded.

He glanced over her shoulder at Brad, who was watching the two of them with interest. "I don't think it would do any good. Just be careful, sis. You could be playing out of your league."

"I thought so, too, at first."

"Not anymore?"

She felt herself smiling. "No. I think I'm right where I belong."

"I'm happy for you, then."

"Thanks."

She closed the door behind him and leaned back against it with a sigh of relief. Brad came over and pulled her into his arms. She nestled against him, awed by how right it felt for her to be there.

"That wasn't so awful, was it?" he whispered.

"It could have been worse," she admitted. "Frank would have slugged first and asked questions later."

"Then I'm glad Tim was the brother who showed up. Did you mean what you told him? Are you feeling comfortable with what's happening between us?"

"More and more every minute."

She could feel his sigh. "I'm glad, sweetheart." Brad tilted her chin up and touched his lips to hers in the lightest of caresses. But the passion that had been kept at bay all night flared into full flame, the heat swirling through them. Karyn lost herself in the enveloping warmth.

It was Brad who pulled away eventually. "We'd best slow down or those brothers of yours will really have grounds to take me apart."

Karyn's knees felt so weak without Brad's arms around her that she sank down on the sofa. "I don't understand what you do to me." She cast a look of appeal in his direction. "I've always been in control of myself, but when you touch me, it's like I just float off to some incredible place."

"And you see that as bad?"

"I see that as terrifying."

He sat down next to her. "I promise you that you have nothing to fear from me. I meant what I told your brother. I won't hurt you."

The comment was reassuring, but hardly realistic. "You can't possibly guarantee that."

"There you go again. You've obviously had too much legal training. Let me correct myself, then. I will do my very best never to hurt you."

"I think I liked it better when you were making more adamant claims."

"You can't have it both ways, sweetheart. Now, how about getting out of here? We're wasting our vacation."

"Just let me take a quick shower and change."

"I don't suppose," he began, but his voice trailed off at one quelling look from her. He grinned. "I didn't think so."

Still shaken by the intensity of the feelings that Brad had aroused in her in such a short time, Karyn lingered in the shower far longer than she should have. She dressed slowly and emerged from the bathroom with her hair curling damply about her face.

"You had a call," Brad told her. "Your office. Someone named Mary Lee wants you to call back right away."

She didn't waste time worrying about what impression Brad's answering her phone might have made on her boss's secretary. She dutifully picked up the phone and dialed.

"Mary Lee, it's Karyn. Did Mr. Wetherington need me for something?"

"Hi, hon. Yeah, he wondered if you could work this afternoon. He knows it's your vacation and all, but since you're in town, he thought maybe you wouldn't mind. He said he'd make up the time later."

Karyn looked at Brad. Clutching the receiver more tightly, she said, "I'm sorry. I can't make it. I have plans for this afternoon."

It was the bravest thing she'd ever done. Conscientious Karyn Chambers did not turn down requests from her boss. She waited for Mary Lee to announce that she was to get to the office at once or else face immediate firing.

"Okay, no problem," the secretary said instead. "See you next week, hon. Enjoy the rest of your vacation."

The breath she'd been holding escaped on a sigh as she hung up.

"Saying no was really tough for you, wasn't it?" Brad said.

She nodded. "In my family taking risks did not extend to career matters. We've always needed the money too badly."

"You don't any more, Karyn. Don't ever let yourself feel that someone has that kind of power over you. There are other jobs."

"Rationally, I know that. And I know I have a little savings now to fall back on. It's difficult, though, to break old habits. I keep seeing the worried expression on Mama's face when payday would come and the money wouldn't quite add up to cover the bills. If one of us got sick, it threw the budget into turmoil for months."

"But the world didn't come to an end when you said no just now, did it?"

She shook her head.

"Most bosses respect people who have their priorities straight and who stand up for their own needs. Remember that. Your time is every bit as important as your boss's."

She grinned. "Then why are we wasting it on this silly discussion?"

"Because every once in a while, you obviously need to be reminded how important you are and that you deserve to be taken care of."

"Yes," she said more seriously. "I suppose I do." For the first time in her life she was actually beginning to feel that way. She felt as if she were Cinderella at the ball, but like the fairy-tale heroine who'd finally savored magic, she felt as though she were watching the clock tick away the final seconds of her dream. A part of her wanted to cling to the excitement she was discovering with Brad, but another part knew when the time came, she would have to let it go.

As if he'd caught her melancholy mood, Brad planned a day designed to touch the romance in her soul. He took her on the spectacular Seventeen Mile Drive along the rugged coast of the Monterey peninsula. Each setting they passed was more breathtaking than the one before. Finally, he pulled into a parking lot designated as a lookout point. It was crowded with tourists snapping pictures of the glorious scenery. Thrilled by the view, Karyn leaned back against the convertible's seat and sighed.

"It's beautiful," she declared softly.

"I'm glad you like it. I wasn't sure if you'd been here before, but it was the closest I could come to Hawaii on short notice. It's not exactly the same, but you do have beaches and endless vistas of deep blue water."

Tears filled her eyes at the sentimental thought. "You really brought me here because you wanted me to experience Hawaii?"

He brushed a strand of hair back from her face, his fingertips caressing her jaw. "I want you to experience everything. Will this do for a start?"

"It's almost perfect."

"Almost?"

She grinned at his indignant tone. "The only thing missing is the scent of frangipani," she confessed wistfully. On rare special occasions she indulged in scented bath salts that filled the steamy bathroom with the fragrance. Then she'd lie back in the tub and soak, imagining herself on an island beach surrounded by the soft, sweet scent of plumeria blossoms. She looked at Brad and caught a flicker of satisfaction in his eyes.

"That's where you're wrong," he said, clearly gloating as he reached into the back seat for a box that he'd hidden from view.

Karyn's eyes widened when she saw the name and address of a Waikiki florist embossed on the side. "But when? How?"

He laughed at her astonishment. "You were in that shower long enough for me to fly to Hawaii and back," he teased.

"Seriously, where did you get it?"

"I called first thing yesterday and had it flown in. It really did arrive while you were in the shower. I ran down and tucked it into the car while you were dressing."

With trembling fingers, Karyn awkwardly opened the box. The remembered scent of the waxy, fragile blossoms wafted up. She lifted the lei gently from the box and held it to her face, breathing deeply.

"Oh, Brad, it's the nicest present anyone's ever given me," she whispered. "They're just the way I'd always imagined." She turned eyes that were misty with tears toward him. "Thank you."

"You don't have to thank me, sweetheart. The look in your eyes is thanks enough. Let me put it on for you."

Brad settled the lei around her neck, then kissed her on each cheek. Then, while staring deep into her eyes, he must have seen her longing or perhaps what he saw there merely mirrored his own desires, because slowly, he bent his head and his lips deliberately covered hers. Instead of satisfying the yearning, though, the kiss merely fueled the keen awareness of the textures of his skin, the silky moistness of his lips, the faint stubble on his cheeks. A sweet, insistent ache spread through her and she moved closer still, seeking the fulfillment that her body somehow knew Brad and only Brad could provide.

Lost in the building passion, Karyn was unaware that the fragile blossoms were being crushed. When Brad reluctantly pulled away, his body taut, the touch of his fingertips still lingering against the sensitive peak of her breast, only then did she see that the petals of her extravagant gift were damaged.

But nothing—nothing, Karyn thought with a sense of wonder and conviction—could harm the love that was flowering between them.

Chapter Six

Karyn had a good, long, heart-to-heart talk with herself before Brad picked her up for the next-to-last day of their vacation. She reminded herself that when it was over, he would go back to his life and she would return to hers. She was merely a diversion for a man used to a more sophisticated woman. Even those who dined regularly on caviar and beef Wellington occasionally yearned for fish and chips—and vice versa. Happily ever after only happened in storybooks.

There were to be no regrets. She had indulged in a once in a lifetime dream. She had savored each moment of delight stirred by his kisses, but that's where it had to end. Even Brad seemed to understand that and had not pushed for a deeper intimacy. The day before he had even chosen activities that had kept them safely amidst people—from the vast displays of Oriental art at the De Young Museum to the twisting, jumbled streets of Chinatown. If their other adventures had touched her heart and soul, yesterday's had reached out to fulfill her thirst for knowledge.

In front of each intricately carved jade figure, as they had looked at each delicate painting on silk, Karyn had questioned Brad endlessly about the Orient. He had answered tirelessly. Worlds that she had only known through books came alive through his eyes. They had settled for a time into the comfortable roles of tutor and student. She had been grateful, not only for his enthusiastic teaching, but for the chance to regain her equilibrium, to forget the delightfully enticing way it felt to have his arms around her, his breath whispering against her cheek.

Once more today, sleeping late had been ruled out. Brad had insisted that the day begin with a hot air balloon ride over the Napa Valley. Flights lifted off just after dawn, which meant that the night had been all-too-short. Drowsy and still flushed from sleep, Karyn was waiting in the lobby when Brad arrived with a picnic basket.

"Comment allez-vous?" he asked, his eyes lighting up at the sight of her.

She blinked sleepily at the unfamiliar language. He grinned. "How are you?" he translated. "I was just trying to get you ready for our trip to France."

"Let me know when we get there," she mumbled unappreciatively and climbed gratefully into the car. "This vacation stuff is wearing me out. You may be used to burning the candle at both ends, but I'm not used to late nights and early mornings."

"Believe it or not, neither am I anymore."

"At least you look alive." Actually, he looked quite a bit better than that. With a teal blue sweater over a bright yellow polo shirt and hip-hugging jeans, he looked as devastatingly handsome and virile as ever.

"You'll feel that way, too," he promised, pulling her into his arms and raining gentle kisses on her forehead, eyelids, cheeks and finally her waiting lips. Her pulse quickened at once and her senses were instantly alert. It was better than any alarm clock she'd ever owned and twice as addictive as caffeine.

"Amazing," she whispered, linking her hands behind his neck.

A faint smile curved his lips and a quizzical look flitted through his eyes. "Isn't it, though?" he murmured. "Karyn..." he began, then shook his head. "No. Not now."

"What?"

"Nothing. We'll talk later. Right now we need to get on the road."

They drove through the darkened streets at Brad's usual breakneck pace, crossing the Golden Gate and heading north on U.S. Highway 101. As they came to the narrow, two-lane roads that took them into the heart of the Napa Valley, he finally slowed down.

"Have you ever been ballooning before?" Karyn asked.

"Once, over France. It's a gloriously free feeling to be soaring just above the earth."

"Not like being in a plane?"

"No. For one thing you're not nearly as high up. Nor are you going anywhere near as fast. And it's just you and maybe a few other people up there all alone. You can feel the air rushing past. You feel as though you could touch the clouds. The weather has to be just right, the clouds no more than wisps. I think we're going to be okay today. It looks as though it's starting out to be a perfect day."

When they arrived at the site, several balloons were stretched out on the ground being slowly filled with air. Couples and families were sipping coffee and waiting for the last streaks of a pink and golden sunrise to give way to end-less blue. Fascinated by everything that was happening, Karyn plied Brad with more questions. When he ran out of answers technical enough to suit her, he laughingly intro-duced her to the pilot of the balloon he'd hired for the morning.

Moments later Brad lifted her into the gondola and fol-lowed her in. Filled with anticipation, Karyn held on to the side and peered down, then up into the vast interior of the cloth balloon. The tethers were removed, flames shot up heating the air and they were off. Theirs was the second balloon to rise slowly from the ground. More cumbersome than she'd anticipated, it quivered and jostled them until it was fully aloft. Then it floated, drifting through the morning sky like a colorful cloud.

Karyn's breath caught in her throat as the earth fell away. Eyes wide, she clung to Brad's hand. It was only when they'd been in the air for several minutes that she shifted her gaze from the panorama below to Brad's face. He was watching her intensely, his eyes mirroring her excitement.

"Happy?" he asked quietly.

"I'll never forget it," she said, touching a fingertip to his cheek. It was morning-shave smooth and warmed at once beneath her touch. "Thank you. No one has ever had such a special vacation."

"It's been special for me, too. Seeing things through your eyes has reminded me how important it is to stop and find the joy in living again."

"I'm glad, if I've given you that," she said. Their gazes met and held, unblinking, searching. Yet another timeless moment was captured forever in her memory. Then she remembered that she'd brought along her camera. She could fill her scrapbook with images of Brad and years from now, when life seemed tedious and mundane, she could look at the photos and remember magic.

As Karyn tried to break away, Brad held her hand more tightly. "Up here, you can't run away," he teased lightly, though there was an intensity underlying the words that she didn't fully understand.

"I'm not going anywhere," she said, sidestepping wherever he was heading with the pointed remark. "I just wanted to get my camera from my purse."

With an indulgent amused expression, he watched as she took the inexpensive camera out and aimed at the distant fields below, then at the magnificent balloon above.

"Now you," she said, positioning him where she could capture his dimpled smile.

"Now one of us together," he insisted, turning the camera over to the pilot. He pulled her back against his chest and they faced the camera. Just before the shutter clicked, he tickled her so that the snap captured her gasp of surprised laughter.

"I think that's the one I'll carry with me always," he said. "Maybe I'll have it blown up and put on the wall in every one of my offices."

"First you have to get the negative away from me," she reminded him.

"No problem." He reached over and with no effort whatsoever plucked the camera out of her unsuspecting grip and tucked it into his pocket.

She lunged after it before she realized the precarious balance of the gondola. When it dipped and swayed, she fell against the solid wall of Brad's chest.

"Yet another way to get you into my arms," he said delightedly, holding her tightly against him. "I'll have to remember it."

Little did he know that he could get her into his arms with just the slightest hint that he wanted her there. He would never know the power he had gained over her in just a few short days. She would walk away from him with dignity, her pride intact, even if her heart was in pieces.

The whole day was a collage of such moments, a sudden burst of melancholy counteracted by carefree laughter, heart-stopping embraces followed by breathless chases that always ended in yet another embrace, another fiery memory.

After the balloon ride they toured half a dozen vineyards and ate their picnic lunch with the warmth of the sun beating down on their shoulders and the warmth of the wine curling seductively inside.

Karyn stretched out lazily on the blanket Brad had brought, her face turned toward the sun. "What a rare treat this is," she said, and sighed with pleasure.

"And this?" Slowly, Brad lowered his mouth to hers. She could taste the burgundy they'd had with lunch, the full-bodied flavor almost as intoxicating as the caress of his lips.

"Definitely a treat," she murmured, though the words were lost in yet another stolen kiss, this one deeper and far more urgent. His fingers slid beneath her shirt, lingering against bare flesh before seeking the tautness of her breasts. Her breath caught as his insistent strokes stirred wonder deep inside her.

Aching with a need more profound than any she had ever known, she turned sideways until her body was aligned with his, her hand resting against his chest where she could feel the heat of his skin and the quickening beat of his heart.

"I want to make love to you," he said quietly, searching her expression for a response. She tried desperately to cling to reason in the face of his entreaty, but the heartfelt plea in his eyes matched the yearning that was growing inside her.

"It would be a mistake," she said, trying one last time to make him see what was so very clear to her.

"Why?"

"Because after tomorrow you'll be gone. I don't want that much of my heart to go with you."

"I will only be gone, if that's the way you want it."

She shook her head. "It's not what I want. It's just the way it has to be."

"How can I convince you that's not true?"

"You can't," she said sadly, wishing she were wrong.

He levered himself away from her with a sigh, but his touch lingered at her breast. He squeezed gently, watching the darkening of her eyes, witnessing the power he had over her. Karyn could almost hate him for that, hate him for proving to himself and to her that he could overcome her resistance easily, if that's what he chose to do.

She brushed his hand away angrily and straightened her shirt. "You can make me want you," she admitted. "So what?"

"I think that says quite a bit about where we stand."

"Passion's easy. Even animals experience lust."

"And you think that's what it is between us? Nothing more than lust?"

"Of course. You come charging into my life like a white knight and sweep me off my feet. It's no surprise that I respond to you physically."

"So you see this as just part of the vacation package. Join Brad Willis on his tour of the San Francisco area, complete with a quick tumble in the hay. Satisfaction guaranteed or your money back."

Karyn was startled by the bitterness in his voice. Before she could respond he said angrily, "Let me make one thing perfectly clear. If that's all that was going on, we would have been in bed together that very first night. I've held back because I knew you felt some uncertainties. I wanted you to have time to get used to the idea of the two of us together, but I'll be damned if I'll let you go on thinking that we're just a couple of animals in heat. You may not know it, but I do. What we have is special. I will not let you throw it away because of some misguided notion that we're from such different worlds that we couldn't make a go of it."

"Make a go of what? An affair? We could probably manage that, but how long would it last? A few weeks, maybe a couple of months, until you got bored."

He shook his head. "I'm not sure which makes me angrier, your lack of faith in me or your own insecurities."

Tears filled her eyes as he lashed out furiously. This wasn't the way she wanted it to end between them. "Brad, I'm sorry."

"Sorry for what?"

"Because..." She realized then that she wasn't at all sure what she was apologizing for. She'd only been trying to be honest with him. "Maybe I'm not sorry," she said quietly. "I only wanted you to know how I felt. I think your response just proves my point. We are worlds apart on the things that count."

His body taut with anger, Brad got to his feet and began gathering their things. "Let's go."

Suddenly cold inside, Karyn shivered, but she stood and followed him to the car. The long ride back to San Francisco was made in tense, angry silence. It seemed somehow fitting that as they reached the outskirts of the city, a cold, damp fog began to roll in, turning the beautiful day to a gloomy gray. It reminded her all too closely of the very first day her Hawaiian vacation plans had been dashed.

Feeling alone and miserable, Karyn paid little attention to the road, looking out only when the car had stopped. Brad was parked on a hill in front of his small hotel in Pacific Heights. Staring straight ahead, his white-knuckled grip still tight on the steering wheel, he said, "I'm sure you can find your way home from here."

She nodded. Then she looked again at the angled line of his tense jaw, at the stubborn set of his shoulders. The thought of never being held in his arms again stirred an aching emptiness so overwhelming that she nearly gasped aloud in dismay.

"Brad..." she began hesitantly.

Only a slight tic in his jaw indicated that he'd heard her whisper his name.

"Don't you think we could talk about this?"

He sighed heavily. "We're past talking."

"I don't think so. I'd like to try."

After the longest sixty seconds of her life—she heard them ticking away on the car clock—he said simply, "Where?"

She took a deep breath, recognizing the risk she was taking, not only with the suggestion, but with her future emotional well-being. "Here. Now."

Brad turned a startled gaze on her. "In my room?"

"I trust you," she said simply. There was no need to say that she didn't trust herself nearly as much.

"You shouldn't," he retorted bluntly. "My body is aching for you right now. I can't make any promises about what will happen once we get inside."

"You would never hurt me."

"Not intentionally."

"Then there's no reason to be concerned. We need to talk. We're here. It seems like the logical place."

"And you're very big on logic," he said with a touch of wry humor. "I hate to tell you, sweetheart, but this time I think you may have outsmarted yourself."

Nerves alive with anticipation, Karyn nodded. "Maybe so," she admitted. It didn't keep her from being the first to open the door and head up the walk into Brad's hotel.

Chapter Seven

Karyn was charmed by the small hotel, which had once been an old Victorian house. The staff was welcoming, greeting Brad by name when they went inside. He and Karyn climbed the steep, curving staircase to his room, her heart pounding harder with each step. She knew exertion wasn't responsible for her breathlessness. The fluttery feeling in the pit of her stomach warned her that she was entering dangerous territory. Her resolution was wavering. Like shifting sand, the arguments pro and con slid in and out of her mind. Desire and sensation were easily winning over caution.

Brad opened the door to his room. She stepped inside, holding her breath as the door shut quietly behind her. The click of the lock jangled her nerves and she shot an anxious look at Brad before looking hurriedly away and studying the intimate, unique surroundings.

Old-fashioned lamps cast a romantic glow in the dusky light. Soft music played from an old radio. The setting was perfect for seduction. A window was open to the damp breeze and the air practically throbbed with their mutual hunger. She realized at once that there was no question of talking first, of resolving differences. There was only this white-hot flame that melted the very core of her. She began one last, halfhearted protest and then she was in his arms.

The minute he held her, Karyn knew this was the right choice. No matter what happened between them after this week, she wanted the magic of the vacation to be completed. Brad's touches had been so tender up until now, his kisses as alluring as springtime. She wanted to know the power of his caresses in passion, the wild intoxication of his deep, hot kisses at the height of loving. She would never forgive herself if he left and she never knew.

Brad backed a step away, stood facing her and waited.

"There's still time to change your mind," he said, his voice gentle, though his eyes blazed with desire.

Karyn shook her head. The decision had been made before the door to the room had closed behind them. "Not a chance."

The defiant lift of her chin seemed to amuse him. "Are you absolutely sure you're here because you want to be?" he said. "Only a little while ago, you were so sure this wasn't what you wanted, that this was the last place you wanted to come with me."

She met his gaze evenly. "I have to know," she said helplessly.

"Know what?"

"What it's like to make love with you. I realized driving here that I didn't want to go through life not knowing."

"How will your family feel about this?"

The question irritated her all the more because it was fair. She had put her family between them. "My family has nothing to do with it," she snapped, then sighed. "I'm not trying to defy them, if that's what you're afraid of. This is just between you and me. I swear it, Brad." She heard his breath catch, saw the tension begin to ease. Her voice dropped to a whisper as she moved into his embrace. "Just you and me."

"I hope so." With a touch that trembled against her cheek, he brushed a strand of hair from her face. "I've discovered this week just how selfish I can be," he said in a voice that was raw with emotion. "I don't want to share you, Karyn, not even with your family."

The words seduced as effectively as his caress. No one had ever wanted her so much. No man had ever treasured her above all others. That this man did—even for this timeless moment only—staggered her. Karyn felt herself melting, the last lingering doubts swept away.

"Kiss me," she pleaded, gazing into his eyes. "Show me how much you want me."

The request seemed to shatter the last of his powerful restraint. His arms tightened around her waist as he captured her lips on a sigh of pure pleasure. The hot, moist invasion of his tongue was as sweet as honey, the heat of his body as warm as a January fire. When his strong hands slid beneath her sweater to span the bare flesh beneath, the sensation was as wicked as a million midnight dreams. Her body hummed with the unfamiliar music of his touch, quickly in tune, delightfully in sync.

Karyn was so absorbed by the soaring sensations that captivated and teased, she was hardly aware of the precise moment when her clothes were stripped away. Only the sudden chill of the air against burning skin shocked her into awareness and then she was lost again, clinging to Brad as he led her into a sensory world she'd only dared to imagine.

The sweet throb of tension low in her abdomen grew until it was her only reality. As glorious as it was, she knew there was more, knew that until Brad's body was united with hers, she would remain incomplete. Burning with fire and too shy to say the words, she used her body with some shockingly instinctive expertise to tell him how badly she needed him, how desperately she wanted him.

Brad heard her frantic, unspoken plea and with one powerful thrust he moved inside her, causing the tiniest instant of pain, then filling her, carrying her to the edge of

wonder and then beyond. Their exultant cries came together, born some place deep within each of them, unifying
them for all time . . . no matter what the future held.

Joy spread through her as she collapsed at last against the
pillows, Brad heavy on top of her. When he started to shift
his weight, she held him tight. She'd waited a lifetime for
this sense of absolute harmony and completion, and she
didn't want it to end.

"Don't move," she begged. "Not yet."

"I'm too heavy."

"No. You're perfect. Holding you like this makes everything more real. I want this moment to last forever."

"Maybe that's something we could arrange," he said, his
tone so serious that Karyn's breath snagged in her throat.

"Brad, don't . . ."

He interrupted the whispered plea. "Listen to me. I think
it's time I met the rest of your family, time we talked about
the future."

"No!"

At the single, harsh exclamation, he did roll away, leaving her feeling bereft. She dragged at the sheets to fight the
sudden chill, but it was bone-deep.

"Dammit, Karyn. Don't tell me even after this that you
think what we've shared isn't lasting."

"It can't be," she insisted adamantly. "And I won't have
you dragging my family into it. It would only upset them,
if they knew I was having a wild, impossible fling—"

Brad's harsh, muttered oath cut her short. "Impossible!
It is not impossible."

"It is." She met his furious gaze without flinching. "I will
not . . ." She tried again to make him see reason, but the
phone rang before she could complete the warning. She
didn't want promises. Despite what she'd said, she wasn't
expecting forever. She couldn't involve her family in some-

thing as tenuous as what she and Brad had. She had hoped for a little more time—just this one tender, romantically sensual night—before reality intruded. The insistent phone already precluded that.

Brad swore again as he reached across her to answer it. Scowling down at her, he was clearly every bit as angry with her as he was at the interruption. "Yes," he barked at the hapless caller.

As he listened to Tim Chambers's urgent warning, Brad's impatience gave way to wariness. He glanced at Karyn, who was still regarding him with indignation. "She's here," he admitted tersely. "Do you want to talk to her?"

"No. Just get her out of there. You haven't got much time. Frank and Jared are on their way over. I tried to stop them, but Frank wasn't inclined to listen to reason. If he owned a shotgun, he'd have it with him."

"Don't worry. I'll handle it."

"Look, Willis, I'm not too crazy about this situation myself, but I'm warning you. Get Karyn out of there. She doesn't deserve to be embroiled in some messy scandal."

"What the hell makes you think I'd let that happen?"

"Because some sleazy tabloid guy is hot on your trail. That's how Frank found out in the first place. The guy called here looking for dirt. I don't know exactly what he said, but it was enough to send Frank rampaging out of here. I've never seen him so furious."

"Thanks for the warning. I'll take care of it on this end."

"Don't thank me yet. I have a few questions about all of this, too. I'd just rather ask them when everyone's calm and rational."

Another dragon to slay, Brad thought as he hung up the phone. The timing, however, was lousy.

"Who was it?" Karyn asked.

"It wasn't anything for you to worry about."

"But you said something about my being here."

"It was just the concierge," he improvised quickly. "He wanted to know about breakfast."

She regarded him skeptically. "If that's all it was, why are you pulling on your clothes as if the demons of hell are snapping at the door?"

Brad leaned down and kissed her. "Stop worrying. I'll be back in a minute."

"You have to go downstairs to discuss breakfast? It's not even dinner time."

He cursed himself for not being more inventive. He should have known she'd have a million questions about any excuse that flimsy. He tried another deep, drugging kiss. "Back in a minute," he said when she was breathless. He was out the door before she could react.

Puzzled, Karyn stared after him. Something very odd was going on, something Brad clearly didn't want her to know about. It wasn't until she heard the sound of raised voices that she figured out exactly what it was. Her brothers! Dear God, how had they found out? More important, why hadn't Brad told her? She had every right to know that her family was on the warpath. The very last thing she needed or wanted was another man intent on taking care of her. She had just barely gained her independence.

Not waiting for the battle to escalate into the crashing sound of flying furniture, she jumped out of the bed and began yanking on her clothes. She was still hopping on one foot, trying to get her other leg into her jeans, when Brad returned. He was wearing a very self-satisfied masculine smirk. If she'd had any strength left after their love-making, she'd have smacked it off his face. Instead, she gave one final tug on her jeans, slid the zipper up and faced him squarely. In her bare feet, she barely reached his chin. She had to look up to glare at him properly.

"My, my," Karyn began scathingly, "That was some argument. Couldn't you agree on whether or not to poach the eggs?"

She caught a first flicker of doubt on Brad's face. "You heard?"

"Not everything, but enough to guess that my brothers were here. I'm amazed you're in one piece."

"They're not unreasonable men, Karyn."

"Are you sure you're talking about *my* brothers?" she said incredulously.

"That's who they said they were. Frank and Jared."

"Oh, God," she moaned. Even though she'd known it, she'd been hoping against hope that she'd been wrong. "Then they were here?"

"Oh, yes. They were definitely here. Actually, Jerry had held them at bay for five or ten minutes before I even came downstairs. The man's so discreet, I doubt if he'd admit to a fire if he thought the arrival of the firemen would compromise a guest's privacy."

"Then why on earth didn't you just come back upstairs and let him handle them?"

"Because they were not buying Jerry's story for one second. Frank already had one foot on the first floor landing and Jared was holding Jerry three inches off the floor. I figured there wasn't a door in the place that was safe until they found their baby sister."

"So, what did you tell them?"

"That I was in love with you."

Even as her pulse leaped, her common sense kicked in. "How dare you tell them something like that?" she shouted. "Don't you get it? Now they'll expect you to marry me."

"No problem. I told them we were working out the details."

Karyn buried her face in her hands. "I will never hear the end of this. They'll track you, Brad. They'll make you go through with it. They'll camp outside your office door at the car dealership. You'll never be able to show your face there again."

He grinned. There still wasn't the slightest evidence of anxiety. "Then you'll just have to make an honest man of me, won't you? What would you think of an August wedding? For that matter, we could fly to Las Vegas tonight. How about it?"

Something snapped inside her at his presumption. Not only had he marched off to fight her family war for her, now he'd backed her into a corner. "What kind of proposal is that?" she raged.

"I was *trying* to propose when Timmy called," he reminded her calmly.

"That's not the point. Dammit all, Brad Willis, can't you see that you're just as bad as my brothers? You haven't once given me credit for being able to make up my own mind about things. I've spent my whole life letting other people fight my battles for me, make the decisions about what's best. Not this time. I'll be damned if I'll jump from the proverbial frying pan into the fire."

She picked up her purse and with one final, furious scowl in Brad's direction, she yanked open the door.

"Karyn," he said quietly. She turned back and saw that he had stretched out on the bed, his back propped against the stack of pillows, his hands behind his head. "I wouldn't go down there quite yet, if I were you," he warned with lazy nonchalance.

Karyn regarded him warily, trying to decide if he was honestly warning her or attempting to trick her into staying. He sure as hell didn't seem to be taking her seriously. "Why not?"

"Because unless I miss my guess Frank and Jared are still planted in the parlor like a couple of giant redwoods."

With a heartfelt sigh, she closed the door slowly. "They're still down there?"

Brad nodded. "I don't think they trust me entirely." He didn't exactly sound broken up about it. He sounded more like a man who was confident of the eventual outcome of this mess.

Karyn wanted very badly to walk out on him, but if he was right about Frank and Jared—and he probably was—she needed to buy herself some time. She looked around for a place to sit. There was only the bed and Brad was occupying a rather intimidating portion of that. She perched on the side as far from him as she could.

"Are you staying?"

"Only until the coast is clear."

He shifted his body until he was sitting next to her, thighs touching. "How about we put the time to good use?"

Every nerve in her body leaped to life at the contact and at the seductive tone of his voice, but she wasn't giving in. Not about this. "No, Brad," she said. Her voice was firm, but she didn't dare meet his gaze. Those green eyes of his could be her undoing. "I am waiting here just long enough to avoid some sort of public scene with my brothers. Then I am going and you and I will never see each other again."

"You don't mean that," he said, but there was the tiniest hint of uncertainty in his voice.

"I do mean it. I do not need somebody to fight my battles for me, Brad. I do not need somebody to support me or take care of me. All I ever wanted was someone who'd love me."

"But I do love you."

"That's not love, Brad. That's smothering. I ought to know. I've lived with it all my life."

Because she couldn't bear the confused, hurt expression in his eyes one single second more, she got up and walked away. Whatever the consequences might be of encountering her brothers downstairs, they couldn't be any worse than sitting here with a man she loved after discovering that he didn't know the meaning of the word.

Karyn had thought her pain couldn't possibly get any worse, but it did. Her brothers had left the lobby of the hotel, but as she emerged, she ran smack into the man who'd gotten her into this mess in the first place. A rumpled, but extraordinarily persistent photographer was waiting at curbside. Lazing against the fender of a car, he was instantly alert at the sight of her. He snapped several shots before Karyn realized what was happening.

It was the final straw. She slung her purse as hard as she could, hitting the man upside the head, then took off down the hill toward Fillmore at a run. She was almost at the bottom when she heard a familiar shout.

"Karyn," Frank yelled from his car. "Get in here!"

She whirled on him. "I think I've been rescued quite enough for one day. Just go home!"

She began walking again, the car creeping alongside. "Come on, sis," Jared pleaded. "I know you're upset, but we were just trying to protect you."

"You have no right to interfere in my life. None. I am twenty-six years old. If you all would get on with the business of living your own lives, maybe I could live mine. Now go away. I want to be by myself."

"What about Willis?"

"You don't have to worry about him anymore. He's as bad as the rest of you. I just finished telling him off, too. I trust that makes you happy. You've done your duty. The relationship is over."

She glanced sideways just long enough to see an exchange of guilty looks flash between her brothers. It gave her a fleeting instant of satisfaction before she dashed across the street behind them and caught a bus going in the opposite direction. She didn't really care where it was going. Just about any place today was going to feel like hell.

Chapter Eight

How in the name of everything holy were you supposed to prove your love to a maddening woman like Karyn Chambers? The question had reverberated though Brad's head so often since his return to Los Angeles, he thought he was going nuts. What had he done that was so terrible? He'd tried to protect her from her brothers' wrath, tried to shield her from embarrassment. She'd reacted as if he'd committed a crime.

For days he paced through the LA car dealership, in and out of his office and around his house muttering under his breath about women who didn't know the first thing about accepting love. Then he finally tried putting himself in her shoes. While Karyn struck him as being an innocent in need of protection, she saw herself as a woman in desperate need of asserting her independence. She was still trying to prove to herself—and her brothers—that she could stand on her own two feet. His actions, well-intentioned as they'd been, had knocked her feet right back out from under her.

Brad was used to fighting fiercely for what he wanted, charging after it with everything that was in him. He hadn't won races by being cautious. He'd won them by taking chances, by wanting them so badly that no risk seemed too great. He wanted Karyn Chambers. He needed every stubborn, feisty inch of her. She'd snagged a part of his heart that had been lonely and untouched for a very long time. Every fiber of his being wanted to roar back up the California coast and claim her.

But some gut instinct told him that would be exactly the wrong thing to do with Karyn. She didn't need to be pressured right now. She needed to work through what had happened between them and reach her own conclusions about the depth of their love. He vowed to wait, to maintain his distance, while she did exactly that.

He had no doubts, none at all, about the eventual outcome. He only hoped he wouldn't go mad in the interim.

The clear, color picture on the front page of the tabloid showed a startled, wide-eyed woman emerging from a familiar San Francisco hotel. A second photo was a close-up of Brad's face. As she stood in the check-out line, Karyn felt a moment of sick uncertainty before she realized that she was the woman who appeared above the headline: Hot Driver Brad Willis Races Toward New Love.

The story below added the lurid details, including Brad's complete and seemingly endless list of romantic conquests, her name and occupation and the recent discovery of their love nest at the Pacific Heights hotel. "Is this the lady who finally lured Brad Willis away from fast cars?" the newspaper asked. "Karyn Chambers might be beautiful, but can she compete with his Porsche? Others have tried, but none have succeeded."

They made it sound like some tawdry competition. *Love nest!* The very phrase left her trembling and feeling sick to her stomach. It was bad enough that she'd made a fool of herself over the domineering jerk, but now the whole world knew about it.

After putting the paper back on the rack, Karyn turned and walked out of the store, leaving behind a shopping cart filled with frozen low-cal meals and three pints of chocolate-crunch ice cream. The dinners had been for her conscience. The ice cream had been a futile attempt to fill the void that Brad's departure had left in her life.

He'd only been gone for a few days and already she was lonelier than she'd ever been in her entire life. He hadn't called, not even once. Though she'd been the one to break things off, she regretted it hourly as the minutes dragged by and she missed hearing the sound of his voice. Maybe if she'd been wiser in the ways of love, she'd have recognized what they had sooner. Maybe she'd have fought harder to work things out, rather than running at the first hint of trouble. Brad's actions might have been wrong, but she was a coward.

For one fleeting second she was almost tempted to go back for that awful newspaper just so she could stare at Brad's picture. Though her memory was good, it didn't capture him as vividly as that sleazy photographer had. Even she was able to recognize the irony in that. As for her own pictures, they had remained in the camera that Brad had nabbed from her while they were on their balloon ride.

Still dazed by the discovery that love didn't vanish immediately upon the arrival of disillusionment, Karyn was even more confused at finding herself a media celebrity. She walked slowly home, her thoughts in turmoil. At her apartment she was greeted by the sound of the phone ringing and the sight of the light on her answering machine blinking insistently. Incapable of dealing with either until she'd sorted out her thoughts, she ignored both and sank down on the sofa.

"Now what?" she murmured. How was she going to live down this latest fallout from her brief affair with Brad? The law firm had been supportive and lenient during her long struggle to complete the training to become a paralegal, but it was a staid, old organization. Seeing her picture by every grocery store checkout stand was not something her bosses would condone. The partners didn't even like to take divorce cases in which they expected a lot of dirty laundry would be aired publicly.

As for her brothers, she had no doubt at all that once one of them had spotted the report, they'd begin pestering her all over again about moving back home. She wouldn't be surprised if they personally packed her bags for her or at the very least permanently locked the hinges on her fold-out bed.

One thing was certain, she wasn't going home again. If she had to find another job, so be it. Nothing was going to make her regret her week with Brad. He had opened new worlds and no matter who tried to turn that into something dirty and capricious, she knew better. She believed in her heart that what they had shared was a kind of love, fleeting perhaps, but love nonetheless. If only he hadn't been so overly protective. If only she'd listened to his explanations. If only he'd fought harder to overcome her doubts.

There were those two sad words again—*if only*.

The rattling of the doorknob warned her that the family onslaught was about to begin. There was no place to run, so she sat right where she was and waited. She refused to help by getting up and opening the door.

Fortunately, it was Tim, who came in holding a copy of the paper.

"Hi," she said in a flat tone.

"I take it you've seen this," he said.

"I've seen it."

"Frank is going to blow a fuse."

"I don't doubt it."

"And Mom. What is she going to think?"

At that moment the doorknob twisted again and Karyn's mother came in. If she'd worked to learn her cue, she couldn't have timed the entrance any more effectively. Only the worried furrow between her brows indicated that she was troubled. Her smile was as bright as ever as she sat next to Karyn and wrapped her arms around her.

"Are you okay, Karyn Marie?" she said, studying her intently.

"Fine, Mom. I assume you didn't just drop in. You've seen the paper."

"Mrs. Murtaugh brought it by."

"I'm sorry."

"Don't you be sorry, baby. That old woman's nothing but a busybody. I'm not one bit concerned about what she thinks. I'm just worried about you. Timmy, go make a pot of coffee, while your sister and I talk."

"But—"

"Go. And make it a big one. I expect the others will be here before long."

When Tim had gone into the kitchen area, Karyn's mother laid a work-roughened hand against her cheek. "You in love with this man?"

"Yes," she admitted, relieved to have it out in the open at last. "It doesn't make much sense, though, does it?"

"Whoever said anything about love making sense? The one thing I do know is that those special feelings aren't something you turn your back on."

"But he's *exactly* like Frank and the others. He thinks I need looking after."

"And that's so bad?"

"I want to be on my own, be my own woman, make my own decisions."

"Don't you think he'd let you do that? There's a big difference between caring what happens to you and taking over your life. A man who cares too much, why he might make a mistake every now and then and push too hard, but it's usually in the name of love. That's not control, Karyn Marie. Not by a long shot. Maybe the very first decision you ought to make to prove you're all grown-up is whether you really want this man enough to fight for him. Now why don't you tell me about him."

Despite herself, Karyn found that she was eager to talk about Brad, anxious to say his name aloud, to pour out everything to a sympathetic ear. "Actually, we just met," she began.

"When?"

"A couple of weeks ago," she admitted sheepishly.

"Oh, my."

"Exactly."

She patted Karyn's hand. "Well, never you mind about that. Where is this Brad Willis now?"

"Back in Los Angeles, I guess."

"Is he coming back?"

"I don't know. I haven't talked to him."

"Oh, my."

"No, it's not what you think. I told him I didn't want to talk to him. I told him I couldn't love a man who wanted to run my life the way my brothers always have."

As if on cue again, the entire Chambers part of the world descended en masse, led by a scowling Frank. Before he could say a word, though, Tim asked, "Coffee everyone?"

"Beer," Frank corrected tersely, sitting down and eyeing Karyn as if she'd grown two heads.

"Don't you dare sit in judgment on me, Frank Chambers," Karyn snapped. "Did I interfere in your life when you got involved with that two-timing little tramp from Oakland? Have I said one word about the fact that it's taken you five years to get around to proposing to Megan, even though she's head over heels in love with you and actually thinks you're the smartest, handsomest man on the face of the earth? Have I? And what about you, Jared? Do I tell you how to live your life?''

''It's not the same,'' Frank grumbled.

''No, it's not,'' Jared agreed. ''You're our—''

''Don't you dare finish that,'' she ordered. ''I am no longer your *baby* sister. I am no longer a baby. I am a woman and I may make a few mistakes now and then, but they're mine to make.''

''You have to admit, sis, this one's a doozy,'' Tim said gently as he handed her a cup.

''Et tu, Brute?'' she said, flashing him a hurt look.

''Sorry, but it's the truth. Maybe if I hadn't warned Brad—''

Shocked eyes turned on him. ''*You* warned him?'' Frank said, aghast.

''Warned him about what?'' her mother asked.

''Yes,'' Timmy said defiantly to Frank. ''I told him you were playing outraged father of the year. I didn't see any need for Karyn to be embarrassed.''

''Well, maybe if she'd been a little more embarrassed last weekend, her picture wouldn't have been right up there beside Cher's today.'' Frank looked ready to explode. ''Good God, Timmy, what were you thinking of?''

''Will one of you explain?'' their mother ordered.

Karyn shrugged. ''They found out I was with Brad last weekend and they came charging over to rescue me. Only Timmy called and warned us and Brad went down to meet them without telling me they were coming, which is why I got mad and left him.''

''He *lied* to us,'' Jared interjected indignantly. ''Let's not forget that the man told us a bald-faced lie. You were obviously upstairs when we were there. It wasn't an hour later when we found you running down the street.''

"I think whatever Brad told you was justified under the circumstances," Karyn countered, just as the door opened and the man in question walked through. Her heart did an untimely somersault in her chest. Despite everything, she was very glad to see him. She figured if she showed it, though, Brad would be lynched before he could cross the room to kiss her. That was really too bad, too. She could have used one of his kisses about now. They still had a lot of talking to do, a lot to work out, but this time she wasn't going to run away from it. This time she was going to behave like a woman who knew exactly what she wanted from life.

Frank and Jared were already on their feet. Her mother looked slightly dazed by the tall, handsome man who was regarding her daughter with a passionate gleam in his eyes. Timmy took a protective step closer to her.

"What do you want, Willis?" Frank demanded.

Brad met his gaze evenly. "To see your sister. We need to talk."

"She doesn't want to see you," Jared said.

"I can speak for myself," Karyn interrupted firmly.

"Well, you don't want to see him, do you?" Daniel said, speaking out for the first time and taking a defiant step toward Brad. He balled his hands into fists at his sides.

"Yes, I do want to see him," Karyn said. As she looked at the shocked faces turned toward her, her stomach rolled over, but she insisted, "Privately, please."

Her mother regarded her intently, then nodded in satisfaction. Apparently she saw something that no one else in the room saw, including her daughter. Karyn just wanted to be alone with the man behind the chaos in her life.

"Come on, everyone," her mother insisted. "It's time we get out and leave these two alone. They have things to talk about that are none of our concern."

"I am not leaving her alone with him," Frank said.

Her mother reached over and grabbed him by the ear, oblivious to the ridiculous picture it presented. "Out! Now!" she ordered. "The rest of you, too."

"Thanks, Mom," Karyn said, giving her a hug.

"Just remember what we talked about. Don't worry about what makes sense. Just worry about doing what feels right."

"You can't be serious," Jared blustered, just as his mother latched on to his arm and yanked him toward the door.

"Nice to meet you, young man," Mrs. Chambers said politely. "Don't mind this troupe. Sometimes they just don't have sense enough to know when to butt out."

"I appreciate your help," Brad said.

"Don't be fooled," she retorted. "Right now, I'm on your side. Hurt my girl, and I'll be the first one to load a shotgun."

Brad grinned. "I'll keep that in mind."

While everyone was getting out, Karyn went into the kitchen area and poured herself another cup of coffee. She held up the pot and gestured toward Brad.

"Please," he said, then took the cup she held out for him. "Are you coming back in here or are you going to hide behind the counter?"

"I think I'll stay right here," she said, refusing to be taunted.

"Coward."

"I think I have every right to be a little cautious with a man who apparently changes women more often than he changes shirts."

"That's overstating things a bit, don't you think?"

"I wouldn't know. All I know is what I read in the papers."

"I may be a great defender of freedom of the press, but that doesn't mean those particular rags have much interest in accuracy. Besides, I never pretended to be a saint prior to our meeting."

"But now you've gone and sprouted the wings of an angel?"

"No, sweetheart, I'm only a man. There have been a lot of times in my life when I've been a very lonely man. Relationships have helped to fill the empty hours."

"And is that what I was doing, filling the empty hours? You had a few days off and didn't want to spend them alone?"

"You know better than that. I had to turn a few things upside down and backward to get that time off. I thought it was worth it to get to know you."

"Was it?"

He smiled for the first time since he'd walked into the apartment and Karyn felt something shift inside her, making the way for the first ray of hope that he wanted to work things out as badly as she did.

"You know it was," he said. "I fell in love with you. I thought I was going to teach you a lesson, that I was going to bring a new perspective on living into your life. Instead, you're the one who taught me. I learned something about loyalty and loving that will make all the difference in the rest of my life."

"Glad to be of service," she said dryly. "Should I charge for this lesson?"

"You won't be giving it again, except to me. Marry me, Karyn. I swore I wasn't going to come back here and pressure you, but I couldn't stand being apart another day."

"If you hadn't come, I would have come after you," she admitted.

"You would have?"

"I finally realized what I was thinking of giving up. I couldn't do it. Not without talking things out, at least."

"You want to talk now?"

She nodded, never taking her eyes from his.

"Okay. I understand why you blew up at me for taking over and trying to handle things with your brothers. I promise it will never happen again. It's just that you're so much more innocent, so much less jaded than other women I've known, it brings out a protective streak in me. I guess I've always wanted to be a dragon slayer for someone."

"I can slay my own dragons," she said quietly. "And even when I can't, that doesn't mean I want you to step in and do it for me."

"I'll try to remember that. I really will, but I don't know if I'll ever be able to sit by and let you be hurt, not if there's anything in my power that I can do to stop it."

In a way Brad's promise seemed only to bring them to a stalemate. "I'm not sure I'll be able to recognize the difference," Karyn admitted. "I'm so scared of becoming dependent on you for my happiness, of taking the easy way out and letting you do things for me."

"I have a feeling you'll never hesitate to tell me when I'm getting out of line. You're stronger than you think. You walked out on me, didn't you? Even though you wanted to stay."

The hint of masculine self-confidence grated. "You're awfully sure of yourself."

"I'm sure of what we feel," he corrected. "Even your mother could see it. That's the only reason she left you here alone with me."

Karyn sighed. "Despite everything she's been through, my mother appears to be an incurable romantic."

"So am I," Brad said. "I believe with all my heart that we have the makings of a forever love. That's why I came back." He grinned ruefully. "That and the fact that my father swore he'd wind up having another heart attack if he had to watch me pacing around the office much longer."

"Your father's back at work?"

"Part-time. Long enough for us to go on a honeymoon, in fact."

"But we've just had a vacation." As soon as she uttered the mild protest, Karyn knew that what she'd really said was *yes* . . . to their love, to working on their problems together, to marriage, to a honeymoon filled with long, lazy hours in Brad's arms.

"Consider that practice," he said, stepping closer until she could feel the whisper of his breath on her cheek. "This time we'll do it for real."

"You could take me to Paris or Greece or Tahiti, but you will never give me a more romantic vacation than the one we just had," she murmured as she found herself back in his arms, her head resting against his chest.

"Then we'll stay home for our honeymoon. I'm not choosy. As long as you marry me. Will you?"

"I will," Karyn said with absolute certainty.

Her acceptance was captured and stolen by Brad's kiss. As their breath mingled and their hearts pounded, Karyn had second thoughts.

"Maybe I spoke too soon," she murmured against his marauding mouth.

"Oh?"

"I think Paris would be a fine idea."

"No problem," Brad said, nibbling on her lower lip.

"And maybe Greece."

"Whatever you want."

"And I've always wanted to see the place where Gauguin painted all those wonderful pictures."

"Tahiti. Absolutely, if that's what you want."

Karyn sighed happily. "Let's not leave just yet, though."

"Okay, when?"

"I ought to be ready to leave this bed right here in another five or ten years."

* * * * *

Sherryl Woods

Romance writer. I think of the label some days and wonder exactly how it came to be. This was not the road I set out to travel on. As with most lives, however, the twists and turns of getting here have been far more fascinating than the straight path I'd set out to take.

I was one of the few people I knew at Ohio State University back in the turbulent sixties who knew exactly what she wanted to be when I walked into my freshman dormitory: a journalist. Ironically, even then I harbored no particular desire to write. I wanted to design the pages of a newspaper. It was the closest I could come to art with no artistic skills.

However, sometime between the freshman dream and graduation, I discovered that a journalist could poke into the most interesting facets of life, changing focus from one day to the next. It was a tantalizing discovery for someone whose curiosity about the quirks of human nature is never satisfied. As a general assignment reporter, I covered a heart transplant in a frog conducted by a high school science class one morning, and suburban zoning regulations the following night. I reported on the launch of *Apollo XI* to the moon one day and worked a police beat the next night. In my spare time, I did movie and nightclub reviews.

The discovery that I could be paid to be entertained was a major turning point. The realization that I could be on the fringes of a fascinating industry without having to get on a stage myself was too great a lure to ignore. I became a television critic, first in Palm Beach, then back in Columbus, Ohio, and finally in Miami. For ten years I made regular trips to Los Angeles and New York to interview stars and talk to network executives. I watched more hours of television—from the sublime to the absurd—than the most committed couch potato. I loved it.

And then I discovered romance novels. Always an avid reader, I found something special in these books. Perhaps it was the thrill of adventure. It might have been the consistently happy endings. Most likely it was their ability to capture that magical instant when two people discover that fate has meant for them to be together. I wanted to tell stories like that.

I took nine months off to try. I wrote two manuscripts and a proposal for a third book. I sent them off. And then I got a job, this time working at the University of Miami/Jackson Memorial Medical Center. I began a whole new phase of my life. I wrote copy for the employee newsletter. I wrote about the hospital's challenges and commitments in the annual report. And then I took over a unique position designed to motivate and solve the work-related problems of the nearly eight thousand employees and physicians in the Medical Center. It was one of the most frustrating, demanding and rewarding jobs imaginable. I loved it.

However, along the way a publisher bought my first book. And my second and third and on and on. I became a romance writer. After nearly five years of attempting to combine both careers, I had to make a choice. You know which one I made.

Perhaps the most intriguing aspect of all has been the realization that so many vastly different roads can answer the needs of the soul. The road now seems straight. If there's a twist ahead, I can't see it.

But I anticipate the possibility.

EASY COME...

Patricia Coughlin

A Note from Patricia Coughlin

The best-laid plans of mice and men often go astray. I'm sure there are people in this world who don't know that—no doubt *their* vacations always proceed exactly according to plan, without last-minute crises. Fortunately, I'm not one of them, and I have the snapshots, family jokes and treasured memories to prove it.

Among my most vivid childhood recollections is a family picnic somewhere in Maryland. All seven of us had piled into the station wagon at dawn for the drive from Rhode Island to Washington, D.C. Many hours, a New York City traffic jam, and a wrong turn later we searched for a place away from the highway to eat lunch. Not until we had nearly finished our sandwiches did my sister Kathie notice—and point out—that the reason the quiet, peaceful road we'd discovered was so quiet and peaceful was that it ran through a cemetery!

Mention Lake Winnipesaukee and I remember the time my sister Debby and I begged to take the rowboat out for a quick spin before getting ready for an air show the family was to attend later. Naturally, our "quick spin" spun out too long, and in our frenzy to head back, we got stranded directly in the path of what looked like an oceanliner. I don't remember much about the air show, but I'll never forget that rowboat ride!

My husband, Bill, and I have continued this time-honored tradition . . . starting with our honeymoon in Jamaica.

Our travel agent was unable to book us a room in the hotel of our choice—the one with the glossy brochure depicting waterfalls in the lobby and bar stools in the pool—but once we arrived on the island, we discovered a room was available there, after all. However, our accommodations were part of a package deal; changing them required a great deal of trouble, paperwork and—although we didn't know it beforehand—a ride through Montego Bay in a bus that carried not only locals and naive honeymooners, but also livestock. Noisy, smelly livestock...

Was it worth it? You bet. I planned on having only one honeymoon, and I'd had my heart set on sipping piña coladas on one of those underwater bar stools. Bill, bless him, understood... even when all that sipping led to a sunburn.

Fourteen years after the honeymoon, we're the parents of two sons, Billy, ten, and Ryan, eight. A couple of summers ago, in direct defiance of common sense, we accepted an invitation to go camping with my brother and his family. Experienced campers smirked when we told them we'd be renting a pop-up trailer, informing us that that wasn't "real camping." Perhaps not, but it's as close as I ever hope to get...

For weeks ahead of time we planned, we organized, we checked and double-checked our lists. Finally we were off—smack in the middle of a record-breaking heat wave that made the Maine campground hotter than Miami. Almost as bad as the heat were the afternoon downpours. Hot and wet is an ugly combination when there's a long dirt road between you and the bathroom....

Maybe, during a good week in the right spot, camping might be as clean and comfortable as it looks in the L.L. Bean catalog. And just maybe, as my brother Tom insists, those fist-sized bugs hovering in the shower stall each morning were not mosquitoes. But no one will ever convince *me* of it. And, although no one will ever convince me to go camping again, either, I wouldn't trade my memories of that horrible, fun-filled week for anything.

When it came time for me to write a story for the *Silhouette Summer Sizzlers*, it never occurred to me to give Merrill Winters and Win Deverell what I've never had: a perfect, trouble-free vacation. I liked them way too much. I knew that, in the end, they'd have a lot more fun my way. I enjoyed watching them making the best of a bad situation—and falling in love along the way. I hope you do, too.

Best,

Patricia Coughlin

Friday, 3:37 p.m.

It was a split second decision that had been months in the making. The very notion was so implausible it was laughable, maybe even impossible, and, therefore, to Win Deverell, an absolutely irresistible challenge.

Leaning back in his chair, he eyed Merrill Winters across the long mahogany conference table and pretended to be engrossed in the technical jargon of her presentation. "Exclusions . . . aggregate . . . limits . . . self-insured retentions." Riveting stuff. What really held Win spellbound were his own thoughts. He turned the idea over in his mind, examining it from every angle and warming to it more and more.

In the three months since he'd been forced to take full control of Haigh and Deverell Marine Claim Services, he'd felt a number of urges toward the prim, ever-efficient Ms. Winters, the most prominent being the urge to strangle her. This new impulse, though, was something entirely different. Win suspected the idea had been simmering in the back of his mind for quite a while, and he wasn't entirely certain what had brought it to such a full, rolling boil this afternoon.

Outside, the Fourth of July weekend was getting off to a fine start. The afternoon was hot and sunny and so perfect for sailing he could close his eyes and feel salt spray instead of air conditioning, could feel polished wood decking beneath his feet instead of pricy Persian carpet. Wishful thinking. Lately his only glimpse of such perfect days was what filtered through the fashionably narrow blinds on his office windows. The sheer monotony of this week-long business trip to Providence might account for his sudden inspiration.

Or it might be the result of something more subtle, like the intriguing blend of silk blouse, tailored suit jacket and soft, soft skin he had been staring at all day, every day for the past week. For him, staring at Merrill had been the one bright spot in these snail-paced negotiating sessions.

She was tall for a woman, maybe four inches shorter than his own six feet. Tall enough to look him squarely in the eye if she lifted her chin and wore high heels—both of which she was wont to do. Her hair was a shade he couldn't name. Blond, he supposed, and yet so far from that common-place description that he never tired of looking at it. Merrill's hair made him think of apricots, honey and silk. It glistened in the sunlight and would probably look softer and more touchable if she'd only find herself a new hairstyle.

Now that he took a closer look, it occurred to him that raw potential was something Merrill had in spades. Behind the shield of her oversize dark-rimmed glasses, her face was delicate and animated, beneath the armor of those severe business suits her body was curvaceous and inviting. In fact, if she were to loosen up a little she might not be half bad to be around.

As it was, personality flaws and all, she wasn't too hard to look at in any situation. When she was the only woman in the room she was downright mesmerizing.

Merrill presented a classic mystery, one that had been driving men crazy since time began. Win was no exception. On the surface she was all cool control, but at odd moments he caught glimmers of something else, something suppressed. A look, a smile, a flash of awareness in her eyes that suggested a deeply sensual nature. He sometimes thought she wasn't at all aware of this, and sometimes he was absolutely certain she was. Experience at sea had taught him to beware of the dangerous currents often lurking beneath a placid surface, yet he couldn't help wondering what sort of currents moved beneath the self-possessed surface of Ms. Winters.

Boredom, hormones, curiosity—a potent combination to be sure. Then again, maybe it was none of those. Maybe what his third-grade teacher used to say about him was still true: he just couldn't resist stirring up trouble. Whatever the catalyst for the idea, there it was, full-blown and utterly irresistible. Someday soon he was going to seduce Merrill Winters.

Friday, 3:42 p.m.

As Merrill spoke, she frequently reminded herself to make eye contact with each of the ten men sitting around the table. And to speak slowly. And to occasionally punctuate her remarks with a confident, but never giddy, smile. Remembering to smile was the hardest part. Just to be on the safe side, she threw one in now.

Devising settlement proposals for marine insurance claims and then pitching them to skeptical, sometimes hostile attorneys was her job, and she was very good at it. Stick a cocktail in her hand and plop her down in the middle of a social gathering and chances were she would fumble and become tongue-tied, but here, in a business situation, armed with a calculator and an insurance manual as thick as the New York Yellow Pages, she was eminently capable. She knew exactly what to say and when to say it and, equally important, what not to say. Eight years of hard work and experience had given her a sixth sense that served her well in high-pressure negotiations.

Right now her sixth sense was telling her it was going to take a miracle to settle this claim today. Soon she would have to excuse herself to catch her flight—or take her chances getting a seat on a later one. Given that this was a holiday weekend, those chances would be slim at best. This claim had been dragging on for months, and the only thing Merrill wanted more than to settle it was to begin her vacation according to plan...by sipping something tall, cool and tropical on the 7:10 flight to Jamaica.

So, she decided, doing her best to follow the exchange taking place between two of the attorneys, she would have to produce a miracle. Not for the first time in the three months since Ted Haigh had left the company, she wished he were around to help.

Nodding in agreement with a point made by one of the men, Merrill allowed her gaze to wander in the direction of Win Deverell's impeccably—if inappropriately—clad body. She instantly dismissed all hope of his being any help. Insurance tradition dictated dark suits and light-colored shirts, but more often than not Win got that twisted. In dress, as in everything else, he bent rules like pretzels and somehow got away with it.

Like right now, for instance. Physically he was present, but his thoughts were somewhere else. A casual observer might not notice it, but to Merrill's disgust, she had sunk to being anything but a casual observer of Win Deverell.

She tried telling herself it wasn't her fault, that all the women at Haigh and Deverell found Mr. Winston Robert Deverell fascinating. Certainly more fascinating than plain-looking, dependable Ted Haigh, Win's former partner and her former boss, who was now off somewhere in Alaska in search of youth and adventure and who knows what else.

The fact that she wasn't the only one interested in Win didn't make her any happier. She felt she ought to know better. Hadn't she seen through him from day one? Hadn't she resolved never to be charmed by him, never to be amused, never to give an inch? It wasn't easy. Win Deverell was charming and amusing. And sexy.

Sexy, not to be confused with handsome. His face could best be described as interesting, inspiring questions about the small nick at the inside corner of his right eyebrow and another longer scar on his jaw. At least it inspired questions in Merrill. Questions she'd bite her tongue off before asking.

Long hours in the sun had left him with a deep tan and creases that on anyone else she would describe as character lines. The tan made his unusual eyes appear even more arresting. They were pale green with charcoal-colored flecks, and he had a way of focusing them on a woman that was so distracting she might not immediately notice his body. Once she had, however, she wouldn't turn away in a hurry.

He had the sort of lean, hard-muscled body that would look more at home shirtless and sweaty and digging ditches than sitting behind a desk. Yet Merrill had never seen Win look anything but comfortable no matter where he was or whom he was with. It was one of the things that aggravated her most about him.

Just once she would like to see his self-confidence collapse. She might get her chance right now if she were to jar him from his daydream with a strategically-placed kick under the table. He was sitting directly across from her, his long legs encroaching on her space. She could do it so easily.

But she wouldn't.

For one thing, she was twenty-nine years old, too old for such childish antics. Also, while it appeared she no longer had a future with Haigh and Deverell, marine insurance was the only business she knew and—something most people found impossible to comprehend—she enjoyed it. One day she may have to face these same gentlemen across another conference table, and she wanted to be remembered for what she was—a mature, competent professional.

With that in mind, she sacrificed the satisfaction of kicking Win in the shins, settling instead for spearing him with her thorniest look of disapproval.

Her silent reprimand was not lost on Win. Though he'd been letting her words roll past like dandelion puffs in the wind, for some time now Merrill had succeeded in holding his undivided attention. He'd been watching with all new interest as she proceeded in her own organized, predictable, ordinarily guarantee-to-set-his-teeth-on-edge style. The look in her dark blue eyes was unwaveringly sober and earnest. Until it flicked to him.

The change that occurred when she glanced his way was concentrated in her eyes and so fleeting that it was likely no one else at the table even noticed, but Win knew that look. He knew it meant that she was aware of the fact that he wasn't listening to a word she was saying. Smart lady. In her own proper, understated way she was warning him to shape up, and his response was instinctive.

First, just to throw her off balance, he sat up in his seat as suddenly as if the icy darts she'd shot at him had been real. Then, he grinned.

Friday, 4:01 p.m.

The sight of his smile made Merrill's skin prickle with irritation, like an itch she couldn't scratch in public. It took
every ounce of self-control to continue addressing the group
in her most serene tone, when inside she was burning to tell
Win exactly what she thought of him...that he was the most
useless, irresponsible, absolutely unprincipled excuse for a
professional she had ever encountered.

Having achieved his objective, Win settled back in his seat
once again. Though his grin had not produced so much as
a ripple of annoyance in Merrill's smooth voice, he knew
he'd gotten to her. It was obvious in the way she squared her
shoulders as she flipped open the policy manual in front of
her. It came as no surprise to him that she took her time
consulting it before responding to a question put to her by
one of the attorneys. The cautious Miss Winters never risked
shooting from the hip.

The first time Win had provoked her into that same indignant reaction he had been startled, having been of the
opinion that the human spine couldn't get any stiffer than
hers was naturally. Since then, he had learned a hundred
different ways of rubbing Merrill Winters the wrong way,
often without having to say a word. Sometimes he didn't
even have to smile.

Three months was plenty long to find your way under
someone's skin, and in his own defense he had to say that
where he and Merrill were concerned it had been a two-way
trip. Before Ted took off, their contact had been limited, but

strained. These days their working relationship was one of mutual inconvenience, full of friction and best characterized by the sound of fingernails being dragged across a blackboard. The woman could be as irritating as hell.

Of course, he hadn't been his most charming, either. Much of the time he stalked around the office feeling ornery and frustrated. Ted's departure had put a definite cramp in his style by tethering him to a desk and a mountain of paperwork for which he had neither the temperament nor the taste.

The business had been Ted's brainstorm from the start. Win's best friend since high school, Ted had convinced Win it was the perfect way to combine the business acumen Ted had developed during his stint working for a national insurance company with Win's passion for boats. Haigh and Deverell Marine Claim Services had been founded eight years ago, when they were both twenty-eight, and had become a success because they'd adhered to a strict division of labor. Ted dealt with figures and shuffled papers and Win did all the legwork, the on-site boat inspections and appraisals.

When two ships collided in the middle of the night and someone had to eyeball the damage immediately, it was Win who got the wake-up call. When the IRS had questions, it was Ted who toiled around the clock to come up with the right answers. The arrangement worked perfectly until three and a half months ago when Ted's wife, Marjorie, left him for a twenty-two year old tennis pro at the country club, sending poor Ted into an instant midlife crisis.

Under the circumstances, Win didn't blame his friend for chucking everything and taking off. He understood . . . hell, right about now he envied him. Understanding, however, did not make him any happier about stepping into Ted's

shoes. Just last week he woke in a cold sweat from a nightmare in which the payrolls and billings and scores of other
tasks Ted had managed so effortlessly melded into an endless black sea that was slowly dragging him under.

The sad truth was that, although he was a full partner in
the business, he didn't know a statutory filing from a filing
system and he was beginning to crack under the constant
strain of pretending that he did. With Ted gone, there was
no one to whom he felt comfortable admitting his insecur-
ity, and so it swelled inside him until he felt if he didn't get
out of the office for a few days, he would go over the edge.
It was the morning after the nightmare that he'd decided to
accompany Merrill on this trip to Providence.

None of his troubles were her fault of course, but she
added to his annoyance because she seemed to thrive on all
the minutiae of this business that made his head spin. She
was the epitome of organized and alphabetized and priori-
tized. Sometimes on a Monday morning, after another
rough weekend when what he really wanted to do took a
back seat to his new responsibilities, just the sight of her
upswept hairdo, every strand glued in place, made his fingers itch to do damage. How would she respond, he suddenly found himself wondering, if he pulled out her hair
pins, took off her glasses, unbuttoned that choke chain-
collared blouse she was so partial to and . . .

He was gone again, thought Merrill, noticing his glazed
expression and the hint of a speculative smile at the corners
of his mouth. What sort of absurd fantasy could he possibly find so engrossing? By now nothing Win did surprised
her, and it certainly shouldn't upset her. But it did. She tried
not to think about it as she fumbled for an answer to the
question regarding policy limit put to her by Richard In-

graham, the attorney in whose plush office this meeting was being held.

Ingraham frowned as Merrill finished her explanation. "I understand all that, Ms. Winters, but it really doesn't address the point I raised."

As a man, Ingraham was all reptilian charm and capped teeth; as an attorney, he was crafty and tenacious. Merrill had known that from the start when he insisted on holding these negotiations on his turf. It was something she shouldn't have forgotten, and she wouldn't have, she told herself, if Win hadn't distracted her.

Concealing her irritation, she reached for the file containing her copies of pertinent policy sections. "To answer you in more detail, Mr. Ingraham, I'll have to check the actual wording of that section of the policy."

"Very well." Ingraham nodded impatiently as Merrill opened the folder and struggled to consolidate her thoughts. She couldn't resist sneaking a sideways glance at Win. Ted would have been right with her on this, but where Win was concerned, it seemed that when the going got tough she was on her own.

Why on earth had he insisted on accompanying her to these meetings in the first place if he was going to sleepwalk through them? Oh yes, to gather a little hands-on experience. Right. By playing games and then leaving her to take the heat. Well, not this time, Merrill decided impulsively. He'd wanted hands-on experience and she was going to give it to him. She hoped he'd brought along asbestos gloves.

Closing the three-inch-thick policy she'd been riffling through she turned to face him.

"I seem to have misplaced my copy of that particular policy section, Mr. Deverell," she announced apologetically. "May I trouble you for yours?"

If life had a sound effects department, there would have been the clash of raised swords at the instant their eyes met.

"No trouble, Ms. Winters." The cordial response poured from him as smoothly and easily as warm syrup.

As recently as two weeks ago she never would have dreamed of pulling a stunt like this. Win was still her boss, after all, and she put great stock in protocol. But two weeks ago she hadn't known about his secret plans for the company.

Straightening up, he reached for his hitherto untouched briefcase and bestowed upon her that wide, bright smile she knew had the power to melt the knees of office stenographers. *Smile away, Deverell*. It had been a long time since she'd been a stenographer, and she'd never been susceptible to smiles from men who were all style and no substance.

"What policy section was that again?" he asked her.

"Section WA1032," Merrill told him with sweet composure. She could afford to be sweet. This time she had him cornered.

"Let's see," he murmured, flipping open the dark leather case and examining the papers on top.

Stalling. Perhaps even sweating a little inside that expensive, dark gray cotton shirt. She loved it.

"1032 . . . 1032," he murmured. "Here you go."

It couldn't be. Merrill hadn't expected him to even recall the policy section, much less have a copy of it at hand. In fact, she wouldn't have been surprised if the only thing in his briefcase was the sports section from the morning paper. She snatched the sheet he held out to her and glared at the heading. WA1032.

Damn, he was lucky!

Damn, she was something!

Win had never before noticed how full her lips were. When she was ticked off, like now, she pursed them in a way that filled his mind with thoughts of all sorts of tactile adventures. That voice she'd used on him a minute ago didn't help to calm his imagination, either. One of these days, he promised himself, she was going to talk to him in a soft, sultry voice and mean it.

Somehow Merrill managed to formulate a satisfactory answer to Ingraham's question. Or so she thought until, with his brows beetled in consternation, the lawyer proceeded to ask her the same thing in different words. Before she could come up with a tactful response, Win amazed her by leaping to her defense.

"I believe Ms. Winters just explained the aggregate limit in complete detail."

"Perhaps to your satisfaction, Mr. Deverell, but I'm here to look after the best interests of my clients."

"Then do it," Win said quietly. "Right now all you're doing is spinning your wheels and wasting Ms. Winters's time."

Ingraham's thinning lips conveyed his shock at being addressed so bluntly. "Is that so? I was under the impression the insurance company your firm represents was interested in preventing this matter from going to trial. However, if my efforts in that direction are wasting your time, perhaps I shall have to pursue a court hearing after all."

"That would be a very foolish move," Win told him, his shoulders resting against the back of his chair, elbows on the padded leather arms, fingertips pressed lightly together. Although the expression in his eyes now was alert and sober, he didn't appear overly concerned about what was happening and that only alarmed Merrill further. "The settlement Ms. Winters has spent the greater part of this week explaining and amending, in deference to your many objections and requests, is a fair one. But if your clients want a court battle, that's their right."

"I realize, Mr. Deverell, that you're somewhat... ah...new as an active participant in negotiations of this sort." Ingraham's tone was balanced on the fine line between polite and confrontational. "So perhaps I should point out that the expense of a trial will greatly raise the final cost of this claim."

Win's eyes narrowed with hostile intensity. "I'm new, not ignorant."

"Then I'm sure you're also aware that if court-awarded damages exceed the policy limit, it could result in the seizure of the vessel."

The vessel in this case was the Hope Ferry which had been at fault in a collision with a fishing trawler. Lurching forward in his seat at the far end of the table, the attorney representing the ferry company glared at Merrill as if she were a ventriloquist and Win the dummy. She shot back a what-can-I-do? look, causing the man's face to turn purple, as if something were caught in his throat.

Her sixth sense was working overtime, scrambling to keep up with the undercurrents in the room. Within seconds the meeting had taken on the aura of a poker game. The papers scattered on the table might have been playing cards, the glasses filled with whiskey instead of ice water.

For nearly a full minute after Ingraham had delivered his thinly-veiled threat, the room was filled with a deafening silence. Merrill had no doubt that if this actually had been a poker game, Win would shatter that silence any second by unfurling a fan of aces. His expression was one of calm certitude and his voice, when he finally spoke, was as soft as distant thunder, with the same unmistakable power.

"Seize it," he said.

Merrill nearly leapt from her seat. *No, no, no,* she wanted to shout at him. *We're here to see that the vessel isn't seized.*

Again the silence. Awful and tight. At last Ingraham curled his lips into the semblance of a smile, displaying teeth as straight and even as ivory piano keys. "All right. If the proposal Ms. Winters presented is indeed your final offer, I will relay it as such to my clients." He paused before adding, "With my recommendation that they accept."

Merrill sagged in her seat, numb. Clients almost always followed the recommendations of their attorneys, and if Ingraham's clients agreed to the settlement she'd proposed, the other claimants would very likely follow suit. It was over...and it appeared her side had won. She'd gotten everything she wanted. The claim was settled, she would be able to make her flight with time to spare and enjoy her vacation without second thoughts about what she should have said or done during this meeting.

So why, instead of rejoicing, did she feel a peculiar blend of relief and amazement? The answer came to her through the resentment beginning to churn somewhere deep inside her. After weeks of her hard work and research, of compiling data and planning strategy, the entire matter had been reduced to a bluff, a reckless high-stakes game of chicken. A game orchestrated by Win Deverell, which, not surprisingly, he'd been lucky enough to win. That rankled.

The meeting wrapped up quickly. Soon everyone was standing, stretching stiff arms and legs and hurriedly sliding papers into briefcases. Merrill followed suit, but while the others broke into small groups, lingering to talk, she nodded perfunctorily to those nearby and followed a direct path to the door. Since Win had handled Ingraham single-handedly, surely he could handle the niceties the same way.

She closed the office door behind her with a single thought: she was free. Less than two hours from now she would be airborne and on her way to Jamaica for seven glorious days without any meetings to attend or reports to write or Win Deverell to worry about.

A new thought intruded, stretching like a late-afternoon shadow across her rapidly lifting spirits. When she returned, there would be plenty to worry about. She would have to make decisions and plans. Decisions and plans she desperately did not want to face. But that was still a whole week away, she reminded herself, doing her best to push the prospect from her mind. She hadn't had a real vacation in over a year, and starting now, she didn't intend to waste even a moment of this one.

Letting her mind drift to her plans for the week ahead she hurried along the crisscrossing corridors to the elevators. The huge office building seemed oddly deserted until Merrill remembered that since this was the start of the holiday weekend, most offices had closed early. She gave the elevator button a jaunty push and while waiting for it to make the long crawl to the top floor, she conjured up images of sun-soaked beaches, jewel-toned waters speckled with brightly striped sails, with her in the middle of it all.

Just thinking about getting away made her heart race with anticipation. She smiled to herself, suddenly recalling a raucous Pointer Sisters song about feeling excited and losing control and liking it. The melody filled her head and spilled over as she unconsciously began moving her feet in time to her own soft humming.

She was well into her impromptu dance solo when an amused, all too familiar voice somewhere behind her drawled, "Bon voyage."

Friday, 4:51 p.m.

Merrill froze.

She prayed the elevator would come to her rescue. Naturally it didn't. Finally she turned slowly to find Win standing—if you could call propping one shoulder against the wall for support standing—behind her.

The patiently speculative way he was watching her gave her a suffocating feeling. His tie was loosened, his top button undone, his mouth curled into quite possibly the most irritating smile he'd ever bestowed upon her. She wondered how long he'd been standing there, letting her make a fool of herself before saying anything, and decided that of course he had been there for quite awhile. This was Win after all.

"Why did you follow me out here?" she blurted out and immediately realized what a ridiculous question it was as he shot a glance at the elevator doors behind her.

"Impulse," he said dryly. "Usually I take the fire escape when I leave a building, or spin a web and lower myself to the ground, but today I decided to make an exception just so I could follow you to the elevator.

"That was supposed to be a joke," he said when she failed to respond.

"Oh."

"Why do I have the feeling you're not pleased with me?" he asked around a gritty chuckle.

"Probably because you've given me reason to tell you so every day for the past three months." She jabbed the elevator button again.

"I mean . . . even less pleased than usual. Usually it's just annoyance I sense, like when I use the wrong size brads on a file or screw up your diary notes. This, however, is serious hostility."

"You want to know why I'm hostile?" she demanded, as usual losing the battle against letting him provoke her. "I'm hostile because you jeopardized weeks of research and planning by trying to steamroller Ingraham into a settlement."

He shrugged. "It worked."

"It could just as easily have backfired."

"But it didn't."

"That's no reason..." She stopped with a grim-sounding laugh and shook her head. "No. No, I absolutely will not start off my vacation by getting into a sparring match with you. I refuse."

Turning her back to him, she willed the elevator to arrive. Though the plush carpeting muffled his footsteps, she could feel him closing in.

Win figured he had to move. It was in bad taste to continue standing behind her, visualizing the way she'd been swaying and bumping just a minute ago. Besides, no way would she do it again now that she knew he was watching. If he'd harbored any doubts at all about his plan, they'd been overridden by all the muscle-flexing that had gone on beneath her straight, snug skirt. She had the nicest, firmest, roundest . . . muscles he'd ever seen.

"You know, Mel," he began.

"I've told you not to call me that."

"Right, sorry. You know, Merrill, I'm glad you don't feel like sparring, because it's much too hot."

He loosened his tie another notch, drawing Merrill's attention to the suntanned length of his throat and the shadow of dark chest hair below, stirring unwelcome memories of a morning a few weeks ago when she had arrived at work early and walked in on him while he was washing up in the office bathroom.

It had been an extremely embarrassing moment. For her, not Win. He'd appeared totally unconcerned by whatever suspicions might arise in her mind at finding him in the office, bare-chested and soapy, at seven in the morning. He hadn't even bothered to turn around. He'd simply grinned at her in the mirror and said good morning.

Merrill wasn't sure what had shocked her more, finding him there half-dressed or the snarling red-and-black sea horse tattooed on his right shoulder. Without a word she'd slammed the door shut and retreated, putting his audacious grin firmly out of her mind. It hadn't been so easy to wipe away the memory of his sinewy, soap-slicked chest. Or that tattoo.

She hit the button again. Hard.

"So," he said, "you're off on vacation."

"That's right."

"I don't even know where you're going, which isn't really surprising since vacations fall into the forbidden realm of personal matters. I know how you feel about discussing personal matters during working hours."

"That's right," she said again, glancing at her watch. "Working hours which technically don't end for another six minutes."

"Maybe I'll get lucky and this will be a really slow elevator."

"Oh, I don't think there's ever been any question of your being lucky." She flicked him a pointed look, recalling the meeting that had just ended and other occasions lately when he had made dangerous professional leaps and had still managed to land on his feet.

He arched his brows as she reached in front of him to pump the elevator button. "I take it you're in a big hurry."

"More or less."

"You sure flew down that hallway in a big hurry."

Her eyes flashed. "So you did follow me."

"I already admitted I did."

"But you didn't tell me why."

"Would you believe me if I said I wanted to catch you before you left to apologize for the way I took over in there?"

"No."

He sighed. "I was afraid not."

"I would only believe you if you said you chased after me so you could gloat over how once again you managed to—"

"Snatch victory from the jaws of defeat?"

"And in the process you might easily have blown all my hard work. Not to mention—"

"Our hard work," he interjected softly.

"What did you say?"

"I said *our* hard work. My reports on the hull and the collision were good, Mel...Merrill, damn good. You've never said so, but I'm sure you're aware of it."

"So I'm aware of it. It's your job to be good. I could have hired an independent marine appraiser to do the same thing with a whole lot less aggravation."

"It's not just the reports. During the past three months I've done all I could to help you put that proposal together."

Merrill shrugged that off. A matter of perspective, she told herself, albeit a trifle uncomfortably. The fact was that she *could* have done it alone. In fact she would have preferred it that way. She could easily do without the teasing and bickering and clashes of work styles.

"I didn't notice you being much help this past week," she commented.

"Only because you made it clear after Monday's session that you would prefer to handle the actual negotiations yourself."

"I had no choice. It was obvious you still don't understand that there is a certain protocol for these meetings. There are things you say and things you don't say."

"You mean there are things *you* don't say. I call 'em like I see 'em."

"Which is precisely why I tried to keep you out of it. I didn't want to spend the entire week having to listen to you spout sports philosophy."

"I told one lousy sports story. And I was trying to make a point."

"Well, it was lost on me."

"That's not surprising. If something doesn't fit into one of your narrow little molds, it might as well not exist." His grin was cocky. "That's what really fries you about me, isn't it, Merrill? That I don't play the way you think I'm supposed to? That I don't get the job done by following the rules, but somehow I still manage to get it done?

She glared at him, and Win wondered how much more shocked and disapproving she would be if he admitted the truth, that much of the time he didn't follow the rules because he wasn't sure what they were.

"Your work habits don't bother me in the least," Merrill lied. "Except when they threaten one of my settlements. What bothers me is having to work with someone who thinks common sense and self-control are character flaws."

"I wouldn't say flaws exactly. I do think they can be overdone in some cases."

She chose to ignore the implication. "It also bothers me that you sleep through important settlement negotiations while I do all the work."

"I wasn't sleeping. I was thinking."

"About what?"

His grin softened to a silky, seductive smile. "You."

"Oh, please."

"Please tell you more?"

"Please go away."

"I can't until the elevator gets here. It's also too hot for climbing fire escapes or spinning webs."

She didn't laugh this time, either, leading Win to conclude that the witty, lighthearted approach was definitely not going to work. What the hell would? he wondered, thinking that in a sense spinning a web was exactly what he was doing. He wasn't sure yet how big or cleverly designed or successful it would ultimately be, but his blood was already racing with the challenge of it.

There was a long silence. This time, when Merrill reached for the elevator button he beat her to it. "I suppose you have a flight to catch," he said.

"That's right."

Silence.

"So where are you headed?" It took great restraint not to ask what he really wanted to know, namely who—if anyone—she was heading off with. The existence of a steady man in her life would ruin everything.

Merrill tried ignoring him.

"Oh, I get it, you want me to guess. All right. Let's see, I probably ought to start with A...Alaska? Alabama? Arkansas?"

When she turned her head away he calmly strolled around to her other side in pursuit of her attention. "Albuquerque? Alcatraz? Albania?"

"Stop. You win. Jamaica."

Since she was clearly already at the teeth-clenching stage, Win figured what the hell. "Bringing anybody special along with you?"

Lifting her hostile gaze to meet his, Merrill countered with, "Why do you ask?"

"Just interested."

"You mean nosy."

"That, too. So are you?"

"No."

"That's a shame," he said, elated by the discovery. "Jamaica is a lot more fun if you have someone to party with."

"I go on vacation to relax, not to party."

That was a shame, too, but he didn't think it would help his cause any to point it out to her this soon.

"I've been to Jamaica a few times," he announced.

Merrill made a noncommittal sound, continuing her silent study of the steel-gray elevator doors.

After a strategic pause, Win made a sudden gesture with his briefcase, as if inspiration had just struck. "Why don't we have a drink, and I can give you a few tips, fill you in on some of the local customs?"

Merrill turned her head slowly. "I'm sure I wouldn't be interested in any local customs in which you participated."

"Right. Of course." His shrug might have been mistaken for apologetic if not for the smile shadowing it. "But there's also this great legend about an island witch that I'll bet you haven't heard."

"The White Witch of Rosehall?"

"Oh, you have heard."

The note of disappointment in his voice was subtle and unexpected. Without knowing why, Merrill found herself explaining.

"Before I go anyplace I always read up on the history, the people and the local attractions. That way I can plan exactly what I want to see and do ahead of time so I don't miss anything."

"Sounds like you probably know more about Jamaica than I do. Why don't I buy you that drink, and you can tell *me* all about it?"

She shook her head and smiled reluctantly. "Thanks, but no. I should head straight back to the hotel and then go to the airport. I have to confirm my reservation and check one bag and my laptop computer onto a flight back home to Sarasota. And the airport is bound to be crowded because of the holiday." *Why on earth was she justifying her refusal to him?*

Behind Win's nonchalant smile, his mind was working overtime. He had already decided not to take no for an answer. He might have to put his plans for Merrill on hold for a week—it was tough to seduce a woman who wasn't around—but he could at least give her something to think about while she was gone.

"No problem," he said. "I'm heading straight to the airport myself. We'll grab a drink there. We can even share a taxi. I'm surprised you didn't think of that first, Merrill. It's such a logical solution."

It was logical, which is probably why Merrill wasn't able to come up with a polite, plausible excuse not to go along with the suggestion before the elevator doors slid open.

"I'm already packed," she told him. "I'll be downstairs in front of the hotel at 5:30. If you can be ready by then, I suppose there's no reason we can't ride together."

"A man couldn't ask for a more gracious invitation than that," he replied, his dry tone underscored by the slant of his mouth. "I'll hurry."

"Suit yourself."

"I always do."

The soft, ominous remark made Merrill turn away apprehensively. Even though they'd agreed it was too hot to spar, it seemed inevitable that they would whenever they were alone together. All she wanted was to relax and enjoy her vacation, and that wasn't going to happen as long as Win was around. She couldn't do much about the ride to the airport, but sharing a cozy little drink and island legends was another matter. One way or another, she resolved as he held open the elevator door for her, she was going to wriggle her way out of that one.

Win smiled at her back as he followed her into the elevator, his blood warming as his gaze traveled over her hips and down the length of her legs. Nice legs. Great butt. His smile deepened as the memory of her dancing erupted in his mind.

It struck him that in trying to spark Merrill's interest, he'd fueled his own. A week suddenly seemed a very long time to wait. Maybe he'd been too quick to decide to put the matter on hold. There remained, after all, an entire weekend before he had to be back in the office. Two whole days. Forty-eight promising hours.

They were alone in the elevator. If Merrill were a different sort of woman he might have thrown caution to the wind and kissed her, then confessed that he'd been on fire for her for weeks. Women loved to see you burn. It made them feel powerful. Instead, he reached for her briefcase, letting his fingers rub against hers as he curled them around the handle.

"You must be beat," he said. "Let me carry this for you."

"No, really, there's no need..."

She held on tight, as if the case contained her life savings; he tugged harder.

"Win, you really don't have to..."

Banishing any trace of a smile, he lowered his voice and looked straight into her startled eyes. "If I thought I had to, I wouldn't. I want to."

"Oh. Well, all right, I suppose." Grudgingly she allowed him to slip the case from her grasp. "I...thanks."

Her tone was one he hadn't heard before. Like her expression, it was slightly bewildered and very suspicious. Clearly he had his work cut out for him.

What were his chances, he wondered, of moving a woman like Merrill from an adversarial position to a horizontal one in forty-eight hours?

Friday, 5:17 p.m.

The line at the hotel registration desk stretched all the way to the revolving doors, blocking the wide, brass-railed staircase that was the centerpiece of the Biltmore's newly restored lobby. Many of those in the crowd milling about were lugging bulky, odd-shaped cases. One robust-looking older gentleman had a soup ladle stuck in his back pocket.

"Chefs from around the country," the bellhop explained in response to Merrill's inquiry. "This year Providence is host to the Great Fourth of July Chowder Cook-Off."

It figures, she thought, deciding she better not take time to change into something more comfortable for the trip after all. Her flight didn't leave until nearly seven o'clock, but she wasn't about to miss the 5:30 deadline she herself had set for meeting Win. Somehow it seemed important not to reveal to him even a small chink in her armor.

Predictably, he managed to pack, check out and make it out front on time. He'd even hailed a taxi and was leaning on the fender when she got there, his luggage already stowed in the open trunk. It was with some annoyance that Merrill noticed he had found time to change.

He looked cool and comfortable in khaki slacks and a white shirt with the sleeves rolled up to the elbow. His loafers were soft, worn leather, and inside them his feet were bare. Just looking at him filled her senses with the fresh aroma of clothes dried outdoors and made her feel even more overheated and wilted in the gray linen suit she'd been wearing all day.

Wilted and hot and sticky. A perfectly awful way to start a vacation. She consoled herself with the thought that the reason he'd been able to pack so quickly was because the clothes he wasn't wearing, dirty and clean alike, had undoubtedly been rolled up in a ball and jammed into his suitcase.

The taxi driver remained slouched behind the wheel as she swung her bag into the trunk. She let her garment bag slide from her shoulder to land on top of it, then stopped short when she heard a sharp gasp. Glancing down, she saw Win's fingers wedged between the taxi and the hard plastic computer case still in her hand. She was leaning on it in her efforts to straighten her suitcases, thereby trapping him.

"Oh, my gosh, I'm sorry!" she exclaimed, quickly yanking the case away.

"No problem," he muttered, curling his fingers into a fist and cradling it against his chest.

"I didn't realize you had moved and were standing so close and—"

"I was trying to help you with your bags." He sounded funny. Sort of winded.

"It really does hurt, doesn't it?" she asked.

"Not too bad. I think it will stop throbbing if I sit down."

"Of course, go right ahead."

"I will . . . as soon as you put that in the trunk." He nodded at the computer case as if it were a hand grenade.

"Oh, right." She placed it beside her suitcase and reached to close the trunk at the same moment he did. This time they both gasped with pain as their heads collided.

"Oh . . ." she said drawing back. "I'm sorry. I didn't realize . . ."

"No problem." He winced as he rubbed his head with his injured fingers. "I'll shut it. Just get in the car."

"But your hand..."

"Get in the car, Merrill." He forced a smile. "Please."

"If you're sure..."

At his expression, she hurriedly climbed into the back seat, feeling foolish and peeved with him for causing it. How was she supposed to know that after months of subtle warfare he would suddenly want to help with her bags? Just the same, as soon as he was settled beside her, she once again politely inquired about his hand. It was fine, he insisted, just fine. Merrill wasn't so sure. It looked a little swollen to her, and he looked a little pale. Although that could have been as a result of the heat. She fanned her hand in front of her face, feeling a little woozy herself.

The air conditioner in the taxi wasn't working, so it was either melt into a puddle on the sticky vinyl seat or ride with the windows rolled down and be whipped by a hot wind that smelled and tasted like asphalt. She opted to brave the wind. After only a few minutes on the freeway, she had second thoughts. Her hair was being blown from the combs holding it in place faster than she could tuck it back in. Loose tendrils tickled her neck and got caught behind her glasses.

"If you slid over this way a little, the wind wouldn't be hitting you right in the face," suggested Win, observing her struggle.

"I'm fine," she replied as a thick clump of hair landed in her mouth.

Before she could fix it, he reached over and peeled it loose. "Right, you look like you're having a hell of a good time. Will you listen for once and slide over here next to me?" Without giving her a chance to refuse he grasped her elbow and hauled her to the middle of the back seat.

Her indignation flared, then quickly faded as she realized how good it felt to be out of the line of fire. Deciding to stay put after all, she smoothed her hair as best she could and carefully repositioned her legs so that her thigh wasn't touching his.

"You missed a piece," he said, sweeping his fingers across her cheek to tuck the errant lock of hair behind her ear. In the process, he bumped her glasses and without hesitating, pressed gently on the bridge to settle them back into place. There was something natural, almost companionable about the way he did it. Coming from a man who was more nemesis than companion, it invested the moment with an unexpected and disturbing intimacy.

"Now isn't that better?" he asked.

"Much," she admitted. "Or at least as good as things will get until I'm out of Providence."

"What do you have against Providence?"

"It's the home of the annual Fourth of July Chowder Cook-Off."

He chuckled. "Lobby a little crowded for you, was it?"

"Yes. But it isn't only that, it's too damn hot here."

"Sarasota is hot."

She shook her head at the comparison of her beloved adopted city with this one. Hot, cold, crowded with tourists or peaceful, as it was during the off-season, Sarasota was home. Growing up, her life had been a constant series of moves, of new neighborhoods, new classrooms, new faces. She loved her family dearly, but when she thought of home she thought only of her own place in Sarasota.

"Not this kind of hot," she said simply, knowing she could never explain all that to him. "This is dirty, noisy cityhot."

"I think it's what's known as a heat wave. Happens to the best of places every now and then." He shifted so that his shoulder was pressed against hers. "Actually there's a lot to be said for good old steamy summer heat. When I think of heat waves I think of hot breezes and ice-cold wine and long lazy afternoons. How about you?''

She thought for a moment. "I guess I think of heat rashes and frizzy hair and my ice maker overheating."

"Quite the romantic, aren't you?"

"I never considered heat waves very romantic," she said, her expression drawing into a frown of consternation.

"You see, it's exactly as I said earlier. You have these fixed preconceived notions of the way things ought to be and you refuse to see around them. For instance, I think you were predisposed not to enjoy this trip to Providence and so you didn't give the place a chance."

"I gave it a chance. A whole week. It felt like a lifetime."

He laughed. "How can you dislike a place you've barely even seen?"

"I've seen enough."

"You've seen the four blocks between the Biltmore and Ingraham's office. You can't taste a city from the back seat of a cab, Merrill. You should have at least come along and had dinner with me once or twice. I did ask," he reminded her.

"I told you I was—"

"I know, working."

"Someone had to prepare for the next day's meeting."

The look she gave him suggested that he'd spent his evenings in Providence engaged in more enjoyable activities. Win smiled, saying nothing of the stacks of reports he'd worked on each night until he was glassy-eyed and had to get out of the hotel room for an hour or so. "What are you trying to do? Impress the boss with your diligence?"

"There wouldn't be much point to that, would there?" she countered.

It was obviously a confrontational remark, and an impulsive one. To Merrill's relief, if Win noticed or wondered what she meant by it he didn't ask. Instead, he drew her attention to the gigantic blue plaster roach looming over the freeway from its perch atop an exterminator's headquarters. The yellow-eyed monster was a local landmark, he explained as she shook her head in disbelief. As they rode along he pointed out others, trying to convince her the city had its own brand of charm.

He told her about a great Italian restaurant he'd discovered and about his search for a decent blues club. He entertained her with a story about how a few nights earlier the hotel bartender had steered him to a storefront nightspot that turned out to be little more than a private hangout for some very big, very ornery-looking bikers.

"The moment I walked in I knew I'd made a mistake and ought to turn right around and walk out, but I was too..."

"Embarrassed?" she supplied, recalling similar moments in her own life.

"Yeah, and dumb. You know, stuck in that *nobody's going to scare me off* mode that I should have outgrown back in high school. I'll tell you, though, I was plenty scared standing at that bar trying to choke down what looked like the tallest shot of tequila ever poured." He gave a sheepish shrug. "Turned out the band stunk, too."

Merrill laughed. She couldn't help taking a perverse pleasure in picturing Win in a tight spot for once. Beneath the laughter, however, her thoughts were tangled. She had long ago formed a very definite opinion of Win Deverell and hadn't seen any reason to alter it. But this—telling an embarrassing story about himself with the same ease he did everything else—did not fit with that opinion.

When they arrived at the airport, Win made a point of escorting her to the sidewalk a cautious distance away before helping the driver unload their luggage. In view of what had happened back at the hotel, she decided it was probably a good idea to stay out of the way while he tipped the baggage handler at the outdoor station, taking pains to make sure the man understood that her bags were going on two different flights. Accustomed to doing everything for herself, she couldn't deny there was a certain thrill in having someone else handle things for her.

She thanked him as they entered the terminal, which was wall-to-wall with holiday travelers. The crowd pushed them together so their shoulders bumped and rubbed as they walked side by side.

"I've been having nightmares about ending up in Jamaica with a suitcase full of business suits while my bathing suit is sitting in the airport in Florida," she confessed. "Usually I take along a carry-on packed with essentials, but on the flight up here I was already saddled with my laptop and a briefcase full of notes."

"I usually make sure to keep a clean shirt and socks handy myself," he said with an understanding nod. Turning, he caught her in a speculative gaze. He lowered his voice. "But then I suppose to a woman 'essentials' means things like fancy silk underwear and French perfume?"

"Oh, no."

She shook her head as if totally oblivious to the teasing note in his voice and the heat and charisma he was doing his best to project. With amazement Win realized it was because she *was* oblivious to it. Lord, this was going to be even tougher than he'd anticipated.

"Underwear, yes," she continued, "but not silk. Silk just isn't practical when you're traveling and constantly rinsing things out in the bathroom sink.'' He noted that she blushed, as though she'd said something risqué. Keeping her gaze pointed straight ahead, she added, ''And I'm allergic to perfume.''

Allergic to perfume? What kind of woman is allergic to perfume? The same kind, he thought, whose memories of summer centered around heat rashes rather than long hot kisses in the sun. She wasn't just a challenge, she was hopeless. And he was an idiot for trying to prove otherwise, especially now, when he needed to focus all his attention on the business.

It went against his nature to admit he'd probably bit off more than he could chew, but he was on the verge of doing exactly that when she came to an abrupt halt beside him. When he turned to look at her, she gazed at him with an expression that tugged at his memory. He'd seen it someplace before.

''What you said in the taxi is true. I'm really not romantic, am I? Not at all?''

''Well . . .'' he said, stalling.

Her blue eyes held his. They were wide and sober and full of hope, and suddenly Win remembered where he'd seen that expression before. It had been a few months back as he was leaving a pre-season Pirates game. A little kid had been hanging around the players' exit, his face pressed to the chain link fence with that same yearning look, as if getting an autograph from one of his baseball heroes was the most important thing in his life. He remembered wanting to slug the players who drove by without giving the kid so much as a wave. Now he saw that same expression on Merrill's face, and it was he who held the power to turn it into a smile.

''Maybe you're not romantic in the classic sense,'' he told her, hoping she didn't press him about what the hell he meant by that. "But there are other ways a woman can be romantic. Deeper, more mature ways."

Her eyes narrowed dubiously. "Really?"

"Definitely," Win repeated, gently moving her forward. "Take my word for it." *Just don't ask me to name them right this minute,* he prayed. In an effort to distract her, he gestured toward the ticket counters ahead. "Will you take a look at those lines? C'mon, we'd better step on it."

Hurrying along beside him, Merrill felt a new rush of dismay. The lines were long. From the look of the one snaking its way to the Coastways Airline desk, she'd be lucky if she managed to confirm her reservation and make it to the boarding gate in time. One thing was certain, there wouldn't be enough time to have a drink with Win.

Thinking about it caused a tight feeling in her chest, which she told herself was relief. Certainly not disappointment. Relief, that was it . . . and irritation. After all, delays of any sort were one of her pet peeves. She planned carefully for whatever she did and expected the rest of the world to cooperate. When it didn't she became grouchy.

That's how she felt now. Grouchy and relieved. The last thing in the world she wanted to do was spend a moment longer than necessary with Win Deverell. Especially in view of the strange way he'd been acting since they left the meeting. True, being with him hadn't turned out to be quite the ordeal she'd expected, but though she couldn't define it, something about his manner left her feeling off-balance. He seemed to have a knack for making her say things and think things that wouldn't ordinarily occur to her. Like this romance notion.

It was something she never thought much about. Working to establish herself in a male-dominated industry took up a substantial portion of her time and energy, and she never squandered what was left over worrying about whether or not she was romantic. It had never really mattered to her and it didn't now, except... Except no woman wanted to be considered completely unromantic, some sort of sensual dud. Especially by someone who, by all accounts, was something of an expert where women and romance were concerned.

It turned out that Win was also flying Coastways, and he claimed the place directly behind her in line. As they slowly inched forward they talked, and when they weren't talking Merrill found herself thinking about him. By tacit agreement they didn't discuss business, and without work-related friction the mood between them remained friendly—very friendly. Almost...

She caught herself. Either she was suffering from heatstroke or was more desperately in need of a rest than she'd realized. It would be a mistake to forget that no matter how different he seemed, this was not a new, improved Win Deverell. It was simply a side of the same old Win that he'd never bothered to show her before. She'd known all along that the man could be irresistibly charming when he wanted something. The question was, what could he possibly want from her?

"Next." With hardly a pause, the impatient voice barked the word a second time. Loudly. "Next."

"That's you, Merrill," Win said, lightly touching her shoulder.

"Oh...sorry," she said, hurriedly stepping up to the counter and handing her ticket to the clerk. "My name is Merrill Winters. I have a reservation for the 6:55 flight to Atlanta. I'll be changing planes there and going on to—''

She broke off as the clerk, after barely glancing at her ticket, detached the top sheet and pushed the remainder back across the counter.

"I'm sorry," he said, "but there's going to be a delay in departure time for that flight. Until we have a definite time, I won't be able to confirm your reservation."

Merrill frowned. "A delay? But what about my connections in Atlanta?"

"I wouldn't worry about that. You see all Coastways flights are temporarily delayed."

For the first time she noticed that the young man's smile seemed distinctly frayed, his manner strained. She looked at him uneasily. "All flights?"

"Yes, ma'am. We're experiencing a temporary staffing problem as a result of a job action and there will be a slight delay in all flights when it's resolved."

"A job action?" Her mind was slow to digest the grim implication of his rote speech. "Are you talking about a strike?"

"No, ma'am, not at this time. I can only tell you that new departure times will be posted on the overhead monitors as soon as they are made available to us by the home office in Newark."

"But when will that be?"

"With any luck it will be only a slight delay."

"Can't you tell me anything more definite than that? I mean, my flight will be leaving sometime tonight, right?"

"I can't say for sure, ma'am. Only that new departure times will be posted—"

"All right, all right," she cut him off as he gestured once more toward the monitors behind him. "What about Coastways' policy of arranging for a seat on another airline if a ticket can't be honored as scheduled?"

"Our policy is that we'll make every effort to do that," he explained mechanically, as if for the thousandth time that day. "And we will. But we've been snapping up empty seats on other airlines all afternoon, and I can't offer you one yet."

Merrill persisted. "What about a flight out of Boston?"

The clerk shook his head. "Boston's worse. Between holiday travelers and the staffing problem, it's passenger gridlock all along the coast." Reaching for his clipboard, he flipped through page after page of names before stopping. "I'll put your name here on the waiting list, Ms. Winters, and hope that if your original flight isn't rescheduled soon, we'll be able to find a seat for you on another airline sometime later tonight. We'll make every effort to minimize the inconvenience."

"I'm already plenty inconvenienced. And I absolutely have to leave tonight."

"You and everyone else around here," he countered wearily.

"You don't understand. This is my vacation. I had to make reservations months ago to get the room I want in the hotel I want. I'm scheduled to take a bus tour of the island at eight o'clock tomorrow morning. I've booked a scuba diving lesson for Sunday. I..." Merrill sighed. This wasn't his fault. "Sorry. It's been one of those days."

"Tell me about it," he muttered.

"If you do find a seat for me, how will—"

"We'll page you," he interrupted, picking up her ticket and handing it to her.

It was a nightmare, thought Merrill. After all her careful planning, instead of being on her way to paradise she was stuck in Providence. Not even in Providence. She was stuck in someplace named Warwick. For who knows how long.

Already she could hear the precious seconds of her vacation ticking away.

Shoving her ticket into her purse, she turned from the counter without looking where she was going and collided with a solid and even more alarming aspect of her predicament.

She was stuck here with Win Deverell.

Friday, 6:51 p.m.

There's one thing that really puzzles me about all this," said Win.

They had circled the overcrowded seating area like vultures until a couple of molded plastic chairs became available. The seats were attached in rows of eight, the rows arranged at right angles to form cozy squares. Beside them sat a family of four children and two battle weary parents. The rest of the section was filled with members of the Golden Agers Social Club en route to Las Vegas.

Merrill fanned herself with the copy of *Forbes* she'd planned to read on the flight. The terminal's air conditioning system was overtaxed by the crowd of detained travelers clustered anxiously beneath the persistently blank monitors, sitting on planters, and lined up to use the rest rooms. Already the air was thickly saturated with the mingled scents of cigarette smoke, perfume and overheated bodies.

"What puzzles you about all this?" she asked him.

"How you could book a scuba diving lesson before you've even arrived in Jamaica...before you've even left home, for that matter."

"You book it through the hotel," she explained around a yawn.

"I don't mean that. I mean how do you know that on Sunday morning you're going to feel like learning to scuba dive?"

She looked at him blankly. "Because that's what I planned to do."

"What if you wake up and feel like Windsurfing instead...or shopping...Don't you ever just let things roll? Let life rise up to meet you?"

"No. Never."

Frustrated, Win raked his hand through his hair. "What if on Sunday morning you meet the man of your dreams, a guy who makes you want to do nothing except spend the rest of the day alone with him, lying in the sun on a secluded beach?"

"If that happened," Merrill replied, the corners of her mouth raised in a wry smile, "I guess I might consider forfeiting the deposit on my scuba lesson. But it won't happen."

"How can you be so sure?"

"Because things like that never happen to me," she replied innocently. "I know this must be hard for you to grasp. Life unfurls before you like a red carpet. But I have to make good things happen. The only thing that ever rises up to meet me is disaster. Sometimes even with all my planning, it's there waiting for me anyway. Like now."

"Things could be worse."

"I suppose." Arms folded across her chest, she glanced at the four human jack-in-the-boxes on her left. "There could be twenty kids stampeding over my toes every time they make a trip to the water fountain. And they would all be in the contagious stage of chicken pox."

"Disaster agrees with you," he said, chuckling. "I don't think I've ever heard you joke before."

Merrill raised her brows. "Who was joking?"

"Oh. Sorry. Anyway, by 'worse' I was thinking more along the lines of being here alone. If I have to be stuck in an airport, I'm glad I'm stuck with you."

"Why?"

"There's no need to squint at me like I'm about to pick your pocket. Take it as a compliment. Working with you so closely this week I've come to see you in a different light."

Her eyes widened. "Really?"

"Without a doubt."

Guilt came with a swift stab as Merrill recalled her first thoughts on being stuck here with him. "Well, I guess you're not as bad as I thought, either."

His mouth curved in a smile. "Fancy that. What do you say, Merrill, want to declare a truce?"

She hesitated. Without warning, his tone had turned warm and beguiling. The look in his eyes seemed hopeful and—God help her—sincere. She was shaken by her response to his appeal. Since stepping into the elevator with him, her feelings had been confused...and confusing. Now, in the space of a smile, they had become sharp and sweet and dangerous. Her stomach twisted with the power of sudden, unexpected attraction.

Unexpected, her conscience needled, *or repressed?* Was it possible that she had been attracted to Win all along? That her animosity toward him had been motivated by the fear that if she let herself, she could be as taken in by his charm as any other woman? And maybe, just a little, by the realization that the odds were he would never waste his charm on her in the first place?

"How about a limited truce?" he suggested, mistaking her preoccupation for silent opposition to his proposed truce. "We could try and get along just for the duration."

He stuck out his hand and it seemed petty to refuse to grasp it with her own. It was obvious he was doing his best to be friendly.

"Deal?" he asked.

"Deal.

"Good." His warm hand enveloped hers and held it far longer than required for a friendly handshake. "I'd suggest sealing it with the drink I promised you, but the lounge seems to be overflowing at the moment. Would you settle for a coke and a candy bar from the gift shop?"

"Thanks," Merrill replied, slipping her hand free, "but I think I'll wait and eat on the plane." She still wasn't ready to surrender all hope that there would be a plane that night.

Win opened his mouth as if to say something, then closed it, shrugging. "Okay. How about if I bring you back another magazine? A book? Or maybe you'd like to come along for the walk?"

"No, you go ahead. I'll save your seat."

The truth was Merrill didn't know what she wanted. Free time wasn't something she was confronted with very often. *Don't you ever just let things roll?* Win had asked her. She'd been telling the truth when she replied that she never did. Her entire life was orderly and well-planned, right down to the day and time she did laundry, watered plants or paid monthly bills.

She suspected her need for a familiar routine had to do with having moved around so much when she was growing up. Her father and two sisters had adapted easily to new cities, new jobs and schools, but Merrill was more like her mother. Mary Winters had coped by turning each new house into an exact replica of the last, right down to the color of the carpets and the paper on the walls.

Merrill had found the stability she longed for in developing routines she could carry with her from Boston to Atlanta to Santa Fe. She had her own precise way of arranging her drawers, of numbering her homework papers, of facing the dreaded ordeal of walking into a classroom where everyone but her knew everyone else. Making new friends didn't come easily to her, and she had to plan ahead which table she would sit at in the lunchroom and where to stand when teams were being chosen in gym class and to take along a book when going out to recess in case no one talked to her.

Somewhere along the way, planning and organizing had stopped being a conscious effort and had become an integral part of her. Now, for the first time in years, she was faced with a block of time without every minute accounted for. There was no neatly printed list telling her what she had to get done and in what order to do it. Actually there was a list, tucked away in her billfold, but until she reached Jamaica it was useless.

Predictably, the delay left her feeling impatient and frustrated, but what concerned her most was what she sensed lurking just beneath those feelings. It was an almost giddy sensation, what you might expect from a kid skipping school. Anticipation, Merrill decided, thinking how the feeling was totally at odds with her situation. She didn't want to explore too deeply the suspicion that it might be directly attributable to Win's presence.

For the time being she had nothing to do but kill time however she chose to do it. There was no set agenda, no deadline, not even an image to maintain. No one here except Win even knew her, and in a few weeks ... She pushed thoughts of the future aside. For now she was free to follow her impulses and the idea held much more appeal than she expected.

Before second thoughts could intrude, she stood and looked around for a trashcan where she could dump the copy of *Forbes*. On the way back to her seat, she slipped off her jacket. The air, warm as it was, felt heavenly on her arms and the back of her neck. Not until Win returned and she saw his eyes widen in surprise as they drifted over her did she consider the fact that the sheet white fabric of her blouse became transparent when damp.

Lace. That was really all Win could see through her blouse, but it was plenty. His nerve endings tingled as if he were back in sixth grade catching his first glimpse of Rita Duhammel's bra strap. With one difference. Instead of the vague, unfocused desires he'd felt for Rita, he knew with erotic detail what he wanted to do with Merrill.

First he wanted to touch that lace, trace with his fingertips and with his tongue where it curved above her breasts and where it dipped between them. Where there was no lace, her skin looked moist and rosy and he wanted to touch that, too. He wanted to taste...

"Win?"

He jerked his gaze up to meet hers. "I'm sorry, were you talking to me?"

"Yes. I asked where your Coke was."

"Coke? Oh. The machine was empty. I think people are beginning to hoard supplies."

"Sure sign of a full-fledged disaster."

"No, a sure sign of a full-fledged disaster would be if the airline passed out dinner vouchers."

"What would it mean if they sent everyone to a hotel for the night?"

"The end of the world," he replied, his expression deadpan. "One of the commandments of airline deregulation was *Thou shalt not make waiting passengers comfortable.*"

That became increasingly obvious as the wait dragged on. Merrill began to wish her seat didn't face a clock. After a while, the hands seemed to move in time to the theme music from *The Twilight Zone.*

The Golden Agers were driving her crazy. With their trip to the Vegas gaming tables delayed, they passed the time by betting among themselves on everything from the length of the wait to how many times each of the kids next to her would trek to the bathroom in a ten-minute period. The kids were worse. They whined, slouched in their seats and picked fights with each other—in general, doing all the things she felt like doing. The prospect of spending the night in that very chair became increasingly, depressingly real.

Gradually she became overwhelmed by all the petty annoyances she had been stoically trying to ignore. The strap on her white sandals pinched her toes and the high heels made her arches ache. Her slip felt as if it had become a Saran Wrap tourniquet around her hips and she was starting to get a headache from having her hair tightly pulled back all day. Even her jewelry chafed.

At 8:44 she couldn't stand it any longer. Yanking the pearl studs from her ears and the matching necklace from around her neck, she stuffed them into her handbag.

"They scratch," she explained when she caught Win's intense gaze.

He stared at her throat so hard for so long that she wondered if there was something there. An ink smudge maybe. She was forever poking herself with her pen. At last, with what appeared to be tremendous effort, he dragged his attention away from her throat. His tone was rough. "I see. Feel better now?"

"Yes."

She did. For a while.

At 9:02 she took off her watch. Then, on impulse, her belt.

She felt Win's eyes on her and turned to find him watching her again, with a disturbing intensity. "Do you have to stare?"

"Yes. I do. I don't want to miss seeing you take off whatever scratches next."

"The belt buckle didn't scratch," she felt obliged to explain, "but it does dig into me when I sit for a long time. Some of us didn't have time to change into comfortable clothes for the trip."

"Some of us ought to learn to make time for the things we really want to do."

"Oh, that's so easy for you to say," she snapped as she coiled the belt to fit in her bag.

"Why? My hour has sixty minutes, same as yours, Merrill."

"Yes, but I..." The belt buckle snagged on something and without thinking she gave it an impatient yank. It was then that she felt her stocking unravel in a two inch wide run from her shin to above her knee. "Now look what you've done."

"How clumsy of me," Win quipped, his tone thick with suppressed laughter. "Let me see if I can fix..."

She swung her legs to the side as his fingertips brushed her knee. "Stop," she ordered, bending forward to inspect the damage. "You've done enough. If I hadn't been bickering with you, I never would have pulled on the buckle that way."

"I see."

Suddenly so did she. She lifted her face to him with a sheepish expression. "Sorry. I guess it wasn't entirely your fault." She gave an indistinct groan. "Look at this mess...as if I didn't look grubby enough already."

"You look fine."

"Sure, terrific."

"If it bothers you that much, take them off."

She rolled her eyes at the suggestion as she continued to fuss with the broken threads of pale gray silk.

"What's the matter? Do bare legs clash with your professional image? Or is it just that you have removing your stockings scheduled for 11:03 tonight? Here's your big chance to be spontaneous, Merrill. Cut loose. Be a real daredevil and take 'em off now."

Their gazes locked. "You think I won't do it, don't you?"

"That's right."

"Well, I just might."

"Then do it."

She caught herself anxiously dragging her tongue across her bottom lip and stopped. "I'm certainly not going to take them off here. I would have to go to the ladies' room."

"Go on, then."

"There's a line waiting to get in."

"So there is. And it's not getting any shorter."

He sat waiting for her response with his hands casually hitched in his front pockets, his legs sprawled before him with ankles crossed. But somehow Merrill knew he was feeling as far from casual as she was. His gaze was black and so intense that she felt it like a depth charge in the pit of her stomach. Now she knew how Ingraham must have felt facing him down during the meeting.

"I knew you wouldn't do it," he taunted.

Merrill smiled. It might have been the heat or the proximity of the Golden Agers or simply the desire not to see him bully his way to two victories in the same day. "Do you want to bet?"

"Sure."

"Dinner?"

"You're on."

"I'll be right back."

With her chin held high she stood, smoothed her skirt and strode toward the rest rooms. With each step she grew more determined. Daredevil indeed. She'd show him daredevil. His taunting voice replayed inside her head. *"Did you have removing your stockings scheduled for 11:03?"* As if she would go so far as to schedule a time to take off her stockings.

What he thought of her was obvious, and the long wait outside the rest rooms gave her plenty of time to stew about it. He thought what most people thought. That she was prim and rigid, uptight, a drone...*unromantic*. It wasn't true. At least not completely. She was simply cautious. Whether it was at work or in her social life she liked to plan and consider all her options and take things one step at a time.

It worked. She hated to think where she would be right now if she had thrown caution to the wind where Peter Habershaw was concerned. Omaha, that's where. Her relationship with Peter constituted her last great affair. Actually, it was also her only great affair. And now that she thought about it, *affair* didn't seem quite the right word. *Affair* conjured up images of wild moonlit nights and mad, passionate rendezvous.

What she and Peter had shared was more of a Wednesdays at her place, Saturdays at his sort of thing. On those rare occasions when they could both get away, they would spend a weekend in Orlando. Their relationship was safe and comfortable, and neither of them ever complained. It seemed to be such a sure thing that Peter had been stunned last year when the accounting firm he worked for offered him a very lucrative promotion to manager of their Omaha office and she'd refused to accompany him.

If she really loved him, he'd insisted, she would think of their future and do what was best for both of them. She would put aside her love for Sarasota and her dedication to her job and go with him. She'd felt sad and guilty, but in the end she'd had to agree that he was right. If she really loved him she would have gone.

At least she liked to think she would have. For weeks after he left, she lay awake at night worrying that some of his bitter parting shots might have been on target. Maybe she was rigid and uptight and hopelessly stuck in her ways.

At last it was her turn in the ladies' room. She located an empty stall and stepped inside, feeling reckless, ridiculously so. After all, taking off her stockings wasn't that big a deal. But the stockings and whether or not she took them off were not the real issue here.

As silly as it was, taking off her stockings would be a signal of sorts. It was a small, safe way to demonstrate to Win—and maybe herself—that there were hidden facets to her personality, that if she chose, she could be spontaneous and uninhibited and who knows, maybe even romantic as well. For now, it was enough just to win this bet. He would look surprised when she strolled out there barelegged, then he would grin in a sort of grudgingly admiring way and then....

That was as far ahead as she'd thought. She wondered what might happen next and she felt a tingle along her spine that could be either apprehension or anticipation.

What *would* happen next? Part of her was afraid to find out and part of her was afraid that if she didn't, she'd regret it forever.

Friday, 9:11 p.m.

Would she do it? Win wondered as he watched her stride away. It didn't really matter. If he won, he got dinner. And if he lost, he'd get to spend the night looking at Merrill's long legs, bare and up close. He'd never wanted to lose a bet so badly in his life.

In another way, however, her response mattered very much. The Merrill he'd thought he knew wouldn't even have considered his suggestion. She would have narrowed her eyes, straightened her glasses and shot him a look that meant she was not interested in playing his games. So if she went through with this now, would that mean she was interested? Was the woman who'd sat beside him tugging off her jewelry and belt as if she were shedding protective armor the Merrill he knew?

It seemed to Win that she was taking forever, even allowing for the long line and the slow-motion disease all women seemed to develop when they passed through the door of a ladies' room. He could have shaved, showered and donned a tuxedo in less time, right down to the studs that always gave him trouble. Or so he thought, until he saw her striding toward him. If he had the rest of his life, he couldn't imagine himself accomplishing such a metamorphosis. She didn't just look different, she looked transformed. She looked spectacular.

At first, he didn't even notice who'd won their bet. His gaze touched on her hair and lingered. He'd been right about her hair. With the combs gone, it tumbled to her shoulders in a tousle of dark-and-light-gold waves that looked silky and infinitely touchable. She had tugged her blouse loose so that it hung like a soft white T-shirt over the gray skirt that looked snugger and shorter than he recalled.

Her glasses only enhanced the overall impression of sensuality. She looked both sexy and sophisticated, and to Win it was a devastating combination. Utterly captivated, he got to his feet as she approached. And at last he thought to check out her legs. He grinned at the sight. They were long, tan, smooth and enticingly bare.

In the end, however, it was her toenails that answered his question about whether or not there was a side to Merrill he'd never seen around the office. Her pale gray stockings had concealed the fact that her toenails were polished a glossy hot-pink. The very last thing he imagined Merrill Winters doing was sitting on her bed, painting her toenails the color of cotton candy. But obviously, she did.

In that instant, what had started as a whim became desire, fierce and hot. It was a dangerous sort of desire, the kind that pushed everything else, including common sense out of its way. The kind that made a man reach out and take first and worry about the cost later.

"I believe you owe me dinner," she said, coming to a stop only a few inches in front of him.

Her scent engulfed him. It was fresh and clean, like soap, and more intoxicating to his senses than the sweetest perfume. "Yes, and all of a sudden I'm ravenous."

"Good, then let's go eat."

A shock wave passed through Merrill as he reached for her hand, followed by a sudden rush of heat. Of course he was only doing it because it made it easier to stay together as they crossed the crowded terminal, but that didn't lessen the pleasure she felt. Every nerve in her body seemed to begin and end at that spot where their palms were pressed together.

She was utterly distracted by the warmth of his skin and the strength of his grip. His thumb stroked across hers and it was impossible to ignore the tingly pleasure that rippled upward. She felt the strip of rough calluses at the base of his fingers and across the tips. Caused by working the ropes on his boat, she mused, reminded of how little she really knew of how he'd spent his days before taking over for Ted. It had always stretched the limits of her imagination to think of Win as an equal partner with Ted.

He hardly acted the part. He would show up in the office only when he absolutely had to, to drop off a late report or sit in on a meeting where his technical marine knowledge was essential. The women in the office considered him a dashing and vaguely untamed figure in his jeans and T-shirt. Merrill always told herself that self-indulgent and irresponsible were closer to the truth, but it was hard to hold on to that thought now with him holding her hand as if...as if he were trying to lead her through the crowd, she reminded herself firmly.

Even at this late hour the airport's only restaurant was crowded, but they finally found a tiny table tucked way in the back corner, about a foot from the dirty dish deposit and within firing range of the swinging kitchen door. A harried-looking waitress dressed in a tan and beige uniform slapped two menus on their table with a promise to return. Win took only a moment to read his, closed it and looked across the table at her.

"I figure a hamburger is always safe. What do you want?"

"I want chicken roasted with pineapple, a raddicio and papaya salad, and a piña colada."

He frowned as he quickly flipped his menu open. "That's on here?"

"You didn't say it had to be on the menu. You asked me what I wanted. I also want to take a hot shower and I want my suitcase so I can change into something that isn't wrinkled and sweaty and...and gray," she said, wrinkling her nose as she plucked at her skirt. "And I want a flower—a fresh hibiscus bloom—to stick in my hair."

It had started as a grim joke, but by the time she'd finished she felt embarrassingly close to tears. She heard them pooled in her voice, and worse, she knew Win heard them, too.

The concern she saw in his eyes was unexpected. It made his tone even deeper than usual. He reached across the small table to cradle her hand between both of his. "Merrill? What's wrong?"

"What isn't? This is my vacation. I should be sitting on a moonlit beach drinking something tropical instead of dodging a kitchen door to eat a hamburger."

"You're right," he said softly. "You should be."

It occurred to her that this was the first time she had ever seen Win look nonplussed, and she was too miserable to enjoy it.

The kitchen door swung open, missing her shoulder by inches. Their waitress emerged, plopped two glasses of cloudy water in front of them and grabbed her pencil from behind her ear.

"Okay, what'll it be? I should warn you, we're out of cheese, so I hope you didn't have your hearts set on cheeseburgers or grilled cheese sandwiches. We're also out of L for the BLTs. Other than that, you're in luck."

"Do you have any hibiscus?" asked Win. He was looking directly at Merrill. Startled, she tried to pull away, but he only tightened his grip on her hand.

The waitress lifted her gaze from her order pad and scratched her head by inserting her pencil into a crack in the lacquered and hennaed helmet of her short hair. "What is this? A joke?"

"How about piña coladas?" Win inquired.

Merrill averted her gaze from the woman's, but couldn't prevent the small smile that formed as the waitress flipped her pad shut and snapped, "The bar's upstairs."

"Thanks," Win replied. "We'll try there." Pulling a five dollar bill from his pocket, he placed it on the table. "Thanks for the water, too. Come on," he said to Merrill, pulling her to her feet. "Let's get out of here."

"Are you out of your mind?" she asked him after they had made their way through the maze of tables to the door. She was feeling a little confused, a little breathless. "We lost our table and there's no way we'll get another one before closing."

"It doesn't matter. They didn't have what you want. I'll find someplace that does."

His expression was not the teasing one she'd come to expect, and staring into his eyes, Merrill felt a rush of emotion she couldn't identify. It made her mouth dry and her palms damp. "Win, I was only kidding."

He shook his head before she could say more. "No. No, you weren't."

"All right, I wasn't. I am disappointed about the way my vacation has started, but that's no reason you should go hungry."

"I don't intend to. I told you, we'll find someplace else."

"You mean leave the airport?"

"Don't sound so shocked. We're not prisoners here."

"No." She shook her head firmly. "No, I can't leave. What if they reschedule my flight and I'm not here?"

"Merrill..." He broke off and ran his fingers through his hair, his exasperated frown softening to a smile. "All right. I have a better idea." Before releasing her hand, he lifted it and slowly brushed his lips across her knuckles. "Wait here." Then he was gone.

She stood, slightly dazed, watching his quick, rangy stride carry him out of sight. All right, she thought, explain this one. This wasn't as easily dismissed as his polite offer to carry her bag or buy her a drink or the way he held her hand to steer her through the crowd.

Taking it all together, one might conclude that Win Deverell was flirting with her. Unless one remembered that for eight years she'd watched him flirt with almost every woman in the office except her, and that ordinarily their shared chemistry more closely resembled acid than honey, and that, no matter how you looked at it, she wasn't his type.

That was the bottom line. Never mind that he had kissed her hand and that she was finding it harder and harder to remember that he wasn't her type, either.

He had kissed her hand. Catching herself massaging the spot his lips had touched, she dropped both hands to her sides and self-consciously walked over to pretend to look in the windows of the closed gift shop.

So he had kissed her hand. Big deal. He could just as easily have saluted. Or tipped his hat if he'd been wearing one. It had probably been his idea of a joke. Or maybe he just felt so sorry for her that he got carried away. Whatever his motive, it had been nothing more than a meaningless gesture. It couldn't have been more. She just wasn't his type.

Even as she thought it, Merrill was brought up short by a glimmer in the darkened gift shop window. She hadn't been able to get near the mirror in the ladies' room and had crossed her fingers that the quick brush she'd given her hair and her blind efforts with lipstick and blusher had left her presentable. However, presentable was not quite the adjective that jumped to mind as she came face-to-face with her own reflection.

While the features were the same ones she faced each morning in the bathroom mirror, there was something unmistakably different about the woman who stared back at her now. It was in her eyes and in her smile, Merrill decided, startled by the eerie sensation that she was staring at a stranger.

This woman looked like the type who laughed easily and made love with abandon and would impulsively take off on a trip around the world. She looked to be the sort who traveled light, with a favorite pair of jeans and a fabulous silk scarf that on a moment's notice she could transform into an evening skirt or a beach cover-up or anything else the occasion might demand. She looked exciting and alive. She looked, Merrill realized, like exactly the sort of woman Win Deverell would flirt with—and who was perfectly capable of flirting back.

Leaning forward she touched the glass, finding it hard to believe the reflection was real and that it was really her. It was.

"Oh, my," she murmured, drawing back as if scorched. Her startled rush of breath fogged the glass, but not enough to erase the other woman's lingering smile of anticipation. "Oh, my."

Friday, 9:58 p.m.

During the hour or so that Win was gone, many of Merrill's fellow airport inmates staked out any available seat or piece of floor and settled in for a couple of uncomfortable hours of sleep. Some even gave up and went home. She made use of the time alone to try to order herself to be sensible.

Although she had accepted the fact that, incredulous as it seemed, Win was indeed flirting with her, she told herself it would be foolish to go getting all starry-eyed over it. There was a simple explanation for what was happening. It had to do with being stuck here together. Win was looking for a way to pass the time, and she quite obviously was not herself. She was tired and hungry, disappointed and vulnerable. Her resistance couldn't be much lower, and it would be just like him to take advantage of that fact.

Win's reputation with women was no secret. Everything she'd ever heard reinforced her conviction that whatever happened between them—if anything should happen between them—would fall under the general heading of a one-night stand. Merrill wasn't sure she could handle that. And she wasn't at all sure she could handle him. If working with him was difficult now, afterward it might well become a nightmare. She might even be forced to leave Haigh and Deverell sooner than she feared.

Was she fool enough to risk all that for a one-night stand? Even if—as some deeply feminine intuition told her—a one-night stand with Win turned out to be a night of the most arousing, passionate, uninhibited sex she would ever experience?

Somehow she convinced herself she wasn't that big a fool. it wasn't easy. It was difficult to silence the part of her mind that kept saying *But suppose, just suppose, this is all for real.* . . . Images flashed in her head. Win smiling at her, touching her face in the startlingly familiar way he had in the taxi, the tenderness in his eyes when he tried to order a hibiscus in a coffee shop because she'd wanted it.

Trying to get hold of her senses, she conjured up different images instead, moments from the past few months—the goading, the clashes of will, all the annoying little incidents she'd endured because of him. She thought about how his lack of routine had turned hers upside down, about the way he borrowed things from her office without asking—her stapler, her secret stash of Snickers, sometimes even her secretary, for heaven's sake.

Things might be tranquil at the moment, but only because they were both being forced to make the best of a bad situation. Together, she and Win were a time bomb. He was a man who only wanted to play and she was a woman who had no time for that.

Not even on vacation? Merrill squelched the mutinous voice inside. Not even on vacation. At least not with a man she would still have to face at work each day, long after the thrill of a summer fling had faded.

Well, maybe not for that long after, if Win had his way. Just thinking about that rekindled her resentment so that by the time he returned she'd succeeded in talking herself into a state of reasonable self-control. Then she felt him tap her on the shoulder. She whirled around in her seat, took one look at him, and her shored up defenses collapsed in a giddy, excited tumble, like rebellious children somersaulting downhill.

From the looks of him it was obvious that the late hour hadn't done much to lower the humidity outside. His dark hair was rumpled and damp. It tumbled across his forehead and collar in appealing disarray. It was also obvious he'd been rushing around. But it was the look in his eyes, a blend of pleasure at seeing her and unabashedly wicked intent, that tugged at her imagination and turned her strong moral fiber to jelly. *Suppose, just suppose....*

Win yanked playfully at her sleeve. "Come with me," he ordered.

It pleased Win that for a change she didn't argue or question his motives, just as he was pleased by the spontaneous smile with which she'd greeted him. It wasn't her usual response to seeing him. Of course, to be fair, it wasn't the response he usually tried to elicit. When, he mused, had he gone from wanting to tease Merrill to wanting to please her?

Wanting to please her? He almost laughed out loud at that as he led her toward the exit. Running his ass off to please her was more like it, considering the events of the past hour. And, he reminded himself, all of this had started back in Ingraham's office, for a very specific reason. He kept forgetting *why* he was being nice to her and found himself simply doing it.

Walking through the automatic doors that led outside was like walking into a wall of heat. Still, he preferred the heavy night air to the stuffiness inside. The airport terminal was a long building, all glass and sand-colored stone. On one side, amid the pebbled concrete and asphalt, was a small oasis of green. Situated in a dead spot between two floodlights, it was bathed in shadows, making the shrubs and grass appear almost black. Against that dark background, the yellow tablecloth he'd spread on the ground seemed to glow. Arranged on it were the fruits of his frantic search.

"Win, what is all this?" Merrill asked as they approached.

"Dinner."

"Dinner," she echoed, staring at the array of containers spread out before her. There were even cellophane packets of knives, forks and spoons. She eyed what appeared to be a potted shrub in the center of it all. It stood about three feet high, its expansive branches in full bloom. "Quite a centerpiece you chose."

"Actually, it's what you chose."

She moved to take a closer look. "What on earth ...?"

"You mean you don't know?" he asked, his tone deadpan.

Biting her lip to control the giggle that threatened to escape, she shook her head.

"You mean I could have brought you a damn rose? Or a carnation, and you wouldn't have known the difference?"

She hitched her chin up haughtily. "I certainly know this isn't a carnation."

"No, a carnation would have been too easy. This, sweetheart, is a hibiscus." His look sharpened. "That is what you said you wanted?"

Merrill nodded, still dealing with the fact that he'd called her sweetheart. "Yes. Yes, it is, but I just said that because I thought it sounded tropical." She touched one of the glossy emerald leaves and brushed her fingertips across a white bloom the size of a grapefruit. Impulsively she bent to sniff it, murmuring with delight.

Along with the sweet, intoxicating scent, she was suddenly overwhelmed by the fact that Win had gone to such trouble to find it and bring it to her. She didn't usually inspire wild impulsive acts in others any more than she succumbed to them herself.

"Thank you, Win. It's beautiful. But where in the world did you find it at this time of night?"

"The taxi drive brought me to one of those all-night super-supermarkets with a flower shop. They wouldn't sell me one flower," he explained, breaking one off now, "so I bought the whole thing."

He held her head still with one hand and slipped the stem behind her ear with the ease of a man accustomed to doing such things. His fingers lingered, toying with her hair. Isolating a single curl, he slowly coiled it around his finger, tighter and tighter, lifting her face to his. Just as slowly, his head bent. She quivered with anticipation.

Instead of claiming her mouth, he touched his lips to the lock of hair wrapped around his finger. As he did, his gaze met hers. Merrill felt herself sway with the force of a sensation that was more emotional than physical. In a daze, she realized that what he had just done was more arousing than even the most passionate kiss could have been. It left her wanting, aching, buzzing with expectancy.

Gently unwinding her hair, he stood back to inspect his handiwork in the moonlight, his eyes dark and caressing.

"Beautiful," he whispered and smiled. "The flower, too."

"Thank you."

Win took note of her flustered shrug and of how quickly she lowered her gaze. Was she so unaccustomed to receiving compliments, he wondered, or was it simply compliments coming from him that she didn't quite trust?

Turning, he dropped to his knees on the tablecloth and began removing the lids from the plastic cartons. Following suit, Merrill sat down across from him.

"I know this isn't a moonlit beach," he said, "but it's about as close as we're going to get to one tonight. At least it's relatively private. You can pretend the tablecloth is beach sand. There also isn't much of a moon, so we'll have to improvise."

He struck a match to light the white candles he'd planted in the hibiscus pot. "See? Instant atmosphere."

"Beautiful," Merrill agreed, mesmerized by the way the flame silhouetted the sharp angles of his face against the night sky.

"Let's see," he continued, "there's chicken from the supermarket deli and potato salad and coleslaw. I wasn't sure what you liked."

"I like everything. It sounds heavenly."

He shot her a surprised look. "Aren't you going to tell me that you ordered chicken roasted with pineapple?"

"Of course not."

"Why the hell not? You always tell me when I screw something up."

"Not when you're being so nice to me, I don't." She pursed her lips thoughtfully. "Not that you've ever actually been nice to me before."

"That's more like it, Mel. Now ask me about the pineapple."

"Okay, where's the pineapple? And don't call me Mel."

He held up the only things remaining in the box, a tall glass jar and two plastic glasses. "In here. Piña coladas. You hold the glasses, I'll pour."

"Are you sure this is all right?"

"Sure. I watched the bartender make them myself."

"Not the drinks. I mean being here. I just noticed the security guard staring at us and I wondered if..."

"If we were breaking some rule by being here?"

"Something like that."

"Would it matter so much if we were?"

She thought for a moment. Then, with a bewildered shrug, admitted, "Tonight...I'm not sure."

The answer seemed to satisfy him.

"You don't have to worry," he told her. "As a matter of fact, that security guard is the one who showed me this spot. If he's staring at us, it's probably because he knows what I'm trying to do and he's wondering if it's working."

He finished pouring and glanced over his shoulder to give the man a wave. The guard waved back and quickly disappeared around the corner of the building as Win returned his attention to the jar in his hands.

"Win?"

"Mmm?"

"What *are* you trying to do?"

He looked up, met her suddenly serious gaze, and knew she wasn't asking what he was doing fiddling with the jar. Damned if I know, he thought.

"Trying to cheer you up," he said. "Is it working?"

"Yes." Her smile came slowly, giving the unexpected thrill it incited in Win plenty of time to jangle up and down his spine. "Yes. Perfectly."

"Good." He returned his attention to the jar and finally succeeded in extracting the two long wooden skewers threaded with cherries and chunks of pineapple that had been floating inside. He plunked one in each glass. "The lady wants pineapple, she gets pineapple. And as a bonus..."

Grinning, he pulled from his shirt pocket a small tissue paper umbrella of the sort usually used to adorn frothy cocktails. He stuck it into the pineapple on top of her drink. "There. Now close your eyes and when you open them again you'll be exactly where you want to be."

Either he was a magician or she was desperate enough to grasp at straws because it worked. At least for now her feelings of frustration and longing to be in Jamaica had subsided.

He lifted his glass to touch hers. "Happy vacation, Merrill."

"Win, this was such a nice thing to do. I don't know what to say."

"Don't say anything. Eat...so that I can. I'm starving."

They ate hungrily, happily, with a minimum of conversation. When their glasses were empty, he refilled them. Savoring her final mouthful Merrill deposited her empty paper plate into the box, wiped her mouth and fingers and leaned back with an utterly satisfied sigh. "Wonderful."

"The meal?" Win asked, his look both pleased and indulgent.

"The meal, this place. You were right, I'd never have believed it, but at this moment this is exactly where I want to be."

He lifted his glass, amusement in his voice. "Here's to unexpected pleasures."

"Go ahead and laugh. That's exactly what this night has turned out to be. This—" She broke off with a bewildered sweep of her hand. "This is not the sort of thing I ordinarily do."

"I know that. You're not exactly what I would call a free spirit."

"It's not that I don't want...I just never..." Her voice trailed off, and she shrugged. "Anyway, this is the sort of thing Mickey would do and then tell me about, and I would shake my head and wonder why things like this always seem to happen to her and not me."

"Mickey?"

"My younger sister...the pretty one. When we were growing up Mickey was always entering beauty contests and winning them. Now she's starring in a soap opera, playing this gorgeous, zany, totally outrageous character. Perfect typecasting." She grinned at him. "You would like Mickey."

Win felt his heart turn over at her easy assumption that he would prefer her actress sister to her. "I like you, Mel. And as far as I'm concerned, you're the pretty one."

The slow, low-pitched way he said it transformed his words into a caress. Merrill warmed with pleasure as they washed over her, and for once didn't protest his use of her nickname.

When her eyes met his, she felt a dizzying rush of sensual awareness. Drawing a deep breath, she waited for it to pass. It didn't. Instead, it built, becoming stronger, picking up elements of longing from someplace deep inside her, carrying them to the surface. Finally she had to look away in order to catch her breath.

"You said she's your younger sister," he said after a few minutes. "Do you have another one?"

"Mmm-hmm. Donna. She's two years older than I am. Donna's the smart one."

"Now I definitely would have figured you to be the smart one."

Her laughter was a clear, slow sound that rippled over him like warm water. It occurred to Win that he'd never before heard her laugh so unreservedly or seen her look so relaxed. It might be the effect of fatigue or the liquor or both, but whatever it was he liked it.

"Oh no, not even close. Donna's a certified brain. She's a research biologist. Every time we talk she's a heartbeat away from discovering a cure for something momentous."

"Three of you." Win's mouth curved. At the moment, he was finding one of her quite overwhelming. "So tell me, Mel," he said, stretching out so that his long legs hung off the edge of the cloth. His head was resting on his hand only inches from her lap. "Which one are you?"

"Brace yourself," she warned. "I'm the tall one."

"The tall one?" Win's eyes narrowed as he turned that over in his mind. "I think that's fine, Merrill, just fine. But the fact is you're not all that tall."

"I know, but it was all that was left." She giggled softly as she lifted her glass to her lips. The drink was sweet and frosty and, she was certain, greatly responsible for this pleasant drifting feeling inside her. "Oh, please don't feel sorry for me," she said, catching sight of Win's somber expression. "It's sort of a long-standing family joke."

"Right...at your expense," he said with surprising sharpness.

"It never bothered me," she explained truthfully. "I've always understood that both Donna and Mickey have extraordinary talent in their own fields. Just as I've always known that I have to work harder to succeed. That's what I meant earlier when I told you that I've never been able to just take things for granted. To get what I want I have to plan and organize and...but not tonight," she said suddenly. "Tonight is for unexpected pleasures. Tonight I can forget all that and be as impulsive and reckless as I want."

Win studied her face as she gazed off in the distance to where headlights occasionally streaked across the black horizon. There was something heartrending about the pleasure she was taking in all this. Her life must be even more restrictive and uneventful than he'd supposed, if this was her idea of reckless and impulsive.

"If I had a car right now," she said suddenly, "I would get on the freeway and drive very fast."

"Thank goodness we're grounded," muttered Win noticing her empty glass. He lifted the jar to refill it, and then thought better of it.

"I love to feel myself racing forward and see the world outside going past so fast that I don't have to think about who or what is out there. So that everything is just a nice bright blur. When I was little, that was the only thing I liked about having to move all the time, the long drives to get where we were going."

"Did you move around a lot when you were young?"

She nodded. The shimmer of her hair caressing her shoulders made Win long to reach out and touch it, but something about the way her expression had tightened stopped him.

"We moved all the time," she explained. "My father was a salesman, a good one evidently because he was always getting offers to work for other companies selling something new, something bigger and better. He'd come home with this sort of strange, wonderful light in his eyes. *This is the big one, Mary,* he would say to my mother, and the next thing I knew we'd be packing again."

As she spoke, she had unconsciously drawn her legs up and hugged them, and tipped her head back. More white lace teased him from beneath her skirt. Her bare legs gleamed in the candlelight.

"It took me years to realize there would never really be a big one," she said, shaking her head. "At least never one big enough for Dad. He thrived on the constant challenge of someplace new and something new."

"I take it you didn't thrive on it."

"I hated it," she revealed, meeting his eyes. "I hated always being the new kid and never having a real best friend and..."

She paused, her breath a fractured sigh that told Win that for her this was an emotionally charged subject. Part of him wanted to spare her by steering the discussion in a different direction, but another part of him wanted to know more about her. So he remained silent, resolving to let her find her own way through it or away from it as she chose.

"It wasn't so bad for Donna and Mickey," she said after a while. "Donna just naturally gravitated toward the other brains in her class and Mickey always has a zillion friends wherever she goes. She's that kind of person. But I...it took time for me to fit in. It seemed like just as I was getting close to someone, Dad would come home with that look in his eye."

Win wasn't fooled by the forced lilting tone in her voice. "That must have been rough, Merrill."

She shrugged. "I survived. Mom always attempted to make our new house look like our old one, trying to trick everyone into feeling at home, I guess. Anyway, she used to say she hated to hang that final picture, because as soon as she did, as soon as it really looked like home, Dad would decide he'd rather be selling tractors than electrical components. We all laughed, but I knew what she meant. It got so I avoided making close friends with anyone, because that only made it harder to go when the time came.

"You want to hear the funniest part of the whole thing?" she asked him.

Win nodded, suspecting it wasn't going to be at all funny.

"Since my mother died a few years ago, my father has stayed put. Same job, same city, same house, with all the damn pictures she loved hanging on the walls. Now, when she's not around to enjoy it."

"It could be because he doesn't have her with him anymore that he needs to stay in one place," suggested Win. "A place that reminds him of her and feels like home."

She thought that over before nodding slowly. "I never looked at it that way. Maybe as long as my mother was around, he had all the stability he needed. Home was wherever she was, wherever we were all together. She was sort of an emotional anchor for him, and now..." She stopped and glanced at him apologetically. "I'm sorry. This is beginning to sound like a bad episode of *Family Court*. Am I rambling?"

"A little. I like you this way."

"Drunk?"

"Do you feel drunk?"

She shook her head, her eyes heavy. "No. I feel good. Relaxed."

"Then that's how I like you—relaxed. It's a change. I don't feel as if every word you say is calculated. And that if I say the wrong thing or make the wrong move, you'll let me know about it in no uncertain terms."

She rolled her head to the side, gazing at him from beneath her lids in a speculative way. He ached to touch her. "I didn't think you ever made a wrong move," she told him.

"If it looks that way, it's because I've learned to avoid failure. You dig your heels in and find a way to succeed. Not me. Any time I'm not absolutely sure of what to say or do, I walk away. But luckily," he said, at last giving in to desire and reaching for her, "this is not one of those times."

Before the words were out, his hand was at the back of her neck, pulling her down. She responded gracefully, willingly. He turned toward her so that they lay stretched out on their sides, facing each other. His fingers tunneled through her hair, holding her still as his lips brushed across hers.

Feeling the tension in her, he restrained his kisses for as long as he could. His lips met hers in brief exchanges of breath, barely touching, landing as lightly as rainwater. Gradually, his self-control slipped. With each trembling stroke of mouth against mouth, each shuddering breath, desire swelled inside him. A wild need throbbed in his head and filled his lungs. It felt as if he would suffocate if he didn't kiss her the way he wanted to, needed to.

With his shoulder, he pressed her down so that she lay flat on her back. Her hair swirled around her head, glistening like spun silver. Win gathered a handful and it was like holding moonbeams. He leaned closer, rubbing his face in it, inhaling her scent until he was intoxicated with it, with her and the crazy paradox of her.

Impatiently, he pushed her glasses to the top of her head, out of his way, and at last bent to claim her mouth in a hard, driving kiss that instantly made him want more, made him want everything. His tongue plunged deeply into her, filling her mouth. He slid it back and forth against hers. The friction was rough and wet and electrifying.

Win had a sense of vaulting through space and standing still at the same time. Real time had no meaning. What he was feeling went beyond the real world. Kissing Merrill and feeling her submit beneath him put him in touch with an intoxicating sense of absolute connection.

His hands moved over her, enhancing the sheer pleasure of touching her. He caressed her shoulders and the curve of her waist. Slowly he brought his hands higher so that his thumbs were pressed to the swell of her breasts.

Her body rippled against his, languidly molding itself to him. Her curves and hollows complemented his angles as he'd known they would, as if she'd been made for him. She was warm and soft and womanly.

And she was trembling. Her hands pressed against his chest and when he kissed her again he could swear he tasted fear mixed with her excitement.

Fear was not at all the response he wanted from her. With great effort, he brought the flood of desire pumping within him under control. Brushing a final kiss across her cheek, he lifted his head to smile down at her.

He intended his tone to be light and jovial, but it came out rusty instead. "So, what do you want to do now?" he asked her.

"I'm..." She was breathless. "I'm not sure. Only that we can't do it here."

He swept the hair from her face and looked hard at her, realizing that it wasn't what they were doing that had alarmed her but where they were doing it.

"How could I have forgotten about your finely tuned sense of decorum," he teased. "And here I stopped because I thought I was scaring you."

"You were, a little," she confessed, "but..." Her tongue licked her bottom lip the way he wanted to. *Don't do that,* he pleaded silently. "But I liked it, too," she finished in a rush.

"You liked it." His voice was mellow with wonder. "But not here?"

She shook her head.

"No, of course not." His mind instinctively scrambled for an alternative. He thought of the motel a few blocks away and just as quickly dismissed the idea.

Right now Merrill was pliant, seduced by the night and the rum and his attentiveness. Suggesting a quick taxi ride to a motel room would shatter the romance of the moment. Win was startled by how fervently he did not want that to happen. There was no reason to rush things.

"In that case, I guess we ought to go back inside," he said softly. "You can check on your flight, maybe get some sleep...and you can stop trembling," he added, running his hands over her lightly. "You're safe. For now."

Saturday, 8:14 a.m.

Merrill shifted on the plastic waiting area seat, slowly coming awake, unkinking her neck.

She was not safe. Instinctively, almost before her eyes were fully open, Merrill knew that. Even if Win could be trusted, and she wasn't convinced he could be, she could no longer trust herself when she was with him.

He possessed some irresistible power over her senses. Just being near him unleashed in her an avalanche of responses. She had been attracted to men before, had even thought herself in love with Peter, but never before had she been gripped by desire with such speed and power.

So, what do you want to do now? he had asked last night after kissing her until she felt raw.

I'm not sure, she had said. She'd lied.

She knew exactly what she wanted. She wanted him. And she wanted him in ways she hadn't known she could want anyone. She thought about him in ways she had never before thought of a man. And she thought about him without relief. The fact that they were trapped here together, with nothing to distract them but each other, didn't help. Whenever she looked into his eyes she vibrated with the knowledge that his thoughts reflected the hunger of her own.

So this was lust, she mused wryly. This feeling of wild obsession.

Watching him eat breakfast led her to fantasize about long, coffee-flavored kisses in bed. He crossed his legs and she remembered the thrill of having his hard thighs pressed against hers. The sight of his hands holding a magazine was all it took for her to feel them sliding over her body, brushing her breasts, sending her into a passionate frenzy.

Desire licked at her like flames, growing hotter all the time. It was like the gravity-defying tower of plates in a magic act she'd once seen. With each recollection of the night before, each delicious plunge into fantasy, each collision of watchful stares, it grew higher and more precarious until she feared that all it would take to send it crashing was the feather-light touch of Win's hand.

She couldn't allow that to happen. Could she? Win was still her boss. But not for much longer, a voice argued. For the first time, she found a bright spot in his plans for the company. Besides, boss or not, he was also the most exciting man she'd ever known, and she could no longer pretend she wasn't aroused by him. He was also the most aggravating, of course. She shouldn't even allow herself to be thinking the things she was thinking, and she certainly would never act on them.

Or would she? It was so hard to think straight when everything inside you was in chaos. All she knew for sure was that if Coastways Airlines didn't get their act together soon, she would be lost.

Saturday, 2:14 p.m.

Win was riding a wave of heat that had nothing to do with the tropical weather and everything to do with the woman beside him.

Merrill Winters made him hot. Somewhere between Ingraham's office and here, his whim to seduce her had become hard-core desire. Last night had pushed him even beyond that, to a need that was raw and immediate.

They had ended the night on a harmonious note. Today the tension was back. But something was different. The mood between them was strung tight, but it was not hostile. It pulsed. It sizzled. There was something elemental about their emotional circling of each other. They were like bull and matador, two opposing forces destined to clash.

He craved hearing the sound of her voice because it had the power to raise the hair at the back of his neck. He intentionally sprawled in his seat so that her shoulder would rub against his and send pleasure leaping through him. Simply looking at her made his senses pound. He felt like a randy stallion straining at a bit that was growing weaker by the minute. He felt like an idiot.

Of course he'd experienced this blinding need for women in the past, but ordinarily it built slowly over the course of a pleasant evening, reaching a peak and lasted only as long as it took him to satisfy the woman he was with and himself. This was different. This was relentless.

Win tried telling himself that the reason it felt different and special was because of their circumstances. He was attracted to Merrill and was picking up unmistakable signals that the interest was mutual, but for the time being there was nothing much they could do about it. It was like dating back in high school, knowing that no matter how the night turned out, what you wanted most was off-limits. Actually, this was even more frustrating. Sitting there between the kids and the Golden Agers he couldn't even grope her the way he yearned to.

Suppressed as they were, his fantasies grew wild and textured, like some exotic forbidden fruit. The hell of it was that as his craving for her became sharper, it became sweeter as well. Part of him was savoring this mounting anticipation. Even if it wasn't by choice, it was enticing to learn all over again how good it can feel to hold hands, how potent a look can be, how a casual touch from the right woman can be more arousing than a thousand meaningless caresses.

It was the romantic side of him that was enjoying all this, Win supposed. He wasn't sure what to call the part of him that felt like a pressure cooker, trapped between heaven and hell and about to explode.

Saturday, 6:19 p.m.

The announcement that negotiations between Coastways management and labor had been suspended until the following morning and that they were therefore providing passengers with room vouchers and bus service to the nearby Holiday Inn was greeted with cheers, immediately followed by a stampede to the ticket desk.

Merrill turned to Win and her breath caught as a single shared thought connected them. A bed.

"I never imagined I'd come to this point," she said, "but right about now a room voucher sounds better than a flight to Jamaica."

"I was just thinking the same thing."

Reeling from the heat in his gaze, she instinctively backtracked to dilute her comment. "I mean because it'll give me a chance to freshen up, of course."

"Of course," he said, his smile mocking. "What else?"

"Nothing." She told herself she meant that every bit as firmly as it sounded. "I feel so grungy."

"Me, too." And horny, he thought.

"And I'm a little tired."

"Yeah." And horny, he thought.

"This will be nice."

"Mmm." Nice? It was going to be like all the Christmas mornings of his life rolled into one.

Walking beside him to pick up their vouchers, Merrill supposed it was true that she *was* feeling grungy and tired. She couldn't be sure, because desire was dulling all other sensations. She might have been wearing burlap and ashes and coming off a three-week insomnia jag. If asked at that moment what she wanted most, her answer, amazingly, insanely, would be Win Deverell.

It took an hour and a half to distribute vouchers, sort luggage and fill the first bus. As the last ones to board, she and Win were lucky to find a single seat to share. As he drew her onto his lap, she curled an arm around his neck for support. He put his arms the only place there was room, around her middle. Then they both sat there with their faces innocently blank, as if totally oblivious to the way their bodies were pressed together, as if his palms weren't flattened on her belly, as if his warm breath weren't raising goose bumps along her neck. As if an explosive passion, connected by a single fuse, wasn't ticking inside each of them.

Like everything else lately, the bus was hot and overcrowded. The ten-minute ride to the hotel seemed to last forever and cover the bumpiest, most winding stretch of Interstate 95. Taking the curves was the worst. Each time the bus veered left, so did Merrill, crushing her breasts against Win's chest. And each time she tried to right herself, her fanny ground against the hardest part of him. By the time she finally peeled herself off him in the Holiday Inn parking lot, she was breathless and Win looked like he needed a drink. Or something.

At least being last to board enabled them to be first off. After collecting their bags they hurried inside. As they crossed the lobby of the sprawling brick hotel, Merrill eyed the elevators longingly, picturing the pleasure waiting above—a cool, comfortable room and a lovely, big bed. Unbidden, her imagination painted Win into the scene, and a sensual energy she'd never known before surged inside her.

She needed a cold shower and a nap to pull herself together. She needed to be alone.

This time they were at the front of the stampede, among the first to reach the lobby and the first in line at the registration desk. So they were the first to hear the apologetic announcement that there had been an unfortunate breakdown in communication between the airline and the hotel. Merrill listened in disbelief as the solemn-faced hotel manager recited something about the overflow from the Great Chowder Cook-Off and unanticipated arrivals and holiday travelers. The bottom line was that there were nowhere near enough vacancies to accommodate the people still streaming into the lobby.

In response to an angry question, he regretfully predicted that all hotels in the vicinity were feeling the same crunch. He continued, explaining that after consulting with the airline representative, it had been determined that the only fair way to handle the matter was to assign rooms in the order the vouchers were originally distributed, according to the number printed in the top right-hand corner.

Merrill didn't even bother to check the number on hers. Recalling the way she and Win had waited out the initial rush to get vouchers back at the airport, she turned to him dejectedly.

With a quick glance at the crowd surrounding them, he succinctly summed up their chances of getting a room. "No way."

They had come so close, she thought, dragging herself toward the door. She was alarmed not by how disappointed she felt, but why. Her desire for a shower and sleep were dwarfed by her desire for Win, which had become a sharp ache at her core. She hadn't wanted to admit even to herself the real reason for the almost giddy anticipation she felt coming here. Now, denied, the craving became even stronger. She was like a dieter trapped with a box of chocolates, a drunk with a bottle of whiskey. Just this once...just this once...the refrain pounded in her head.

As they reached the hotel door, a black stretch limousine pulled up under the canopy outside. The driver quickly came around to open the door for the passengers who were invisible behind the tinted glass. Looking cool and unruffled, a tuxedo-clad groom, followed by his bride in pristine white lace, emerged from the air-conditioned luxury of the limo.

Merrill and Win stepped aside to let them enter. The young woman's expression was joyful and animated. She laughed, looking up at her new husband as she took his arm and swept past.

"Nice to see someone's having a good day," Merrill grumbled.

"Let's hope they don't plan on flying Coastways for their honeymoon."

"I didn't think things could possibly get any more awful than they already were, but this is definitely worse."

"No, worse is going to be climbing back on that bus for a ride back to the airport."

"But at least if we go now," she pointed out as they walked outside, "we might get seats near a window that opens."

"Somehow that doesn't make me feel significantly more enthusiastic."

"Well, enthusiasm aside, I don't see that we have any alternative.

Win caught at her arm, bringing her to a sudden halt as she started along the walk. Turning, Merrill found him staring at the long black limo with a slightly wild, very determined expression.

"I do," he said.

lowered to curl tightly around the back of her neck, it exploded inside her, unleashing a cathartic madness.

He yanked her forward just as she began to melt against him. The combined force sent her crashing into his chest. He gripped her upper arms, her arms wound around his neck, and they fell on each other hungrily.

He kissed her mouth, tugged on her hair until she arched her neck for him to kiss her there. He dragged his hot mouth higher to kiss her ear, thrusting his tongue deep inside. It was rough and wet and it was driving her into a frenzy. Merrill moaned with the force of the pleasure ripping through her. He bit her earlobe, then framed her face with his palms and held her still as he kissed her mouth again and again.

His kisses were explicit, and in between them he murmured to her in a frankly sexual language. Merrill could barely hear him above the frantic rasp of their breathing, but she liked it...she liked all of it. She liked the impatience in him, the hint of roughness in the way he handled her, her own fierce hunger. She liked the feeling of being on the edge of something dangerous. Somehow his wildness sanctioned the new wildness inside her.

She found the buttons on his shirt and ripped them open, pushing the fabric aside to circle his chest with her palms. He felt rough and hairy and wonderful. When she plucked at his nipples he grunted with pleasure, then tipped her backward to take her mouth in a deep, tongue-thrusting kiss.

She sucked hard on his tongue and felt a tremor rock him. It was passion without pretense. A heady eroticism. Nothing was out-of-bounds. For the first time in her life, she felt free to do anything, feel anything, dare anything.

With his hands on her shoulders he pressed her back against the seat hard enough to make her eyes fly open.

"Admit it." He lifted his mouth off hers only far enough to speak. "I want to hear you say the words."

She stared at him in a sensual daze, her eyes blinking rapidly.

"Come on, Merrill. I can feel it when I touch your skin and you tremble. I can taste it. I can even smell it, for God's sake. You want this as much as I do. Say it."

Before she could form any words, he ducked and bit her bottom lip, scraped his whiskered jaw across the smooth skin of hers. Exquisite punishment, it made her burn inside. She licked her lips. They felt swollen and tasted of Win.

"I want you," she whispered. "Now." The admission quickened her need. Her fingers wrapped around the edges of his shirt, dragging him closer. "Right now."

Without a word he pushed her down onto the seat, arranging his knees so that he was straddling her. Hooking his thumbs under her blouse he pushed it up so that it was bunched at her armpits, then swept aside the lacy white camisole and bra she wore underneath, baring her breasts to his gaze. She watched his face while he strummed the soft pink aureolas with his fingertips. As they hardened she whimpered with pleasure and saw passion swirl darkly in his eyes.

Bending his head, he caressed her with his tongue. His hair fell forward, tickling the flushed and sensitive skin of her chest and throat. When he drew her nipple into his mouth Merrill's hips lifted off the seat, thrusting into him. She clutched at him, settling her hands on either side of his waist for support.

Taking his weight on his knees, Win straightened. He held her gaze as he slid his hands over her hips, skimming down her thighs to find the hem of her skirt and hike it up to her waist. He slipped his hand between her legs and touched her through her panties. She felt hot and damp. The musky scent of their arousal swirled around him. He pressed with his thumb, seeking, and knew when he found the spot because her head fell back and her teeth clamped over her bottom lip.

Seeing her respond so uninhibitedly inflamed him. As quickly as he could, he worked her panties off and planted both his knees between hers. He reached for his buckle, then stopped and lifting her hands placed them there instead.

"You do it," he urged.

He liked watching her fingers unfasten his belt. He liked feeling the backs of them pressed to his belly as she undid the button at his waist and enjoyed seeing her eyes widen with delight as she lowered his zipper, freeing him, exposing the height of his desire for her.

Still watching her, he braced his weight on one hand and with the other played with the pale gold curls between her legs. A deep, primitive urge he'd never known before reared up inside him, driving him on. Roughly shoving his pants lower, he covered her and with a single powerful thrust made her his. The pleasure he felt being inside her was so pure that sweat beaded his forehead, and for a minute he had to hold absolutely still or he felt he would die.

Her body drew him in and held him. The friction was nearly too much as he slowly pulled almost all the way out, teasing her and himself, then plunged again. As he moved he slipped his hand between their bodies, his palm on her belly, his fingers pointed toward her breast. With each stroke he worked it lower until the heel of his hand pressed the spot that held the power to make every muscle in her body grow taut with anticipation. He kneaded her there, his touch sure and rhythmic.

Merrill's head thrashed on the seat as the sweet pressure within grew unbearably strong. Electric sensations whipped through her, gathering into a combustible knot down low, near the place where his hand still moved relentlessly, imparting a sweet magic that was driving her toward the edge. Perspiration dotted her upper lip as her fingers found the leather handhold above her head. She clung to it as the fiery pleasure finally exploded.

Never had she climaxed with such fury. This was all sensation and all new and a little frightening. She cried Win's name sharply as she felt herself free-falling through total blackness. Like magic he was there. His arms were around her, his chest crushing her breasts, his hoarse moan of gratification long and resplendent and sounding so close it seemed to be coming from someplace deep inside her.

After a while Win sat back, pulling Merrill along so that her weight rested on him. He kept his arms around her. With one hand he stroked her head where it lay cradled against his chest, smoothing the tangled waves of her hair.

His heart hadn't stopped thundering when he felt her move. Without lifting her head, she reached up and pulled her blouse down to cover her breasts. Then she tugged at her skirt. He began to feel uncomfortable about the fact that his own pants were still bunched around his thighs, and he had to fight an urge to scramble to cover up like some insecure schoolboy.

Something was definitely wrong and he realized that he probably should have expected it. He'd wanted Merrill so badly he'd blinded himself to everything else. Belatedly, he considered what had just happened in the context of all he was beginning to learn about the woman in his arms.

Last night, for the first time, he had discovered that beneath that cool, capable veneer Merrill was extremely vulnerable. She had no idea how beautiful and intelligent she really was, and she had admitted that she didn't think she was particularly talented or lucky. She had tremendous faith in hard work, but none in her own instincts and so was convinced that acting impetuously invariably led to disaster.

He had an uneasy feeling that by Merrill's standards what had just happened was not simply impetuous, but in direct defiance of a precise code of behavior that undoubtedly included a precept dictating that a woman shall not screw her boss. Especially in cases where she and her boss have mixed like bees and vinegar since day one.

He read her thoughts at that moment as if he were a blind man and they were written in Braille on the soft skin beneath his fingertips. She was berating herself, telling herself she never should have let matters go so far, refusing to feel any of the joy she ought to be feeling...that he so badly wanted her to feel.

She might even be experiencing a little guilt. That would explain her big rush to cover up and the way she was feeling around on the seat for his displaced glasses, clearly in a big hurry to put the world back into focus the way she thought it ought to be.

Lifting the glasses from the seat, he tapped her on the shoulder with them. "These what you're looking for?"

"Yes. Thanks." She sat up to put them on. She smoothed her hair, her blouse, her skirt, and dragged her hand across her mouth. Finally she lifted her head.

For all her fussing, thought Win, she still looked beautifully disheveled and sweetly dazed. In that instant, he knew
that one way or another there would be a next time and a
next. Perversely, he wished the first time was still ahead of
them. He would go about things very differently.

The urge to make this easier for her rose up strongly inside him. He couldn't undo what was done any more than
he could go back and do it in a slower, more conventional
way that would placate her sensibilities. But he could soothe
her conscience a bit by telling her the truth, that he was more
to blame for this than she was...if you could use the word
blame in connection with something that felt so right.

An awkward confession, but a necessary one.

"Merrill?"

"Mmm?"

She rested her head on the seat and stretched her legs.
Pretending to be relaxed, Win thought tenderly.

"There's something I have to tell you. I probably should
have said something before...or gone about things differently. I just didn't think..."

She turned to him. Her eyes, a dark, hypnotic blue, held
a shade of embarrassment. "Win, I'm not promiscuous, but
I'm also not naive. I don't rely on men for birth control
protection, if that's what you're getting at."

"Always planning ahead, hmm? Always prepared?"

She nodded.

"Well, I'm glad to hear you're protected, because the
truth is I was so caught up in what was happening I forgot
all about using something."

Her eyes widened in response to his serious tone. "Is that
a problem? You're not trying to tell me..." She halted, but
her expression conveyed a string of fearful questions.

"No," he snapped, feeling injured that she thought she had to ask and at the same time flattered that, being Merrill, she hadn't demanded a complete medical history up front. He really had swept her off her feet. "It's nothing like that. It's just that I think you should know that the reason this happened is because I wanted it to."

His heart clenched at the sight of her small, awkward smile.

"I wanted it, too," she confessed.

"But not the same way I did. You talk about planning? I planned for this, Merrill, every step of the way." Saying it out loud made him feel as greasy as old currency. Which was all the more reason he had to say it before they went any further. "Since the moment we left Ingraham's office yesterday afternoon I've had just one thought in mind... seducing you."

I know."

Win's head snapped as if it were mounted on a spring. "You know?"

"Of course. Is that all you wanted to tell me?"

He nodded slowly.

"For heaven's sake, Win, for a second you had me worried."

"I can't believe you knew."

"Well, I did."

"All along? You knew all along?" He seemed to be having a lot of trouble with such a simple fact.

"Of course." Wearing a subtle smile, she gazed at him from beneath slightly arched brows. "Think about it, Win, the hibiscus, the romantic dinner, all those sweet compliments that you would have choked on just a few days ago. You weren't exactly subtle."

His expression flickered as he absorbed what she was saying, revealing a series of emotions as clearly delineated as textbook diagrams. Surprise, disbelief, confusion, disbelief and, finally, acceptance, which quickly turned to annoyance. Apparently the notion that his legendary charm could be so transparent didn't mesh with Win's image of himself.

No doubt he fancied himself some sort of seducer extraordinaire, thought Merrill, telling herself it served him right to have the tables turned by a woman who saw through his game and elected to play it as blithely as he did. For her sake, she only wished that were the case.

Oh, yes, on one level she had known all along what he was up to, but knowing hadn't saved her. He had been charming, and she had been charmed beyond reason. He'd been bent on seduction, and she had been seduced. Expertly, passionately, utterly seduced.

In those final sane seconds before he started kissing her, she had warned herself that was all there was to it, that what she felt was simple lust, a biological urge easily satisfied and then forgotten. Her mind had spit forth a rapid-fire stream of circular logic to justify what she burned to do.

She was on vacation. She was exercising her sexual equality. Her freedom of choice. It was a good way to vent frustration and pass the time. And it wasn't as if she had picked up a stranger in the airport lounge. Technically she had known Win for years. He was a very attractive man, and she was a normal woman. It would be fun, and she deserved some fun.

So she had done what she never did: she'd succumbed to impulse. It had been fun, and it had been soul-shattering. It had been everything she'd ever read or heard that making love could be, *should* be, but had never been for her. What it had not been, she realized too late, was anything as simple as lust.

How could something that meant nothing have meant so much? she mused, watching Win yank his pants up and shove his shirt back inside. And how could she have been foolish enough to think her emotions could be controlled as easily as the water flowing from a garden hose? With jerky motions he zipped and buttoned and buckled. She smoothed and tugged and patted until they were both tidy and composed, sitting side by side as if nothing monumental had occurred.

For Win that was probably an accurate assessment, and she'd rather chew nails than give him the satisfaction of knowing how much more it had meant to her. Hiding her feelings was a self-defense mechanism, and years of practice, years of saying goodbye and leaving friends behind had made her an expert at it. If you pretended not to care, it didn't hurt so much. Sometimes if you pretended hard enough for long enough you even began to believe it. For now, she was only concerned that Win believed it so that she could survive this with her dignity intact.

It had grown dark outside the limo. His face averted, Win stared out his window in silence at a landscape that was exactly what she'd requested last night...a shadowy blur pierced by hazy points of light. She used to feel a sense of tranquility seeing the world outside reduced to fast-moving streams of color and light, but the trick wasn't working tonight. The problems she faced now weren't out there, but deep inside her.

Finally, Win turned to face her, and Merrill was startled to see his eyes narrowed to dark slits and a confrontational set to his mouth.

"Let me get this straight," he said. "You knew all along that I was trying to seduce you?"

"How many times are you going to ask me? Yes, I knew, all right?"

"No. No, it isn't all right at all. You knew what I was doing and yet you went along with it?"

She gave a smile she hoped looked worldly and enigmatic. "Obviously."

"Why?"

"It was an impulse," she replied with a shrug.

He looked indignant. "That's no reason."

"Last night you seemed to think it was a perfectly fine reason for doing something, even a philosophy to live by."

"That is different."

"How is it different, Win?" She held her breath, yearning for him to say something to convince her it was different, that it had been special to him, too. For a moment it almost seemed he would. Then he turned away, shoving his fingers through his hair.

"It just is," he muttered. "This was more than some bet over taking off your damn stockings. It wasn't some sort of game or contest."

"Wasn't it?" she countered, everything inside her longing to hear him deny it.

He opened his mouth, his eyes locked with hers, then abruptly averted his gaze. "I don't know. I guess maybe it was . . . in a way."

"Under the circumstances, don't you think it would have been simpler—not to mention more honest—just to ask me straight out to go to bed with you? Then we could have approached it like two adults."

He flushed, his stubborn expression reminding her of a child not getting his own way and not quite sure what to do about it. "I don't want to approach it like two adults, damn it. I want to know the real reason you let me make love to you. The truth this time."

"I've told you the truth," she lied.

"No. There has to be more to it than that. I know you."

"All right." She leaned back against the seat, her eyes glittering. "But first tell me, why did you want to make love to me?"

"Because you're beautiful, and I'm attracted to you."

"I feel the same way about you."

"And because you always seem so...unattainable."

"Yes," she said, her nod slow and thoughtful, "you seemed that way to me, too."

Frustration with her tactics flashed in his eyes, dark and lethal. Clasping her upper arms he drew her closer, lifting her off the seat. "And because you make me hotter than I've been in a long, long time."

It was all she could do to nod without letting her teeth chatter. Her voice was a whisper. "You make me hot, too, Win."

Even before he bent his head she knew he was going to kiss her. He didn't look like he wanted to exactly, it was more like he was being driven from within.

It was a hard, rough kiss, more punishing than passionate. It didn't matter. The taste of his lips thrilled her. Without planning to, she opened her mouth. His tongue thrust between her lips, ravenous, demanding. A low groan escaped her as her body began to sink into his. Merrill wasn't sure what response he was seeking, but that clearly wasn't it.

"Damn you," he hissed, releasing her so abruptly she fell back against the seat. "Just because you're hot is no reason for you to start rolling around in the back of a limo with me."

"Why not?" She tossed her head to clear it, a gesture that looked supremely self-assured. "It was evidently a good enough reason for you to rush around buying flowers and dinner and rubbing up against me every chance you got and renting the damn limo in the first place."

"That's different. I always follow my impulses and do just as I please. But not you. You had to spend half an hour debating whether to take your panty hose off, for Pete's sake. You need a reason and a game plan to say good morning. You expect me to believe you made love with me on impulse? I just don't buy it.''

"Well, whether you buy it or not, it's a fact. And frankly, since you got what you wanted, I don't see why you're so angry."

"Who the hell is angry?" he shouted.

He was. And it suddenly occurred to Merrill to wonder why. Preoccupied with concealing her own feelings, she hadn't considered how very out of character his reaction was.

When he first confessed to intentionally seducing her, she'd assumed he was gloating. She wondered now if it might have been prompted by guilt instead. But why should Win feel guilty for doing what he set out to do? Unless—a fascinating explanation uncoiled inside her—unless his feelings had changed. Unless what he'd thought he wanted was no longer enough.

If that was true, what did it mean for the one-night stand she had braced herself to accept? Tantalizing possibilities presented themselves to her. *Suppose, just suppose...*

"So that's really all I am to you?" he asked, interrupting her private thoughts. "Just an impulse? No more than a convenient way to scratch an itch?"

"I'm not sure I would choose those exact words," she replied, her suspicions raised by the lazy nonchalance that had replaced the anger in his tone. "But, yes, I suppose that's basically it."

"And how about right now?" he asked, cupping her chin in his warm, rough palm, scouring her face with eyes that were intense and yet revealed nothing of what he was feeling. His voice was soft and smooth. "Now that you don't *itch* anymore, you have no regrets? No second thoughts?"

Who doesn't itch? she thought. Pushing aside all semblance of the truth, she shook her head. "None."

"Well, that's good. That's real good, Merrill. You've come a long way. Tell me..." With the pad of his thumb he stroked her lips, dipped inside for moisture, painted them with it. "Have you given any thought to what you'll do if this impulse strikes again?"

Anticipation shivered up and down her spine. "I guess I'll decide when—and if—that happens. I am on vacation. I think that entitles me to a little spontaneity."

"Ah yes, vacation."

"Yes. Vacation. And I've decided to take your advice."

"What advice is that?" His hand was on her throat now, his fingers teasing, caressing.

"At least for this week I'm going to let life rise up and meet me. I'm going to stop analyzing every move I make."

"Really? Still, it must please you to be able to file me in the nice neat category of a vacation fling." His mouth was smiling, but not his eyes.

"Does that upset you?" she asked.

"Any reason it should?"

Her mouth went dry under his close scrutiny. "None that I can think of. We are adults, after all. We know our own minds, can make our own decisions. We certainly have the right to share a fling. If we should decide we want to, that is. It doesn't have to change anything."

"Doesn't it?" His brows lifted. "How about when the vacation—and the fling—is over?"

"I expect we'll both survive." Would she really? Right now she wondered if she would survive the next few moments. His touch was making her senses vibrate. His leg had slid close to press against hers.

"How about next week," he continued, "when we're back at work? Remember, I am still your boss."

His voice was low, like an echo in her head. His hand was inside her blouse. She was fighting for breath when she was struck by an ugly suspicion about what he was suggesting. She tried to straighten up, but the pressure of his body made it difficult.

"What are you getting at?" she asked. "I hope you don't think that the reason I . . . we . . . that it's because I work for you that I . . . Win? *Is* that what you think?" Maybe that was the reason for his anger a few minutes ago.

"What I think," he murmured, putting his lips to her throat, "is that you are the sweetest, most . . ."

"Stop." Marshaling her self-control, she shoved at his shoulders. "I want an answer. Do you think the real reason I made love with you is because you're my boss?"

"Of course not, Merrill." He drew back a few inches, holding himself absolutely still against her. "I know I'm no more than an impulse to you."

"I meant what I said, Win," she told him, not trusting his denial any more than she did the challenging glint in his eyes. Beneath both, she sensed layers of something she didn't understand. "I don't expect this to change anything. I'll still do my job. You'll still be my boss. I'm sure we can both behave like professionals."

"What if this impulse should strike again, while we're at work?"

"We'll control it," she said firmly.

"And if we can't?"

She still had the feeling he was testing her, but when he rubbed his whiskered jaw along her neck she shivered with pleasure, which only made her angrier. With him. With herself.

Somehow she found breath to lash out at him. "I wouldn't worry about it. I'm sure that with your luck you'll manage to find a buyer and sell Haigh and Deverell before it becomes a problem."

Win appeared neither shocked nor upset by her words. He studied her carefully, as if *her* response to them were of greater interest than his own.

He leaned back, putting distance between them. With his touch withdrawn Merrill's skin felt cold.

"So," he said finally, "you know about that, too. It seems you're much more perceptive than I gave you credit for."

"It's not a matter of perception," she told him. "A friend of mine is a broker for companies looking to buy or be bought. She mentioned hearing that you had put out feelers."

"It's gone beyond that actually. I've hired a broker, and we've had several interesting offers."

The hollow feeling that stole over her was reflected in her voice. "So it's not just a rumor."

"Come on, Merrill, you never really thought it was."

"No," she agreed. "Oh, maybe at first I did. I didn't want it to be true, so I told myself it was simply speculation, that not even you were crazy enough to sell a successful company for no good reason."

"I have a good reason."

"Which is?"

He hesitated, as if weighing his reply, then shrugged and said, "I don't want to run it anymore."

"You don't want to run it anymore?" Merrill's tone was tinged with disbelief. "What about Ted?"

"I'd say it's pretty obvious that Ted feels the same way. Otherwise he'd be here instead of in Alaska."

"That could be temporary," she argued, expressing one of her fondest hopes. "He might come back any time."

"I don't think so, and frankly, after sitting in his seat for the past three months, I don't blame him."

"Why? Because running Haigh and Deverell is a job that requires you to be responsible and wear a suit and meet deadlines and..."

"And schedule your life away down to the last second and be nickeled and dimed by slimy attorneys. Exactly. It sucks."

"It might seem that way to you now, sort of overwhelming, but if you hang in there you'll develop your own system. I know you will."

"Maybe that's what I'm afraid of. Maybe I don't want any system. I like waking up in the morning and not knowing exactly what my day will be like. I like getting my hands dirty when I work. I hate the thought of spending my life sitting in an office pushing papers."

Her temper went off like a rocket. "I don't push papers. And neither did Ted. I settle claims involving millions of dollars. That requires skill and patience and experience. I get a feeling of real satisfaction from bringing order to a complicated case file and seeing it through to completion."

"I don't." His expression was implacable, his tone as final as an auctioneer's gavel. If she hadn't before, Merrill knew now that Haigh and Deverell was as good as gone. Frustration heated her blood.

"Fine, so you go ahead and accept one of these interesting offers you've received. What then?"

"I'll probably take some time off, do some sailing."

Her laugh was short and sarcastic. "Won't that be a nice change?"

"Yes, as a matter of fact it will be. I know you think my end of the business has been all fun and games, but while you're sitting in your nice, air-conditioned office anguishing over something critical, like whether it's more efficient to file by date of loss or policy number, I'm crawling around the belly of a ship, slopping through seaweed, inspecting greasy broken-down engines, all to make sure nothing blows up in your face in the middle of one of your stuffy meetings."

She folded her arms across her chest stiffly. "Thank you."

"I don't want you to thank me. It's my job. Just don't turn your nose up and act like because I don't wear a suit and tie what I do is a joke."

"I never intended to imply that. And actually when I asked the question I wasn't asking what you're going to do now, I was thinking about the people who work for you."

"I see." His harsh laugh took her by surprise. "Suggesting that I haven't thought of them, right? Well, I have. One of my priorities in making a deal will be that the new owners retain a high percentage of the staff."

"They may keep on the clerks and typists, but you know as well as I do that anyone with any authority will be replaced with their own people."

"I've anticipated that, and I've already looked into providing very generous severance packages, as well as help with résumés and placement. I know a lot of people in the business, and I'll do everything I can to see that everyone lands on their feet."

"How noble."

Win didn't feel noble. Sitting in the direct line of her contemptuous glare, he felt guilty for the first time since he'd made the decision to sell out. Which was ridiculous. He also felt the urge to say whatever it took to erase the bitter disapproval from her eyes, but he had no idea how to go about it. He wasn't particularly introspective, and he sure as hell wasn't interested in resurrecting a bunch of painful memories right now.

"I just have one more question," Merrill told him.

Her tone was so mild he was instantly suspicious. "What's that?"

"If everything is going to be so wonderful for everyone, why are you keeping the sale such a big secret?"

"It's not such a big secret. You found out."

"By chance. You could have announced it and given everyone plenty of time to make plans."

"Your favorite word again, *plans*. What are you really worried about, Merrill, having enough time to transfer the payroll deductions for your IRA?"

"Yes," she shouted, "that's one thing I'm worried about. I'm also worried about finding another job and starting over at a new place with new people."

"I know how you feel about that and I understand. But you're not a little girl now, Merrill. You're smart and experienced and very good at what you do. I can name a half-dozen companies that would snap you up tomorrow."

"Companies located in Sarasota?"

"No, but..."

"You just don't get it do you? There are some of us who don't think it's exciting to be uprooted and packed off to someplace new, who don't like living life by the seat of our pants."

"And there are some of us who do. Do you honestly expect me to plan my future and the future of the company around whether or not a handful of employees might have to relocate?"

"No," she said turning away. "I don't honestly expect anything from you at all."

Afraid that if he touched her she'd flinch, he resigned himself to talking to the back of her head. "Just for the record, I wasn't being underhanded by keeping this quiet. I planned to make an announcement as soon as I had something solid to announce. For all I knew, it might not have worked out. Do you blame me for not wanting to alarm people unnecessarily?"

"I suppose not," she said, then shrugged. "Look, it's your company, handle it however you like."

"But you think I'm handling it wrong? You think I'm wrong to sell?"

"Does it matter what I think?"

"Yes." Then, because he'd made up his mind never to be less than truthful with her ever again, he added, "And no. Merrill, I'd go crazy sitting behind that desk forever, and I'd drive you crazy right along with me. In fact, I'm already doing that...admit it."

He was driving her crazy, but not exactly in the way he meant. His smile, his sexy drawl, the memory of their passion a few moments ago and the vibrations he was giving off even now...all of it was driving her crazy.

Even more upsetting, to her amazement, she was beginning to understand him. She didn't want to understand. It would be easier to go on disapproving of him. She wanted to resent him. Hell, she wanted to hate him. Instead, she was being drawn closer and closer to him. And a big part of what she was drawn to was the part of him she'd deplored most heartily, the part that couldn't be shackled to a desk and nine-to-five life-style. Win wasn't Rolodexes and wing tips. He was physical and sensual and unpredictable. He was everything she'd always avoided in life.

"Admit it," he ordered again. "I drive you crazy."

"You drive me crazy. Satisfied?"

"It's a start." His grin came slowly. "A thank-you would be nice."

"You want me to thank you? What on earth for?"

"For coming up with the idea of selling in the first place. If I don't, if we have to keep working side by side, day in and day out, we don't have a chance."

"Be serious, Win. What happened a few minutes ago was..."

"Fantastic."

"A freak accident. A once-in-a-lifetime experience. You and I are like oil and water, day and night..." She fumbled for words. "Ship and shore. Face it, Win, any way you look at it, we don't have a chance."

hey drove all night, leaving the freeway somewhere in
ew Hampshire to travel south along the winding New En-
and coastline that would eventually return them to the
rport. They might have been moving in circles for all Win
1ew or cared. Merrill had finally dozed off with nothing
solved between them, leaving him feeling frustrated and
1certain.

He looked at the matter a hundred different ways and it
ill looked the same. What had started out as a lark for
m—and maybe for both of them, although he still wasn't
nvinced Merrill had acted on impulse alone—was now
mething much more. Making love to Merrill had left him
1ysically satisfied, but hungry in ways he hadn't known
isted. His feelings for her were complicated and tangled,
id he was determined to sort them out.

There was only one way he could do that. Somehow, he
id to make Merrill face up to the truth, that what she felt
r him was something more than desire and that what they
id shared was more than a vacation fling. Once she had,
would be safe for him to admit it, too.

At dawn, they stopped for breakfast at a roadside diner.
ack in the limo afterward the mood between them was
iendly, but guarded. Try as he might, Win couldn't steer
e conversation onto a more intimate track. Half a dozen
nes when their eyes met and clung he was tempted to let
s instincts dominate, to tumble her onto the seat and make
r his all over again.

Ironically, however, he found himself taking a positi
that had always mystified him when he'd been on the
ceiving end of it in the past. He was determined not to ma
love to Merrill again until she gave some sign that s
thought of him as more than a convenient way to sow so
wild oats. He'd always been the one to argue that pleasu
for pleasure's sake was enough. He knew now that som
times it was not.

They had only been back at the airport a half-hour wh
Merrill was paged to the Coastways ticket counter. S
didn't invite him to tag along, so he squelched the urge to c
so. Negotiations to end the work action had resumed th
morning, and the official word was that the two sides we
close to agreement. In the meantime, the public-relatio
minded airline was still honoring room vouchers as soon
rooms became available at three nearby hotels.

When she returned, instead of sitting down, Merr
reached for her suitcase and stood before him looking ve
ill at ease.

"They have a room for me," she announced.

Win's heart soared, leveled, crashed. She hadn't sai
They have a room for *us*.

"Great."

Silence.

She shifted her suitcase to her right hand, wiping t
sweaty palm of her left hand on her skirt.

"I'm sure you'll be called up there any minute," she sai
"They're going by that list they made and filling rooms
quickly as guests check out of the hotels. You were rig
behind me in line."

"I remember."

"So you're probably next on the list."

"Makes sense."

"I'm sure it won't be long."

"I'm sure you're right."

"Maybe we'll even end up at the same hotel."

And maybe they wouldn't. Did it even matter to her? Win wondered.

He managed a smile. "Stranger things have happened."

"Yes, well, I'll see you. And thanks, you know, for last night . . . I mean for breakfast, and the limo and . . ." She stopped short, her face coloring. "I mean . . ."

"I know what you mean," Win said gently, wanting to ease her embarrassment at that moment nearly as much as he wanted to grab her and shout, *What the hell is going on with us?*

"So if I don't run into you at the hotel, I guess I'll see you in the office next week," she said, backing up a few steps.

Next week. She might as well have said next year or next century. The thought of being without her for even a few minutes made him ache with something he suspected was loneliness. He didn't want her to walk away, but even more, he didn't want her to *want* to walk away from him.

"Right, next week. I hope you get a flight to Jamaica soon." About as much as I hope to be swallowed up by the Bermuda Triangle, he thought. "If you don't, we can work out something, arrange for another week for your vacation."

"Thanks. I contacted the hotel there and had them hold my room, but if this thing drags on past today I'm going to cancel it."

She sighed with such feeling her chest shuddered, as if the prospect of altering her damn vacation plans was tearing her up inside, thought Win.

"That's probably a good idea," he told her.

"Yes, I think so. Well, so long."

Her smile, her shrug, the way she tossed her hair back, all of it was strained, as if she'd be relieved when this awkward scene was over.

Well, that made two of them, he told himself, reaching for the newspaper someone had abandoned on the seat next to him. He gave a dismissive nod. "Yeah, see ya."

He looked at the newspaper so he wouldn't have to watch her walk away and then gave in and watched anyway, feeling a knifelike twisting in his gut with each step she took. As soon as she was out of sight he chucked the newspaper and stood up. His emotions were racing frantically and in too many opposing directions for him to sit still.

Curbing the desire to torture himself further by standing at the door and watching her climb into a taxi and drive away, he paced around the terminal instead, staring at all the glass display cases advertising local businesses and seeing nothing. He went into the men's room, splashed water on his face, cursed himself in the mirror and came out.

He checked the clock on the wall. 11:26. She hadn't been gone five minutes and already his need to see her felt like a crushing weight inside his chest.

He walked to the gift shop and looked over the racks of candy and magazines. What he wanted wasn't there. He was staring at the paperbacks when it occurred to him that he hadn't thought to ask which hotel she would be staying at. If he knew he could always decide to wait until a room there became available. If he ran, he might be able to catch up with her to ask now. At least it gave him a half decent excuse to go after her.

Spinning from the book rack, he collided with someone rushing into the gift shop. Instinctively his arms went out to steady them both. Win recognized her before he even looked down, from her scent alone. It was staggering to realize how deeply her essence was woven into his.

"Merrill." He kept his hands on her upper arms, first to balance her and then just for the thrill of touching her. "What's the matter?"

She was breathless. The rapid pulse point in her throat made him want to touch her there with his tongue.

"Nothing. I came back because I started thinking that it's already after check-out time and there might not be another room available today. Or they might not be going as scrupulously by that list as they claim. It seems a shame for you to be stuck here if you don't have to be. I thought you might like to..." She suddenly hesitated, her breath catching in her throat, her eyes like melting sapphires.

"Yes?" he prodded.

"Share my room. I don't mean...that's all, really. I thought it would only have to be until you get a room of your own. You can leave word at the desk where you can be reached. That is, if you want to."

She was more than breathless now. Her cheeks were flushed, her expression anxious and alert. Any fool could see she was pumped up with excitement. Win wanted the words.

"Do you want me to?" he asked.

She licked her lips. Shrugged. "Only if you want to."

He quickly decided to take what he could get. After all, she could have walked away and left him here, but she had come back. If she were the sort of woman she'd pretended to be, the sort to have sex with a man on impulse alone, the sort to offer to share a room just for the sake of another roll in the hay, she'd also be the type who could come right out and say so. The very uncharacteristic way she blushed and stammered at even a loose reference to their lovemaking was all the proof he needed that her feelings about it ran as deeply as his own.

"Besides," she said just as he was about to accept her offer on any terms, "I always did hate saying goodbye to friends."

"In that case I would very much like to share your room," he told her in a world-class understatement.

"Then come on. I have a cab waiting outside."

Somehow he managed to keep his hands off her all the way to the Airport Inn a few miles down the road. A long, gray and green one-story building, the Airport Inn was the sort of place you spent the night when you absolutely had no alternative.

They were given a room the size of a shoebox overlooking the black-top parking lot of the adjacent office building. Someone with a fetish for bright orange and lime green had handled the decor and the closest thing to a touch of luxury the room had to offer were the double sinks outside the bathroom. But it was clean and cool, observed Win, resting his back against the closed door. And it contained not only Merrill and a bed, but a room service menu, which at that moment and for the foreseeable future were all he needed to be deliriously happy.

He stood watching as she opened her suitcase and took a few things out. He was thirty-six years old. In his life, he'd been in at least a half-dozen hotel rooms with a half-dozen different women. He could not recall ever being spellbound watching one of them place make-up bottles by the sink or shake out her nightgown. Here, with this woman, the extraordinary intimacy of such ordinary tasks filled him with a deep pleasure.

As she turned from the open closet, she chanced to meet his mesmerized gaze in the oval mirror above the sink.

A frown puckered her forehead. "Don't you want to sit down?"

Win shook his head. "No. No, I don't want to sit down. What I want," he said, uncoiling his spine as he came away from the door, "is to know how long I'm supposed to go on pretending that the only thing you invited me here to share was your room?"

Letting the hairbrush she'd picked up slide from her fingers and clatter into the sink, Merrill turned to face him. She swallowed. Her jaw trembled. Her voice was little more than a whisper. "I'd say if we both tried real hard, we could keep it up for maybe another three seconds."

"One," he said, starting toward her. He waited until he had swung her into his arms to say, "Two."

Crossing the room in a couple of long strides, he lowered her to the bed and came down on top of her. Even before she had rolled onto her back, her soft laughter wrapping around him like smoke, his hands were busy locating the buttons on her blouse, and plunging inside. His mouth was discovering the hottest, wettest path from her lips to her breasts.

"Three."

Sunday, 3:02 p.m.

Would you like to do something kinky?"

They were lying on their sides atop a tangle of love-scented sheets, facing each other. They were both satiated from their afternoon of lovemaking, yet already fresh passion was stirring in response to the gentle, ceaseless play of their hands over each other's bodies.

At her words, Win came up on his elbow to stare down at her with a look of such sheer amazement Merrill had to smile. His fingers fell still on her breast. "Why? Do *you* want to do something kinky?"

"Actually, it's up to you. You see, what I have in mind is something that you have to do. Alone."

His eyes widened at that. Shades of gray and green swirled in them. Merrill saw herself reflected there, looking thoroughly debauched and contented. Well, nearly contented.

"Name it," he said, his mouth widening in a familiar grin. "I'm not shy."

"Good. I want you to go over there to the sink..."

"Yes?" he encouraged, clearly intrigued.

"And wash up."

He cocked an eyebrow. "Should I brush my teeth and gargle while I'm at it?"

"I didn't mean it that way," she said with a laugh. "It's just...a fantasy of mine." She paused, reaching for the sheet to cover up. "It's silly...let's forget it."

"No way." Win drew the sheet away. "I want to hear all about this kinky fantasy of yours. What happens after I wash up?"

"That's it. I told you it was silly. It's just that a while back—right after Ted left and you began coming to the office every day—there was one morning when...you probably don't remember this, but I arrived a little earlier than usual and walked in while you were washing up at the sink."

"I do remember. You gave me a dirty look and ran out as quickly as if you'd seen a ghost. I figured I'd gone and done something else wrong."

"Oh, no, not wrong. You took my breath away and that scared me. Afterward, every time I remembered how you looked standing there, with no shirt on and soap suds all over your chest..." She trailed her hands across his chest and biceps and over to the back of his shoulders, relishing the knowledge that for the moment he was hers to touch. "And this very fearsome tattoo on your shoulder...it took my breath away all over again."

He gazed at her for a long time, his expression full of wonder, elation, disbelief. "You were thinking of me like that, way back then?"

"I guess I was." She averted her gaze. "Why a sea horse?"

"The *Sea Horse* was the first boat I built. We had a huge celebration the night we launched her. I got loaded."

"And succumbed to a lifelong desire to visit a tattoo parlor?"

"I never wait a lifetime to satisfy my desires." Their faces were inches apart. She could feel the intensity in him gather, then slowly diffuse. "Anyway, the tattoo was there when I woke up."

"Quite a surprise, I'll bet," she said, running her fingers over the finely detailed artwork.

"Yeah, hurt like hell, too. But I've made peace with it." His eyes clouded. "Does it bother you?"

"Oh, no," she assured him. "I like it. I never knew a man with a tattoo before." A deep sigh lifted her breasts. In a hushed voice she added, "I never knew a man like you."

Win's smile faded. Cupping her jaw in his hand, he gently drew her face toward his. His mouth touched hers, the contact warm and tender. He eased his tongue between her teeth and stroked in and out with slow deliberation. Withdrawing, he brushed his lips lightly across hers, drawing his next breath from deep inside her.

With his fingers still curled around her jaw, he pulled away enough to study her face. "I can't believe you fantasized about me."

"I can't believe I confessed it," Merrill countered, her wry smile tenuous.

"Seeing as you did, I have a confession, too. Richard Ingraham never insisted that I accompany you up here for the negotiations."

"But you told me..."

"I told you that," he broke in, "because I wasn't about to tell you the truth, and I knew if I simply said it was my idea you'd fight me every step of the way... telling me how cold a day in hell it would be when you needed my help."

"So what is the truth?"

"That I wanted to come."

"Why?"

"I'm not sure exactly. I've been telling myself it was strictly business. I never thought I'd confess this, either, but the fact is *I* need your help. The details of this business make my head swim. I'm no good at interpreting policy clauses and deciding which report has to be filed with who and by what date in order to prevent a legal disaster. I couldn't imagine a whole week in the office trying to answer questions and pretending to know what I was doing without you to turn to for help.''

''But you never ask me for help.''

''Of course not,'' he said, grinning at her look of consternation. ''Why should I, when it was so much gentler on my ego to goad it out of you instead? I push the right buttons and you're so busy being defensive and snarling facts at me that you don't know how much you're really helping.''

His words conjured up a familiar, maddening, oft-repeated scene. ''Of all the sneaky, underhanded...''

''I may be sneaky and underhanded,'' he admitted, snaring her arms so she couldn't land the punches aimed at his chest. ''But it's for damn sure that if I had walked in on you washing up, naked from the waist up, it wouldn't have taken us all this time to get where we are.''

''Even so,'' she grumbled with a haughty toss of her head.

He rubbed up against her. Her irritation melted. His voice was playfully gruff, as bristly as the chin he scraped across her shoulder. ''Even so, what?''

''Even so, are you going to go stand at that sink or not?''

''Yes, ma'am, I am going to do that for you. On one small condition.''

''What one small condition?''

''That as soon as I dream up a fantasy of my own, you'll indulge me.''

''Deal,'' Merrill foolishly agreed, and watched as he swung himself off the bed. ''To be authentic you have to put your pants on,'' she reminded him.

Glancing over his shoulder to quirk his eyebrows at her, he did exactly that, eschewing his underwear and stepping into his slacks.

"Uh-uh," she coached, shaking her head as he buttoned the waist. "Leave them unbuttoned."

"Your memory is faulty. I'm sure my pants were fastened that day."

"But I like them better open."

"What happened to authenticity?"

"It takes a back seat to artistic license. This is my fantasy."

"So it is," he said, unbuttoning his pants. His belt hung loose at his waist. Above it his chest was a broad, tanned expanse of ridged muscles, covered with a wedge of softly curling black hair. "Better?"

"Perfect."

Smiling wickedly, he turned away and crossed the room without looking back. Merrill placed his pillow on top of her own and propped her back against them. From the center of the bed, she had a clear view of the small area outside the bathroom where the sink was located. The light illuminated the mirror below it and Win's shoulders, making the sea horse riding his right shoulder blade stand out sharply against his smooth dark skin.

For a second he met her gaze in the mirror, then slowly, deliberately, he turned his attention to the fresh bar of soap he picked up from the edge of the sink. He held it under the running water, rubbing it back and forth in his strong brown hands. With white lather dripping from between his palms, he lifted them, still holding the soap in one, and spread it across his chest.

If he'd appeared awkward or embarrassed, she would have felt the same way and the fantasy would have been ru ined. He didn't, and inside Merrill's excitement began a slow, steady beat. The memory of that morning and the fantasies it spawned paled beside the reality of that moment.

The muscles of his back and shoulders flexed and rippled as he rubbed his palms up and down his arms. Unhurriedly he soaped his armpits, his neck, his belly as far down as his zipper. His biceps rolled and swelled. The hair on his chest and under his arms clung to him in dark, wet curls. His skin became slick and glossy. He moved much more slowly than he had that morning, his movements more graceful than vigorous, intended not to cleanse, but to arouse.

It was working. Merrill's breathing had grown quick and shallow. Her hips twisted restlessly. She bent one leg at the knee, stretched the other until her toes curled into the mattress, and felt between them a hot, pulsating desire to feel those strong caressing hands on her body, to have his fingers gliding over her damp flesh, moving inside her. She refused to think beyond the moment.

As if reading her mind, Win turned from the sink and started toward her at a lazy pace. His smile was insidious and he was still holding the soap in his dripping hands.

"Oh no," she said, half laughing as she pressed her back against the pillows.

"Oh yes." His knee dimpled the soft mattress. "I want you as slippery as I am." Instead of putting his hands on her as she expected, he held the soap out to her expectantly. "It's all yours."

She nibbled her lip, torn between her excitement and her inhibitions. "Is this your fantasy?"

"Nope." The sensual heat in his gaze prevented her from bristling at his next words. "It's an order."

She supposed that was as good an excuse as any to do what the newly discovered reckless spirit inside her wanted to do. She stretched out her hand and Win placed the bar of soap in it. It felt hot and slippery against her palm, and even more so when she touched it to the sensitive skin near the base of her throat. She trailed it along her collarbone and her shoulders. Win, leaning on one hand, traced the path she took with the fingers of his other.

"Mmm. That's real good," he murmured in approval. His eyes were heavy-lidded with passion, his voice husky. "Now do your breasts."

Holding her breath she moved the soap lower, circling first one breast then the other. Her flesh tingled and tightened. Merrill knew the response was ten percent a result of the physical contact and ninety percent her awareness that Win was watching.

He dipped his head to nuzzle her soap-slicked breasts, groaning with pleasure. "Now lower," he urged in a strangled whisper.

Her hand skated down the center of her body. When she reached her belly the soap tickled, causing the muscles there to quiver. Win sucked in his breath. When she hesitated, looking up, he smiled.

"Chicken?" he teased.

"This is as far as you went."

"Only because you made me put my pants on."

"Hand me my suitcase and I'll do the same," she pleaded breathlessly.

Win shook his head. "Oh, no you don't. Here, I'll help."

His hand closed over hers where it had stalled low on her stomach, pressing it inexorably lower. At the same time he drew her knees apart, shifting on the bed so that he was kneeling in the wide vee of her thighs. Merrill's head fell back against the pillow as the soap held in their linked hands slid across the most sensitive spot on her body.

Holding it there, Win increased the pressure perfectly, rotating in small circles until her breath was coming in small desperate gasps. Her hand fell away, lifting to clutch at his shoulders for support, leaving him to continue the magic. He was so good at it. Her hips lifted in time with the gentle thrusts of his agile fingers.

When she felt as if she were poised at the edge of a high cliff, unable to make the final exquisite leap, he bent his head even lower, replacing his hand with his mouth, replacing heat with fire, and sent her soaring into oblivion.

While her heart pounded and aftershocks rippled through her, his mouth caressed its way back across her belly and breasts. He gently grazed her nipples and the side of her throat with his teeth, finally claiming her mouth in a kiss that tasted of soap and absolute possession. The passionate tenderness of his every touch pierced her heart and brought tears to her eyes. She hadn't counted on this happening, not at all.

Smiling up at him afterward, she slid her tongue over his lips. "You taste like soap."

"So do you ... all over," he informed her with a devastatingly sensual grin. "So tell me, was that as good as your fantasy?"

"Fishing?"

"Desperately."

"It was better, stupendous, unequaled. Best of all, this time when I watched you I knew you weren't washing away traces of a night with another woman."

He arched back to look at her. "Fishing?"

"I guess I am," Merrill admitted, her expression wry. "You have a reputation, you know."

"Is my past a problem for you?"

"I know it shouldn't be . . . I certainly have no right . . ."

"I'm giving you the right . . . all the rights in the world."

A thrill—one she knew was unwise to feel—shot through her. "I guess I have this fear about measuring up."

His eyes darkened. "I was never running a contest. But even if I had been, it would have been over the moment I took you in my arms for the first time. I'm having trouble even remembering anything that happened before that. Don't," he ordered, gripping her arms to hold her still. "Don't pull away from me."

"Then don't say things like that."

"Like what? The truth?"

"Things that make it sound as if there's more to this than there is. As if this . . . as if *we* have some sort of future."

"We do," he said, sounding stubborn. "Merrill, you have me feeling things I've never felt before."

"For the moment, maybe. It won't last. You crave excitement, Win, and I can't deliver that—I'm not sure if anyone or anything can—on a long-term basis."

"I don't expect you to."

"No, but you would expect me to smile and move on once the excitement begins to wane. The trouble is, I'm no good at smiling and moving on. Things come so easily for you that you don't need to place too great a value on security." She snapped her fingers. "A new woman . . ." She snapped again. "A new business. For you, everything is easy come, easy go."

"Not this time," he growled fiercely. "Not you."

"No? A few flowers, a few kisses and there I was . . . how did you put it? Rolling around in the back of a limo with you. If that's not easy I don't know what is. Don't get me wrong . . . I don't regret it, not a second of it. But this . . ."

She threw her hands up expansively, "What's happened between us is an aberration for me. For you, it's just business as usual. We're different, Win."

"What's wrong with being different? We'll work it out."

"That's just it, you won't work it out. Sooner or later you'll get bored and move on to the next challenge, the next impulse."

"I'm not your father, Merrill. Doesn't the fact that I've stayed in one job, in one place for eight years prove that?"

"Not when you consider that the minute Ted was no longer around to take care of all the drudge work so you could be footloose to come and go as you please, you decide to sell out."

His hold on her tightened. "You're wrong about that . . . and about me. How can I convince you of that?"

"You can't." Frustration tightened the set of his jaw. She tried to smooth it away with her fingertips. "Please, Win," she said, "we've already been over all this. Please let's not spoil tonight by arguing."

His eyes flashed, signaling his reluctance to let the matter drop. She kissed his lips, stroked his chest. Finally, with a ragged sigh, he said, "All right . . . for tonight."

Room service stopped serving at seven. Driven by hunger, they ventured out for a walk along the four-lane strip that ran in front of the motel. It was all neon lights and drive-through windows, a fast food paradise. Settling on a deli that featured foot-long submarine sandwiches, they found a booth in the noisy, fluorescent lit back room.

They ate straight from the wax paper wrappings, and the meal tasted better than anything Merrill had ever been served on china. They traded bites and played the jukebox, oldies that had never sounded so good to her, and touched each other the way lovers do. Light, frequent, casual touches that reverberated with intimacy.

Back in their room, the message light on the telephone was flashing. It was for Win.

"They have a room for me at another hotel," he told Merrill, holding the receiver away from his ear as his gaze locked with hers across the room. "Want to hand me a pencil so I can take down the information?"

She shook her head, making no move to do as he asked, and he understood that it was because she wanted him to stay. At least she was no longer hiding behind an excuse, he thought. It was another small step. Smiling, he thanked the operator and hung up.

Another night, thought Merrill, he was hers for another night. And maybe longer. Who knows how long the strike might drag on? She no longer felt morose over her ruined plans. Jamaica would always be there.

They made love again before falling asleep—slow, coaxing, floating sex—and fell asleep with their bodies still comfortably entwined in a way Merrill was convinced their lives could never be.

Monday, 8:08 a.m.

It was the Fourth of July and it was going to be his best one ever. Win knew that even before he opened his eyes. Today was that different from other years. There wouldn't be any sailing for him today, no parties or barbecues, probably not even any fireworks. He smiled. At least not of the sulfur-smelling, gunpowder variety. There would be only Merrill, and to his amazement that was fine with him.

Everything was different now. This thing with Merrill had changed everything. It was as if he'd been swept up in a cyclone and dropped back down somewhere far away, where everything looked new from the inside out.

For a while he lay quietly, watching her sleep, thinking about what she'd said last night and reassuring himself that it wasn't true. Everything in him railed against the suggestion that he had no stick-to-it-iveness. He'd built entire boats, for God's sake. At first nearly single-handedly and then as foreman of his own crew. For over a year he'd trained and been part of a team challenging for the America's Cup. He'd sailed a good part of the world alone. Those were not the kind of things accomplished by a quitter. Deep inside, however, he knew that was not the sort of quitting Merrill was talking about.

There had been some truth in what she'd said. It was true that he was used to getting what he wanted, and on his own terms. He supposed that was the way he wanted her, on his own terms. But not, as she was convinced, on a whim or for only a little while. He wanted Merrill in a way he couldn't name, a way he'd never wanted another woman. He couldn't foresee a time when he would not want her this way. It was a momentous and slightly daunting thought and he couldn't understand what was so wrong with letting things roll from there.

By the time Merrill began to stir, he had showered and shaved, grinning in the mirror as he scraped the black whiskers from his face. There was something unmanly, almost unconstitutional, about shaving on a holiday, but there was no way around it. Merrill's delicate skin had been ravished enough. He had just pulled on a fresh pair of jeans when the breakfast he'd ordered arrived.

The knock on the door disrupted the fragile, uppermost layer of sleep where Merrill had been languishing. Yawning, she rolled to her side and watched as Win took a tray from the bellhop and tipped him. He carried it toward the bed, preceded by a delicious aroma of fresh coffee, and lowered it to the nightstand.

"Good morning," he said, his bright gaze touching all of her.

"Morning."

He grabbed her arm as she swung her legs off the other side of the bed. "Where do you think you're going?"

"The bathroom," she shot over her shoulder.

He let her go. "Okay, but come straight back. I plan on having breakfast in bed with you."

"Win," she said, pausing to glance around the room, which contained not even the usual small round table tucked into a corner, "I don't see that we have any choice."

"True." He looked around, too, wearing a smile of deviant satisfaction. "Great hotel, isn't it?"

Merrill rolled her eyes, grabbing her nightgown on her way to the bathroom. It seemed silly to be putting a nightgown on after getting out of bed, but she wouldn't be comfortable sitting there naked with Win looking so fresh and gorgeous. She washed her face and brushed her teeth and returned to find her coffee poured and waiting for her. Win lifted the plastic plate cover to reveal a selection of muffins and croissants.

"I'm afraid the breakfast menu is limited," he explained apologetically. "It was this or Sugar Pops."

"Wise choice," she said, reaching for a flaky croissant and a small tub of strawberry jam. There was also a tub of butter on the tray, a bud vase holding both a plastic rose and a miniature American flag, and a neatly folded newspaper. She gave the management an A for effort.

"So what do you want to do today?" he asked her between bites. "It is the Fourth of July."

Merrill didn't care if it was Christmas. They were doing exactly what she wanted to do. "I don't know. What do you want to do?"

Make love to you, thought Win. All day long. "We could walk around, see the sights here in Warwick," he suggested.

"I have a feeling we already have."

"Right. How about going to a movie?" He liked the idea of sitting beside her in a cool, dark theater, putting his arm around her shoulders. If he could talk her into seeing something scary he'd be able to hold her reassuringly and let his fingers occasionally brush across her breast.

"A movie sounds good," said Merrill, envisioning her head resting on Win's strong shoulder as some wildly romantic story unfolded on the screen. She reached for the newspaper. "Let's see what's playing."

At first she was so intent on checking the table of contents for the entertainment section that she didn't notice the headline. When she did her fingers froze. "Agreement Puts

Coastways Back in the Air.'' It was blazoned across the top of page one in inch-high letters.

"Look," she said, moving the paper so Win could see it as well. "The strike is over."

"So it is." His voice was subdued, but colorless, registering neither joy nor disappointment. "Does it say anything about when they'll be able to resume flights?"

Swallowing in an attempt to ease the lump forming in her throat, Merrill scanned the article. It was ridiculous. She ought to be elated. Instead, she was struggling to read through a film of threatening tears. "It says the full flight schedule will resume immediately."

"That's bull," snapped Win. "These things take time. Ten to one it'll be Wednesday before they're up and operating full steam."

"Just the same," Merrill replied, folding the paper and placing it carefully on the tray beside the croissant she knew she wouldn't be able to swallow another bite of. "We ought to get back to the airport and check on our flights."

"Why?"

A shiver of dread passed through her. He wasn't going to make this easy. But then, she'd known from the start that nothing with Win would ever be easy. No, that wasn't fair. Falling in love with him had been appallingly easy. "Because otherwise, how will we know if our flights have been rescheduled?" she demanded as calmly as she was able to.

"We won't." He pushed the tray from between them, spilling coffee onto the muffins and into the tub of butter. Bridging her body with his unbending arms, he pressed her back onto her pillow. "The world won't stop spinning if those planes take off without us. We can stay right here, no one will care. We can go to that movie. We can make love. We can find fireworks tonight and watch..."

"No," she exclaimed harshly, not wanting to hear any more of the way things could have been. Her hands pushed at his shoulders. "We can't... *I can't*. Win, this was wonderful... but it wasn't real. It was like a gift, a few days' reprieve from real life, like being under a spell of some sort."

Your spell, she thought, knowing she was still under it and would be for a long time to come. Suddenly the prospect of finding a new job, away from Win, no longer seemed an ordeal, but a blessing. Another survival technique. She would never be able to go on seeing him every day and resist getting involved, deeply involved. She refused to be dragged through the emotional wringer of a full-fledged affair with him, letting herself be torn between the hope that it could be more and the knowledge that it never would be, that he wasn't interested in, perhaps wasn't capable of, real commitment.

Win listened to Merrill in silence, forcing himself to pull back in response to her resistance and in defiance of his aching need to touch her. The distance between them was killing him, but he was determined to let her get it all out, to hear all her sensible, well-thought-out reasons why they couldn't be together. Then he would slowly, logically disassemble each one.

"It was wonderful," she said again. He shifted impatiently. He already knew that. "But now the strike is over... and so is the spell."

She stood up, leaving Win dumbstruck. That was it? That was the extent of her sensible argument? He was on fire for the woman and she was going to walk away with some ridiculous line about magic spells? How was he supposed to argue logically against that?

He stared out the window while she showered and dressed, but there were no easy answers written on the pavement out there. Whatever he said to Merrill was going to have to come from inside. He'd decided to wait until she was dressed so they could discuss it without any distractions. No more impulses, no more clever seductions that backfired. He wanted Merrill to want him as much with her eyes open and her adrenaline at a normal level as she did in bed.

He pulled on a shirt and shoes and waited until she emerged from the bathroom fully dressed, checked her reflection in the mirror, then disappeared again after first snatching something new from her suitcase. It became a pattern, and he began to recognize the same pieces of clothing in different combinations as he realized she was intent on creating exactly the right look for walking out of his life.

She'd always appeared so impeccably put together, he'd assumed achieving the effect was effortless. He knew now that she worked at that as diligently as she worked at everything that mattered to her. Nothing of any importance would ever be an impulse for Merrill. When she fell in love with the right man she would give herself body and soul and she deserved to be loved the same way in return. Body and soul.

She finally settled on black slacks with a clingy looking royal-blue top and a jacket the same hot-pink shade as her toenails. Avoiding any glance at his sprawled out form, she began to gather the debris she'd strewn about in the process of dressing, packing it neatly into her suitcase.

Watching her, a strong, increasingly familiar feeling of possessiveness spread through him. He wanted to matter to Merrill. He wanted it so badly his chest ached. And he wanted to be the man to love her the way she should be loved, body and soul. God, he was slow. Not until the sound of her suitcase shutting brought the metallic taste of panic to his throat did he at last find his way through the maze of new and bewildering feelings and realize that he already did love her exactly that way.

He rolled off the bed, leaving all his carefully chosen words of persuasion behind.

"No," he said roughly and succinctly as she approached him carrying her suitcase. He moved to stand between her and the door. The word *no* certainly summed up his feelings about her leaving, but the anguished, slightly confused look she turned on him made it clear that it wasn't eloquent enough to convince her to stay. "Nothing is over, Merrill. I won't let it be over. I don't think it will ever be over. And I'm sure as hell not going to let you walk out on me."

"Please, Win, I have to leave. Right now," she said, visibly gathering her courage. He marveled at her determination and control even as he resolved not to let them get in his way. "You can come with me to the airport or stay here," she continued. "But I have a flight to catch and plans for the rest of this week."

His mouth twisted. "Plans that don't include me."

"You knew that from the start. We both did."

"You're right. I did. And I know how much you like making carefully considered plans. So you go right ahead. But from now on, factor this into every plan you make...I love you."

Merrill's heart took off so fast she felt dizzy. Her fingers clenched around the handle of her suitcase. "Win, please..."

"No," he said, pressing his fingertips to her lips to silence her. "Before you say anything, let me finish. I love you and I won't give up and I won't go away and I won't change my mind."

"How can you be sure of that?"

"I don't know how...I've never been in love before." His grin was fleeting, devastating. "I only know that I am. And I believe that deep down you feel what I feel, but you're afraid. Don't be. Take a chance on what you're feeling. Give me a chance."

"A chance to do what? Break my heart?"

"I will never do that," he swore, framing her face with his hands. He searched her eyes, seeking and finding a glimmer of hope beneath the sadness and skepticism.

"All right," he said, searching for a way to nurture her trust, "as long as you're not ready to hear that you're wrong about me or to take a chance on the future, we'll have to start by straightening out the past.

"Where to start?" he muttered, his expression wry. "I suppose my reputation is as good a place as any. I'm no saint, Merrill, and I did my share of running around when I was younger... okay, maybe more than my share, but at some point my reputation became self-perpetuating."

His expression grew solemn. "For instance, that morning you walked in on me at the office, I hadn't been out all night partying with a woman, which is apparently what you assumed. I was dousing myself with cold water to try and stay awake and clear my head after spending the night—the entire night—at my desk."

"You brought a woman back to the office with you?" Merrill asked, purposely being obtuse while she tried to keep the spurt of optimism caused by his revelation from surging out of control.

Win silenced her with a look. "I was working." He tipped her chin up, refusing to permit her to look away. "What's the matter, Merrill? Doesn't that jive with your bad opinion of me?"

"I don't have a bad opinion of you." She shrugged sheepishly, twisting from his grasp. "Exactly. I did assume that you were only hanging around, marking time until you could unload the company. I never knew . . .''

"Now you do," he said when she faltered, being pulled under by her own thoughts. "Now you know you can be wrong about me."

"But it doesn't make sense. If you were willing to work that hard . . . to spend all night at your desk, why are you so determined to sell out now?"

"That's not what we're talking about here," he snapped with an impatient gesture. "We're talking about us, damn it. Will you forget about the damn business?"

Merrill couldn't forget it. Her mind was suddenly filled with a single, crystalline thought. It made everything clearer and at the same time it blew through her head like a strong wind, tossing everything she'd known about Win—or thought she knew—up in the air again.

"You're not selling out because you've lost interest in running the business, or because you're tired of it." She was talking as much to herself as him, focused inward, concentrating on the jumble of puzzle pieces sliding into place in her mind. Finally her eyes widened in astonishment. "You're not bored at all. You're afraid."

He didn't blink for several seconds, only held her in a stare. When he released his breath at last, it did nothing to ease the tension in his stance or in the air between them.

"Afraid?" he drawled. "Me, afraid?"

"Yes. Of course." She shook her head, stunned by a realization that shattered her image of Win as a man for whom everything came easily. It didn't, and when it didn't he could feel the same panicky lack of confidence she'd often felt herself. "Why can't you just admit it?" she asked gently.

He looked as if he'd sooner confess to being Jack the Ripper. Any second Merrill expected him to hook his thumbs in his belt and call her out. She had to fight back a smile at the belligerent thrust of his jaw. Suddenly she was able to smile again. Win might be ready to do battle with her, but gradually, for the first time in days, she was beginning to feel at peace with herself.

"Afraid of what?" he demanded.

"Failing. You're selling out because you're afraid you'll fail."

"That's the craziest thing I ever heard. It's a riot."

But he wasn't laughing, she noticed. Beneath the arrogant stance and disparaging glare, he looked troubled.

"I am not afraid," he insisted. "Cautious, maybe. A little uncertain, sure. Maybe a little concerned. But I'm not afraid."

She couldn't suppress a smile as she stepped closer, lifted her chin and locked gazes with him. "Admit it, Deverell. You're scared as hell."

She didn't flinch from his furious glare. Both her instincts and her knowledge of him told her that whatever he was feeling wasn't directed at her, but at himself. She watched as he struggled with it.

"Yeah, I'm scared," he finally admitted quietly. "Not for me . . . for you . . . for all the people who depend on a paycheck from Haigh and Deverell to feed their kids and pay their bills every month." He looked past her, drawing in a deep breath, focusing on a corner of the ceiling Merrill suspected he didn't even see. "You said you hated the way your father kept moving from one job to another. Well, when my father lost his job there wasn't anything to move to, not for a long time, and I don't ever want to be responsible for that happening to another man, to another family."

"Is that why—"

"Yeah, that's why," he cut in, returning his gaze to her. "I was fifteen when the shipyard where he was a foreman shut down. Things had been rocky for a while, ever since the old man who owned the place died and his son took over. He didn't know crap about running a shipyard and he had no right doing it except that it was his name on the letter-head."

She said nothing, knowing he was thinking of his own situation the same way.

"I remember my father coming home every night with another horror story," he told her. "Missed delivery dates and screwed up supply orders. *The inmates are running the asylum,* he'd say and we'd all laugh. After a while he didn't say anything anymore and we all knew it was bad. Then one morning he went to work and the gate was locked. No no-tice, no severance package. Twenty-seven years and he shows up and finds the gate locked."

Merrill touched his arm and felt the tension there. "With all that experience surely your father could find work at another shipyard."

He shook his head impatiently. "The economy was just starting its long downward slide back then, and not too many people were interested in buying pleasure craft. Dad and the other foremen had tried telling this guy that. They tried to talk him into looking into government contracts, but he said he'd handle everything his way.

"My dad lost his truck," he said after a minute. "I re-member him standing in the driveway a long time after they drove it away. I remember my mother's face the day they sold their bedroom set to make the mortgage payment on the house." His bitter laugh sent a shiver through Merrill. "And in the end, they lost it anyway. Everything.

"Eventually we moved to Trenton and Dad found a job as a welder in a factory there, but things never went back to being the way they had been. It was as if we'd lost something, trust, security, I don't know. But it changed him, and my mother. It changed all of us, I guess."

"I know what you're thinking," she said, "but it wouldn't be like that with you running Haigh and Deverell. For one thing you recognize up front that you don't know everything there is to know about the business and—"

"There's an understatement for you. I know almost nothing about the day-to-day business side of things. Merrill, face it, I'm just no good at juggling figures and dates and people. So I'm getting out before I ruin everything, before the business that my best friend and I worked to build goes belly-up in disgrace and a lot of people get hurt in the process. If you want to call that being afraid, go right ahead. I call it being smart."

"You are smart," agreed Merrill, grasping his arm to stop him from turning away. "That's why I know you could do anything you want."

"Thanks for the vote of confidence. If it was just me involved I might be willing to take a chance, and you might be willing to take a chance on me, but there's no way I'm going to play around with other people's lives, people who have kids and responsibilities, people who are depending on me."

"You wouldn't be playing around. We all know how to do our jobs and we're damn good at them. I think you're savvy enough to let us do them and to listen when we come to you with suggestions." Her fingers tightened on his arm as she sensed him considering what she said. "Win, you could learn this side of the business a lot more easily than Ted or I could ever hope to learn what you do."

"Maybe," he conceded. "But I can't totally dismiss the fact that I don't want to. That's something I wasn't lying about. The thought of doing Ted's job every day for the rest of my life makes me feel claustrophobic."

"It wouldn't be so bad. After things settle down, you ould go back to doing fieldwork at least part-time. Now 1at I understand how you feel, I could be more of a help to ou. Ted wasn't such a whiz with figures, you know. A lot f the time I would do the actual—"

"Of course."

His tone and the look on his face startled her.

"You needn't look so smug," she told him. "I wasn't riticizing Ted. I'm sure he would tell you the same thing."

"He did. All the time." Capturing her hand between his e brought it to his lips. "That's why I can't believe it took 1e so long to see the solution to our problems. There's only ne possible explanation for my lapse," he said, pulling her loser, sliding his palms up and down her arms. "You have 1e transfixed."

Laughing, he hugged her hard, running his mouth over er hair, her face. "I know now what my fantasy is," he said etween kisses.

She blinked at him. "Fantasy?"

"Our deal, remember?"

"Win, really..." She tried to wriggle away from him. "Is ex all you ever think about? We were having a serious, very nportant discussion."

"I consider sex to be very important and I take it very se- ously. And yes," he continued, his grin spreading, "since met you it is all I think about."

She looked askance. "You've been thinking about sex ith me for the past eight years?"

"I'm convinced that I was, subconsciously. Of course I'm lso convinced you were thinking the same thing."

She tried to frown, giggled instead, then gasped as he round his hips closer to hers. "You're weird."

"But you like it?"

"I like it." She sighed.

"Good. Now for my fantasy."

"Now?"

"You promised."

"Only under duress."

"Tough. A deal is a deal. My fantasy is that everythi[ng] goes back to being the way it was before Ted took off."

"Join the club. What do you propose we do? Go [to] Alaska and kidnap him?"

"No. Ted's made it clear he's happy where he is. He h[as] no objection to selling the company. Only instead of selli[ng to] Haigh and Deverell, we're going to buy Haigh out. You'[re] going to take his place." Before Merrill's jaw had finish[ed] dropping, he added, "You're going to be my new partner[.]"

"Me?"

"Right. It's perfect. I know you're capable of taki[ng] Ted's place. I'll get to go back to doing the work I'm go[od] at, work I love. The company won't fold. No one will lo[se] a job. Best of all, while we won't be constantly under ea[ch] other's feet—or at each other's throats—we will be t[o]gether. Partners."

He said the word with such utter satisfaction Merrill hat[ed] to pierce his daydream with reality.

"Win, I can't afford to be your partner. I don't ha[ve] anywhere near enough money to buy Ted's share of t[he] business."

"I do."

"But then we wouldn't be partners," she pointed out. "[It] wouldn't be fair to call it a partnership when you're taki[ng] all the financial risk and risking the failure you're so det[er]mined to avoid, while my involvement is basically risk free[.]"

"Oh, but you will be taking a risk," he announced res[o]lutely, reaching for her hands. "I'm asking you to ri[sk] everything, Merrill. I'm asking you to marry me."

Monday, 2:30 p.m.

The man ambling across the screen was long and lean and sexy. The woman in his arms was blond, slightly terrified of his recklessness and slightly intoxicated by his animal magnetism. A clear-cut example of how art imitates life, thought Merrill. She watched, utterly captivated, as the man drew the woman closer, murmuring to her in his soft, *big-easy* drawl.

The television sent flickering patterns of light across the walls of the silent hotel room. The tightly drawn drapes and the air conditioner kept the heat and light of the afternoon sun at bay. It might have been any hotel room anywhere. It might have been an ocean-front suite at the Jamaican Princess, the sort you have to reserve months in advance. At some point, hours ago, it had ceased to matter.

She reached for popcorn and got a handful of Win's lap instead.

"Ahhh," he said.

"Cut it out and put the popcorn back where it was," she hissed. "This is one of my favorite parts."

"This is my favorite part," he countered with a pointed glance at where her hand and his hard body met.

She snatched her hand away as the man on screen began to teach the woman the lazy, shuffling steps of a traditional Cajun dance. Win's leg rubbed against hers in an invitation to a dance of a different sort.

"Why is it," he asked, putting his lips close to her ear, "that every movie set in the south has to be as long as *Gone with the Wind*?"

Smiling indulgently, she checked the time. "Win, it's only been playing for fifteen minutes."

"Really?" he queried, using his glance at the clock as an excuse to nuzzle her breasts. "Seems like hours."

"Watching a movie was your idea," she reminded him.

"Yes, but at the time I suggested it I was still courting you and trying to be my most charming." He rolled onto his side, facing her. "Now that we're officially engaged, I have more pressing matters on my mind."

"That's not your mind," she told him dryly in response to the warm pressure he was applying to her hip. "And if this is what being engaged is like, I'm not sure I have the stamina to be married to you."

He smiled, running his fingers through her hair, loving the silky feel of it, loving even more the fact that it was his to touch—that she was his—now and forever. "Speaking of which, we never did settle on a date."

"Because you're being unreasonable and impractical... as usual."

"I think I'm being eminently reasonable. I'm not the one who refuses to compromise."

"Wait just a minute," she said, punching the pillows behind her as she wriggled to sit up, the drama on the screen forgotten in favor of her own. "I suggested Labor Day. You want to get married tomorrow. I'd hardly call giving me a choice between Thursday and Friday of this week a compromise."

"Friday is the perfect compromise," argued Win. "That way our honeymoon can pick right up where your vacation ends."

"You're doing this on purpose, so I won't have time to get caught up in making elaborate wedding plans."

"It's true that I don't relish the prospect of spending weeks trying to decide whether it ought to be a bell or a couple of plastic dolls sitting on top of the cake," he admitted, citing just one of the matters she'd broached in the short time since she'd thrown herself into his arms and agreed to become both his business partner and his wife.

"So instead, you expect me to plunge into a lifetime commitment without time to catch my breath, much less rummage up something borrowed and blue, for no better reason than that I'm madly in love with you?"

"That's it."

"A week from Friday," she offered.

He smiled and kissed her. "This Friday. No later."

She tipped her head back to assess the determination in his voice and eyes and privately resigned herself to a hasty search for a wedding dress. She would let the formal surrender wait until she'd enjoyed his attempts to persuade her, however. While his hands and lips went about it, she closed her eyes and thought about marrying Win.

She had a blue teddy in her suitcase that would make him drool. That left borrowed, old and new. Donna might not be able to get away to attend the ceremony on such short notice, but Mickey would be there, and Merrill could borrow a pair of earrings from her. She frowned, picturing the watermelon slices that had been hanging from her sister's ears the last time she saw her. Well, she could always borrow panty hose. Finding something old and new would be no problem.

Win's lips were hot and damp at the side of her throat. She couldn't hold out much longer. She hoped all her family would be there to share in her happiness, but if they couldn't be, she and Win could always visit them later. She liked the idea of that.

In fact, as long as Win was involved, she liked the idea of spur of the moment weekend trips and impulsive, private midday rendezvous. She liked the idea of working with him and locking horns with him as she knew they inevitably would—and forgetting all about it when she went to bed with him that night. Every night.

Life with Win was not going to be predictable or well-ordered. Instead, it would be spontaneous and exciting and exactly the way she wanted it to be. And he would always make her feel secure in his love, in the only way that really mattered. She could get used to following her impulses, she thought, sighing as he worked the sheet down her body using only his teeth.

"I never did have much luck with sex."

The awkward, regretful admission came from the actress on the television screen. Merrill glanced over Win's shoulder, her attention captured once again.

"Well, sugar," the good-looking rogue sharing his bed with the woman assured her, *"your luck is about to change."*

The first time she'd watched this movie she had been alone and had thought that was the most romantic line she'd ever heard, and the most ludicrous. Luck wasn't such a simple thing to manipulate, she'd thought at the time.

She'd been wrong. She knew now that your luck—your whole life—could change overnight. All it took was a combination as simple as an airline strike and the right man. One thing she hadn't been wrong about. When you fell in love you knew it, no doubts, no second thoughts. She loved Win, and at long last life seemed to be unfurling before her like a red carpet. She snuggled closer to him.

"What's that smile for?" he asked, moving to cover her.

"I was just thinking about how one person can get real lucky real fast."

He narrowed his eyes at her. "Oh, yeah? And what inspired this sudden philosophical thought? Me or that movie?"

"A little of both, I guess."

"Well, let's see if I can't change that."

He bent his head and rubbed his parted lips against hers until they opened invitingly. Winding his hand into her hair he pulled her head back and drew her slowly, deeply into the kiss.

His other hand slid over her shoulder, fondling her breast, coasting down to brush as delicately as falling petals against her thighs and between them. Their bodies strained together to the sultry beat of the Cajun ballad coming from the television. He kissed her with passion and tenderness and promise.

Leaning back a little, he framed her face with his hands, looking down at her for long, silent minutes. "I love you," he said finally, his words neither impulsive nor glib.

Merrill bit her lip, emotion pooling inside her. "I love you, too. And I won't change my mind and I won't give up and I won't go away."

"I won't ever let you." He smiled down at her, tracing the frame of her glasses as lovingly as if they were a part of her body. Pinching the bridge between his fingers, he paused before removing them. "May I?"

She nodded.

"You won't be able to see your movie," he teased, slowly sliding them away as she reached to draw him closer.

"That's all right. I know exactly how the story ends."

* * * * *

Patricia Coughlin

For reasons I've never completely figured out, I began writing my first romance in 1981. My sudden impulse to write took a lot of people by surprise, including me.

Whenever I'm asked if I always wanted to be a writer, I'm tempted to answer something about brilliant childhood scribblings and being chosen to edit my college yearbook. The truth is, I never considered writing until I actually started doing it.

Like most writers, I was always a voracious reader, and perhaps it was because I loved books so much that I never dared to think I could write one. One of my biggest thrills came the day I walked into a bookstore, saw my first novel alongside books by authors I'd read and admired for years, and watched as someone actually bought it! Granted, it was my mother purchasing so many copies that the novel should have made the bestseller list, but I was thrilled just the same.

My mother is one of my greatest supporters, even if her initial support was offered with an equal measure of bewilderment. When I first told her I was writing a book, her response was, "That's nice, Pat, but if they wanted someone to write a book, why wouldn't they choose a real writer?" With only three chapters under my belt, I was privately asking myself the same question.

Luckily, around this time I realized I had one thing in my favor—an addiction that has plagued me all my life, an addiction that turned out to be an asset. Daydreaming. I'd been doing it for years without knowing it was great training for a fiction writer. I did it all through school. I do it while shopping, cooking, driving. (I chose WRITER for my license plate as fair warning to anyone sharing the road with me.) Daydreams occurred so naturally to me that I never thought much about them until I started writing them down. "Where do you get your ideas?" people would ask, and I would stare at them, thinking the answer rather obvious. Didn't everyone walk around with a story spinning in her head at all times? It came as something of a shock to me to realize that everyone does not. I just happen to be one of the lucky ones.

A newspaper article, a snatch of conversation overheard in line at the bank, a glimpse of an interesting character, and I'm off and dreaming. If a movie leaves me wondering what will happen next, I can't help but think of the way I would have ended it. When I finished reading *Gone with the Wind*, I was certain Scarlett was going to get Rhett back, and I knew a dozen different ways she could go about it. I'm constantly asking myself *what if?* and reworking reality to suit me. Bill says that living with me has taught him two questions you never, ever ask a writer: "How's the book coming?" and "What *really* happened?"

Writing has changed my life. Now when someone intrudes on one of my fantasies I can say, "Don't bother me, I'm working." Also, through my characters I'm able to travel around the world and take part in their schemes and adventures. I get to know them and care about them, to laugh and cry with them and—best of all—I get to hear from readers who say they enjoyed reading a book as much as I enjoyed writing it. That's what it's all about.

Sixteen books later, I finally know the answer to my mother's question. I *am* a real writer, and I love it.

"Easy Come..." is for the Maddens,
Tom, Mary, Beth, Tommy and Sarah,
vacationers *extraordinaires*.

 *Silhouette Romance* ®

DIAMOND JUBILEE CELEBRATION!

It's the Silhouette Books tenth anniversary, and what better way to celebrate than to toast *you*, our readers, for making it all possible. Each month in 1990 we'll present you with a DIAMOND JUBILEE Silhouette Romance written by an all-time favorite author! Saying thanks has never been so romantic...

The merry month of May will bring you SECOND TIME LUCKY by Victoria Glenn. And in June, the first volume of Pepper Adams's exciting trilogy Cimarron Stories will be available—CIMARRON KNIGHT. July sizzles with BORROWED BABY by Marie Ferrarella. Suzanne Carey, Lucy Gordon, Annette Broadrick and many more have special gifts of love waiting for you with their DIAMOND JUBILEE Romances.

January: ETHAN by Diana Palmer (#694)
February: THE AMBASSADOR'S DAUGHTER
           by Brittany Young (#700)
March: NEVER ON SUNDAE by Rita Rainville (#706)
April: HARVEY'S MISSING by Peggy Webb (#712)

Double your reading pleasure this fall with two Award of Excellence titles written by two of your favorite authors.

Available in September

DUNCAN'S BRIDE
by Linda Howard
Silhouette Intimate Moments #349

Mail-order bride Madelyn Patterson was nothing like what Reese Duncan expected—and everything he needed.

Available in October

THE COWBOY'S LADY
by Debbie Macomber
Silhouette Special Edition #626

The Montana cowboy wanted a little lady at his beck and call—the "lady" in question saw things differently....

These titles have been selected to receive a special laurel—the Award of Excellence. Look for the distinctive emblem on the cover. It lets you know there's something truly wonderful inside!

FOUR UNIQUE SERIES
FOR EVERY WOMAN YOU ARE . . .

Silhouette Romance

Love, at its most tender, provocative,
emotional . . . in stories that will make you laugh and
cry while bringing you the magic of falling in love.

6 titles
per month

Silhouette Special Edition

Sophisticated, substantial and packed with
emotion, these powerful novels of life and love will
capture your imagination and steal your heart.

6 titles
per month

SILHOUETTE Desire

Open the door to romance and passion. Humorous,
emotional, compelling—yet always a believable
and sensuous story—Silhouette Desire never
fails to deliver on the promise of love.

6 titles
per month

Silhouette Intimate Moments

Enter a world of excitement, of romance
heightened by suspense, adventure and the
passions every woman dreams of. Let us
sweep you away.

4 titles
per month